The
Murderer's
Apprentice

By Ann Granger and available from Headline

Inspector Ben Ross crime novels
A Rare Interest in Corpses
A Mortal Curiosity
A Better Quality of Murder
A Particular Eye for Villainy
The Testimony of the Hanged Man
The Dead Woman of Deptford
The Murderer's Apprentice

Campbell and Carter crime novels
Mud, Muck and Dead Things
Rack, Ruin and Murder
Bricks and Mortality
Dead in the Water
Rooted in Evil
An Unfinished Murder

Fran Varady crime novels
Asking for Trouble
Keeping Bad Company
Running Scared
Risking it All
Watching Out
Mixing with Murder
Rattling the Bones

Mitchell and Markby crime novels
Say it with Poison
A Season for Murder
Cold in the Earth
Murder Among Us
Where Old Bones Lie
A Fine Place for Death
Flowers for his Funeral
Candle for a Corpse
A Touch of Mortality
A Word After Dying
Call the Dead Again
Beneath these Stones
Shades of Murder
A Restless Evil
That Way Murder Lies

The
Murderer's
Apprentice

Ann
Granger

HEADLINE

First published in Great Britain in 2019
by HEADLINE PUBLISHING GROUP

1

Cataloguing in Publication Data is available from the British Library

ISBN 978 1 4722 5269 2 (Hardback)

Typeset in Plantin by Palimpsest Book Production Limited,
Falkirk, Stirlingshire

Printed and bound in Great Britain by Clays Ltd, Elcograf S.p.A.

HEADLINE PUBLISHING GROUP
An Hachette UK Company
Carmelite House
50 Victoria Embankment
London EC4Y 0DZ

www.headline.co.uk
www.hachette.co.uk

This book remembers Jack Martin. He repaired shoes in a workshop set up in a garage made of corrugated metal sheets. When I was a child, I spent a lot of time watching him at work. He explained to me exactly what distinguished a good piece of leather from an inferior example. I watched, fascinated, as he drew the shape of a sole freehand, cut it out and pared it down until it was an exact fit. He allowed me to collect up fallen nails and tacks from the floor with the help of a large magnet, sort them, and put them in jam jars. Occasionally he let me put the finishing touch to a repair by using heelball to bring the heels to gleaming perfection. I was not allowed to do this very often because I used too much.

I sometimes think writing a book is very similar to that shoe repair process I watched so many years ago. The assorted ideas picked up here and there wait in the equivalent of jam jars in my mind. The plan of the book is sketched out roughly and then it is pared down, reworked, and when it is right, all put together and finished off with a final polish.

Writers owe a lot to the sympathetic support and eagle eye of their editors. My thanks go to the present one, Clare Foss, for her encouragement and support. I hope you enjoy this book, Clare!

I must also thank my friend and fellow writer, Angela Arney, who drove me to Salisbury and accompanied me visiting the town.

One note concerning the description of the monument known as Stonehenge, on Salisbury plain, which Ben Ross has cause to visit in the course of this book. When he would have seen it, in 1870, its appearance would not have been as it is now, following extensive restoration work in the 1900s. I have based Ben's sight of it on the painting of 1836 by John Constable.

'Fog everywhere. Fog up the river, where it flows among green airs and meadows; fog down the river, where it rolls defiled among the tiers of shipping, and the waterside pollutions of a great (and dirty) city . . .

Most of the shops lighted before their time – as the gas seems to know, for it has a haggard and unwilling look.'

Charles Dickens, *Bleak House*, 1853

'Criminal cases are continually hinging upon that one point. A man is suspected of a crime months perhaps after it has been committed. His linen or clothes are examined, and brownish stains discovered upon them. Are they bloodstains, or mud stains, or rust stains, or fruit stains, or what are they? This is a question which has puzzled many an expert, and why? Because there was no reliable test.'

Sherlock Holmes in *A Study in Scarlet*,
Arthur Conan Doyle, 1887

Chapter One

Inspector Ben Ross

LONDONERS ARE rightly proud of the gas lighting that has made the streets so much safer at night than in their grandfathers' day. Respectable Londoners, that is to say. There are plenty of residents who do not want any kind of light shining on their activities. They are the folk who interest me and any other police officer.

Unfortunately there is one thing that renders the gas lamps almost useless and provides plenty of cover for wrong-doing: it is the London fog. It is as though evil had found its natural milieu, creeping its way unseen into every nook and cranny. Fog is the villain's willing accomplice and the murderer's quick-to-learn apprentice.

The early months of 1870 had tested our hardiness to breaking point. We were now in March, yet still the snow lay banked up and soot-coated in sheltered corners. The bitter wind nipped at noses and ears; and even the best of gloves couldn't protect chilled fingers. People had begun to murmur wistfully about spring, many as if remembering an old departed friend. More optimistic hearts spoke of it not being many weeks away, at least according to the calendar.

Well, you would never have guessed it. London, in addition to the cold, had been assailed for the past week by a foul-smelling, suffocating pea-souper. Sea mists rolled upriver and encountered the pall of coal smoke belching from every chimney, whether domestic or industrial. Also contributing were the engines puffing in and out of our great railway termini, odours from the giant gasometers, the noxious vapours from the Thames mud at low tide, the rotting heaps of rubbish in the slum courtyards and nameless refuse running in the gutters, and there you have it: a 'London Particular' as it's known. It wraps itself around everything like a dirty yellow blanket, slips into a house the moment a door is opened; and finds any chink in a window frame. Londoners are perversely proud of that, too. Fog is something they do better than anyone else.

Beggars and vagrants froze in the streets overnight. Drunken revellers stumbled from the alehouses and sprawled on the cobbles. Unable to aid themselves, and unseen in the murk by passers-by, their stiffened corpses were often discovered when some other person tripped over them.

Where it had melted, snow had now turned to icy slush. The horses had pieces of sacking tied over their hooves to prevent them slipping and would have looked comical in these winter boots if they could have been seen in the gloom. As it was, the familiar clip-clop of their approach was muffled and you couldn't always hear them coming. There would be a sudden rattle of wheels out there in the greyish-yellow curtain, and a dull thud, perhaps a sudden nervous whinny, followed by a shout from the cabbie or other driver. The pedestrian had to leap aside, hoping, as he did so, that he leaped in the right direction. Understandably, accidents had become commonplace.

The swirling monster breathed sickness and death on its clammy intrusive breath. The very young and the very old were its first victims but no one was safe. On all sides the coughs and wheezes of the stricken could be heard in the murk; and served better than any lantern in locating pedestrians. It sometimes seemed as if most of London was ailing. The casual wards of the workhouses were full. Hopeful queues formed every evening but most were turned away. The children of the poor were sewn into bodices of wadded cotton to be cut free and emerge like moths from a chrysalis in spring – if they survived until then.

At Scotland Yard, that Monday morning, the week had not started well. We had our fair share of casualties, brought about by the cold and damp. Even a seemingly immovable fixture like Superintendent Dunn had succumbed. He was at home in bed with a mustard poultice on his chest and his feet on a stone hot-water bottle, under the watchful eye of Mrs Dunn. His absence freed us from his demands to know what we were all doing; and why this or that criminal had not yet been brought to book. But it also slowed the making of decisions. This meant much day-to-day business fell to me. I did not mind; but I did wonder what would happen when Dunn returned, restored to vigour, and turned his eagle eye on everything I'd instigated in his absence.

Another inspector and three constables were absent sick,

adding to my load. Worryingly, stalwart Sergeant Morris, on whom I depended, was croaking like a bullfrog. He kept saying he was all right but he didn't look it. And Constable Biddle had a cold.

You might think that Biddle's cold was the least of my worries but in reality it was not. It struck very close to home because Biddle is walking out with our maid of all work, Bessie. He had been discovered in our kitchen the previous evening, with his head over a bowl of steaming water laced with Friar's Balsam, and a towel over the lot. Standing over him was Bessie and every time he threw back the towel, and raised his scarlet, perspiring face to complain, she pushed his head down again and covered it over. His muffled cries attracted Lizzie, my wife, who came upon the scene. While sympathetic to Biddle's plight, she promptly banned him from the house until his cold was better. 'Or we'll all have it,' she said briskly.

Bessie was distraught, but Lizzie unrelenting, pointing out that Biddle had a mother to take care of him. Bessie bridles at talk of Mrs Biddle. There is some friction there. Mrs Biddle claims Bessie wants to rob her of her only support, her son, and leave her all alone. 'And me with my knees', as she is wont to add.

This was the situation when, at two o'clock on a dark afternoon and all gas mantles in the building already hissing, the officer on the downstairs desk was startled by an apparition which burst through the front door.

The combination of a Scotch cap pulled down about his ears and a red muffler wound round his neck hid the visitor's face. Most strangely, he wore a shabby floor-length fur coat of considerable age. Billows of smoky moisture swirled around him.

'I thought at first it was a performing bear on its hind paws, and wearing a hat,' said the desk officer later. 'It gave me quite a turn.'

The newcomer unwound the muffler and declared, 'I come to tell you about an 'orrid murder!'

Chapter Two

THE VISITOR went on to declare that the body of a young woman had been discovered in the kitchen refuse bin kept in the yard behind the restaurant where he worked as kitchen boy. All this was more than enough for the desk officer. The visitor was brought up to see me.

Now we had been joined in my cramped office by Morris, and by Biddle, who brought with him his cold, but also a notebook ready to take a statement.

Divested of his motley outerwear, the informant proved to be about sixteen or seventeen years of age. He still wore his grubby apron. He was a stubby youth whose build suggested he made short work of any leftovers that came back from the dining room. I was surprised there was anything left to go in the refuse bin. His head only reached the middle button of my waistcoat and, with his generous girth, gave the impression that, supported by his short legs, the rest of his body measured pretty much the same in all directions, like a dice. His name was Horace Worth.

'It's not my fault, gents,' said Horace, deeply aggrieved at being expelled from the warm kitchen on such an errand,

and what he took as a lack of sympathy on our part. 'I don't know why everyone is blaming me.'

'We're not blaming you, my lad,' rumbled Morris, 'not unless this turns out to be a load of nonsense.'

'I didn't put her there. I didn't know she *was* there. If I'd known she was, I'd have stayed in the kitchen and not put my nose outa the door. I swear on a stack of Bibles I don't know how she got there. It's not my fault, is it? But first O'Brian goes hitting me over the head with a ladle...'

'Who is O'Brian?'

'He's the cook. He's a bad-tempered b—. He's bad-tempered at the best of times. When I ran in and told him what a horrible shock I'd had – and it frightened the life outa me, you can believe that! Well, O'Brian, he hit me over the head with a ladle.' The speaker rubbed his skull at the memory. 'And then Mr Bellini comes and he starts on me. He's the owner. Worst of all, *she* turns up, his wife. She's a dragon, that's what she is! A regular dragon. She keeps her eye on the money,' he added confidingly. 'The fruit and veg merchants know her for the way she haggles over the price of every potato.'

'What's the name of this chophouse?'

'We're called the Imperial Dining Rooms,' Horace replied grandly. 'We're in New Bond Street and we are a quality establishment. So, Mr Bellini says I'm to go to Scotland Yard. Never mind how much trouble I had getting here. You can't see your hand in front of your face out there. Half the time I didn't know if I was going north or south.' He pronounced 'th' as if it were 'f', the directions coming out as 'norf' and 'sarf'.

'You had only to stop the first constable you met and inform him,' croaked Morris, unsympathetic to our visitor's hardship. 'He would have returned with you to your place of employment and found out a bit more about it, before making a detailed report in an official manner.'

'I already told you, Mr Bellini said I was to come to the Yard,' retorted Horace with dignity. 'He said he didn't want no ordinary bluebottle poking about. He wanted an officer who'd know what to do with a dead 'un. I was to come here to the Yard and nowhere else. Anyway, I didn't see any constable. I heard one. He was out in the middle of Piccadilly trying to sort out some mix-up between a cabbie and a costermonger's cart. I couldn't see him, only heard him shouting. They was all shouting, the cabbie, the costermonger and a few other people. There was veg rolling about all over the road. I trod on a parsnip.'

By way of proof, he burrowed in his coat pocket and produced a squashed shape that might once have been a parsnip.

'Why did you pick it up and carry it here?' asked Morris, still hoarsely.

'I'm taking it back with me,' retorted Horace. 'It can go in the soup.'

'Wherever this establishment is,' I muttered to Morris, 'I don't think I'd care to dine there.'

Horace had sharp ears. 'There ain't nuffin' wrong wiv our place!' he declared sternly. 'You can come and look round our kitchen and it's all as clean as a pin. Half the time O'Brian, he has me clearing up, washing pots and dishes and scrubbing down the table. I don't do the floors, mind,' he added. 'Because there's an old girl comes in of a morning and does that. I'm not a skivvy; I'm learning the cooking. I watch O'Brian. Mostly, he has me peel spuds and stir things. When he's in a good mood, he explains how to make pastry and so on. I'll be a proper cook meself one day.'

'Heaven help us!' murmured Morris.

'Tell it all again to the constable and he'll write it down!' I ordered and Biddle got ready with his pad and pencil. Aside to Morris, I asked, 'Who is there to send?'

'Mullins is out looking into a burglary,' Morris informed me. 'Jessop reported for duty this morning; but he was sniffing and snorting something awful so I sent him home. The others have all been called to other matters, robbery mostly. It's this fog. Every villain in London is taking advantage of it. We're very short-handed, Mr Ross.'

'Constable Biddle?'

Biddle emerged from behind a large handkerchief and blinked red-rimmed watery eyes at me. 'Sir?'

I sighed. 'You had better stay here. But arrange for a police surgeon to meet us at the scene, will you? Well, then, Morris, it's up to you and me, I suppose!'

It did take us a good while to get to the spot. We had to go on foot. Horace Worth led the way, shouting out all the time so that we knew where he was, because the fog swallowed him. Sometimes we could dimly make out his sturdy form in its fur wrapping, but mostly he was only a voice, 'crying in the wilderness', as Morris observed, in a gloomy attempt at some humour. Morris and I both carried bull's-eye lanterns. Their yellow glow in the fog served to identify our position, but that was all. We cannoned into other pedestrians and stumbled over unseen obstacles. At long last, we arrived at the Imperial Dining Rooms.

The entrance to the chophouse was narrow. But once inside we found the building ran back through the block in a suite of three small dining areas, justifying the name of the place, though empty at that moment of customers. Beyond that we debouched into the kitchen where there was a welcome heat, a less welcome steamy atmosphere, and a hostile reception awaiting us.

They were three in number and their faces shone with perspiration. I soon began to feel the sweat trickling between my own shoulder blades beneath the heavy greatcoat I wore. I began to regret having exchanged one extreme of temperature for another.

O'Brian, the cook, was a small man wearing a stained white apron over check trousers, and a chef's white hat. He scowled at us and gestured with the ladle he gripped; it was unclear whether this was in greeting or defiance. Beside him stood a stout gentleman who turned out to be Mr Bellini, the owner of the establishment. He had luxuriant dark moustaches and looked very much the popular idea of an Italian eating-house proprietor, until he spoke in the purest of London accents. Beside him stood Mrs Bellini, also generously built and clad in black bombazine. Her face was red and her hair even redder. It was piled in an intricate mound of braids that put me in mind of a nest of writhing adders. Perched on top was a small lace cap with dangling ribbons framing her broad features.

Taken all together, we pretty well packed the kitchen, and the crush was soon made worse by the arrival of a newcomer. The back door opened, admitting a gust of fog and a constable in a greatcoat. He must have been standing guard over the body.

'Mitchum, sir,' he said to me, when he'd managed to squeeze in and Morris and I had identified ourselves. 'This place is on my beat.'

'They did go and find you, then!' growled Morris, with a glare at Horace Worth.

'Not exactly, sir,' explained Mitchum. 'A passer-by in the street stopped me and told me there was a problem at the chophouse. He'd just come from there, he said, and there was a lot of disturbance in the kitchens. He couldn't make out exactly what was going on, but someone was shouting out that a corpse was in the backyard. So, I thought I'd better come and have a look, sir. It's a body, all right, a girl.'

'I want it out of there!' snapped Mr Bellini. 'I want that thing off my premises. I can't have customers while it's here and I'm losing trade.'

'I shouldn't think there's much trade to be lost, sir,' observed Morris. 'Not in this fog.'

'There's always trade near Piccadilly!' retorted Bellini.

'We're famous for our steak puddings.' Mrs Bellini spoke up. 'We make the best in this part of town.'

'I've been making them since six this morning,' broke in O'Brian. 'But who's going to order steak pudding when there's corpses on the premises? They all know the story of Sweeney Todd, don't they? They won't touch those puddings, you can put your last penny on it!'

'She's got nothing to do with us, that girl!' shouted Mrs Bellini furiously. 'She's a common prostitute, that's what she is – or she was. They're always ending up dead in alleys, those girls. But this one's ended up in our backyard and it's not right!'

'Ruined, that's what we'll be, ruined!' lamented her husband.

'Mitchum,' I said to the constable. 'Perhaps you could take us to the body? The rest of you, stay in here. We'll take statements from you all later.'

'What have we got to say about it?' yelled Mrs Bellini, her already florid complexion now an alarming magenta colour. 'It ain't nothing to do with us! We just want her taken away!'

'So she will be, eventually, madam,' Morris soothed her. 'We'll just take a look, first. Why don't you all go into the dining room there?' He pointed at the door through which we'd entered the kitchen. 'Perhaps a nice cup of tea would help restore your nerves.'

Morris's calm manner and concern for her nerves placated Mrs Bellini, who observed that she was glad someone had some concern for her feelings. She then barked an order for tea to O'Brian. We left them to it.

The yard was small and surrounded on three sides by the walls of buildings. On the fourth side a wooden gate gave on to an alley. The gate was closed to keep out the curious, but we could hear voices muttering excitedly from the other side and smell tobacco smoke. Word had got round. A large metal receptacle stood just by the back door into the kitchen, wedged between the wall of the chophouse and a ramshackle privy. It looked as if it might once have been a water cistern. All this we could make out with difficulty by the light of our bull's-eye lanterns. The fog swirled around us and found its way into our throats. I pulled up the muffler I wore to cover my mouth as I began to cough.

'Is this it?' demanded Morris of Mitchum. 'This rubbish bin or whatever?'

'It's only rubbish to those who have no use for it, Sergeant,' said Mitchum. 'They throw all the refuse from the kitchens into it. Then the scavengers move in. Someone comes from the glue factory to take away any animal remains, bones, skin and trimmings. There's another fellow who keeps pigs nearby and he takes anything of a vegetable nature or what the glue factory don't want. A pig, as you'll know, will eat most anything. The chophouse never has to concern itself with emptying it. They just keep throwing stuff in it. But today, when that boy came out to tip away a pail of kitchen bits, he found this.'

Mitchum held his lantern out over the bin and we all peered in.

It was a desperately sad sight. She looked little more than a child but was probably about eighteen. Whoever had left her in this grimy apology for a resting place had, from appearances, simply scooped her up in his arms and tossed her in. She had landed curled up on her side and looked as if she was asleep, except that her eyes were open and unseeing. A tall and strong man did this unaided, I thought. If two fellows had lifted her and tipped her in, she would very likely have fallen in face down. No, he held her cradled in his arms, lifted her over the rim of the tub and let her fall. Her pimp, perhaps? Had she tried to escape him? Or a violent customer?

Her fair hair had escaped its pins and fell around her face but did not obscure it completely, so that I could glimpse her small nose and her mouth, half open as if to take a last breath. So much could be made out in the orange glow of the lantern. The poor light played havoc with colours and her dress could have been any shade – it appeared grey. I couldn't make out any kind of bonnet, hat or shawl.

As a scene of a serious crime, conditions could not have been worse. In the fog there was no question of making a photographic record. At least the rats hadn't got to her. That would be because she rested in this smooth-sided metal bin. The creatures would know she was there but they hadn't worked out a way to scramble in. Given time, they would. But she would be gone before that happened.

I lowered the lantern. 'Write as detailed a set of notes as you can, Morris,' I told him. 'Make a diagram of this yard with the location of the refuse bin, the gate, anything else you can think of. If you want to try your hand at being an artist, make a sketch.'

A low growl from somewhere in the fog indicated that Morris was not feeling very artistic at the moment.

'Do what you can,' I consoled him. 'Where is that lad?'

'I'm here,' came a voice from within the bundle of moth-eaten fur that was Horace Worth.

'What time did you find the body?'

'I told you,' said the fur coat. 'A bit more than an hour

before I got to Scotland Yard. About half-past twelve it was and normally we'd be really busy. But it's the fog, and we weren't.'

'Are you telling me you had no cause to look into this bin earlier than that?'

'I came out a couple of times and tossed in some peelings. But I didn't look in proper, as you might say. I just got back indoors as fast as I could. Then the last time, I did look in and, well, she was there.'

'Looks as if we'll have to assume she was put there during the night, or very early on this morning, sir,' croaked Morris. 'That boy there might not have noticed her before, but either him or that cook would have noticed someone carrying in a body and putting it in there. Must've made a bit of a noise.'

It was a reasonable deduction and I agreed. 'I'll go inside and talk to the Bellinis. I don't know whether they've taken a proper look at her or just glanced in. They might, I suppose, recognise her if they look properly. Constable!' I turned to Mitchum. 'This your beat. You must know by sight most of the girls who work these streets. You haven't seen her before?'

'Don't think so, sir.' Mitchum shook his head. 'I know a few of them by sight, like you say. But they come and go. Besides, there's so many of them in and around Piccadilly.'

I went back into the building and found the owners and the staff still gathered together, sitting at one of the dining tables. A middle-aged waiter in a striped waistcoat and white apron had joined them. The top of his head was bald

and the hair still growing around the sides had been carefully combed forward over his temples and stuck down
with grease. He stared at me with resentful pouched eyes
and greeted me with, 'I don't know nothin' about loose
women. I'm a Methodist.'

They might have started by drinking tea, or Mrs Bellini
at least had drunk some and her cup with the dregs was
by her elbow. But they had moved on to stronger stuff and
a bottle stood on the table.

I put my questions: had they taken a proper look? If
not, would they mind all going out and taking a good look
now? In case they recognised her.

'Recognise her?' Mrs Bellini recoiled as if threatened
physically. 'How should we recognise a doxy like that? This
is a quality chophouse, not a brothel!'

'If she worked the area, you might have noticed her.
She might even have come in with a client, you know, a
man she'd persuaded to buy her a meal.'

'Not in here!' retorted Mrs Bellini tightly. 'If a customer
brought a girl like that in here, he'd be told to take her
outside again, straight away.'

'A painted harlot,' said the bald waiter. 'Know 'em
straight off!'

Still all grumbling they allowed me at last to chivvy
them outside into the yard where, one at a time, they peered
into the bin, Morris standing nearby holding up the lantern.
I reached down and pushed back the curtain of fair hair
so they could see more of her face. My fingers brushed
her cheek. She was icy cold.

Mrs Bellini took the briefest glance and muttered that

it was downright disgusting before she fled back indoors. Of the others, O'Brian at least showed some respect, crossing himself and hoping God would rest her soul. But he sounded cheerfully philosophical about it. The bald waiter stood there for the longest time, staring down at her. I expected a suitable Biblical quotation, but he only shook his head and shuffled away. They all denied having seen her before.

I returned indoors with the Bellinis to find a newcomer awaiting us. He was wearing a heavy ulster overcoat, but he had taken off his hat to reveal a youngish face and a head of bright red hair.

'We're closed, sir,' declared Mr Bellini in tragic tones. 'But we'll be open later for business as usual, sir, as soon as – as soon as a little problem has been cleared up. I trust we shall have the pleasure of your custom then?'

'I am Dr Mackay,' said a Scottish voice. 'And I don't want anything to eat. I'm the police surgeon.' He turned his gaze on me. 'Are you Inspector Ross?'

'Yes, I'm Ross, and thank goodness you've arrived. We're in the backyard here, behind the kitchens, follow me!'

The Bellinis watched us go with gloomy faces.

Mackay proved a practical fellow and not one to waste time. He took off his coat and handed it to Morris. Then he clambered athletically into the bin to examine the corpse. It didn't take him long before he scrambled out again and retrieved his coat. As he shrugged his way into it he said, 'I hope you're not going to ask me when that lassie died?'

'Even an estimate would helpful,' I told him.

'Aye, I dare say it would. Rigor is well advanced. In

normal conditions I would expect it to have passed off by tomorrow morning. However, if she has been lying there all night in near-freezing conditions, that confuses the issue. When I examine her in decent light I might be able to tell more closely than that.'

'Morgues are all full, sir,' Morris put in hesitantly. 'It's on account of this fog.'

'That's true enough,' agreed Mackay. 'You could try the local undertakers. There must be a funeral parlour around here somewhere. They might agree to let her be taken to their premises for the time being.'

'Well, there must be somewhere. Mitchum! You must know where the local funeral parlours are. Perhaps you'd take Sergeant Morris with you to find one.'

I bent over the bin to take a last look at the victim. When I straightened up and turned, Mackay was eyeing me. He said in his brisk way, 'You'll not need me any longer at the moment!' With a nod, he strode back into the dining rooms.

At that moment came a loud and very confident rapping on the closed wooden gate into the alley beyond.

'No admittance! Police business!' shouted Mitchum.

'If that is a constable,' replied an elderly but confident female voice in educated tones, 'then kindly open this door. I wish to speak to someone in authority.'

Chapter Three

'TAKE A look, Constable,' I ordered.

Mitchum approached the gate cautiously, opened it a crack and peered through. I heard him give an exclamation and then he reached out, pulled someone through the narrow gap, and shut the gate again before anyone else could follow.

'I didn't know it was you, Ruby!' he said. 'What are you doing out and about in this fog? You should be at home by the fire.'

'I'll thank you to address me as Miss Eldon,' snapped the newcomer. 'Is there a senior officer here? If so, I wish to speak with him. Inform him.'

Mitchum came to where I stood and said in a low voice, 'Her name is Ruby Eldon, sir. She lives locally. She's – er –' Mitchum lowered his voice. 'She's a bit of a character, sir.'

'Bring her into the kitchen,' I ordered.

Mitchum conducted the visitor into the kitchen with some ceremony and seated her on a wooden chair. She was revealed as an extraordinary-looking person, very small, about the height and build of a twelve-year-old child. She was dressed with care but in the fashions of the 1830s, a bell-shaped skirt and overmantle, with balloon sleeves and sloping shoulders. A large bonnet and ringlets, bursting from the brim like foliage from a basket, framed her face. I assumed the ringlets to be false, because they were very shiny and a russet colour, showing no grey hairs, although I judged the visitor to be quite elderly. Her skin was very fine and unblemished but with the texture of crumpled tissue. She sat very straight with her hands folded on the handle of a large umbrella planted upright in front of her. Her bright eyes fixed me intently and I was put in mind of a squirrel. She seemed to be waiting for something and I realised I was meant to introduce myself. I hastened to do so.

'Very good,' said Miss Eldon with a gracious inclination of the bonnet and the ringlets. 'By your voice, you are not a born Londoner. Who was your father?'

'He was a collier, ma'am, in Derbyshire.'

'Then why are you in London and why are you a police officer?'

'A long story, ma'am. How may I be of service to you?'

'They are saying, out there . . .' She took one tiny, gloved hand from the umbrella and gestured in the direction of the backyard. 'The populace are saying that the dead body of a woman has been found here. Is that so?'

'I fear that it is, ma'am. Not in the building, but in the yard.'

'I wish to view it,' said Miss Eldon calmly.

'I hardly think that would be wise, ma'am, or seemly.'

'Your delicacy does you credit, Inspector Ross, but I still wish to see the unfortunate. I may know her.'

Mitchum had remained and stood behind the chair in the manner of a footman. He met my eye, raised a fist to his mouth and cleared his throat. 'Miss Eldon lives over the Queen Catherine tavern, just a couple of streets away. She does know, at least by sight, many local residents.'

Miss Eldon rapped the ferrule of the umbrella loudly on the flagged floor and snapped, 'I do not live *over the tavern*, Constable Mitchum. I have taken rooms in the building, on the topmost floor. The landlord and his family live over the tavern, as you would put it, on the floor below.'

I hesitated. 'It would be a distressing sight, ma'am.'

'I am not easily distressed, Inspector Ross.' She rose to her feet. 'Lead on.'

'Very well,' I agreed. I had realised she was not to be put off.

We conducted her to the backyard where we found a problem. The lady was not tall enough to see into the bin.

'Constable!' ordered Miss Eldon. 'Assist me.'

'Yes, ma'am,' said Mitchum. He wrapped his arms round her waist and lifted her up as one might a child, so that by tilting forward she could see into the bin. Morris, bemused, held out his lantern.

'Dear me, no,' said Miss Eldon. 'That is not the girl.'

Mitchum set her gently back on her feet.

'Which girl is this you mean?' I asked quickly.

'Not the one I thought it might be. I cannot help you, Inspector Ross. Constable Mitchum, open the gate, if you will. I wish to go back to my rooms now.'

'Miss Eldon!' I said on impulse. 'I wonder if I might send someone to see you – to call on you.'

'I do not receive men in my lodgings,' said Miss Eldon stiffly. 'My father was a gentleman.'

'Of course, ma'am. I wonder if I might send my wife, Elizabeth, if that would be acceptable.'

'Between two and four of an afternoon,' said Miss Eldon. For the first time she appeared momentarily disconcerted. 'The Queen Catherine is indeed a tavern. The landlord and his wife are very decent people, but the same cannot be said of all the clientele. Mrs Ross should not come unescorted.'

'Our maid will come with her.'

'Very well, then. I have no objection.' She gave me a gracious nod and walked off through the gate out into the fog to be swallowed up instantly.

'Right, Constable Mitchum!' I said. 'Perhaps now you'd go with Sergeant Morris to hunt out somewhere to take the body.'

'You want me to go and talk to this elderly lady?' Lizzie asked me that evening. We were sitting by the fire and I had narrated the events of the day. 'Will she make any sense?'

'I suspect she will make perfect sense, provided you keep an open mind,' I told her. I saw Lizzie's eyebrows twitch and added hastily, 'And I know you to have such a mind.'

All right,' said Lizzie thoughtfully, 'I'll go. I admit I'm curious to meet her. You'll come with me, Bessie.'

'Yes, missis!' said Bessie eagerly, from the door where she lingered to hear my news.

'You'll find Miss Eldon rather eccentric, perhaps, but she didn't strike me as . . .' I hesitated.

'Potty?' suggested Bessie.

'Not in the slightest bit potty, just, as Constable Mitchum had it, a bit of a character.'

Lizzie concentrated on the flames flickering up from coals in the grate. The brass implements dangling on the companion set glowed like gold. I had first set eyes on her when she'd been a child, long ago it seemed, although it was probably no more than five-and-twenty years. Events had separated us and, after time and many changes, brought us back together again. Yet now, looking at her, I could still see that tomboy of a little girl.

Then she looked up and asked: 'What is it in particular you want to know? You say she denied recognising the dead girl.'

'And I believe her. She didn't know her. But I suspect she knows of some other girl; and she has reason to think that girl might be in some danger, I am sure of it. I would like to know what she suspects. My impression was that Miss Eldon is no fool.'

Suddenly, Lizzie asked, 'What has become of the dead girl?'

'The body lies in the mortuary of an undertaker's establishment nearby to where she was found. The public mortuaries are oversubscribed with the deceased at the moment. It is this confounded fog. Morris was pleased to find one so near to the scene. A police surgeon by the name of Mackay will examine the corpse in the morning, as there is no one else free to do it. He thinks that because the body was lying for some hours in that bin, in outside temperatures near freezing, it may be difficult to say when she died with any exactitude.'

Speaking of how cold the weather was, I felt an apology was in order. 'I am truly sorry to ask you to pay Miss Eldon a visit, Lizzie, particularly to go out in such wretched conditions. You will need to cross streets to get to Piccadilly and have your wits about you. There have been so many accidents. I'd suggest you take a cab; but even with your friendly cabman, Wally Slater, to drive you, it wouldn't be any safer at the moment. There was a horse down, with a cab tipped over, not far from Scotland Yard. They were cutting the traces to release the animal as I came upon it.'

'Better off on our own two feet,' observed Bessie sagely. 'Don't you worry, sir, we'll be all right.'

'Yes, well, aren't you supposed to be washing up, Bessie?'

Bessie sniffed and withdrew to the kitchen. Shortly thereafter a clash of pots and rattle of crockery signified she was washing up in her own energetic fashion.

Lizzie was still staring into the fire. 'Do you think the girl was working as a prostitute?'

'The Bellinis have no doubt about it. Piccadilly is a known haunt of ladies of the night, and of the daytime, come to that. She probably was, yes.'

'What was she wearing?'

I had to admit I couldn't give details. 'It was barely visible out there in the yard, what with the fog and darkness already fallen. A dress of some sort.'

'What about a hat?'

I know my wife well enough to realise she doesn't ask

questions without a good reason, but that one left me puzzled.

'I didn't see a hat. It must have fallen off.'

'Then you will need to find it. If it fell off when she was attacked, that could give you the exact spot, couldn't it? I mean,' Lizzie added. 'They all wear hats, don't they? All those girls?'

It was true. Dressing up to look one's best was part of attracting trade. I had seen prostitutes, soliciting the wealthier clientele, dressed like fashion plates. Even poor little drabs loitering round the docks and tavern doors wore some sort of headwear pinned to their curls, real or false. Remembering the crowd that had already gathered in the alley by the time Morris and I had arrived, I thought our chances of finding anything, let alone such a desirable lost object as a hat, were slim.

'Someone will have found it and made off with it,' I said. 'To have searched for it last night in such poor visibility would have been useless.'

'How about a shawl?'

'No, no shawl that I saw.' Her quizzing was beginning to unsettle me. 'Where are you going with this, Lizzie?'

'Oh,' said my wife vaguely, 'nowhere in particular. Only, you see, I wondered if perhaps she was inside a house when she died.'

Now, that did give me something to think about. I wondered if Morris and I would find ourselves trawling the brothels.

Chapter Four

MY FIRST task the next morning was to call in at the Yard to ask if anyone had reported a missing young woman. No one had and I was not particularly surprised. I had decided that the Bellinis were probably right, and the unidentified body in their refuse bin was that of a prostitute, one of the many girls working in the area. The pimps and brothel madams who control the trade seldom report the death or disappearance of one of their girls. All too often the girl has died either at their hands or at the hands of a client. In either instance, questions from the police are not welcome. Disposal of the body would be the priority for those responsible. But why in the Bellinis' yard? Why not carry the body, under cover of the fog, to the river? Young women were fished from the Thames with depressing regularity.

I next made my way to the undertaker's establishment to which the body had been taken, to meet there with Dr Mackay. I would have preferred Mr Carmichael at St Thomas' to carry out any post-mortem examination, especially as there was the complication of the body having been so long at a cold temperature, and the time of death likely to be difficult to fix. But every medical man in the capital was rushed off his feet. In any event, Mackay had made a good impression on me at our brief meeting.

The fog had lifted very slightly but the day was young. As it progressed it would worsen. The funeral parlour, as might be expected from its Piccadilly location, proved to be an impressive place. Marble pillars framed the door. A plate-glass window, draped in purple velvet, displayed an arrangement of wax flowers beneath a glass dome and a pair of sorrowful stone cherubs.

The undertaker was a prosperous-looking fellow, matching his establishment. He had muttonchop whiskers and wore a good quality frock coat and a figured silk waistcoat, both of deepest black. The sombre colour of the waistcoat was relieved by the splendour of the heavy gold 'Albert' chain draped across it. However, he looked depressed, and not just professionally so. Mr Protheroe felt that his business reputation had just been dealt a blow. In this, he was at one with the Bellinis.

'You must understand, Inspector Ross,' he declared, standing before me with one palm pressed on his waistcoat like the popular image of Napoleon, and using the other to make large gestures. 'You must surely appreciate the embarrassment to us here at having a – a woman of the streets lying on the slab in the preparation room.'

He made a wide sweep of the hand towards the rear of the premises to indicate the location of the slab. 'It is best Carrara marble,' he added, apparently forgetting for the moment that I hadn't come to 'make arrangements'. 'I've had some very distinguished deceased lying on it.'

'We wouldn't have troubled you, Mr Protheroe, but there

is something of a shortage of space in the public and hospital morgues at the moment.'

'Ah, yes, the fog.' Protheroe nodded sagely. 'It's taken off a fair number of people. Of course, we wish to oblige the police. But only last week we made the final arrangements for Sir Hubert—'

I decided to cut short further details of the distinguished dead he'd buried and asked if Dr Mackay had arrived.

The medical gentleman had been about his business for the last hour, confirmed Protheroe gloomily. He then called upon a whey-faced youth to conduct me to the rear of the premises.

Mackay's stocky form was bending over the body. He was in his shirtsleeves; his stretched arms and fists resting on the Carrara marble. His ulster coat hung from a hook on the wall. He looked up as I came in and the frown on his face faded as he stretched his hand across the corpse to shake mine briefly. In better light and more at leisure to study him, I put his age at no more than thirty. He had blunt features and a freckled skin, and even when he wasn't frowning he still looked truculent. Then we both looked down at the corpse. Rigor had almost entirely passed off, as Mackay had suggested it would do, and she lay flat. It was an even more pathetic sight, now that she was stripped.

'How old, would you say, Dr Mackay?' I asked him.

'Seventeen, possibly eighteen.'

'No older?'

'Not in my view.' Mackay spoke crisply.

There was a brief silence. The gas mantles hissed. Even so early in the day artificial light was needed in this gloomy place. I wondered if Mackay was a man of few words. If so, that wasn't helpful to me. I wanted information.

'Any suggestion as to the cause of death?'

'She received a sharp blow to the back of the head. There is clotted blood, beneath the hair . . .' Mackay indicated the spot. 'Also, she has suffered a broken neck.'

'Could a fall on to cobbles have caused both injuries?' I asked.

'The blow to the head could be due to a fall. If so, she fell backwards. That alone might not have been sufficient to kill her, though it is not impossible. The broken neck would certainly have done it. I shall put that in my report as the cause of death.'

Mackay hesitated then admitted, 'I attended the usual number of autopsies when I was a medical student and I've done a couple since then, in my time as a police surgeon. But they don't give us the interesting ones. They send those off to St Thomas' or somewhere like that.'

'For Mr Carmichael's attention?'

'He is the expert,' Mackay agreed, a touch wistfully. Then in a burst of confidence, he confessed, 'My own particular interest is in blood – above all, bloodstains.'

'Bloodstains!' I exclaimed.

For the first time Mackay grew enthusiastic. 'Oh, yes, bloodstains make a fascinating subject for study. We still know so little. There are murderers walking free out there in the streets of London because we cannot confidently identify a stain as blood, particularly if it is old, dry and perhaps degraded. Such methods as are used, you will know about the guaiacum test, are unreliable. Research is being done, particularly on the continent, also in America. I am reasonably sure, from my own work, that I shall soon be able to declare with confidence whether or not a dried stain *is* blood, even if it has deteriorated.'

Mackay slapped his hands together. 'Now then, this is what I *can* tell you. After she was killed she, that is to say her dead body, was propped in a seated position on a flat surface. I suggest on the floor. Her knees were drawn up under her chin, and her hands rested on the floor to either side of her.'

Perhaps I looked startled by this sudden burst of graphic detail. Mackay took my surprise for doubt. He walked to the nearest wall, dropped down and sat with his back against it, his knees drawn up beneath his chin and his hands trailing on the floor to either side, as he had just described. 'Like this, you see?'

He scrambled to his feet and returned to the body on the slab and gently rolled it on to one side. 'Now then, look here, Mr Ross, if you will! Obvious pressure points on the lower buttocks, showing white against the purple. There are similar marks on the palms of the hands and the soles of the feet, particularly in the toes of the feet. That is due to her wearing boots with stacked heels.' He gestured towards a table against the far wall. 'They're over there.

'The purple discoloration tells us how the blood drained and settled following death, the white the position in which the body lay or was propped,' he continued. 'Most importantly, the body remained in that seated position for, oh, seven or eight hours. If it were not so, the pattern of lividity would have been disturbed. Also, during that time, rigor began to spread throughout the body. All the time the body was in a very cold place. After that time it was moved and finally deposited where it was found in that refuse bin.'

'You are sure of this, Doctor? You are very precise.'

'Oh, yes,' returned Mackay confidently. 'Because lividity had time to become fixed. Moreover, she had stiffened in that seated position. Whoever disposed of her body could not straighten her first. So, when she was dropped into the refuse bin, she was already in that curled position as you and I both saw her.' He paused. 'It would have made her body difficult to dispose of, her being huddled as she was. The refuse bin must have appeared the ideal repository.'

'Thank you, Dr Mackay,' I said at last after some moments of silence. 'You have painted a very clear scenario. When I first saw the deceased she lay in that rubbish bin and appeared to be curled up on her side. I thought she had been thrown down in a way that caused that position. Now you tell me that is not so, but she was already stiff with her legs bent both at the knees and hips. If the body had been moved earlier, say, only a couple of hours after death—'

'She might not yet have stiffened; and lividity wouldn't have had time to become fixed. Thus I am satisfied the position in which the dead girl's body was stored, prior to being moved to that bin, was as I described to you. She was propped in that position almost at once following death, and so she sat, or the body did, for the period of time I mentioned, or even less. Lividity can become fixed within six hours, so can rigor.'

Mackay drew breath. 'But it's seldom possible to be as

precise as the police always like a medical man to be! And, as I have already remarked to you, the very low temperature confuses the issue. She was found on Monday morning. She had presumably been moved overnight beforehand. She died on Sunday, therefore. Much more I can't say, well, not for certain. So, don't ask me to look at my watch and tell the hour at which the murderer struck.'

I had been given a lot to think about, even so. I decided to explore a new line of inquiry. 'She appears well nourished,' I suggested.

'Oh, yes, she is,' he agreed. In another burst of loquacity he added, 'And has been since childhood.'

I pushed for more detail. 'The girls who work the streets are normally stunted in growth, from impoverished backgrounds or the workhouse.'

'This girl wasn't working as a prostitute!' Mackay retorted. He looked up and met my gaze directly. His chin had a pugnacious thrust to it. He expected me to argue.

I was startled and must have looked it because Mackay relaxed and gave a wry grin. 'You assumed she was,' he said. 'Well, seeing she was lying dead in a back alley, as I understand it, it's not surprising.'

'In a backyard, with a gate into an alley,' I corrected him automatically and he accepted it with a nod. In my own mind I was bitterly regretting having made a facile assumption, and accepting the opinion of the Bellinis that the dead girl worked on the streets. 'You are sure, Dr Mackay?'

'She was a virgin,' he said simply.

I had a far more complicated case on my hands than first thought; that, to say the least of it. Now the absence of outdoor clothing, that so worried Lizzie, seemed more than odd. It could be deeply significant. Now we must rule out the possibility that the victim had been carried to that cramped backyard from some brothel. Now, much more alarmingly, it was possible she been carried there from some outwardly respectable house in the neighbourhood. This was turning out to be an investigation with far-reaching ramifications.

I walked to the nearby table on which her clothing had been neatly laid out. The dress, which had looked grey in the light from Morris's lantern, could now be seen to be mauve. Did that, I wondered, mean she was in 'half-mourning'? The period etiquette decreed for deepest black was over, but it was not yet acceptable for her to wear bright colours. I felt the quality of the cloth: good woollen weave. If she, or her family, could afford the extensive wardrobe needed for the time of bereavement, and buy the best, well, they weren't poor. They might, of course, have taken out the 'mourning garments insurance' popular among the less well-off. But the tiny contributions to such a fund would result in a limited payout.

Her underthings were also of good quality and her stockings of silk. She'd worn little black button boots, with the high heels remarked on by Mackay, and rounded toes. They held a charm all of their own, and I picked one up. The leather was very soft, again of good quality, and when I peered into it I saw a maker's stamp just below the ankle rim. The boots came from the workbench of Tobias Fitchett and Son of Salisbury. They appeared quite new. I was getting steadily more worried. I knew now from Mackay that these were not the boots of a streetwalker, but clearly neither were they those of a factory worker or a housemaid. These were the boots of a young lady. When such a young female is found bludgeoned in a refuse bin, alarm bells begin to ring very loudly indeed. The newspapers! I thought in dismay. This is exactly the sort of case the gentlemen of the press like. That, in turn, meant it was exactly the sort of case Superintendent Dunn, my immediate superior, did not like.

Mackay had joined me at the table. He'd noticed the bootmaker's mark. 'Trace her from that?' he suggested.

'We might get a lead. I hope so.'

'Sad business,' muttered Mackay, more to himself than to me. 'At least, Protheroe out there will be cheered to learn his Carrara marble isn't being defiled by a strumpet.'

I was still studying the boots, turning them to study the soles. 'It's always a sad business,' I said automatically.

'Yes, of course, I hadn't intended to sound . . .' Mackay's voice tailed away apologetically.

'It's easy to become hardened to such sights,' I consoled him. 'Police detectives and police surgeons both, we see too many like that. Oh, and Protheroe was anxious to tell me about the marble being from Carrara.'

Mackay, perhaps hoping to redeem himself in my eyes, pointed at the soles of the boots. 'Mostly worn indoors,' he said. 'Or just to walk a few steps down scrubbed front steps to a carriage, perhaps? I can see they are fairly new, but in this weather, if they had been worn more than half a dozen times outdoors, the soles would be much more discoloured: mud, water . . .'

'You should join us at Scotland Yard, Dr Mackay!' I put down the boots and turned my head to smile at him, to show I bore him no ill will for his earlier flippancy.

'Oh, a doctor often has to be a detective, too,' he said. Very gently he lifted one small dead hand. 'For example, she has done no manual work,' he said. He turned the hand so that it was palm uppermost. 'The skin is soft. The fingernails are well cared for and intact.'

In a way the sight of that hand was more disconcerting than the sight of the whole body. The way the doctor held it made it appear the girl was asking me for something. Help? It was too late for that. Justice? One could only hope. It would not be for want of trying on my part.

'Cold in here,' said Mackay, setting the hand down again in the same gentle way. 'And cold as charity out there in the fog. She might just as well have been kept on ice the whole time.' Mackay looked up at me and with more emotion than I would have expected from him, added fiercely, 'This is a foul business.'

I nodded.

'Do you think you have a chance of finding the wretch who did this? Or even if you'll be able to put a name to the poor lassie?' he asked.

'We shall do our best. Mr Protheroe will make a fuss, but I must leave the body here until a photographer and his apparatus can be brought. If no one comes forward immediately to identify her, we'll have need of an image of her.'

Mackay looked startled. 'Good grief!' he said. Then he flushed and added quickly, 'You know what's necessary, of course. But, speaking personally, I have never managed to come to terms with this fashion for making photographic images of the dead. I have known bereaved parents who must have such an image made of a child. I suppose it is cheaper than engaging an artist to make a portrait as the wealthy do. But still, I would rather remember a child as the poor little soul was when alive.'

'This will not be a sentimental image and her nakedness will be covered. It will have a practical purpose.' I indicated the girl's garments on the bench. 'All the evidence tells us this girl was not from a poor background, or an institution, nor did she earn a living on the streets. Therefore, someone of consequence is missing her; and will insist on knowing what has become of her. I would expect her disappearance to be reported to the police soon. It may already have been done, somewhere, and the news not yet reached us at the Yard.'

'Fair enough,' said Mackay. 'You know what needs to be done.' He went to a basin in the corner and washed his hands briskly. Then he unhooked his ulster and began to struggle into it. He wanted to be gone from here. I didn't blame him.

I was confident my decision to send a photographer was correct. A voice in my head warned, *Superintendent Dunn will not like the expense!* Nor would he like the expense of my travelling to Salisbury the following day to track down the origin of the boots. But go I must, first sending a telegram to the police in Salisbury to let them know I was coming. The costs were rising and Dunn's voice, in my head, was near-hysterical. Silently I told the voice that it was not in charge of this investigation: I was.

I collected the boots from the table and went to request some brown paper from Protheroe, if he had such a thing, to wrap them in. The whey-faced youth was sent for it and reappeared in a short time. The pair of them watched dolefully as I parcelled up the boots.

'You are going to take *all* her things, aren't you, Inspector Ross?' Protheroe asked nervously. 'We are not a left luggage office. And the deceased herself . . .'

'I am confident a public morgue will be found to take her today,' I assured him. 'Sergeant Morris will let you know. As for her remaining belongings, they are evidence and must not be touched. Sergeant Morris will remove those, too.'

I marched out with my parcel under my arm.

Chapter Five

'SALISBURY?' EXCLAIMED Lizzie that evening, when I arrived home with my parcel and the news that I intended to take the train the following morning for Wiltshire.

'No report of a missing young woman had come in by the time I left the Yard. In view of her quality clothing and physical condition, that is both strange and worrying. I have no choice but to go out and search for her. I have no other real lead and these boots are distinctive.'

I handed my parcel to my wife as I spoke. To my own ear, I sounded a trifle defensive. It was the awareness of Inspector Dunn's probable disapproval that caused my discomfort.

Lizzie had unwrapped the boots and was examining them in detail; watched by Bessie, mouth agape.

'They cost a bit,' declared Bessie. 'They're really nice. I never had a pair of boots like that. I don't suppose I ever will,' she finished wistfully.

'Yes, Ben, these were very expensive,' Lizzie confirmed.

I had had enough reminders of expenses. 'Then they should lead us to their owner!' I declared with a confidence I did not entirely feel. 'At least, that is my hope.'

I sighed as I gazed down at the boots, watched by the two women. Lizzie's wise eyes rested on me thoughtfully. Bessie, a cockney sparrow, almost hopped about in the desire to add her pennyworth of opinions.

'Perhaps she came up to London shopping?' she suggested eagerly. 'Or she wanted to go to the theatre? Or she was visiting someone. Anyway, as I see it, someone came with her. Who? And where's she gone now? Or it might have been a "him"!' Bessie's cheeks grew pink with excitement and the thought of intrigue.

She had asked a pertinent question. If the deceased girl, young and respectable, had travelled up from Salisbury within the last few days, it was likely someone would have accompanied her.

'These are all things I have to find out,' I told Bessie. To Lizzie, I added, 'An investigation into the death of a complete stranger about whom one knows absolutely nothing is one of the most difficult any officer can undertake. First, I have to find out who the victim was. Then I have to get to know her, and her circle of acquaintances. I need to know her as well as if she sat by that fireside.' I pointed at the grate.

Bessie shivered. 'That's really creepy,' she said in awe. 'It's like those boots have brought a ghost in here with them!'

It was time to cease talk of the dead girl, at least until the following day. I turned my attention back to my wife.

'Well, my dear,' I said. 'Did you go to visit Miss Eldon?'

'Of course!' said Lizzie, nettled. 'But we should have supper first, or it will spoil.'

So we ate our evening meal and then I settled back to listen to Lizzie's account of her day.

Elizabeth Martin Ross

I set out with Bessie for the Queen Catherine tavern that afternoon, to make my call on Miss Eldon. Bessie, always keen for what she called 'an adventure', fairly danced beside me, not a bit put off by the clammy touch of the fog on our faces and the smoky stink of it. It was a little thinner than the previous day. But we still found it best to stay close to the buildings, and be guided by a fingertip touch on the brickwork, as though we were blind. Even so, we narrowly avoided colliding with other pedestrians several times, as indistinct shapes emerged from the gloom without warning. Like us, they stayed close by the walls. We muttered mutual apologies and made our way on.

'Spooky, ain't it?' said Bessie with relish, as yet another dark form materialised briefly and swerved just in time to avoid us, before being swallowed up by the mist.

We heard a voice say, 'Apologies, ladies!' But it came as if from nowhere.

'What do you want me to do, missis, when we get there? I mean, while you're chatting to this funny old woman the inspector wants us to pump for information.'

I felt I ought to reprove her for the way she described our outing, but it was difficult to justify being outraged because she was right. Ben had sent me out to gather information. I was beginning to regret being so quick to accept the task.

'We ought not to call Miss Eldon a "funny old woman", Bessie. We haven't met her yet. As to what you should do, well, perhaps I could ask the landlord if you could wait in the warmth of the kitchen while I pay my call? Kitchens are great places for gossip. If the girl Miss Eldon is worried about lives locally, others may have noticed something odd.'

We eventually found ourselves, after several missed turnings in the fog, standing before the Queen Catherine tavern. It was difficult to make much out of the frontage. That was a pity because it must be a very interesting old place. At the moment, all we could discern was that it was a timber-framed building, probably much older than most of the surroundings ones, if we could have seen them to judge. Its antiquity was confirmed when we made our way inside. The ceilings were low with ancient oak rafters. The taproom, in which we found ourselves, was a cramped place crowded with more tables than convenient, although this afternoon only two old men sat there, smoking pipes before the hearth. We welcomed the heat, too. The ancient floorboards were swept clean and polished, the gas mantles burned brightly and the brass work gleamed. The landlord, though clearly surprised at the sudden appearance of two respectably dressed ladies, smiled a welcome.

''Ullo,' he said genially. 'Come inside outa the fog, have you?' He then added warily. 'You ain't come to preach religion, have you? Because there's only those two over there and they're both as deaf as posts. I manage without religion nowadays myself.'

Hastily I explained I had come to call on Miss Eldon. 'I understand she has rooms on the top floor.'

'Indeed she has. Come to see Ruby, have you? I'll fetch my wife. She'll take you up there.' He went to a low doorway in the corner of the area and bellowed, 'Louisa!'

The landlady appeared, a well-corseted figure in dark blue brocade, with intricately piled dark hair.

'This is Mrs Tompkins, my better half,' said the landlord proudly, gesturing towards his spouse. 'They've come to visit Ruby, Lou.'

Mrs Tompkins assessed us with a rapid glance and we passed muster. 'Got visitors, has she? Well, that's really nice. Is she expecting you?'

'Oh, yes, my husband spoke to her yesterday, about my calling on her. I am Mrs Ross. I have my card.' I took a visiting card from my pocket and handed to her.

Mrs Tompkins scrutinised the small rectangle of card, impressed. 'Then I'll take you up.'

I indicated Bessie, hovering behind me. 'I wonder if my maid could wait for me in your kitchen?'

'Maid, eh?' said Mr Tompkins, much amused.

'I don't mind helping out, while I'm there,' offered Bessie.

'That's all right, dear,' Mrs Tompkins assured her. 'You don't have to work to earn a chair by my fire. Glad of your company. I'll just fetch us a lamp.'

I had been right. Kitchens are great places for gossip and Louisa Tompkins, clearly intrigued at Miss Eldon receiving a visit, was as keen to talk to Bessie as Bessie to her. And I had learned something already. Miss Eldon had not warned the landlord and his wife that I was coming. She, too, had anticipated curious questions.

The treads of the twisting flights of the staircase up which I was led creaked noisily beneath our feet, and all around was more evidence of the tavern's age. I remarked on this to Mrs Tompkins, climbing ahead of me with a paraffin lamp clasped in one hand to light us the way, and holding up her bunched skirts with the other.

'Oh, yes, dear, very old,' she called back to me without turning her head. 'This is one of the oldest buildings in this part of town. It was here before most of the other places around, probably before they'd finished building Piccadilly. It makes you think, doesn't it? It wasn't always called that, you know.'

'The tavern was called something else?' I asked a little breathlessly.

'Well, the old records say it was called the Safe Haven. But I was talking of the street, Piccadilly, just a block away. It was called Portugal Street before that, long ago, mind! It was named for the wife of King Charles the Second. She was a Portuguese princess. She brought oranges with her.' She paused in her ascent and turned to look back at me.

'Oranges?' I asked.

'Yes, dear. They were a bit of a novelty at the time. They got very popular. This tavern was renamed after her, too. So the Queen Kate was here when Piccadilly was Portugal Street!' Mrs Tompkins beamed down at me. '"Pubs and churches", my old dad used to say. "Pubs and churches last out when everything else is knocked down!"'

We arrived eventually, with even Mrs Tompkins a little out of breath, at the very top floor, where there was a small landing. A mullioned window that must be original to the building would normally have admitted light. But today the tiny diamond-shaped leaded panes, uneven with age, were curtained by yellow fog. Mrs Tompkins tapped on the door.

'Ruby! You got a lady come to visit! She's Mrs Ross.'

'You may show her in!' commanded an elderly voice.

Mrs Tompkins opened the door and ushered me in with some ceremony. 'I'll leave the lamp, dear. You'll need it when you want to come down.'

'What about you?' I asked anxiously. I didn't want to hear the crash of the landlady falling down the staircase.

'I'll be all right, dear, I'm used to this old place. You'll need that lamp.'

The door was shut behind me and I stood blinking, glad of the lamp's bright glow. Otherwise, the room was lit only by the fire in the hearth and the limited glow of a pair of candles on the mantelshelf.

Seated before the fire in a winged chair I could make out a figure like a large doll.

'Set that lamp there!' ordered the doll, pointing through the shadows to a side table.

I did as bid, finding the table already held a tray with teacups and a plate of ratafia biscuits.

I returned to the fireside. 'I am Elizabeth Ross,' I said. 'I gave my card to Mrs Tompkins.' Understandably, the landlady had not volunteered to climb and descend the winding staircase twice, first to present the card and then again to bring me up.

'Bring up a chair and set it there!' Miss Eldon ordered. She did not sound unfriendly.

I brought a rather spindly chair, hoping it was stronger than it looked, and placed it as bid, seating myself.

'The kettle is nearly boiled. We shall take a dish of tea.'

I saw that a small tin kettle stood on a trivet before the

fire, a spiral of steam slowly rising from the spout. That explained the cups and the ratafia biscuits. I realised that Miss Eldon seldom received a visitor and wanted to make the occasion special.

'You are married to the police inspector who was at the Imperial Dining Rooms yesterday, summoned to view the body.'

'Yes, ma'am, I am.'

'He told me his father had been a collier.'

'Yes.' I added that my own father had been a doctor, because I realised this was information important to my hostess.

'Mine was a gentleman!' said Miss Eldon firmly. 'Although you temporarily find me in reduced circumstances.'

The reduced circumstances had lasted most of her life and were unlikely to change. But I imagined her story. She had grown up in comfort, daughter of a wealthy man; but not a provident one. When he had died, she had been reduced to poverty. Perhaps he had been a Georgian rake, and had left large debts. I could even guess the approximate date he had died from her style of dress. After that, there had been no money to replace her wardrobe, at least not to the same standard, so Miss Eldon had continued to wear the gowns of the 1830s. She wore one now, with sloping shoulders, low-set balloon sleeves and close-fitting wristbands. She must be, I thought, at least seventy years of age.

I felt a deep sense of kinship with her. My father had died leaving me poor, not because he had gambled or frittered away his money, but because he had been kind and generous. Often he had failed to ask patients to settle his bill because he knew they could not. On his death, I had the good fortune to be offered a home in London by my Aunt Parry, in return for acting as her companion. Then Fate had led me to meet Ben again, whom I'd not seen since childhood. Otherwise, I would have been living like this and counted myself lucky.

Miss Eldon had not been without some good luck. Whatever she paid the Tompkins couple for her rooms, heat and probably a modest midday meal, it was unlikely to be as much as she would have been required to pay elsewhere. I guessed Louisa and her husband, kindly souls, had taken her in, as they would have done an elderly relative, allowing her the illusion of independence.

'Business first, then tea,' said Miss Eldon. 'I was naturally distressed to see that poor child lying dead in a bin of kitchen scraps. But, as I explained to Inspector Ross, I was relieved to see she was not the girl I had feared to find there.' She rose to her feet. 'Come!'

I followed her across the room to the front wall, pierced with an unexpectedly large window. I guessed the aperture had originally been either access to a hayloft or to bring in other items for storage, raised by chain and pulley from below in the street. Very likely, the remains of the hoist were still bolted to the outside wall. Only later was the opening glazed and the area converted into a living space. What manner of items? I wondered. Old inns like this one often had a dark history. When it had been built there would have been open heath beyond it. Old tales of highwaymen crept into my brain. The former name of the tavern had been the Safe Haven. But safe for the travellers or safe for those who preyed on them?

'Because I am under the roof here, I can see across and at a downward angle into the upper rooms of that house opposite.' Miss Eldon appeared to realise I couldn't see the house she spoke of for the fog. 'Unfortunately today we can make out nothing,' she added regretfully. 'But *normally* I have an excellent view of the buildings opposite and the street below.'

'It is a private residence?' I asked.

She nodded vigorously, her false ringlets *à l'anglaise* bobbing. 'There is a young girl living there. She never goes out. I don't mean she never leaves her room, she does. But never the building. When she leaves the room it is only for short periods.'

'An invalid?' I suggested.

'No, she walks about unaided in the room and seems perfectly able-bodied. She is something of an artist, sketching at a little desk. To do this she sits by the window to have good light. Poor child, she has little to sketch by way of subject. I often wonder if she draws what she sees from the window, walkers below in the street, possibly the front of this old building. It is very quaint. At other times she sews or embroiders. Sometimes, the door opens and he, the house owner, comes in. Sometimes it is a woman servant come to tidy the room or set the fire of a morning. I have observed no other visitors.'

Speaking with less certainty, Miss Eldon added, 'I have seen her make agitated movements with her hands. I think, when she did so, someone else was in the room with her.

I think she may be gesturing to that person to keep away. Or that she is denying something. I could not see who the other was. At any rate, it is clear she is a prisoner.'

Miss Eldon turned to me, ringlets framing her serious face. 'I do believe that to be the case,' she said. 'She receives no visitors except for the man, and she never smiles.'

'Who is "he"? The man who visits her room? Have you any idea?'

'I believe he owns the house. He is about fifty years old or so, well built, a little on the stout side. He has side-whiskers and is well dressed. I would think him a successful businessman. I see him going in and out of the house. There are two servants who seem to live in. I believe them to be foreign. From my observation, I conclude the servants go to market and run necessary errands. There may also be a scullery maid. I have occasionally glimpsed a poorly dressed scrap with the look of the workhouse about her, using the basement steps. A boy calls from a laundry in the area. He collects a basket of wash and returns it later in the week. Mrs Tompkins uses the same laundry so perhaps the boy could tell us something? Although he never goes into the house, and the manservant generally carries out the basket of laundry to be put on the boy's barrow.'

'You have kept most careful observation, ma'am,' I said to her. I could have said she was a first-class spy.

'Yes,' agreed Miss Eldon. 'I have considered it my duty.'

We left the window and returned to the hearth where, at Miss Eldon's request, I made the tea. When we had refreshed ourselves and eaten a couple of ratafia biscuits each, Miss Eldon asked, 'Well? What do you conclude, Mrs Ross?'

'That it seems very strange. However, sometimes things do appear odd, but there is an explanation. Perhaps the poor girl is, well, simple, and cannot be allowed to go out and about.'

'She sketches, sews and embroiders, as I told you. There is a tapestry frame and she sometimes works at that. But even if she were backward, she ought to be taken out occasionally, to the park perhaps? We have plenty of fine parks in London, some not far from here. Or to church?'

'Does she appear well cared for, fed, suitably dressed?'

'Yes!' said Miss Eldon tartly. 'But a horse in a stable is fed and groomed. A human being requires more.'

'Have you spoken to Mr and Mrs Tompkins about this?'

I fancied Miss Eldon was slightly embarrassed by my question. 'I did ask once who lived in the house opposite. I did not give my reason for asking. Louisa Tompkins says he is a man of business – in finance, a banker, or something of that sort. I did not like to ask more. You see, I did not wish to appear to have been spying, or the sort of person who would spread a rumour. That might rebound on the Tompkinses.'

That made sense. She could not afford to lose the landlord's goodwill. To appear a troublemaker would not help.

'So you will tell your husband?' Miss Eldon asked brightly. 'And he can go to the house and demand to see the girl, question her.'

'It might not be so easy,' I protested. 'If he has no reason . . .'

'He has a reason. I have given more than one.'

'It must be a reason that suggests a crime has been committed or is planned.'

Miss Eldon drew herself up in her seat and gripped the arms. 'You do not consider it a crime to keep a young woman as you would keep a tame animal?'

It would be no use arguing. Miss Eldon had, in her mind, reported the matter to the police and the affair was now in official hands. My heart sank.

Chapter Six

'WELL, WELL,' murmured Ben after I'd concluded my account. He suppressed a yawn with difficulty and rubbed his palms over his face to disguise it.

'You're tired,' I observed. 'Or perhaps the story is not so interesting, after all.'

'No, no!' he said hastily. 'It's a curious story, to be sure. But we can't assume from the observations of Ruby Eldon that a crime has been committed or is being committed. This young woman is clearly well looked after, fed, clothed, not required to do any work about the house. She has been taught what Miss Eldon would think the accomplishments of a young lady. She sketches, embroiders and so on.'

'But she has no subjects for her sketchpad but what she sees in the house or in the street below her window. That has to be odd.' I hesitated. 'I said nothing to Miss Eldon but I have been thinking and well, you know, I am a doctor's daughter.'

'Go on,' Ben encouraged. 'You've worked out a clue to the mystery?'

'No, not exactly. That is to say, I don't want to offer what might be an explanation because it might be wrong.

And then the situation would be worse than it is now. We'd be in danger of congratulating ourselves on our cleverness and stop wondering about the girl. That could spell disaster.'

Ben leaned back in his fireside chair, the flames in the hearth throwing a pattern of dancing shadows on his face and thick black hair. This past year a few flecks of grey had appeared at his temples. This gave him, I thought, a distinguished look. I had not told him this because he would have laughed.

'Miss Eldon has converted you, I think, Lizzie, to her way of thinking. You want to believe, as Ruby does, that the girl is a prisoner. But I'd like to hear the possible explanations you have dug out of that busy brain of yours. What does your childhood medical connection suggest?'

We had eaten our supper and earlier there had been distant sounds from the kitchen indicating Bessie was washing up. But now all was quiet. I called out, 'Come in, Bessie!'

There was a moment's silence and then the parlour door creaked open a crack and Bessie's nose and mouth could be seen. 'You want me, missis?'

'Oh, do come in!' ordered Ben crossly. 'Don't creep about in the hall eavesdropping!'

At this the door flew open and Bessie appeared, bristling with indignation. 'I wasn't,' she snapped. 'I wasn't doing no such thing! I was just walking past the door.'

'Sit down quietly over there,' I told her. 'The inspector and I both want to hear if you learned anything from Mrs Tompkins, the landlady of the Queen Catherine.'

'I was wondering when you was going to ask me about

that!' retorted Bessie. 'I was going to tell you on our way home, but you said to wait until this evening when the inspector was here.' Less combatively, she added, 'So I've waited, like you told me to, missis.'

'Right!' ordered Ben. 'Lizzie, you first. Tell me your medical theories. Then you tell us what you learned in Mrs Tompkins's kitchen, Bessie.'

'I don't have anything so grand as a medical theory, Ben. But I do know how many unusual medical cases there are. I used to keep my father's cash book, the money he was owed and the money he'd earned from attending patients.' I sighed. 'He was often owed more than he had earned in a week. It was always a relief when a patient settled an outstanding bill.'

'He was a generous man,' Ben said quietly. 'As I know well. He never pressed the poor for payment and he paid for my schooling and that of another lad from the colliery.'

'Yes, but it wasn't the money owing from the poor that made our household finances so uncertain,' I said. 'It was the much larger amounts owed by the rich. They were often very slow to pay. But that's not what we're talking about now. My father was scrupulous in keeping his patients' problems confidential but sometimes it was a case that was, well, public knowledge, or I was able to draw my own conclusions.

'There was one lady my father visited from time to time, a Miss Lansley. She lived in a large house with a married sister and her family. The family was comfortably off and I must say that, in their case, my father's bills were always promptly settled. Miss Lansley's brother-in-law owned a factory where soap was made. The factory was well away from where they lived because of the stink from the great cauldrons in which the fats were boiled down.'

'Ugh!' muttered Bessie. 'I've smelled that stink, I have. It's something awful.'

I ignored her to get to the point of my speech, as Ben was beginning to look restless. 'The thing is, Miss Lansley had a great fear of open spaces. She had no difficulties inside a house, or inside a coach. But getting her from the house into the coach was such business, you couldn't imagine! They used to drape a shawl over her head and push her along and into the vehicle and then she was all right again. Until they arrived where they were going, at church for example. Then it was the shawl again and a real tussle to persuade her out of the coach and down the path to the church door. Sometimes it was almost more than her sister and sister's husband, the coachman and the vicar of our parish as well, exhorting her to take heart, could manage. I am afraid some the less well-behaved boys who lived locally would hide behind gravestones to watch and laugh.'

'It's sad, that is,' observed Bessie from her corner.

'Yes, because she was a very pleasant lady and always well dressed. If you had visited her at home, you wouldn't have imagined there could be any problem at all. My father always said Miss Lansley was charming and musical. She played the piano very well. It made life difficult for the sister and the husband if they wanted go out. That is to say, *they* could go out, but they couldn't get Miss Lansley to go out, even into the garden, and they had a large and well-tended garden. She couldn't take the air in an open carriage. The brother-in-law came to consult my father to find out if he could help. As a well-known businessman and factory owner in the area, it was a great embarrassment to him. Besides, you know how people fear gossip.

'But my father, although he would visit Miss Lansley from time to time to try and find out what she feared so much out of doors, couldn't help. She wasn't mad, you understand, as some local people believed. In another family the decision might well have been taken to place her in an asylum of some sort. But the scandal of that would have been worse for her sister. Besides, my father counselled strongly against such an idea. Poor Miss Lansley just had a terror of any open space. So I wondered, just a thought you know, if this girl observed by Miss Eldon might not have the same problem.'

'It's not a criminal matter, if so,' said Ben. 'It is, as Bessie remarked, very sad. But I can't do anything about it.'

'Miss Eldon is sure she isn't simple, because she has skills, like embroidery and tapestry, but that doesn't mean she couldn't a be a little slow. I don't know. I only know that Miss Eldon is convinced the girl is a prisoner and she wants something done about it.'

He looked towards Bessie in her corner. 'What did you learn from the kitchen gossip, Bessie, if anything?'

'Not much,' confessed Bessie. 'That is, I didn't know I was supposed to ask about the house opposite. But Mrs Tompkins, the landlady of the tavern, she does know everyone's business around there. She says there are quite a few wealthy folk living in the area. They don't come into the Queen Catherine, as a rule, of course. But a few of the younger men sometimes show their faces. She always shows them into the snug. They never sit in the public taproom. Anyway, they don't drink ale: they want spirits. They even order champagne when they're celebrating something. Mrs Tompkins says she and her husband *keep an excellent cellar*.' Bessie placed great emphasis on the last words. 'Sometimes the young gents play cards and get a little rowdy. But they spend a lot of money, too, so Mr Tompkins doesn't mind.'

'Well,' said Ben firmly, 'I am glad the tavern is doing such good business! But as regards the girl Ruby Eldon sees from her window, I can do nothing, not without some real evidence or visible cause for alarm. If you want to persevere and try and look into it further, without causing a furore, well, that is up to you. I can only beg you to be discreet. In the meantime, I have a real crime to investigate and a journey to make to Salisbury tomorrow, as I told you.'

'They are forewarned there, that you are coming?' asked Lizzie.

'I'd prefer "informed" to "warned". I don't anticipate I'll cause them any trouble. I do hope they'll be able to direct me. I have sent a telegraph message to my opposite number there. He will meet me and take me to see this boot- and shoemaker, Tobias Fitchett. It means I shall have to rise early and so now –' he slapped his hands on the arms of his chair and stood up – 'I am going to bed.'

He walked out of the room, leaving Bessie and me together.

'What are we going to do then, missis?' asked Bessie eagerly.

It had occurred to me that I was to about to bite off more than I could chew. But Miss Eldon had such confidence that I would do something.

'Bessie,' I said, 'I have to go back and tell Miss Eldon what the inspector has said. She will be disappointed, I know. If you come with me you must try and find out from Mrs Tompkins if she knows a little more about the people living opposite, particularly if she knows anything about the young lady in the house. But Bessie, please, do be very, very tactful.'

'Of course!' retorted Bessie. 'You know me, missis.'

Yes, I did know Bessie very well and it didn't altogether put my mind at rest.

'There is no need to mention Miss Eldon to Mrs Tompkins. Just be curious on your own account.'

'I am,' replied Bessie simply.

'I, too, can only hope,' I told her, 'that the fog will have lifted tomorrow, even a little. It's so difficult trying to walk anywhere and very dirty underfoot. If it's possible for horse traffic to move about the streets, perhaps you could go out and fetch a cab here, Bessie. It would be nice to have Mr Slater drive us to the Queen Catherine.'

Wally was a trusted cabbie and considered himself my guardian when I was on one of what he called my 'investigations'. I thought of Ben setting out for Salisbury in the morning. 'At least Inspector Ross will be leaving the fog behind him,' I said.

Chapter Seven

Inspector Ben Ross

I DISCOVERED, when I stepped out of my house the following morning, well before it was light, that the clerk of the weather had a disagreeable sense of humour. The fog had thinned considerably, but only because it had been dispersed by a cruel wind blowing up the river estuary. The wind brought driving rain on it, striking the face like the slash of a steel blade. It must surely be coming to us from the Nordic lands or even the frozen wastes beyond. Underfoot the slush had formed troughs and ridges perilous to walk on; and the new rain added another layer of ice so that I, and others out and about early as I was, slithered and staggered along like so many drunks. In doorways, the huddled forms of the homeless and itinerants took what shelter could be had. None moved as I passed and some, I feared, would never move again. I hoped the rain did not turn to snow. If Lizzie and Bessie were to return to Piccadilly today, they should engage a cab. Better still, they should delay their visit. But Lizzie would make up her own mind. She usually did.

As for myself, when I stumbled into Waterloo Bridge Station it appeared as a haven. The heat from the great engines warmed the air though they filled it with smoke. After some initial confusion, I was finally directed to a train that would take me to Salisbury and managed to scramble into a second-class compartment moments before it departed. I was lucky to find a seat despite the early hour. It was already almost filled with travellers, each made more bulky by layers of winter clothing. They shuffled resentfully to make a space and I squeezed in. At least so many packed together generated heat, a benefit. I tried to be grateful for that and to ignore a passenger opposite me who was eating a pungent pasty breakfast containing a lot of onion. He had a scarf tied over his head and hat and under his chin and little could be seen of his face but the rhythmic movements of his mouth as he munched on the crust and scattered crumbs around him. He was getting more than a few disgruntled glances. The company clearly thought he ought to be in third class.

Superintendent Dunn, when I put in my claim for reimbursement of my fare, would probably tell me third was the class of ticket I should have purchased. But I dreaded to imagine the conditions in third on a day like this. If I got the cost of my journey back from the Yard, I expected only the third-class amount. I would have to bear the difference myself, but it was worth it. A blast of onion struck my nostrils. Well, I trusted it would prove worth it. I bid the company 'Good morning!' and got back a chorus of grunts of acknowledgment, but not from the pasty-eater. Then we all huddled back into our greatcoats. I did not foresee any lively conversation on our journey.

We drew out of London, slowly leaving behind us the soot-blackened tenements. It was lighter now outside and I began to feel more optimistic. I recalled travelling south on a previous investigation, to Hampshire on that occasion. I looked forward to the rolling countryside of its neighbouring county of Wiltshire, its open countryside uncluttered with bricks and mortar, its pockets of woodland and its clean air. Of Salisbury itself I knew nothing, the only image in my mind being that of Constable's famous painting of the cathedral and its tall pointed spire.

But I travelled on a serious matter and not for pleasure. I turned my mind to the body of the girl I'd last seen lying on Protheroe's Carrara marble slab, (although the body had now been moved to a public morgue), a girl who had been wearing boots made in Salisbury when she died. I carried the little boots with me, wrapped in a paper parcel. I had set it on the rack above my head with other luggage and trusted I would not lose it. The unknown girl, had she lived in Salisbury? Had she travelled up to London by train? Or by road, in a coach? What had brought about her journey? Had she travelled alone or escorted?

Rain still splashed against the windows and gusts of smoke from the engine billowed by. However, the rain soon lessened, the view became unimpeded and my feeling of optimism grew. Then I remembered that, doubtless, Lizzie would be returning to visit Miss Eldon, to report my disappointing lack of interest in the tale of the damsel in the upper room opposite. Rapunzel! I nearly chuckled. The pasty-eater had fallen asleep and gave a snore. His immediate neighbour contrived to kick the sleeper's foot. The fellow snorted, woke, glared suspiciously him and then closed his eyes again. With nothing else to occupy me, I began to think about my wife.

I should have urged Lizzie strongly to engage a hackney cab. The fog was thinner but the rain disastrous to clothes, footwear and general well-being. Surely Lizzie was sensible enough to realise that for herself. I was feeling more than a little guilty because I knew I had been unsympathetic to her concerns about the unknown girl who lived opposite the Queen Catherine tavern. Although, I thought crossly, they aren't Lizzie's worries! They are Miss Eldon's. Could there be anything to that elderly lady's fears? No, probably not.

I had liked what I'd seen of Miss Ruby during our brief meeting, while wary of taking what she said at face value. She was clearly someone who had time on her hands and little to occupy her; other, that is, than taking an interest in what she saw from the windows of her rented rooms. Possibly all her worries resulted from an overactive imagination, although that didn't make them less real to her. Now she had what is sometimes referred to as 'a bee in her bonnet', an idea that buzzed incessantly around her brain. Such people are often keen to attract others to their cause. Getting free of them once you have shown interest can be very difficult. Perhaps I should have urged Lizzie not to return to the tavern and to let the matter rest. She could, if she felt she really must, write a letter, telling her eccentric new acquaintance she had reported the matter to me; and I felt there was nothing to warrant an investigation. But that wasn't my wife's way. Lizzie had been raised by her widower doctor father to look upon the well-being of others as her concern. She and Miss Eldon had that much in common.

The true cause of any guilt I felt was, of course, that I had asked Lizzie to visit Miss Eldon in the first place. I had been made curious by the remarks of the old lady when she had failed to identify the dead girl found at the rear of the Imperial Dining Rooms. Ruby Eldon had so clearly feared to find someone else. My instinct as a detective had been to find out who that person might be; and I had sent Lizzie to make inquiries. It was my doing. I sighed.

We drew into the station at Salisbury in a cloud of engine smoke and steam. Trapped beneath the projecting roof above the platform it formed an atmosphere almost as dense as the fog I'd left behind me in London. I reached up and grabbed the parcel with the boots from the rack. It would never do to forget that. I climbed down to the platform as others jostled past me, coughing and spluttering, and peered into the haze, where a male form loomed up.

'Inspector Ross?'

As he spoke the train pulled away, puffing out a fresh helping of murk, and he momentarily disappeared again from view. But he reappeared almost at once and when the air cleared I saw he was a solidly built man of sporting appearance, wearing a tweed suit and a bowler hat tipped at a rakish angle. He had the alert expression of a gun dog as he scrutinised me. I judged him to be in his mid thirties, a year or two younger than myself.

'It is Inspector Colby?' I asked, putting out my hand.

He shook it briskly. 'It is! We received your telegraph

message. I confess it made us all very curious. It said you wished to visit a bootmaker here in Salisbury, by the name of Fitchett. We could have done that on your behalf. Although,' he added hastily, 'you are most welcome. How may we help?'

The platform had emptied and I became aware of a hammering and pounding in the near distance. 'They are building nearby?' I asked.

'Oh, yes, work on the railway seems never-ending,' he replied carelessly. 'Let us go into the refreshment room. It's fairly quiet in there. You can tell me all about it.'

When we had settled in a warm and well-appointed refreshment room and been provided with tea, Colby asked the question all Englishmen ask of a newly arrived visitor. 'How was the weather in London when you left?'

Perfectly foul,' I told him. 'We have had nothing but stinking fog of late and today it has given way to driving rain. The streets are coated in icy mud; and you can't see a hand in front of your face!'

Colby chuckled. 'We've not been plagued by the fog to that extent. But we might rival you when it comes to mud. We've had snow and it is lying up still in sheltered spots. However, where there is wheeled traffic or footpaths, the snow has melted or been trampled into slush. And are you in need of a new pair of boots to protect your feet and come here to buy them?'

I placed my parcel on the table. I had not unwrapped it and Colby eyed it with keen interest. 'I have come,' I said, 'to inquire about these, with luck from the man who made them, and who will be able to tell me for whom, and who ordered them.'

I unwrapped the parcel, took out one little black boot and passed it across the table to Colby. I rewrapped the other boot and placed it on the floor by my feet, mindful that leaving items of footwear on a table brings bad luck. I could do without any more of that. Colby took the boot and examined it inside and out, even sniffing at it like a bloodhound.

'Tobias Fitchett, eh?' he observed at last.

After such a thorough examination I had begun to hope for something more than that from him. 'You know of this bootmaker? Is he still to be found?' I asked.

Colby raised his eyes from the boot in his hand and looked at me as if I had indeed disturbed a train of thought. If so, he wasn't ready to share it with me yet, and contented himself with answering my question. 'Oh, yes, I know of this workshop. It is near the Butter Cross. That is a medieval construction in the centre of the city. I can take you there. They have never made boots for me, but it is an old-established firm, representing a couple of generations at least.' He handed the boot back to me and I set it on the floor by its partner. 'How did it come into your possession?'

I told him the story of the dead girl found in the refuse bin behind the Imperial Dining Rooms. Colby scowled and shook his head. 'A bad business!' he said. 'So you have reason, because of the boots, to think the dead girl came to London from Salisbury?'

'I hope she did because if she didn't, well, I really don't know how I'll ever arrive at her identity, unless someone comes forward. So far, no one has, although it is early days.

But it's very odd. The boots have little sign of wear. With luck, she was living here until fairly recently.'

'How about the rest of her clothing?' asked Colby thoughtfully, picking up his cup of tea and draining it.

I described it. 'I wondered if she might be in half-mourning. If she was, that might mean she was living here with someone who died within the last year or two. That, in turn, might have led to her having to leave Salisbury and move up to London. But at the moment, I can only speculate. She might have acquired the boots second-hand. There are numerous second-hand clothes dealers in London – some sell from shops, some from barrows at the roadside. But the lack of wear and tear on them inclines me to believe they were made for her. All her clothing was of good quality.' I took an envelope from my inside coat pocket. 'I have a likeness of her. It was taken after death, of course.' I passed it across.

'Well, well,' murmured Colby as he took it and held it up in front of him. 'I see you are up to date in your methods of detection in London!'

'You have never used a photographic portrait to help identify a mystery body?'

'We've occasionally used one, if available, to track down a live suspect. But a dead one? We trust to an artist to work up an image in most cases. Well, we must keep up with the times. If this is what Scotland Yard does, then so must we.'

Colby rubbed his chin and gazed at the image. 'I can't say I recognise this young woman. Of course, I'm not acquainted with every young lady in Salisbury. But if, as you say, she came from our city, someone should know her.' He fixed his sportsman's keen eye on me. 'Has no one reported her missing in London? Isn't that very odd? A respectable family or household, with a well-dressed young lady living in it? Well, they wouldn't overlook it if she just disappeared one evening. They would be raising the alarm before the night was out!'

'I've been hoping for a report,' I confessed. 'But none has come in so far. It might still do so. Respectable households often don't like to involve the police in their affairs.'

Colby startled me by raising his hand and clicking his fingers. I didn't know whether he was attracting the attention of the one elderly waiter, or had been struck by inspiration. I hoped it was inspiration.

'How about an elopement?' he suggested. 'Perhaps the family fears she's run off with some young fellow? They'd do all they could to get her back by their own efforts before they involved the official channels. The scandal would damage her future prospects, if the lover were to desert her, to say nothing of money being involved. Perhaps she is – or was – a young lady with a fortune?' His voice was gaining enthusiasm.

It was for me to take the role of opposition, questioning his theory. 'It wouldn't explain how she came to be dead in a rubbish receptacle. Also, I failed to mention to you when I spoke of her clothing that there was no shawl or outer garment of any kind. And who struck her so violently on the head? Not the lover with whom she was running off, surely? Not if he was a fortune-hunter, as you suggest.'

'You never know,' said Colby seriously, leaning across the table and dislodging a teaspoon that fell noisily to the floor unheeded by him. 'Perhaps someone wanted to prevent the elopement? Perhaps someone chased after them, caught them? There was a struggle . . .' My Wiltshire colleague was proving to have an imaginative turn of mind and his enthusiasm was growing alarmingly.

My turn to quibble. 'Then isn't it more likely some avenging papa or brother would hit the lover on the head? Then drag the girl back home.' I didn't want to pour cold water on his romantic explanation, so I said, 'It's to be considered, of course. Nothing is out of the question. But first I need to find out her identity.'

Colby had the grace to look slightly abashed. 'Of course. I'll take you to the bootmaker.'

We set off at a good pace. It was, as Colby had warned, very muddy underfoot. There was less traffic than in London streets, and much of it seemed to have come in from the surrounding countryside. Cartwheels threw up sprays of dirty slush as they rattled over the cobbles. I began to fear we'd arrive looking a pair of ruffians. As Colby had indicated, the shop was located in the heart of the city of Salisbury in a narrow street crowded with old buildings. The buildings were packed together higgledy-piggledy, many without the possibility of sliding a sheet of paper between them. Ahead of us they gave way to an open area at the centre of which stood a round construction, with Gothic arched openings, surmounted by a short spire rising from graceful stone ribs. It looked rather like a giant's crown.

'That's the Butter Cross,' said Colby cheerfully. 'And here's Fitchett's shop.'

He had stopped by a bay window, displaying a jumble of footwear-related items. In addition, above our heads hung a sign like an inn sign, but this one showed a painting of a gentleman's hessian boot, with a tassel, of the sort very fashionable when men wore knee-breeches. This, and the legend EST. 1772, confirmed Colby's statement that the firm of Fitchett had been making boots in Salisbury for at least three generations.

We climbed a pair of steps to enter the shop, our arrival announced by the jangle of a bell of the sort fixed on a metal spring above the door; and noisy enough to deafen the new arrival for moment or two. Immediately our noses were assailed by the smells of leather and wax, and filled with dust. From the rear of the premises came the sound of hammering. Perhaps that was why such a loud bell was needed. As its urgent clamour died away the hammering ceased, and a voice asked if that had not been the bell?

A pale young man with straight dark hair, wearing a leather apron, appeared in the doorway to, presumably, the workshop itself. He bid us good day and took his place behind a scarred wooden counter, moving in a stately, unhurried way. Behind him, fixed to the wall, were rows of pigeonholes nearly all filled with a paper parcel each. They must do repairs here, as well as make the originals, I concluded, and the paper parcels awaited the owners of the footwear to come in and claim them. But, as this was not a simple cobbler's workplace, I wondered whether they only repaired the shoes and boots they themselves had made, not entrusting this to other hands.

'May I be of assistance, gentlemen?' inquired the young man, resting his hands on the counter. One fingernail was black. A mishap with the hammer, no doubt.

Colby informed him we were police detectives, first introducing himself and then me.

'Oh, yes,' said the young man agreeably. He seemed neither surprised nor curious at the arrival of the police. Perhaps he thought we wanted boots.

Colby hastened to put him right on this, explaining we had come seeking information about a particular pair of boots originating in this workshop.

'Oh, yes,' repeated the young man, his pallid face still showing no curiosity whatsoever. His opposite number in a London establishment would have been alive with interest and peppering us with questions.

I decided it was my turn to speak up. 'Is it possible to speak to Mr Fitchett?' A thought struck me. 'Or are you the present Mr Fitchett?'

At this the young man did appear mildly startled. 'No!' he said. 'My name is Ezra Jennings.' He stretched out an arm to indicate the rear of the premises. 'Mr Fitchett is creating.'

At this Colby uttered a sound that finished as a cough but had begun as a guffaw. Ezra stared at him with disapproval.

I decided to take charge. 'We should like to speak to Mr Fitchett himself. Would you kindly tell him we are here?'

Ezra withdrew silently whence he had emerged and we heard a murmur of voices. Ezra returned and again indicated the doorway to the rear of the premises. 'If you'd care to go through, gentlemen.'

We went through and found ourselves in a long, narrow room. Tobias Fitchett rose from a workbench to greet us.

The bench was covered with scraps of leather, balls of wax, bundles of strong twine, a variety of knives, awls, and bodkins. A row of jars contained all manner of nails and tacks. There was no outside light, only that of a gas mantle projecting from the wall immediately above the workbench. The smell of leather was overpowering, and the atmosphere airless. Mr Fitchett was small, stooped, as leathery as the material he worked with, and he had small dark eyes beneath bushy brows. He assessed us shrewdly over the pair of spectacles perched low down his nose. He was holding a wickedly sharp scalpel-like knife and I was relieved to see him put it down.

'Well now,' he said. 'Here's a thing. Police officers of a quality sort, dressed very gentlemanly, not constables, eh? Ezra was very surprised.'

'He didn't show it,' returned Colby. 'A very cool sort of chap, your assistant.'

'You need to be calm to work with leather,' said Tobias. 'You have to take your time, get it right, can't let your hand slip. Just like that!' He gestured. 'And you can ruin a piece of the best leather. You can cut your hand open, come to that. Ezra tells me you don't want boots. What do you want to ask me, eh?' Then, stressing we were in the right place, he added, 'If it's about making boots, I'm your man. My grandfather made boots in Salisbury, and my father after him, now me. And all of us,' he added, 'carrying the baptismal name of Tobias. It makes things simpler.'

It was my turn. 'It is about boots, these boots.' I produced my parcel and unwrapped it. Watched closely by Fitchett, I set the little boots side by side on the workbench. I wondered, as I did so, if I was returning them to the very spot where they had been created. To confirm this, I added, 'Your stamp is in them. You did make them?'

Mr Fitchett beamed and seemed delighted to see the boots again, as one would old friends, unexpectedly calling by his premises.

'Oh, my, yes!' he said. He picked them up gently and turned them back and forth in his hands, examining them closely. 'So you have come back to see me, have you, my dears?' He gave them an affectionate pat apiece. 'You have been looked after, my dears, looked after very well, I am pleased to see.'

Colby glanced at me with a raised eyebrow and a twitch of the mouth.

'Mr Fitchett,' I said. 'I am wondering if it is possible for you to tell me for whom you made these boots?'

'A lady, they are a lady's boots,' said Mr Fitchett immediately.

'I do know that much,' I told him. 'I was hoping you—'

'You saw our name stamped in them,' Fitchett went on, ignoring the interruption. 'That's what it's there for, so that people can see who made them. We are proud of our boots and shoes. But did you mark the number, eh?' His bright dark eyes, so like boot buttons themselves, gave me a sudden piercing look.

'Number?' I muttered, disconcerted.

He held the boot up with the leather upper around the ankle turned so that I read his stamp and saw, beneath it, a three-figure number. I confessed I had not paid much attention to that, being more interested in the name and location of the workshop.

'Last,' said Mr Fitchett, and noting that Colby looked confused, added, 'That is the number of the wooden last. Follow me, gentlemen.'

He led us into another room even further into the building. We found ourselves in a long narrow area lit by a window at the rear, but no artificial light, so it was very gloomy. It was made more so by being crammed with racks, like the racks one sees in the larger bookshops, except that these racks held not books, but the carved wooden shapes of feet, neatly arranged by pairs, and numbered.

'When we make for you,' explained Fitchett, 'we first make a last for your foot. Then, should you require a further pair of boots, you have but to let us know and we'll make them. Our boots are much travelled. You could be living in Africa, sirs, or in China or India. You have but to write us a letter and we'll get on and make the boots. We'll send them out to you, or you can collect when you return home.'

Colby, who was now showing a lot of interest, pointed to a spot containing a single quite large wooden shape. 'There's only one foot here,' he said.

'Customer lost the other one,' explained Mr Fitchett. 'A naval man, he had his right leg blown clean off below the knee in a sea battle when he was a midshipman, only a lad. But he had a fine career nonetheless, although most of it, I understand, was at the Admiralty. Afterwards he retired here to Salisbury because he was born here. And we always made his boot or shoe, as required.'

Mr Fitchett stood back and surveyed the collection of wooden feet stacked before us. 'Every pair of those, gentlemen, tells a tale. Wherever life takes a man, he goes there on his feet. But if Fitchett's made his boots, those same feet remain here all that same life, in wood.' Fitchett nodded to himself. 'Ours is a craft, you understand, gents, that leads to a philosophical turn of mind.'

He reached out and picked up a pair of much smaller wooden shapes. 'These are yours,' he said. 'Or rather, they are the lady's.'

It was an extraordinary moment. Just briefly, I felt that she stood before me. These were her feet, not just anyone's. My dead girl had been in this very cordwainer's stockroom and had left behind a token in the shape of carved wooden lasts, just as Fitchett had said.

'And are you able to put a name to the lady and find out when the boots were made?' I asked eagerly.

'Oh, yes,' replied Fitchett. 'Follow me, if you would. Ezra!' He raised his voice. 'The order book, if you please! Find number –' He gave the three-figure number.

We returned to the front of the shop where Ezra presided over his counter. On it now was opened a large order book. Mr Fitchett adjusted his spectacles to a reading position on his nose and peered at the columns of spidery entries.

'Here we are, gentlemen! The boots were made for Miss Emily Devray. The order for them was placed by Mrs Waterfield.' He straightened up and removed the spectacles. 'A very charming young lady, Miss Devray. I took her foot measurements myself. Mrs Waterfield herself was an old and valued customer.'

'Was?' I asked quickly.

'The lady has sadly been called to a higher place. Early last year, it was.'

'Is there a Mr Waterfield?' I asked hopefully.

Mr Fitchett shook his head. 'Long gone,' he said. 'Went to Jamaica on business and took a fever on board ship. Never returned. Buried at sea.' He frowned. 'We made his boots, several pairs. I wonder whether they buried him booted. Probably not. A good pair of boots like that? I dare say some sailor slipped them off the body before it went into the water.'

Colby had been examining the book and the addresses given for each customer. 'Mrs Waterfield lived not far from here, just by the cathedral green.'

'Do you happen to know,' I asked Fitchett, 'if Miss Devray was related to the late Mr and Mrs Waterfield?'

'Of that I have no knowledge,' returned Mr Fitchett.

'But you met the young lady, you said, when you measured her foot?' I took out the photograph. 'I wonder, could I ask you to look at this and tell me if this is the young woman?'

Fitchett took the piece of card on which the image was printed and studied it. Then he silently passed it to Ezra. After a similar lengthy study, Ezra passed it back to his employer. Mr Fitchett handed it back to me with some ceremony. 'That is the young lady,' he said. 'But I fear we shall not be making another pair of boots for her, am I right?'

'You are right,' I confessed. The photographer had done his best, but the image in the photograph was clearly that of a corpse.

'I wonder,' said Mr Fitchett, 'why you must come to *me* to know her name?'

'She was discovered dead in distressing circumstances in a— in London. So far no one has identified her or come forward to report a young lady missing. We needed to put a name to her. Now we can, and I thank you, sir.'

Ezra was now showing a lot of interest. He looked quite alert. 'I delivered those boots,' he said, 'to the house. It's been sold since. It had a sign put up outside it. All the furniture was sold, as well. I saw it being carried out and taken off to the auction house. All sorts of stuff, there was, tables, chairs, sideboards, pictures in their frames . . .'

'So I believe!' said Fitchett sharply, turning a severe look on his employee. 'Standing in the street and gawping is not behaviour expected, Ezra, of anyone associated with the firm of Fitchett! Nor is taking an interest in a customer's private business, even if that customer has departed in every sense of the word.'

'All right, Mr Fitchett, but it was all taken out, anyway,' muttered Ezra sullenly.

'Did you hear anyone say, Ezra, what became of the young lady, Miss Devray?' asked Colby hastily.

Ezra shook his head.

I rewrapped the boots and thanked Mr Fitchett sincerely for all his help.

'What will become of *them*?' asked Mr Fitchett sadly, gazing at the parcel. 'Will they find a good home, do you think?'

'They are evidence, Mr Fitchett. Very important evidence.'

'Murdered, was she?' Ezra burst out, his pallid face brightening. 'Up there in London, was she murdered?'

'Ezra!' thundered Mr Fitchett.

'Probably,' I told them with caution. 'If you should think of anything that might be useful to us, you can tell Inspector Colby here, Mr Fitchett. You, too, Ezra.'

We left the premises to the sound of Tobias Fitchett upbraiding his employee. I hoped Ezra didn't lose his position.

'Well,' I said to Colby. 'At least I have a name for the victim. Now to find out how she came to be in London.'

'Gossip,' said Colby thoughtfully. 'That's what we need, Ross, gossip. I have hopes of that young fellow, Ezra. Fitchett will tell him not to speak of our visit for the sake of the reputation of his business. But I am confident that Ezra will have spread the news all over Salisbury by tomorrow morning. You can wager good money on it. You can't keep news of a murder quiet. I'll wait a few days and then go back and speak to Ezra again, preferably when he isn't in the shop. That is, if no one comes forward of his own accord.'

'Thank you,' I said. I thought Colby was right. Ezra would be eager to spread the gruesome news. Perhaps it would lead someone to speak out.

'In the meantime,' went on Colby cheerfully, 'the house formerly belonging to Mrs Waterfield is this way. Come along!' He set off at a brisk pace, his bowler hat at a jaunty angle. Ezra wasn't the only one whose interest had been sparked.

Chapter Eight

THE HOUSE was a stone building in a narrow lane. Ahead of us, as we approached it, I could see an ancient archway and beyond that a view of a wide green sward and a glimpse of the cathedral itself. Then we turned aside to go through a gate and up to the door where Colby tugged at the bell pull. A middle-aged maid of daunting respectability opened it to us. She eyed us with some misgiving. Colby explained who we were and our purpose.

'We understand,' he said, 'that the house previously belonged to Mrs Waterfield. We would like to speak to the present owner, if he is here and would be kind enough to receive us.'

She looked from one to the other of us. 'The reverend Dr Bastable lives here now,' she said. 'I'll let him know you're here. But we are not accustomed, you know, to have the police call, and at the front door. You could have gone to the back!'

And the door was shut firmly in our faces.

'Wouldn't you think,' said Colby to me, 'that respectable people like this clerical gent, and his household, wouldn't be so suspicious of the police?'

'Fear of scandal,' I said, 'and the watching eyes of neighbours. The same thing has led to a delay in reporting the girl missing, perhaps.'

Colby scowled. 'They are all the same. As soon you as you knock on the door of some fine upstanding citizen, he reacts like the guiltiest person on earth. On the other hand, when the person you're calling on greets you heartily and asks what he can do for you, he's probably hiding something. It is similar in London, you say?'

'It's much the same,' I said. 'But once they are reluctantly convinced they have need of you, they remember that you are a public service. They demand you drop every other inquiry to concentrate on theirs!' Miss Eldon came briefly to mind. I wondered if Lizzie would have returned to that lady's lodgings today.

The maid was back. The Reverend Dr Bastable would see us. Would we kindly wipe our feet? This request, I assumed, did not come direct from the reverend gentleman but was the maid's own concern. We made sure to make use of the metal boot-scraper by the door, stepped over the threshold, and were relieved of our hats by the maid, who put them on a hall table. Eventually she directed us into a comfortable room where the walls were lined with bookcases. A fine fire flickered and crackled in the grate.

Dr Bastable had been reading in what was clearly his library when we arrived. He rose now from a wing chair beside the hearth and set down his book on a small side table. Also on the table stood a decanter of what I guessed to be sherry or madeira, and a glass. He could not be pleased at our intrusion into such a comfortable scene, but he hid it well.

'You gentlemen are from the police, eh?' he asked. 'So, then, what's brought you to my door?'

He was probably at least seventy years of age and had once been a tall man and a fine-looking one. Now he was stooped, lean in build, with silvery hair and side-whiskers. A pince-nez was perched on his aquiline nose. He took this off as he spoke and pointed it at us. I suspected he had once been a clerical schoolmaster. If I had been his pupil, I would have been terrified of him. The eyes that fixed on us might need spectacles for reading, but they had a clear, piercing stare.

'Thank you for seeing us, sir,' said Colby courteously. Indicating me, he added, 'Inspector Ross has come down from London today regarding inquiries he is making there about a young lady we understand once lived here. This house did belong to Mrs Waterfield, did it not?'

'Yes, it did, indeed. But Mrs Waterfield is deceased,' said Dr Bastable.

Colby was looking at me. I was meant to pick up the questioning. I did so, and Colby looked relieved.

'The facts are these, Dr Bastable. I am investigating a sad case of violent death. The body of a young woman has been found in London. We have reason to believe she is a Miss Devray and that she previously lived here with Mrs Waterfield.'

Dr Bastable was probably used to hearing alarming confessions. He showed no surprise, only took his chair again and a moment or two to make himself comfortable. He removed his pince-nez and set it carefully alongside his book. Then he placed the tips of his long, thin fingers together and studied us over them. I recognised all the signs of someone taking time to think.

'Indeed?' Bastable said at last. 'Where, in London, may I ask, was this young female found?'

'In a yard behind a chophouse, not far from Piccadilly,' I told him. 'The body was discovered in a large rubbish receptacle used for kitchen refuse.'

Bastable seemed to freeze for a moment, but otherwise did not betray any surprise at hearing what was a shocking statement. He only asked, 'And the cause of her death?'

'She had received a violent blow to the head and her neck was broken. As yet, we don't know the weapon used, nor why, nor anything of the circumstances.'

I did think that, this time, Bastable was about to say something of interest, so I paused. He reached out for the pince-nez he had set down when he retook his seat, and took it up again. He studied the glinting lenses for a moment, turning them this way and that. But all he said was: 'Go on.'

I took a deep breath and explained about the boots and our visit to Tobias Fitchett. 'So that,' I concluded my explanation, 'is how we come to know Miss Devray lived here with the late Mrs Waterfield.'

'I was not acquainted with the previous owner of the house,' Dr Bastable informed us, 'nor the young person in question. I purchased the house after Mrs Waterfield's death, and from the heir to her estate. He had no use for it. I can therefore tell you nothing of Mrs Waterfield or her household.' After another pause, he added grudgingly, 'However, the cook, Mrs Bates, was employed here in the late owner's time. She may know something of it all.'

This was better than I'd hoped. 'She would have known Miss Devray? That is encouraging news!'

'I assume it to be the case.' Bastable disapproved of my enthusiasm. He rose to his feet and tugged at the bell rope hanging beside the hearth. The elderly maid appeared within minutes, so fast that I suspected she had been loitering in the hall hoping to catch a word or two through the door panels. She undertook to fetch Mrs Bates. Bastable indicated we should be seated with a gracious gesture. He had left us standing until now, trusting our visit would be very brief. He sat down again in his original chair, propped one knee upon the other, placed his hand together as in an attitude of prayer and tapped the fingertips together in an irritable way. We were lingering longer than he liked. He was resigned to his public duty to assist the Law. But he didn't like it. We waited in silence.

Most cooks, in my experience, tend to be generously proportioned and Mrs Bates was no exception. She appeared before us, breathless and curious. Her pink face, beneath a mob cap, was perspiring freely, and her stout body was swathed in a voluminous apron.

'Yes, sir?' she addressed Dr Bastable.

'Ah, Bates,' said her employer coolly. 'These gentlemen are from the police. They have come to tell us that Miss Devray is dead.'

Mrs Bates's eyes bulged, her mouth fell open, then she uttered a scream and sank to the floor.

'Oh, my word, I never did!' she exclaimed from the welter of skirts, apron and mob cap. 'The poor blessed young lady! What, dead and gone to be among the angels?

She was an angel herself, I do declare.' She clasped her hands. 'Taken before her time, was she?' Her eyes fairly sparkled in her eagerness to know the lurid details.

'Indeed, she was,' I confirmed. 'And quite possibly as the result of a violent act.'

The cook drew in a deep breath, and unclasped her hands to place one meaty palm on each of her two red cheeks. 'The world's a wicked place, as we all know, and you'll know more than most, sir!' (This was addressed to her clerical employer.) 'But to take an innocent like poor Miss Devray? Why, she wouldn't have harmed a soul. She couldn't watch me take a mouse out of a trap. It is a wicked business, it must be! We'll all be praying for her poor angelic young soul.'

'Yes!' Dr Bastable told her crisply. 'Stand up, Bates. It is a shock to you, I dare say, but these gentlemen have no time for your lamentations. They want to know what you can tell them about Miss Devray! Was she related to Mrs Waterfield?'

'No,' said the cook firmly. 'Not by blood, and I know it for a fact. She was born in sorrow, that's the truth of it. Her poor mama died at the birth. Her papa was a business associate of the late Mr Waterfield and, as he and Mrs Waterfield had no children of their own, they undertook to raise the orphaned infant. It's a blessing, gentlemen, that neither Mr nor Mrs Waterfield are here today to hear the shocking news you've brought. Not, of course, that they are not sadly missed in Salisbury. They were very well regarded, both of them. But if they hadn't been already dead, this horrid news would have killed them.'

'Is Mr Devray, her real father, still alive, do you know?'
I asked.

'Dead and gone,' the cook told me with a shake of the
head. 'Didn't last out more than twelve months after the
loss of his poor wife. His heart was broke.' Mrs Bates
lowered her voice. 'So the poor mite was left all alone and
would have ended up in an orphanage, the workhouse most
likely, had it not been for Mr and Mrs Waterfield. Mr
Devray left not a penny, you understand, to his child. His
money was all lost in some way. I don't know how,' finished
the cook on a note of regret.

Dr Bastable was growing impatient. 'I suppose, Ross,
all this is important and what you need to know?' he
demanded of me.

'Very much, sir.'

'Very well, if it's necessary. But I do not encourage
servants' gossip! Is there anything else you know, Bates,
that would be of interest to the police officers here?'

I was not best pleased at having the conduct of the
inquiry taken over by Dr Bastable and wished I had been
quick enough earlier to ask to speak to Mrs Bates alone.
But it was Dr Bastable's house and his cook, so I had to
make the best of it.

'Mrs Bates,' I said firmly, 'do you know where Miss
Devray went after she left this house, following the death
of Mrs Waterfield?'

'No, sir,' said Mrs Bates sadly. 'But I believe she had
been offered a place.'

'As a servant?' I asked in surprise.

'Oh, no, sir, or not exactly, more as a nurse-companion.

Not to a child, but to an invalid lady, someone who was bedridden. But I don't know where.'

'And Miss Devray told you this herself?'

Now the cook looked a little embarrassed. With an apprehensive glance at her employer, she admitted, 'Not exactly, sir. I happened to overhear her tell Mr Carroway, who was Mrs Waterfield's lawyer.'

Dr Bastable uttered a sound indicating extreme disapproval. It was time to conclude the interview with the cook. I doubted she had anything more to tell us, except one thing. I knew the answer, or thought I did, but it did no harm to double-check.

'Can you confirm for us, Mrs Bates, Miss Devray's first name?'

'Emily, sir, that was her name.'

'You may go now, Bates!' ordered Dr Bastable.

To me, Colby murmured, 'I can take you to this lawyer. I know where his rooms are.'

I thanked Dr Bastable for all his help and apologised for disturbing him. He acknowledged the courtesy with a dignified gesture; but was clearly very pleased to see us leave.

In the hall, as the elderly maid handed us our hats, I asked of her, 'Did you know Miss Emily Devray?'

'No, sirs,' said the maid regretfully. She hadn't wanted to allow us into the house, but she dearly longed to know what it was all about. Well, Mrs Bates would tell her.

Outside in the road again, I looked at Colby. 'What do you make of Bastable?'

'Cold fish,' said Colby. 'But he was very shocked when you told him about the refuse bin, though he hid it well.

A bit sordid for his refined tastes, that. He wants to, let's see, distance himself from the whole affair. Yes, that's the phrase. He didn't even treat us to a bit of suitable scripture. He might be a clergyman but he's not one I'd go to for spiritual comfort. We'll get nothing more out of him!'

'Very well, next we go to see this lawyer. See if we get more out of Mr Carroway?'

'He'll be thinking of his luncheon,' said Colby, consulting his fob watch. 'So should we be. I know a place that will serve us a decent meal.'

Thus it was a little later when, fortified by cutlets and a boiled raisin pudding, we set out for the lawyer's rooms.

Carroway had probably lunched well too, and perhaps had been hoping for a post-prandial nap. He was clearly not pleased to see us and didn't trouble to hide it.

'Police?' he inquired sharply. 'Could you not have made an appointment?'

He was a thickset fellow of medium height and perhaps fifty or so years of age. His clients were probably mostly country squires and better-off yeoman farmers, with some respectable ladies like the late Mrs Waterfield. His reddened weather-beaten complexion suggested he kept a saddle horse and rode out to country clients to give his advice. His red-veined nose suggested he might keep out the cold on these journeys with the contents of a hip flask.

It was my turn to apologise for disturbing him. But I did so in a firm voice. I did not want to encourage him to think he could bully me or overwhelm me with protestations of client privilege. He turned small, angry eyes on me.

'Well, then?' he snapped. 'Tell me what you want.'

I told him that I was investigating a murder in London and had reason now to believe the victim to be Miss Emily Devray, who had formerly resided with a client of his, Mrs Waterfield.

'Yes, she did,' agreed Carroway, leaning back in his chair and staring hard at me. 'But I did not manage her affairs. She had none. She was a penniless orphan. The Waterfields had taken her in as an act of charity. I can't tell you anything about Miss Devray.' Rather too late he added, 'I am sorry to hear of her death, of course. Murder, you say? That sounds deuced unlikely to me!'

Had I imagined it, or did he sound, just for a second, uneasy?

'A broken neck.'

'Not an accident? A fall downstairs, that sort of thing?' he persisted. 'Sure about it, are you?'

He was not the first person to whom I'd given unpleasant news, only to be met with a blank refusal to accept it.

'Quite sure, Mr Carroway. There was also a blow to the head, and the body was moved and abandoned in an attempt to interfere with our inquiries.'

Carroway still hesitated, puffing to himself and fidgeting in his chair. He rubbed his hands together, as if they were cold, although a good fire burned in the grate.

Then he leaned forward, his small sharp eyes fixed on me, and challenged, 'Has the body been identified beyond any doubt?'

I was forced to admit it had not yet been identified officially as that of Emily.

Carroway leaned back and relaxed. 'Let us hope, then,

you are mistaken,' he said. He did not appear disposed to add to that.

If he thought that was it, and there would be no more questions, he was mistaken. I produced the photograph. 'Is this, in your opinion, Miss Devray?'

Carroway took it between finger and thumb with marked distaste and held it away from him. I wondered if he was far-sighted.

'It is somewhat like her,' he said at last with reluctance. 'But I could not swear to it. I had little to do with her directly, as I told you. I cannot make a reliable identification, if that is what you want.'

I was not going to let him fob me off.

'I understand Miss Devray to have spent her entire life from early infancy with Mrs Waterfield,' I said. 'I am wondering if Mrs Waterfield made any provision for her in her will.'

'I am not prepared to discuss the details of my late client's testamentary dispositions,' intoned Carroway. Then, perhaps seeing a combative look in my eye, he added grumpily, 'But I can certainly confirm that she left only a very small amount to Miss Devray.'

'That surprises me,' I remarked. 'Surely Mrs Waterfield might have looked on Miss Devray almost as a daughter.'

'Well, she wasn't, and Mrs Waterfield didn't!' Carroway fairly snarled at me. As I made no reply and Colby seemed intent on studying the law books on a shelf nearby, Carroway grudgingly added, 'There was no cause for her to do so. Had the Waterfields not taken her in as a baby, she would probably have been place in some charitable orphanage.'

'Do you mean the workhouse?' I asked.

Carroway's florid complexion grew even darker. 'That is what the workhouse is for, to take in the destitute and the unwanted. This child was both.'

Suddenly, he seemed to come a decision. He wanted me out of his offices, but had realised I wouldn't go away unless I gained some information from my visit.

'See here, Inspector Ross,' he went on. 'I will be frank. Miss Devray's father was a man of very poor judgement. I must stress that he was never my client, but I knew of him. When he died, he left nothing but debts. The Waterfields fed, clothed, educated, and provided his orphaned daughter with every necessity for seventeen years. That was more than enough, surely? What Mrs Waterfield was not prepared to do was provide the girl with a marriage portion, or take on the expense and responsibility of "bringing her out". *She was a charity case.* When she had almost reached eighteen, it was time for Emily to support herself. Besides, Mrs Waterfield was now elderly, a widow, and her health failing. She decided to find a situation for Miss Devray, as a governess or some such thing.'

'Was that at your suggestion, by any chance?' I asked.

Carroway adopted an air of dignity and replied, 'She consulted me, certainly, as to the good sense of such an arrangement. I told her it made perfect sense. So Mrs Waterfield found Emily a position in London, through an acquaintance of hers. I must stress, I was not involved in making this arrangement. I do not know the name of the acquaintance, nor of the family to whom Miss Devray went. As it happened, no sooner was the arrangement made than

Mrs Waterfield collapsed and died at home. Miss Devray had not yet left to take up the post in London. She remained some few months in the house with the agreement of the heir, and with Mrs Waterfield's cook as a companion, so that the property should not be left unoccupied while the details of the estate were settled.'

'Who then was this heir?' I asked.

Carroway frowned. 'The main beneficiary was a nephew of Mrs Waterfield's, a gentleman living in Yorkshire. He had no wish to move south. Thus, the property was sold up and Miss Devray left.'

There was a silence. Colby at last removed his gaze from the spines of the books of law, and said casually, 'The cook you speak of, formerly employed by Mrs Waterfield, is now employed by Dr Bastable, the new owner of the house.'

'Indeed?' returned Carroway frostily. 'Then the cook is very fortunate to have kept her place. It is most likely that decision would have been taken by Miss Bastable, Dr Bastable's sister, who runs his household.'

'We did not meet Miss Bastable,' I told him. I wondered if that was a missed opportunity but quickly decided it was not. If Miss Bastable were anything like her reverend brother, she wouldn't have told us a thing. She might even have prevented us from talking to the cook as a matter of principle.

Colby was worrying at the point like a terrier. 'The cook seems to think Miss Devray went to take up a post as a sort of nurse-companion to an invalid lady in London.'

'Servants' gossip is seldom reliable,' said Carroway. 'I do not think I can be of any further service to you, officers.'

When we were outside the premises and walking down
the street, Colby remarked, 'I really can't say I took to that
fellow.'

'I didn't like him at all,' I agreed. 'And I believe he was
less than frank. He didn't like it when you mentioned the
cook's gossip. He's like Bastable. He wants to keep his
distance and for us to keep ours.'

'Oh, well, there is murder involved,' said Colby wisely.
'I had my eye on him when you passed across that likeness
of her. He knew her, all right! I would wager you, any
amount you care to name, that the idea to pack the girl
off to London came from him. Similarly, the decision to
leave only a small legacy to Emily was probably made by
Mrs Waterfield on Carroway's advice. Now the girl is dead
and Carroway is covering his tracks.'

'Why would he do that, do you think? Advise against
Emily Devray's interest?' I wanted to know Colby's theory.
I was sure he already had one. He had a creative mind, I
had discovered.

'Plain as the nose on your face!' declared Colby. 'It's
this fellow in Yorkshire, the one who inherited everything
except for a couple of trifling bequests like the one to Emily.
His aunt was old and she was in poor health.' Colby tapped
his forehead. 'Getting a bit muddled up top, perhaps? She
was worth a pretty penny. He stood in line, as the natural
heir, to inherit a tidy sum and a desirable property. But,
wait! There is a fly in the ointment.

'Well,' Colby added apologetically, 'I don't like to
describe Emily Devray so unflatteringly, but from the point
of view of the nephew in Yorkshire, she was a cause of some

concern. A cuckoo in the nest! Suppose his aunt took it into her head to make a substantial bequest to a young woman she had brought up, after all, pretty well as a daughter? He would still come in for the larger amount of the inheritance, I dare say. But he wants the lot. Being rich doesn't mean people aren't still greedy. Well, what would you do?'

'I might sound out my aunt's lawyer,' I said. 'A man on whose advice she had come to depend, and whose opinion she respected.'

'And that's what he did, mark my words!' Colby slapped his hands together in triumph. 'And Carroway, whether to oblige the nephew or for some other reason of his own, artfully suggests to the old lady that it was time Miss Devray was out of the house and financially no longer a burden.' Colby paused. 'I wonder if Carroway really doesn't know where Emily Devray went after she left Salisbury?'

I considered this. 'If you ask me,' I told him, 'he doesn't.' Colby looked at me in surprise. 'The reason I suspect he doesn't,' I explained, 'is because he didn't *want* to be told any of the details. It was a shabby business and he knew it might turn out badly, so he wanted no part in the responsibility for it. After all, if things did go wrong, it might be embarrassing for him. As it is, he can't be accused of playing any part in a disastrous decision, or of concealing what he never knew.'

'You are probably right,' agreed Colby reluctantly. 'But I wager Carroway knows more than he lets on. You noticed he said that Miss Devray left the house once the sale was settled, but did not mention the cook leaving? That's because he knows she's still there, knew it before we told him, and he didn't like it when I reminded him. Downy fellow, that Carroway!'

The darkness was already closing in as I set off back to London. The open countryside through which we passed as the train set off was veiled in a violet dusk. As we neared London this grew ever darker and more sombre, until I felt the train and all its passengers were wrapped in purple velvet, like the cherubs in the window of Protheroe's funeral parlour.

Chapter Nine

Elizabeth Martin Ross

BESSIE AND I had travelled by cab to the Queen Catherine. The rain had been unrelenting and was still rattling at the windowpanes at two in the afternoon. It was already dark enough for evening and an oil lamp had burned all day in our small parlour. I wondered what it was like in Salisbury and hoped Ben would not be soaked to the skin. Bessie, almost invisible under a large black umbrella, had gone in search of a suitable conveyance and returned to the house in triumph in a familiar-looking four-wheeled 'growler'.

She bounced through the front door, exclaiming, 'Look what I found! It's Mr Slater!'

But I had already recognised Wally Slater. You couldn't mistake him. He hove into view, his former pugilist's battered features contorted into a fearsome grimace that I knew to be his smile.

'Miss Bessie here tells me you're off chasing after mysteries again!' he greeted me.

'Well, it might or might not be a mystery. I am very pleased to see you, Mr Slater. I trust Mrs Slater is well?'

'Right as ninepence!' Wally assured me.

'The fog must be bad for your business.'

'Terrible,' growled the cabman. 'Fares can't see me and hail the cab. I can't see anyone waiting, nor what else is on the road. When I do pick up a fare, you can be sure he'll grumble at the cost and how long it takes us to get where we're going. But you can't hurry the journey in these conditions, ice underfoot and all. Most of the time, we're going at the pace of a hearse. But I'll get you to where you're going all right, which, she tells me –' he indicated Bessie – 'is a pub by the name of the Queen Catherine, not far off Piccadilly. Old place, with not a right-angle to it, ain't it?'

'You know it, then, Mr Slater?'

'I know where it is,' Wally told me. 'It's my business to know where everything is. But I can't say I know the establishment on the inside, as you might say. I never took a drink in it. What's your interest in it, then?' he added with his usual familiarity. 'Not in your line of places to visit, I wouldn't have thought.'

'I am paying a call on an elderly lady who has taken rooms on the top floor.'

'Is she deaf?'

'No, she's not deaf!' I exclaimed, startled.

'Living above a tavern, it might be useful to be a bit on the deaf side,' explained Wally. 'Well, let's be on our way. Give me your hand, Mrs Ross, and I'll help you up.'

This time when, safely delivered by Wally, we entered the tavern, Mr Tompkins spotted us as we came in. He broke off his conversation with a customer to hail us.

'You've chosen a nice day for it!' he roared in a jocular

tone. 'I'll fetch Louisa.' He moved away from the bar to put his head through a hatch. 'Lou! Mrs Ross is back to see Ruby.'

The customer he had been talking to at the bar turned and favoured us with a stare. He quickly dismissed Bessie, and didn't take much longer looking at me. I was probably not quite young enough, nor handsome enough, to be of interest to him. He, on the other hand, was a very handsome young man, with fair hair and a fresh complexion, very well dressed, and carrying an air of confidence. I realised at the same time that there were other young men of similar type in the snug beyond the bar. I remembered Bessie telling me that she had learned, from Mrs Tompkins, that there were some young fellows about town who used the snug of the Queen Catherine to gather and drink. They were already making quite a lot of noise. Perhaps Wally had been right: to be a little deaf might not be a disadvantage if one lived here.

Mr Tompkins had returned to say Lou would be out directly, and go up to announce us.

'Come on, George!' shouted one of the young men in the snug, directing his words towards the fair-haired young swell at the bar.

'Yes, Tompkins, what about that champagne?' demanded the customer impatiently.

'Be with you directly, sir!' promised Tompkins. The young man strode back to his companions.

Louisa Tompkins had appeared, encased today in a tartan gown of alarmingly bright colours, fashionably falling smoothly from the waist in front but gathered behind into a generous bunch of material. As she entered the taproom like a ship of the line under full sail, I wondered if this obviously new and probably 'best' gown had been donned in anticipation of my return. I was beginning to admire Louisa. She was neither young nor slender but she had tremendous 'style' and clearly kept an eye on the latest fashions. It was an expensive interest. With that, and their generosity towards Miss Eldon, it suddenly occurred to me that possibly the Tompkinses had no children.

'Ruby will be pleased to see you again, Mrs Ross,' she said as we climbed the creaking stair. 'Did you come in a cab? You look dry.'

I told her, yes, we'd taken a cab.

'Well, when you're ready to go home, just put your head round the taproom door and let my husband know. He'll send the pot man out to find you a cab to take you back. I suppose this rain is better than snow but, if you ask me, we shall see more snow again before the month is out. I do believe it's turning to sleet out there already.'

I replied I was much afraid she was right.

'Put your money on it, dear!' said Louisa cheerfully. She opened the door at the head of the stairs. 'Mrs Ross to see you again, Ruby!'

I found Miss Eldon, as I had on my previous visit, sitting in the chair by the fire. The kettle was coming to the boil on the trivet and emitting little gusts of steam.

'It is very kind of you to return so soon,' Miss Eldon greeted me graciously. 'I hope you are able to bring me some positive response from the police?'

My heart sank because that was just what I had not

brought. The moment of confession was however delayed. We reversed the procedure of the day before, Miss Eldon decreeing that we should take tea first. 'Because, my dear Mrs Ross, you have had the goodness to come in such dreadful rain, and should be restored with a hot drink.'

At last, when we had drunk our dish of tea and eaten our ratafia biscuits, I was obliged to break the bad news.

'I am very sorry, Miss Eldon, but I cannot bring you quite the reply you were hoping for. I explained it all in detail to my husband. But, ultimately, he is bound by the rules of evidence, you see, as much as a judge would be. He must have some solid reason to believe a crime is being committed before he demands entry into the house of a respectable citizen against whom nothing is known. The situation in the house opposite certainly sounds very odd and undesirable. But you have not actually witnessed any act of violence against the young lady—'

'Being kept locked up is not an act of violence?' interrupted Miss Eldon.

'Well, yes, if she were being kept against her will. But we don't know she is being forcibly prevented from leaving the house. Nor has she tried, from anything you told me before, to communicate with the outside world. If you can see her, then probably she can see you, especially if you stand at that very large window overlooking the street. Has she never made any kind of signal?'

Miss Eldon was reluctantly obliged to confess the girl had not signalled in any way.

'But,' she said firmly, 'I shall find a way to communicate with her. It is obvious that is what I must do, since Inspector

Ross is so unwilling to act in the absence of what he considers evidence.'

I was sorry Ben had so badly 'blotted his copybook', as the saying goes. I felt I must do something to make amends.

'Believe me, Miss Eldon,' I told her earnestly. 'I shall not give up. Inspector Ross cannot act, but I can. I shall do my very best to discover exactly the nature of the situation across the road. I have my maid making discreet inquiries, too.'

Miss Eldon considered my reply. 'I suppose I ought not to encourage servants' gossip. But it's true servants are very quick in finding out things. She really is discreet, this maid of yours?'

I assured her Bessie was discretion itself and half expected a bolt of lightning to strike me on the spot. I should have to impress on Bessie that all our inquiries must be shrouded in secrecy.

Miss Eldon moved to a new subject. 'I dare say,' she said graciously, 'that Mr Ross is much occupied in discovering who left that poor child in the bin behind the dining rooms?'

'Well, yes, he is, Miss Eldon.'

'Tell him from me, if you would, that I perfectly comprehend he has such a pressing matter to attend to. However, perhaps, when he has discovered who killed her and left her in such an inappropriate place, he will have some time to investigate the house across the road.'

I had only gained Ben a respite, after all. He was still expected find out what Miss Eldon wanted to know, despite my best efforts to make her understand he could not walk into a respectable citizen's house at will.

Bessie, on the other hand, had gained some information of sorts, although not to do with the house where the girl lived.

'I know who that flash young swell is,' she said smugly on the way home as we rattled through the gloomy streets. 'The one wanting champagne.'

'Go on!' I encouraged.

'He lives with his godmother and she is Lady Temple. Her ladyship has a town house nearby, a really old building. She's pretty old herself, Lady Temple. But she doesn't go out much because she's an invalid. She took to her bed, Mrs Tompkins told me, after a bad fall at home. On a fine Sunday she is pushed out of the house in a chair and loaded up into a growler. That takes her to church. When she comes back, she is unloaded again, as you might say, and put back in the chair and taken back indoors. But not when the weather is bad like it is now. She stays at home. Her godson lives with her when he's in town. Everyone thinks he will inherit one day because she's a wealthy woman and she hasn't any children of her own. Her husband was an army man, a general, but he died in India.'

'Her godson seems already to be a wealthy young man,' I replied. 'To judge by the free way he buys expensive champagne.'

'He's got expectations, hasn't he?' retorted Bessie. 'And the general, the one who died in India and was married to Lady Temple, was his uncle, and that makes her his aunt. So he's family, too.' Bessie drew a deep breath and cast me a look of barely concealed triumph.

'It's not all I found out! As Mrs Tompkins was talking

so freely about Lady Temple I started to ask her about other people living round about. "Who is that over there in that nice house?" I asked. "The one across the road."

'"That's the house of Mr Bernard, the banker," she told me straight off. I could have got more out of her, I'm sure, but as bad luck would have it, the pot man came in and wanted something or other. So when he'd gone, I couldn't go back to asking about Mr Bernard without it sounding a bit too curious. But now I know, I'll have another go next time.'

'Take care, Bessie!' I warned her. Privately, I was thinking that Miss Eldon would be expecting me to return, and Bessie would have her chance.

When Ben returned home that evening it was quite late. Despite that, and the tiring train journeys he had taken that day to Salisbury and back, we sat up until late, talking.

'We have a name for the victim,' he'd said, almost as soon as he came in the door. 'I'll tell you about it after supper. If there is any supper?' he added. 'I realise you didn't know if I'd be back very late or even tomorrow.'

'I wasn't at all sure at what time I would see you this evening,' I admitted. 'So nothing is cooked. But there is a cold ham and plenty of eggs. Or, if you'd prefer, Bessie can run to the pie shop.'

'Ham and eggs sounds splendid. I have eaten once today, quite well.' He grinned suddenly, and added in a dramatic undertone, 'Don't you want to know what I found out?'

'Of course I do! And you've found out quite a lot, since you know who the poor girl is.'

'Yes, her name is Emily Devray— oh, Bessie! Listening at the keyhole?'

The door opened and Bessie appeared, flushed. 'I wasn't! I don't listen at keyholes! I just wanted to say, it wouldn't take more than ten minutes for me to fetch a hot pie from the shop.'

'That won't be necessary, Bessie,' I told her.

'All right, then,' returned Bessie. 'Ham and eggs it is.' She withdrew with dignity.

'One of these days,' said Ben seriously, 'she really is going to overhear something we don't want her to know.'

'She doesn't eavesdrop all the time, Ben,' I defended our maid. 'I expect she'd like to be here when I tell you about our visit to the Queen Catherine. But you must tell me first what you've discovered because that's more important. Was it raining so hard in Salisbury?'

'No, it was very cold with snow lying up under hedges and trees. It was deucedly muddy underfoot. It is an attractive city. One wants to say "town" because, compared with London, it is a small place. But of course it has a fine cathedral and long history. Colby, my counterpart, met me off the train and we wasted no time. Between us, we uncovered a sad story.'

He went on to tell me Emily Devray's history. I knew from my own experience how vulnerable single women without family were, and so I was very much moved by Ben's account.

'You have certainly learned a great deal. It's good you can put a name to the girl. Carroway sounds a disagreeable man. I am sure you are right and he had something to do with Emily being sent away to London, to survive, or not, depending how Fate rolled the dice. What kind of man is Inspector Colby, by the way?'

'Very pleasant, helpful sort of chap. He's got a vivid imagination. I think he'd get on well with Ruby Eldon.' Ben smiled.

But something had occurred to me. 'You learned that Emily came to London to be a nurse-companion to an invalid lady. Well, as it happens, Bessie learned today of such a lady. She lives near the Queen Catherine tavern in an old town house. She is a Lady Temple, widow of a general. Her godson – her late husband's nephew – was drinking in the snug with his friends. They were rather noisy, and drinking champagne. Perhaps they were celebrating some piece of good fortune.'

'Ah, so you paid another call on Ruby Eldon, then? The rain didn't put you off?'

'Oh, we both went. Bessie went out to find a cab and was lucky enough to find Wally Slater's growler, so we kept quite dry.'

'I hope you explained to Miss Eldon I can do nothing to investigate the situation in the house opposite to her? Unless I have more solid information of some wrongdoing!' Ben raised his black eyebrows.

Now was not the moment to tell him that Miss Eldon still expected him to act, once the mystery of Emily Devray was solved. 'Oh, yes, Ben. I did tell her.'

I left it at that. It was too late to begin any argument and we were both very tired. I had long since sent Bessie up to bed.

The clock in the hall, a wedding present from Superintendent and Mrs Dunn, chimed eleven. Ben smothered a yawn. I stood up and went to peer through the curtains into the street. 'I do believe it has stopped raining.'

'I always feel that clock of Dunn's is issuing some order to me. Telling me now to get up to bed, most likely!' Ben muttered, hauling himself from his chair. 'Perhaps Dunn himself will be back in the morning, restored to good health and ready to issue orders in person? And perhaps Biddle's cold will be better and he will stop that infernal sniffing.'

Inspector Ben Ross

Dunn did not return in the morning. But he sent a note saying he hoped to be back by the end of the week. I should have detailed reports ready for his perusal on all the cases I had been charged with investigating in his absence. I was right, that clock of ours did act as Dunn's spokesperson. Accordingly, I drew a fresh sheet of paper from the drawer and began to summarise the progress so far in the murder of Emily Devray. I was glad I now able to put a probable name to the victim, although the body had yet to be identified. That, at least, would satisfy Mr Dunn.

But I had not got very far describing the details of my visit to Salisbury when my fellow inspector in charge of the investigation into the string of robberies that had taken place under cover of the fog came to tell me they had broken up the gang and arrested its ringleader. They had also managed to recover a hoard of stolen items concealed behind a false wall in the attics of a brothel in Limehouse.

He would not be deflected from sitting down and telling me every detail of how he had tracked down the thieves and giving me a lively description of the raid on their hideout. It was some time before I could politely point out I had a workload of my own.

He took himself off, humming a popular music-hall ditty and generally very pleased with himself. I started over again where I'd left off my report on Salisbury and the possibility that our unnamed corpse might be Emily Devray. It meant getting my thoughts in order and consulting my notes. I began to write again, my pen scratching across the paper, but it seemed I was doomed to be interrupted.

About twenty minutes later, Biddle appeared to tell me that I had a visitor.

'Young gent wants very much to speak to you, sir. He is a Mr George Temple.'

Temple? I had heard that name recently. My mind still full of the previous day's trip to Salisbury, I could not place it straight away. Besides, a large inkblot was spreading at an alarming rate across my new and unfinished report.

'What is it about?' I asked, adding, to gain time to deal with the blob of ink, 'Can't it be reported to Sergeant Morris?'

'He's come to report a disappearance,' said Biddle. 'And he must see someone of the rank of inspector at least, he says. No one else will do. He's a very forceful young gent, sir.'

A disappearance! 'Well, show him in, then,' I urged.

He was a dashing young fellow who strode in confidently, obliging Biddle to jump out of his way. He carried his hat together with an ivory-headed cane on an ebony shaft. He shook my hand and took the seat I indicated, then considered whether to put his hat on the floor. Not unreasonably, deciding it would get dusty, he turned instead to hand it to Biddle, ordering him to put it on a table somewhere. Biddle, having first been bundled out of the way, and now being treated like a footman, grew red-faced with indignation and looked at me. 'Just put it on that cupboard, Constable!' I said quickly.

Biddle gave me a wounded look, dumped the hat unceremoniously where indicated, and withdrew 'in good order'. He relieved his feelings by blowing his nose noisily outside the door.

My visitor winced. 'Every damn cabbie has a cold,' he said. 'And my aunt's housemaids are going down like ninepins.'

'I am sorry to hear that, Mr Temple. Is it a housemaid who has disappeared?'

'No!' retorted the young man. 'I shouldn't be troubling you if it was a housemaid. Nobody cares about them! I'll be honest. I wouldn't be troubling you at all, but my godmother, Lady Temple, insists.'

Aha! So this was indeed the young man my wife had seen yesterday in the Queen Catherine tavern, drinking champagne with his friends. I regarded him with renewed interest. Not for the first time, I was reminded that I ought to pay more attention to what my wife told me. I was careful to speak in a neutral professional tone.

'The lady is a relative, as well as your godmother? You have the same name.'

'Her late husband was my uncle, my father's brother.

Otherwise, we are not related by blood. But she looks on me as being such. She doesn't have anyone else.'

'I understand, please go on,' I said. 'And may I have the exact address from where the disappearance took place?'

He told me and watched, scowling, as I wrote it down. I looked up and nodded to him to continue his tale.

'It's like this, Inspector,' he said. 'My godmother is of advanced years and more or less keeps to her bed; or lies all day on a chaise-longue. She took a tumble about two years ago and has had difficulty walking ever since. It's not her legs,' he added, 'it's her hip. It was broken and did not mend well.'

'I am sorry to hear it,' I said politely.

'You will appreciate that I'm telling you a private thing like this so you understand that the household routine is, in every way, arranged to suit her needs. She has a personal maid, who is nearly as old as she is, and has been with her for years. Given that the maid can't help much with lifting the old lady, and it isn't always suitable to call on a footman, my godmother decided to inquire about a nurse-companion, living in. She asked around her acquaintances and about, oh, six months ago, I suppose it was, a young woman arrived to take up this post. Her surname is Devray. Emily is her Christian name.'

Well, now! Had I been given the necessary link between the sad body of a young woman and the equally sad story of Miss Emily Devray? Would I now be able to go back to Carroway in Salisbury, should it prove necessary, and tell him I had unravelled the link he had been so anxious I should not?

'Go on,' I invited Mr Temple. I had done my best to disguise any reaction to the name, but perhaps I had betrayed something, because Temple had stopped speaking and was staring at me.

I stared back and said nothing.

'She has been missing since Sunday evening,' he said bluntly.

'Did she go missing from the house? Or fail to return after going out?' I asked.

He looked slightly disconcerted. 'It's hard to tell. She might have gone out and not come back, but we just don't know.' He spoke with a marked reluctance.

'No servant saw her go out?'

'They say not!' he snapped. 'I don't believe they are all lying.'

'Very well,' I said, 'do go on, Mr Temple.'

Temple went on sulkily, 'In any case, it's dashed inconvenient! The old lady, I mean my godmother, is in a panic about it. She has taken a fancy to the girl. Don't know why. She's a dowdy little thing with no conversation, who goes around looking miserable.'

Whoever his tailor, whatever prestigious school claimed him as an Old Boy, however well connected he may be, I decided, a lout remains a lout. And this young jackanapes is a lout, albeit one with a smart coat, fine linen, an ebony cane, and a wealthy godmother from whom he no doubt hopes to inherit.

'Well then, when was her absence noticed from the house?' I persisted as I glanced down at the address I had written out. Oh, yes, and he drank in the tavern nearby, where he was spending his inheritance before he had it on champagne. He didn't know I knew that.

'Oh, well, not until it was almost time for my aunt to retire to bed. I don't keep track of where Devray is. She's of no interest to me. Anyway, I wasn't there for most of the day!' he finished quickly.

'All the same, if you please try and be more specific, Mr Temple? Inquiries must have been made among the staff and I assume you are aware of the results, even if you weren't there yourself. You have explained that Miss Devray was not seen leaving the house that evening. In that case, when *was* she last seen, by anyone, not just by Lady Temple or yourself?'

He reddened and glowered at me. 'Wilson, the butler says she was certainly in the house at luncheon on Sunday. Wilson generally knows where everyone is. He didn't see her after lunch. But my aunt had given her permission to go out, so didn't expect to see her until later. Lady Temple takes her main meal of the day at half past noon. She does not dine of an evening. She is old-fashioned in her ways. She takes tea with toast or muffins at about six o'clock and not long after that retires to her room. Devray didn't join her for tea, as she usually did. However, as she had permission to go out, my godmother didn't take it amiss.

'I lunched with friends, and didn't return until nearly seven, so can't tell you about Devray. Up to that point, there was no alarm. Then my godmother's maid came to tell us, at about eight o'clock, she needed Devray's help. My godmother had been writing letters, but had decided to retire to bed. That was when it was discovered that

Devray was nowhere to be found. She should have been back by then. It was annoying she was so late returning, but, well, there might be a reasonable explanation. But she didn't return, and, although we all assumed she went out, no one saw her go, as I said.'

Temple heaved an irritable sigh. 'She has never returned and time is passing. On Monday morning my godmother ordered her maid to search the companion's room for any clue as to where she might have gone.'

'What of her possessions?'

Temple shifted awkwardly on his chair.

'The maid reported that all Devray's belongings appear to be in place: her clothes, some books, and a few trinkets in a jewellery box. At first my godmother was reassured that it meant Devray intended to return. When she did not, she became alarmed and instructed me to come to you. So,' concluded Temple casually, 'here I am. But I apologise for troubling you with it. I dare say the girl will turn up. It will be interesting to hear what sort of excuse she manufactures. Whatever it is, I shall advise Lady Temple strongly not to accept it and to terminate her employment at once.'

'Mr Temple,' I said, 'you've taken your time coming here to report her missing. Why did you not come at once? It does not occur to you that she might have come to some harm? Perhaps it has occurred to Lady Temple?'

'It would be like my godmother to fear the worst. She is easily alarmed. But to call the police to the house, well, that is a last resort. One doesn't, well, persons of Lady Temple's social standing don't . . .'

He must have noted the expression on my face. He

115

abandoned his explanation and finished defensively: 'We did – or my godmother did – consult her man of law for advice. He set in hand some private inquiries but they have turned up nothing, so I have come here today.'

He drew a deep breath. 'Look here. Personally I suspect Devray has run off with some fellow. Or why did she sneak out of the house without anyone seeing her go?'

'How about a winter mantle? If she went out during the afternoon, when she had permission, she would not have done so without some warm clothing. The weather has been particularly cold and unpleasant.'

He stared at me as if this obvious detail surprised him. 'I don't know,' he snapped. 'I didn't speak to the maid. She reported to Lady Temple that Devray's things were all in her room.'

He was not being completely frank, I decided, but couldn't say in what way.

'We can ask again,' I said calmly. 'You think she may have left to join a man. Has Miss Devray had a – let us call it an admirer – since she arrived in London?'

'Lord, no, who could it be?' Temple retorted. 'I told you, she's a plain little thing and she dresses as though she were still in mourning. I can't imagine she's been what she would probably call walking out with anyone. She imagined herself a cut above a servant, you know. Well, companions do, don't they? They've all "come down in the world" as the saying goes. She wasn't treated as a servant. At any rate, she sat at table with us, with Lady Temple and myself when I was at home. I have just told you, she was a sort of companion.'

I was married to a lady who had briefly been a companion

to an elderly woman, but Temple didn't know that. I wondered if it would have made any difference if he had known. I was by now thoroughly disgusted with him, but I took care not to show it. Instead, I took the photograph of the dead girl from a drawer and handed it to him.

He looked surprised and raised his eyebrows. But he took the photograph and glanced at it casually. Then he looked again and an expression of alarm crossed his face. He thrust it back at me.

'Where have you that— that horrible thing from?'

'It is the photograph of an as yet unidentified body,' I told him. 'It was taken by a photographer employed by us at the Yard.'

'Where . . . when . . .' he stammered. Drops of sweat had broken out on his brow. He pulled out a handkerchief and mopped his face. By the time he had done this, and tucked away the handkerchief, he had regained some control.

'I wish you hadn't just— just produced it like that, like a damn conjuror with a rabbit out of a hat! It gave me the devil of a turn!'

'Do you recognise the subject?'

'I— well, I suppose you'd like me to say it is Emily Devray?'

'Is it?' I asked.

He had sagged momentarily but he gathered himself together and sat up straight. 'I cannot say for sure. It is— it is a corpse, is it not? I can't be expected to identify a photograph of a corpse!' His voice rose almost on a note of panic.

'But you think there is a similarity to the missing girl?'

117

'Well, I . . . There might be! Look here, Inspector Ross, this must surely be an irregular way for you to go about your investigations. I came here to report a missing nurse-companion. Where did you . . . where was the girl in that ghastly photograph found? When?'

'The body was found on Monday in the early afternoon. You will recall the fog was very thick on Monday and that probably delayed the discovery. We believe the body was abandoned where it was found earlier in the day, or possibly during the previous night. We were informed here at the Yard at four of the afternoon on Monday. As to where it was found . . .' Now I hesitated. 'Not so very far from Lady Temple's house,' I told him.

It might be as well not to say too much, and give him any more information than necessary, should he want later to concoct some explanation. He had his hands folded over the ivory knob of his cane and now began a rapid beat with the fingers of the upper hand on the back of the lower one.

'I cannot possibly say,' he announced at last. 'I cannot identify the photograph with any certainty. There is . . . some resemblance, but then, Devray was . . . is very plain. If that is her in the photograph, all I can say is, she never looked very animated. Not, I must stress, that I did spend much time looking at her.'

Oh dear, I really didn't care for George Temple. It was not just his manner that put me off. He was altogether too keen to make me understand he'd had no interest in the missing girl. But he was a young man and a worldly one. We had been discussing a young woman living under the same roof. A girl of just eighteen, who had no protection other than that offered by an elderly lady who was more or less bed-ridden.

'I need to speak to Lady Temple herself,' I said.

He looked alarmed. 'Must you? See here, she's not strong—'

'Nevertheless, she is the missing girl's employer and so I need to speak to her.'

'You're not going to show her that— that thing!' He indicated the photograph. 'For pity's sake, Ross, my godmother would faint away on the spot!'

'Oh, no, be reassured, Mr Temple, I should not do that. As you say, an identification from a photograph alone would hardly be satisfactory.'

He relaxed. 'No, well, I'm glad you agree with me, then.'

'Therefore, after I have spoken with Lady Temple, and if it seems possible that the body we have is that of Miss Devray, someone must identify it at the morgue, or say for certain it's not her, as the case may be.'

He leaped to his feet, wild-eyed. 'Are you saying I may have to go to a morgue and look at that corpse of yours?'

'If you would be so good, and if it still seems necessary. After all, from what you tell me, I can hardly ask Lady Temple to do it.'

'No, no, she can't, couldn't . . .' He swayed on his feet and steadied himself with his ebony cane.

I took pity on him. 'But take heart, Mr Temple. When we go to your aunt's house, we may find Miss Devray has returned, or sent an explanation for her absence.'

'I suppose so,' he mumbled. He didn't sound convinced.

He hunched his shoulders briefly in a way that was dismissive.

I was even more sure he knew perfectly well she wouldn't have returned. Emily Devray was on a slab at the morgue. Whether he was in any way responsible for her lying there remained to be seen.

I asked Sergeant Morris to come with us. George Temple was obviously not very happy about being driven through the streets of London in a cab with two police officers, as we clearly were. Morris, in particular, who is of burly build and singularly bland expression, could hardly be anything else.

When we arrived at the house, and the butler opened the door to see the three of us, George in the middle, the situation had a moment of grim comedy. Butlers are well trained not to show any emotion. But this fellow was sorely tested. He managed to control his shock, however, and gravely stood aside to let us in.

'Let me go and tell Lady Temple the officers are here, Wilson,' Temple ordered. 'They wish to speak to her. It's better I let her know.'

'Lady Temple has been awaiting your return, sir. She is expecting you to bring the police. She asks that you will all wait in the drawing room and she will join you.'

The man spoke civilly but clearly meant to follow any instructions he had received from his employer. He did not accept any change to those orders from the young gentleman.

'All right, then,' Temple muttered sulkily, foiled. 'Let her know we're here, Wilson.'

This interested me. Was the lady able-bodied enough, despite what her godson claimed, to walk about the house unaided?

The answer was soon known: she was not. After we had waited some minutes we heard the sound of people approaching on the other side of the double doors, voices and the creak of wheels. George stood up. Morris and I did likewise. The pair of doors was opened wide by the butler and we beheld a startling sight.

A cane invalid chair was pushed in. In the chair, well supported with cushions, sat a small, frail-looking elderly lady with white hair under a widow's cap, wearing a magenta gown with a lace collar and cuffs. At her throat was a mourning brooch, a woven pattern of hair preserved in a frame. A sad memento of her husband? Her features were good, her eyes particularly striking, and her skin, though lined, was excellent. She had once been a beauty, I decided. She was also, despite her frailty, clearly of determined character.

But, in truth, my attention was not first attracted so much to the lady as to the servant pushing the wheeled chair. I have already mentioned that Sergeant Morris is of sturdy build and tall, but this fellow was almost a giant. He had the height and physique of a prizefighter, and surely outweighed Morris. His features were blunt, as if roughly chiselled ready for some monumental sculpture, and he had a shock of tow-coloured hair. He looked as if he had emerged from some Germanic folk tale.

Perhaps Lady Temple was accustomed to visitors gawping at her manservant because, although she couldn't have failed to observe our surprise, she chose to ignore it. Instead she gestured to some chairs and asked both Morris and me to be seated. Her voice was firm.

We did as bid. George Temple took a seat nearby. He appeared ill at ease.

'My godson has explained to you the circumstances which have caused my concern?' she asked.

I assured her that, yes, he had. 'But,' I added, 'I would like very much to hear from you, Lady Temple, anything that you can tell me about last Sunday, from the morning until the time in evening when you realised that Miss Devray was not in the house. What time was that?'

'We realised she was not in the house at all at about eight that evening. I intended to retire. I sent my personal maid to find Emily to help. She, Dorcas the maid, came back about ten minutes later to say she couldn't find her. Then I summoned Wilson, the butler, and asked him to find out what had become of her. If necessary, he was to institute a search. Around half past nine, Wilson came to say Miss Devray was not in the house, nor could she be located any-where nearby, despite exhaustive inquiries among the neighbours.'

'If we could go back to Sunday morning,' I requested.

'Emily was certainly here then. I do not always leave the house to attend a church service, Inspector Ross, but I always read my Bible, or the order of service, every day. On Sunday, after breakfast, I asked Emily if she would read aloud to me from the Book of Common Prayer. She did so.' Lady Temple paused. 'She read it very well. She was a young woman of some education. When she had done that,

I told her that, after luncheon, she might have the rest of the day free until the evening.'

'May I ask, did she sit at the same table as yourself? I understand that was the usual routine.'

'Oh, yes,' said Lady Temple immediately. 'She was not a servant, Inspector Ross!'

From the corner of my eye, I saw George Temple shift impatiently on his chair.

'Was it usual, may I ask, for you to allow Miss Devray the Sunday afternoon free?'

'Yes. She did not lack free time, Inspector! I needed her in the morning, mostly, and in the evening. But during the day, unless I wanted her to read to me, or to keep me company, Dorcas was able to manage for me.' The lady paused, and looked briefly sad. 'I shall miss Emily if she does not return, because I liked her company. She chattered to me about her life in Salisbury. She was a thoroughly nice girl.'

More wriggling from George.

'But I sound selfish,' Lady Temple added suddenly. 'My chief concern is for Emily's safety and well-being, not that I lack her companionship. I have found her a very reliable young woman. To simply disappear is quite out of character. Besides, when Dorcas looked in her room, everything was – still is – there, including her outer garments. The weather is bitterly cold. She would not go out without some warm mantle or shawl.'

I had already made that point to Master George; and he looked sulky now at hearing it from his godmother. He very much wanted me to believe in an elopement of some sort. John Colby in Salisbury had also speculated about one.

'I should like to take a look in Miss Devray's room before I leave, if I may,' I told Lady Temple.

She inclined her head. 'Of course. Dorcas will show you.'

'Did Miss Devray mention any friends in London? Did she know anyone here?'

'No one at all,' said Lady Temple firmly. 'I have been a little worried that she might be lonely. I think she did miss Salisbury, having lived there all her life.'

George Temple's fidgeting was getting more obvious. His godmother had noticed.

'What is the matter, George?' she asked with a steely kindness.

'I am sorry, Aunt Charlotte, it is just that, well, I know you are worried about Miss Devray, we all are!' he added hastily. 'But perhaps she decided, on the spur of the moment, to go back to Salisbury?'

'Without her belongings? Don't talk nonsense, George!'

George turned scarlet with embarrassment and rage. 'Well, just, you know . . . She could have decided to avoid having to explain to you that she was leaving.'

'Emily had better manners!' snapped Lady Temple.

George would do well to keep quiet, I thought. He realised it and did not speak again.

'Thank you, Lady Temple,' I said. 'Now I should like to speak to Dorcas, if I may.'

'Do you need my presence?'

'No, ma'am. But I should like to see Miss Devray's room, as I said.'

'Then, if you wait here, I will send Dorcas to you. Michael!'

The giant by the door, who had stood perfectly motionless throughout, stepped forward. The butler, Wilson, who must have been hovering outside in the corridor, appeared without summons and opened the doors. Michael gripped the back of the cane chair in his massive hands and wheeled his employer out of the room and away.

When the doors had closed, and we remained with George Temple, he said, 'You didn't mention finding a body to my godmother.'

'It has not yet been identified,' I reminded him. 'Perhaps you would go now with Sergeant Morris to take a look? The task is unpleasant, I recognise that, but it is urgent.'

'Very well!' he said with poor grace. 'What will you do?'

'Stay here and await Dorcas,' I replied mildly.

I had not to wait very long. Dorcas appeared within five minutes of George's departure with Morris. She was an elderly woman of country appearance, plump and sensible.

'Something's happened to that poor child,' she said immediately to me. 'Her ladyship is very worried. We all are.'

'All?' I inquired.

'All the servants!' she retorted. 'Everyone liked Miss Devray.'

'How about Mr George Temple? Is he worried?'

She blinked and gave me a sharp look. 'Anything that upsets Lady Temple is of concern to Mr George.'

'Dorcas,' I said, 'did Miss Devray tell you, or did anything she said or did lead you to suspect, she had an admirer, a young man? She might not tell Lady Temple, but I think you would suspect it, if it were so.'

'I don't know why you should think that!' snapped Dorcas. 'But the answer is no. She never said a thing.'

'Where did she go, when she had free time?'

'I don't know,' said Dorcas. 'It wasn't my business to know. She did once say she had been to look at some paintings in a gallery. A museum, too, she went to a museum once, she said. The British Museum, it was. She was very impressed by that.'

I nodded. She could have met someone at a museum or gallery, I was thinking. Emily was a young woman of good education. If some young fellow had struck up a conversation about a piece of art, she might have been drawn into discussing it.

'Lady Temple says you want to look at her room, sir,' said Dorcas.

'Oh, yes, I do.'

'If you would follow me, sir?' She turned and led the way out.

They had given Emily a small but pleasant room at the side of the house, overlooking a small walled garden. The area on which I gazed down was laid mainly to grass with some shrubs. A small wooden building in one corner suggested a gardener's shed.

I turned back from the window and looked around the room. It was very tidy. I asked Dorcas if anyone had been in to make it so, but she said it was as Miss Devray had left it. There were some books on a shelf: her Bible, a Book of Common Prayer, three novels by Mr Dickens and two by Sir Walter Scott, plus an account of someone's travels in the Orient: all solid fare, no penny romances. Yes, a serious young woman! Her outer clothes were in a wardrobe and her underthings in a chest of drawers, again all folded neatly. Only one thing surprised me. In the bottom drawer there was a copy of a local newspaper from Salisbury, five weeks old. It had been read, but carefully refolded, and put away to be consulted again. Now, how had she come by that? I wondered. Had someone sent it to her? Had she chanced upon it? Had some other visitor left it in a public place she'd visited? Why had she kept it?

'I will take this with me, Dorcas,' I told her, holding up the newspaper.

She showed no surprise.

'Do you happen to know where she got it?'

'No, sir.'

Wherever Emily had got it, she had kept it. Even prized it? News from home? From the evidence of Lady Temple and from this hoarded newspaper, Emily had been home-sick.

When I left the house, I stood outside taking a moment to study the building. There was a basement and a flight of steps leading down into it from the pavement, to the left of the main front door. That would be the way the servants went in and out. I walked past the frontage, along the pavement, until I reached the end of the building and came to a high red-brick wall adjoining it. There was a door in it but it was locked. I looked up. The bare winter branches of trees showed above it. On the other side of this wall was the garden Emily could have seen from her window. Had that any significance, I wondered?

I went back to the Yard and awaited the return of

Sergeant Morris, who had accompanied George Temple to view the body.

He came back with an expression of grim satisfaction on his face. 'He passed out!' he said bluntly. 'Keeled over and went down like a skittle. We picked him up and someone found some smelling salts. Then I got him to take another look, standing by to catch him if he went again. But he was all right the second them. Can't blame the young fellow, I suppose, it isn't a pleasant task. And she's been dead a few days now and although she's been kept good and cold, she's beginning to look a bit waxen and there's an odour. Body was identified as that of Miss Emily Devray by Mr George Temple, member of her employer's family,' concluded Morris formally.

'Then we'll ask the coroner to rule quickly on allowing her to be buried. Has he been informed?'

'Inquest will be held first thing in the morning, sir.'

'You and I will have to attend. That boy, Horace Worth, too. He found the body. Does Lady Temple know?'

'I accompanied the young gent back to the house but he insisted he should be the one to tell his godmother. It seemed reasonable to me, sir.'

'Yes, I suppose so. We shall have to go back to the house tomorrow, straight after the inquest. I can talk to the old lady again and you can have a chat with the servants, especially that butler. Ask him about the garden. Get him to show it to you.'

Morris looked surprised. 'Didn't know there was one, sir.'

'It's adjacent to the house and there is a door in the

wall giving access from the street. It's locked at present. I want to know if it is always locked and who keeps the key. If there is a gardener, is that the way he comes and goes? If she died in the house, how was the body removed? Not through the front door. Up the basement steps, perhaps? Or through that garden door?'

'Yes, sir, I see.' Morris eyed me curiously. 'Any more ideas, sir?'

'A couple, but nothing definite. I am thinking that, if Emily died in the house, that would explain why she wore no outdoor clothing. Whoever is responsible for the body being dumped where it was found did not think quickly enough, or did not have access to Emily's wardrobe to fetch outerwear. But we mustn't forget Emily had permission to go out. So, did she die earlier in the afternoon, after luncheon, never leaving the house alive? Or later, after she had been out and returned, taking off her warm mantle? What do you think, Morris?'

Morris frowned. 'The young gentleman is very unhappy, sir. I mean, obviously he is at the moment because he's just identified her. But he was unhappy before. To my way of thinking, he couldn't have been altogether uninterested in her. He's human and a bit of a man about town. Surely, at some point, he must have tried to steal a kiss.' Morris looked at me. 'What are you thinking, Mr Ross?'

'I am thinking that the situation in Lady Temple's household was eerily similar to that in the late Mrs Waterfield's.' I leaned forward over the desk to urge, 'Think about it, Morris! Before she came to London, Emily lived with an elderly and wealthy woman to whom she was not related.

That lady was apparently very fond of her, or up to a point. Because when the lady dies and the will is read, Emily receives almost nothing. The chief beneficiary is a nephew living in Yorkshire. That nephew must have known about Emily because Mr and Mrs Waterfield more or less adopted her at birth. A cause of concern to the nephew, up there in the North and not in easy communication with his wealthy aunt?'

'Should think it was!' agreed Morris. 'Of course, we don't know what kind of a man he might be. But rich or poor, no one likes to think an outsider has snatched a family fortune from under his nose.'

'Yes, and now consider the household of Lady Temple. Again we have an elderly lady and a wealthy one. Her heir presumptive is a nephew, her late husband's nephew if you want to be precise, but her nephew by marriage and her godson. In the short time Lady Temple knew Emily, she had become fond of her. She told us so herself. A cause of concern to Mr George?'

'Worried him pretty badly, I reckon,' said Morris.

'After we've visited Lady Temple again, I must write to Inspector Colby, let him know what's happened. The news of Emily's death being confirmed will cause quite a stir in her home town, I dare say.'

'Might jog a few memories?' suggested Morris.

'We can but hope, Sergeant,' I told him.

That evening, when I went home, I told Lizzie that the dead girl was now known for certain to be Emily Devray as we had suspected.

Lizzie was quiet for some minutes and then said, 'I think

I should pay another visit to Miss Eldon. I have only ever spoken to her about the Bernard family and the girl who never goes out. But I wonder if she knows anything about Lady Temple's household. After all, George Temple carouses with his friends in the snug of the Queen Catherine. Louisa Tompkins talked to Bessie about George Temple. She might well have spoken to Miss Eldon about him. Miss Eldon is not a gossip in the usual sense. But she is observant and intelligent. If I ask her and she does know something, I think she would tell me.'

'There is another thing I would ask you to do,' I said. I produced the Salisbury newspaper I had brought from Emily's room. 'This is five weeks old. Someone either gave it to Emily or sent it to her. I would like to know who that was and, also, whether she kept it for nostalgic reasons, or whether there is some item in there that particularly interested her. I have glanced through it and found nothing particular, other than reports from livestock sales and such matters. You might spot something.'

'I'll read it carefully,' Lizzie promised.

'I have to go to the inquest in the morning,' I said with a sigh. 'And Mr Dunn is due back among us at any moment.'

Chapter Ten

DUNN'S REAPPEARANCE among us the next day was not unlike the sudden eruption of a whirlwind in a previously peaceful countryside. The superintendent was more than restored to health; he was brimming with energy and a desire for positive action. In appearance, with his red face and fondness for tweed cloth, he always resembled a farmer. Now he looked like one contemplating a bumper harvest.

'Now, then, Ross!' he hailed me. 'You have a murder investigation in hand, I understand. I want to know all about it!'

'I have written a full report, sir, it is on your desk,' I protested, I knew in vain. I wouldn't escape so lightly.

'Yes, yes, I am sure it is very detailed. I know you to be a conscientious officer.' Dunn rubbed the palms of his hands together briskly, a man getting down to business. 'I shall read it carefully. But I should like to hear your initial thoughts first-hand now.'

'You shall have them, sir. But it cannot be straight away. I have to attend the inquest on the victim this morning. She has now been formally identified as Emily Devray, a nurse-companion. You will find details of her background in my Salisbury report.'

'Glad to hear your jaunt to Salisbury was not in vain, Ross!'

'No, sir, by no means. I learned a lot. A request will be made for the release of the body for burial this morning, following the inquest. There is a shortage of space in all mortuaries and morgues at the moment.'

'Oh, very well, then!' snapped Dunn, thwarted. 'But report to me as soon as you return.'

'Immediately after the inquest I plan to pay another call on Lady Temple, the girl's employer. It is her godson, also resident in her house, who has identified the victim.'

'Well, then, report to me as soon as you get back after that,' was the testy response. 'Are you taking Morris?'

'Yes, sir. I need him to make inquiries in the house – ask the servants more questions.'

Dunn squinted at me. 'You suspect the house to be the scene of the crime?'

'It does begin to look likely,' I admitted. 'But I cannot say for certain. The absence of any warm outer clothing on the body when it was found, together with none being missing from the girl's room, does suggest she hadn't gone out to meet her death elsewhere. Proving that she died in the house is another matter. No one heard anything. No one saw anything. And who is the murderer? Are we looking at some sort of conspiracy? How could the body be taken from the house, if that is the scene of the deed, all the way over to the backyard where it was discovered?'

'I trust you will soon be able to tell me the culprit's

name, Ross.' Dunn gave me a ferocious grin. 'Now, then! Since I must await your return from your pressing engagements elsewhere, I must look at another case. Send me whoever was in charge of investigating those robberies. That matter at least, as I understand it, has been dealt with.'

The weather remained bitterly cold. The fog, though thinner than the monster we had just suffered, was still present in swirls of yellow sulphurous vapour that would infest our coats with its stink. It wrapped clammy fingers round our faces as the chill wind nipped our noses and ears. I was sorry to bring Morris out with me as he was still croaking. At least the rain had gone away for the time being.

We soon found we'd moved from one extreme of discomfort to another. The inquest was being held in a small and stuffy upstairs room. An open fire in the grate smoked vilely, causing everyone to cough and splutter, and created its own version of a London Particular here in the room.

Due to being delayed by Dunn, Morris and I were among the last to arrive. We took our seats just as the coroner entered through a private side door and advanced to take his seat at a table on a podium. The room was already full, about twenty people attending; most of whom had probably come in out of the cold although one, at least, I recognised as a representative of the press. The public likes to read about a murder. In the front row sat George Temple, there, no doubt, because he had identified the deceased and to report back to his godmother. Horace Worth, too, was there, rotund and red-faced. With him sat Mr Bellini, moustaches freshly waxed. And seated by

George Temple was another person known to me. I had not expected *him*. His name was Pelham and he was a lawyer. He and I had crossed swords before.

Perhaps George had seen me arrive. He murmured to Pelham. The lawyer turned his head and stared hard at me. We acknowledged one another with professional nods.

Proceedings began and moved at a brisk pace. The coroner was a busy man these days. I said my piece. Horace said his. George stated he had identified the body as being that of his aunt's nurse-companion, Emily Devray. Mr Bellini then insisted on being heard, solely, as far as I could understand it, in order for it to be set on record that although the body had been discovered in his backyard, the young female had at no time, when alive, set foot in his dining room. Thus her death could in no way be connected with his well-regarded and respectable establishment. Well known, he added, for its steak pies.

A pity he had to mention the steak pies, I thought. He was doing well until then.

The coroner replied sharply, 'Quite so, Mr Bellini! Does anyone else wish to say anything?'

No one did. The coroner, gathering up his papers as he spoke, ruled that he could only return a verdict of murder by person or persons unknown. He trusted that the police would soon be able to identify the culprit and the murderer be brought to justice. Meanwhile, the body could be released for burial, in view of the lack of space in London's mortuaries at the present time. He then looked up and asked, 'Is there a member of the family present to whom the body should be released?'

At this, Pelham, the lawyer, stood up. He was a tall, thin, silver-haired man of distinguished bearing, habitually clad in black. When he stood quite still, as now, I could not help thinking of a heron beside a brook, waiting for a fish to swim unwarily by.

'I represent Lady Temple, the deceased's employer,' he announced. 'Miss Devray had no living family, and no private fortune. So, in order to avoid her being given a pauper's funeral, Lady Temple requests the body be released to her. She will undertake to pay the cost of a funeral and burial plot, in order that it should not fall upon the public purse.'

The coroner was obliged to Lady Temple for her generous offer. He had no objection to ruling as requested.

After the inquest, Morris and I were delayed a few minutes in the empty room by the newspaperman, eager for details. We fended him off and hastened as best we could to Lady Temple's house. But George Temple and Pelham still arrived ahead of us. I suspected they had had a cab waiting.

When we arrived at last, Wilson the butler made to show us both directly into the drawing where, he told us, Lady Temple was awaiting us.

'I will speak alone to Lady Temple,' I said. 'Sergeant Morris has some more questions for the staff.'

'As you wish, Inspector,' said Wilson frostily. 'But there is another gentleman already there.'

They were both awaiting me. When Wilson opened the doors I saw the scene had already been set. I was struck by how theatrical it looked and thought, *I am a spectator now, and the curtain is about to rise.* Lady Temple had been brought in beforehand, no dramatic entry in her invalid carriage this time. She was seated on a silk-upholstered and gilded rococo-style sofa. She was clad in black silk. I wondered for how long she would wear mourning for someone who had been an employee. Probably, I thought, until after the funeral. Then convention would have been observed; longer would give rise to comment.

But she was not the only one in black. Pelham sat nearby and rose to his feet as I entered. I wondered where George Temple was. Possibly he was already in the snug of the Queen Catherine tavern, fortifying himself with brandy after the inquest. I was annoyed to see Pelham here but could do nothing about it. I did wonder, however, just why his services had been called on. George could have requested the body be released to his godmother. He wasn't a boy, for goodness' sake! He must be about twenty-four or -five.

'Mr Pelham will already have given you an account of the inquest,' I said to Lady Temple, once I had taken my seat and Pelham retaken his. I tried not to sound sour.

She inclined her head. 'Yes. After being needed to identify Emily yesterday, George found the further matter of the inquest a trying experience. He has gone to rest and gather his thoughts in his room.'

So he *had* scuttled down to the tavern, I interpreted this. Did his godmother really believe George was still in the house? I looked at her and she met my eye steadily. Yes, she knew he'd gone out and was most likely in a tavern – or even seeking solace with an obliging young female in a house where such women may be found. Lady Temple had been an army wife. She was aware of the ways of young men.

'It is very good of you, Lady Temple, to offer to meet the costs of Miss Devray's funeral,' I told her.

'No one,' she returned sharply, 'will leave this house to be buried in a pauper's grave. That would be quite improper!' Her expression softened. 'Besides which, I was fond of Emily. I confess to feeling a degree of responsibility for her unfortunate death. She was so young, and in many ways I was, if you like, *in loco parentis*. This should not have happened while she was living under my roof.'

'Dear madam!' cried Pelham immediately. 'I do assure you that no one would think you had failed in any duty. The young woman was a paid employee. You owed no duty of care towards her.'

'Nevertheless!' said Lady Temple shortly.

A tinge of red showed briefly on Pelham's pale cheek-bones, but he had the wisdom to accept the rebuke.

'Were you thinking, I wonder, of returning the body to Salisbury for burial?' I asked.

Now she looked at Pelham to reply for her. Perhaps she wanted to soothe any ruffled feelings he might have. He turned his pitiless predator's eye on me.

'Miss Devray had severed all connection with Salisbury. Lady Temple wishes her to be buried in a plot in the Brookwood Necropolis cemetery.'

Now then! The Brookwood Necropolis was a fashionable place to be buried. It lay just outside London and was reached by its own company railway line, with special rolling stock to accommodate mourners and the coffins. This meant it was also an expensive place to be laid to rest.

I was beginning to feel uneasy. I felt there ought to be something I should be asking, but I did not quite know how. Also, Pelham's presence hindered me.

Instead, I asked, 'Have you decided who will make the necessary arrangements?'

'Mr Protheroe, in Piccadilly,' said Lady Temple. She said it briskly and with a touch of relief. Or was that my imagination? Had she feared a different question? Or was she just content the disposal of Emily's body would soon take place and details were in experienced hands?

As it was, her reply gave me a start. Fate, I had discovered several times in the past, had a twisted sense of humour. Emily would be placed in a coffin provided by Protheroe. She would be returned to lie on the Carrara marble slab in the preparation room to the rear of his premises. The irony was complete. The first time her body had been there, Protheroe had been appalled. This next time, her mortal remains would be welcome because Lady Temple would be paying the bill.

Then the lady herself, perhaps because she was relieved I hadn't asked the question she feared, volunteered a further detail concerning the funeral. It was one that really surprised me. If Pelham had known she might reveal it, he would have counselled against it.

'Besides, Mr Pelham has received a letter from a lawyer whose rooms are in Salisbury, a Mr Carroway. Mr Carroway apparently feels that a burial in Salisbury would attract a great deal of local interest of the unseemly kind. There might be a crowd of sightseers. The public has a morbid curiosity.'

I used the word she herself had used earlier. 'Quite improper!' I said.

'I am glad you agree, Inspector Ross,' she replied graciously.

I rose to my feet and bowed. 'I am grateful to you for seeing me, Lady Temple. And now I think I had better go and find my sergeant.'

I bowed to Pelham, who had also risen to his feet. 'Mr Pelham.'

He returned my bow. 'Inspector Ross.'

It was all very dignified and *comme il faut*, as my wife Lizzie might have said. Because Lizzie speaks French and occasionally peppers her conversation with phrases, I've learned quite a few.

The butler appeared in his silent way without – as far as I could tell – being summoned by any bell.

Morris was waiting for me in the hall.

'Mr Wilson has been so good as to show me the garden, sir,' he croaked. 'I thought perhaps you might like to take a look.'

'Thank you, I will,' I said to him, but looking at Wilson. 'Is there a gardener?'

Wilson answered. 'No, Inspector Ross, not at this time of the year. It is a simple grassed area, as you will see, and there is no need of a regular man to look after it. From spring to late autumn a man does come in once a week to keep it tidy, cut the grass and so on. Lady Temple sometimes sits out there when the weather is warm.' He turned. 'If you will follow me, gentlemen.'

We followed him to a morning room at the rear of the house where glazed doors opened on to the little garden.

'I'll return the keys to you before we leave, Mr Wilson,' said Morris firmly.

The butler took the hint and left us to inspect the garden without him.

'Which keys are these?' I asked.

Morris produced a ring on which hung two keys, one large and one small. 'The big one is for the gate in the wall, sir, the one you noticed from the street. The little one is for the shed where they keep odds and ends of tools.'

'Where are these keys normally kept?'

'On a hook in the butler's pantry,' Morris told me. 'Anyone could get at them in his absence and he'd be none the wiser. As they're never used in winter, he probably wouldn't even notice they'd been removed provided they were returned fairly smartly.' He glanced at me. 'How was the lady?'

'Ready for me. She had Pelham with her. George had either taken himself off or she had sent him out of the way.'

'Closing ranks, sir?' asked Morris.

'Oh, yes, most definitely. They have closed ranks.'

'It's what the gentry do,' said Morris, with the wisdom of experience. 'They must realise the poor young woman almost certainly died in the house, that Sunday.' It was not a question but a comment.

'It's my belief they are most definitely aware that must be the case, Sergeant,' I told him. 'No one here will admit it, of course, until and unless the evidence is set out before them in such a way that even Pelham won't be able to reject it.'

It was not the time of year to be in a garden but nevertheless, and despite the chilly weather, it was a pleasant spot. We stood side by side and studied the garden, as men who didn't exactly do any gardening, but liked to think they did.

Underfoot the grass was long, in need of its spring trim, but far too wet. The bushes had not yet begun to sprout any green shoots. There was a birdbath of stone, dark and mossy with age. Much-eroded carving around the pedestal suggested it had originally come from a church. Had it been a medieval holy-water stoup, rejected at the Reformation? In a corner, tucked behind a large and spiky holly bush, was a slatted wooden box. A sodden mulch lurked at the bottom of it: a compost pit for the cut grass later in the year. In the opposite corner stood a small well-weathered shed. Morris asked if he should open it and I nodded. Inside, we found an assortment of tools hanging on nails in the wall, together with a simple oil lamp in a wire cage. There was also a modern contrivance such as I had seen advertised in illustrated magazines. It was a small grass mower constructed as a set of blades in drum shape, with a long wooden handle enabling it to be propelled back and forth. It might only be a small town garden, but its scrap of lawn was cut by the latest thing.

'I've got one of those', said Morris unexpectedly. 'We've not got much of a garden, and Mrs Morris likes to hang her washing out in it. But on a nice day, she likes to sit out there and do her mending. I used to cut the grass with shears, you know, kneeling down. It's very hard on the knees. So, one year, Mrs Morris got me one of those gadgets, second-hand, of course. It makes life very easy.'

'I don't have any grass,' I said. 'Mostly our backyard is paved over. There isn't much of it, half the size of this, and there's a coal-house and a privy in it. My wife likes to grow geraniums in pots out there in the warmer months. Last year she had some success with tomato plants grown in the same way.'

I reached out and took down a hammer from the wall. It was old but serviceable and did not seem to have been used recently. All the same . . .

'What do you think, Morris?'

'Kill someone easy with a blow from that,' he opined.

'We'll take it with us – and that trowel – and get Dr Mackay to look at them through his microscope. He's very interested in blood. I gather he's always carrying out research into the subject. If there are any traces on those tools, I fancy he's the man to find them. The butler won't like us removing anything but we can give him a receipt. Let's take a look at the door in the wall.'

We relocked the shed and progressed to the wall door where the larger key turned easily in the lock. We pulled the heavy wooden door open and found ourselves in the street.

'The whole household must know about this key,' I said as we relocked the door from the garden side.

'Carry the body out through there, in the dark, in the fog?' speculated the sergeant.

'It would be a long way to carry a body from here to the rear of the Imperial Dining Rooms. She was only a young woman but a dead weight is just that,' I murmured, and Morris nodded.

As we had anticipated, Wilson, the butler, received the news that we intended to take the two tools from the shed with us with displeasure. Nevertheless he accepted a receipt.

'He's a worried man, sir,' observed Morris as he and I left the house and set off back to the Yard.

'I imagine it's a very unhappy household,' I replied.

We returned to the Yard, stopping at a telegraph office so I could send a message to Colby to tell him Emily had been identified and the inquest had been held. On arriving back, I arranged for the tools we had brought from Lady Temple's garden shed to be sent to Dr Mackay, with my compliments, and a request that he would be so good as to examine the surfaces for traces of blood. Finally I went to report to Dunn. At last I could go home.

It was now quite dark. The fog was closing in again and horns sounded mournfully from the shipping on the river. The stink of sulphur still lingered in the air. Underfoot it was wet and slippery. I encountered two ragamuffin boys, perhaps ten years of age, probably thieves, with pinched white faces, shaggy hair and motley clothing. For them, the cover of the fog was welcome, a co-conspirator in their mischief. They knew me at once for an arm of the Law and scuttled away into the gloom like rats disturbed in a cellar. Vagrants had already taken occupation of the best nooks and archways for the night. Police patrols would move them on. They'd sidle off into the murk only to creep back later, as would the child thieves. It had been a long day.

Chapter Eleven

Elizabeth Martin Ross

I HAD begun the day by reading, from cover to cover, the Salisbury local newspaper Ben had discovered in Emily's room. As Ben had mentioned, it did not contain anything that appeared in any way significant. It was, after all, five weeks old. The latest editions would be full of news of Emily's death. This seemed to have nothing more exciting than an account of hounds straying on to a railway line; but it opened up a panorama of provincial life for the imagination.

A new milliner had opened a business in the town centre. Ladies were invited to come and view a display of hats already created by the owner and her skilled workers. A gentlemen's outfitters, not to be outdone, offered cambric shirts at advantageous prices per dozen. There was an illustration of a gentleman with a fine moustache wearing such a shirt and looking mightily pleased about it. Readers were also invited to an exhibition of watercolours by A Lady. Otherwise it was paragraph after paragraph of reports of local events, like the agricultural sales mentioned by

Ben, and a general auction; and there was a list of guest preachers at Evensong at the cathedral for the coming month. Here, at last, something caught my eye. I wondered if Ben had seen it. On the Sunday following the appearance of this newspaper, the preacher at Evensong would be the Revd Dr Bastable. Ben had told me about him, with a lively description.

I continued reading. Even better: below the printed list a note informed readers that Dr Bastable was a comparatively new arrival in Salisbury. He and his sister, Miss Agatha Bastable, had taken up residence in the house formerly owned by the late Mrs W.

After I had read all this, I sat back with the newspaper in my hands and wondered. Emily had been homesick, Ben had told me. She could have come by this newspaper by pure chance. Someone might have left it at the British Museum, a place we knew Emily had visited, or anywhere else she had been. But these few words attached, almost as an afterthought, to a list of preachers, threw up an intriguing possibility. There was mention, indirectly, of the house in which Emily had grown up. Had someone, seeing this and thinking Emily in her London exile might be interested, sent her this paper?

'Why send the whole newspaper?' asked Bessie, on whom I tested this theory. 'Why not just cut out the bit about the house and send that? It would cost less.'

'I don't know,' I replied, as I folded the paper and put it aside. 'But I'll bring the inspector's attention to it when he returns tonight.'

Despite the unpleasant conditions in the streets, and

the lingering vapours of the fog, I had decided to return to the Queen Catherine that afternoon. I had another call to make nearby, too.

'What are we going to do, missis?' asked Bessie, as we rattled across the cobbles. We had again taken a cab.

'I feel Miss Eldon expects me to do something about that house across the street from her. We know the owner's name is Bernard and he is a man of some wealth. I am going to be a lady interested in good causes. Men like Mr Bernard are always being approached by a spokesman for good causes. I shall approach him.'

Bessie was clearly impressed, but spotted the flaw in my argument. 'He might not be at home.'

'Then I shall leave my card.'

The growler in which we travelled lurched and shook. A horse whinnied. The driver shouted and there was an exchange of colourful language. Bessie and I held on tightly. When the cab continued on its way I heaved a sigh of relief. I remembered Ben telling me of seeing an overturned cab; and the horse being cut from the traces. Perhaps Bessie and I would have been safer on our own two feet.

We descended from the cab and I paid the cabbie off. As it rattled away Bessie and I stared up at the front of Bernard's house.

'Confidence, now, Bessie!' I instructed her. 'Collectors for charity never lack confidence.'

'What sort of charity is it, missis?' hissed Bessie hurriedly as I reached for the doorbell. 'They might ask.'

'The welfare of cab horses!' I told her on impulse.

Bessie muttered something I didn't quite catch. I didn't

give her time to argue, fearing I might lose my own confidence, and pulled at the bell firmly.

After a few minutes, during which I sensed Bessie's instinct to run away and wasn't far from sharing it, the door was opened by a manservant.

He was of medium height but very strongly built, of swarthy complexion with dark eyes that fixed me in a hostile manner. Hardly the usual sort of butler, he did not even speak to inquire my purpose. He just stood there and stared.

'Good afternoon!' I said briskly. 'Is it possible to speak to Mr Bernard?'

'Mr Bernard is not here.' The accent was heavy but the words clearly distinguishable.

'But this is his house?' I persisted.

'He is not here.'

Had no one told this fellow that he ought to be saying his master was 'not at home'?

'And Mrs Bernard?' I asked in a voice I hoped let him know I was not intimidated.

'No Mrs Bernard.'

'I see. Then I shall leave my card.' I produced my card case, slid out a visiting card and held it out.

He stared down at it impassively and made no move to take it. It was the moment I had either to lose the game completely or make a countermove. I decided that, since he had not been adequately instructed on how to receive visitors to the house, I would let him know what he should do.

'The card tray?' I asked impatiently.

He looked startled.

'Come along!' I ordered.

To my amazement my air of confidence and my indication that he was somehow in the wrong worked wonderfully. He actually stepped back, turned aside and took a small silver salver from a side table. This he held out towards me. He even looked at me a little nervously, as if he hoped he was atoning for an earlier dereliction of duty.

I placed my card on it. He picked it up and scowled at it before looking at me questioningly.

'I represent a charitable group of ladies concerned with the sufferings of cab horses.'

He looked puzzled and replaced the card on the tray.

'Thank you!' I told him. 'I will call again, another day. When is the best time to find Mr Bernard at home?'

Now I had him really confused. 'Five o'clock,' he told me. 'Mr Bernard returns at five o'clock.'

'Thank you. Come along, Bessie!'

'Yes, ma'am!' said Bessie, not to be outdone in correct replies, and not, for once, addressing me as 'missis'.

We walked away, hearing the door close behind us.

'Cor, missis!' said Bessie in awe. 'You're really something, you are.'

Thank you, Bessie.'

'I didn't think you'd get away with it.'

'I thought myself I might not.'

'You didn't show it nor sound it. You were a regular dragon!' Bessie's eyes sparkled.

I accepted this was spoken in admiration and not criticism. Even so, it did make me feel more than a little guilty at involving her in my questionable plan.

'What do we do now, missis?'

I hadn't thought that far ahead, but the confidence I had assumed had not yet deserted me so I replied immediately. 'We walk to the end of the street, wait a few minutes, then walk back on the other side until we reach the tavern. Then we walk in there, confidently, mind! And we call on Miss Eldon.'

'Supposing he spots us, that butler or whatever he was?'

'He will suppose us gone. But, if he should see us, it does not matter. We are spreading information about our charity.'

'Mr Slater wouldn't like you going round saying he doesn't look after his horse properly.'

'I didn't say otherwise. Mr Slater takes very good care of his horse. But you and I have both seen other cab horses in a pitiable state. Come along and stop worrying about it.'

Miss Eldon had not expected to see me and apologised profusely for the lack of ratafia biscuits.

'But of course I am delighted at your visit, dear Mrs Ross. I take it Inspector Ross is in good health?'

'Excellent, thank you. He is very busy, of course.'

Miss Eldon sighed. 'So much wickedness about. Because I sit up here in my rooms, like a bird in a treetop nest . . .' She stopped and smiled. 'That is my little joke, Mrs Ross.'

'You do indeed have a view such as a bird might have.'

Miss Eldon cocked her head on one side and said, 'I see a great deal from my eyrie, Mrs Ross! I observed you call at that house earlier.'

I should have guessed she might be watching from her window above. 'Well,' I confessed. 'I have a little strategy, but I don't know that it will be successful.' I explained about my pretending to call on behalf of a charity. 'Now that I know Mr Bernard returns home at five, I shall call tomorrow at a little after five and we shall see if I manage to gain admittance.'

Miss Eldon clapped her mittened hands in delight. 'How clever you are, Mrs Ross!'

'I have not yet been successful,' I warned her. 'But I don't know what else I can do. I want you to know I haven't given up.'

'I was confident you would not,' returned Miss Eldon, smiling brightly.

'Have you seen the young woman again, the one in that room across the way?'

'She has been working on a piece of needlework. I cannot see exactly what it is. I have not caught her eye.' Miss Eldon sighed.

Suddenly she spoke in a soft, nostalgic voice. 'I was the only girl in a family of four. My brothers, all three of them, were older. When I was born, the first daughter and, as it turned out, the last child, my father declared I was like a jewel. He decided I was to be called Ruby for that reason. I have been told that the parson at first refused to agree to baptise me in that name, because it was not a conventional Christian name. But when my father referred him to the line in Proverbs, about the price of a virtuous woman being above rubies, the parson gave in; and in that name I was baptised.

'My eldest brother, William, was much older. He was in the army and looked so handsome and dashing in his regimentals. He was killed in the great battle at Waterloo, against Napoleon. I remember that, before he left with his regiment for the Low Countries, he came home for a few days. My parents hosted a gathering at our house in his honour. There was a fine supper and dancing. The ladies all looked so beautiful in their silk and satin gowns, their hair dressed with jewels and feathers. I was but six years old and crept from my bed to hide at the top of the stairs with my brother Edwin, who was nearest to me in age, being eight, and we watched the coming and going.'

'The news of his death must have struck your parents very hard.'

'Oh yes, it did, although they were very proud of him. But you see, that young girl across the way, she should be going out to balls and entertainments. She should not be sitting, day after day, alone.'

I was becoming more and more convinced there was some reason for the young woman's isolation. But I knew Miss Eldon would accept no argument. Instead I asked, 'And your other brothers?'

'Oh, Henry was killed on the hunting field in a dreadful fall. We were staying with an uncle and aunt in the country. Henry's neck was broken and he was brought home on a hurdle. I remember that, when he was carried into the house, my dear mother gave a great sigh and sank down insensible. She was never the same again and died herself only a year later. Edwin, to whom I was closest, also chose the army as a career. But, unlike William, he hardly saw a shot fired. He died of cholera in the great epidemic of 1848.'

'What of the aunt and uncle whom you and your parents were visiting when your brother Henry was killed?'

'There was a breach, after Henry died,' said Miss Eldon abruptly. 'Too many painful memories.'

I experienced a spasm of guilt. The story I had invented in my own head to explain Miss Eldon's reduced circumstances had been quite wrong. I had supposed her father to be a rake, frittering away the family wealth. In reality it was all much sadder. But something she had told me led me neatly to the other subject I wanted to broach.

'Two brothers in the army,' I said. 'You must have been very proud of them.'

'Yes,' Miss Eldon replied simply.

I decided to plunge on. 'I have heard there is the widow of a military man, a General Temple, living in the area.'

Mentally, I had my fingers crossed that she would not ask me where I'd heard this piece of gossip. Perhaps she would think I had it from Mrs Tompkins, which in a way was the truth. I did hear from her, via Bessie.

'That is correct,' said Miss Eldon, nodding. 'General Temple, as a young man, was at Waterloo with my brother, William. He wasn't a general at that time, of course! Later he made a good career, but sadly he died in India at the time of the great Mutiny. He, too, died of a fever.' Her eyes had lost their customary brightness and seemed clouded, as she gazed unseeingly across the room.

I was suddenly ashamed of my prying. It was time to change the subject. 'My husband is much occupied in investigating the death of the girl who was found behind the Imperial Dining Rooms. It's now known who she is. Her name is Emily Devray.'

Miss Eldon dismissed the reverie into which she had

fallen and declared fiercely, 'And that's another great wrong. A young girl like that, her life ahead of her, left dead in such . . . a horrid place! I cannot rid myself of the sight of her lying there amongst potato peelings and animal bones. It is cruelty beyond belief. And such wrongs must be put right. Of course, that poor child cannot be brought back to life, but she should have justice.'

'My husband is determined that she shall have that, Miss Eldon.'

'Good!' Miss Eldon nodded. 'Perhaps you would like some more tea, Mrs Ross?' She had regained her self-control; but I didn't think she regretted her outburst.

At any rate, the attention of both us of was drawn to a sudden commotion in the street below. A woman was screeching abuse. I could hear a man shouting loudly, issuing orders. I thought I recognised the voice of the landlord. There was a lull and then another scuffle below. At least one of the participants, a man, youngish by his voice and educated, was apparently resisting an attempt to drag him back inside the tavern. He was protesting vehemently.

'Let go of me! Look here, Tompkins, it's none of your business!'

I could not resist standing up and, with a murmured excuse, hastening to the window. Miss Eldon remained seated tranquilly by the fire.

Below, a small crowd was gathering in happy anticipation of a fight. The woman yelling insults was young, with a mop of henna-red hair. This crowning glory appeared to be wet. Her features were heavily painted and distorted in rage. She was showing herself no mean combatant and as I arrived landed a powerful punch on the pot man's ear. The pot man, a stocky fellow of simian build, responded by wrapping both long arms round his assailant, and lifting her clear off the ground. She kicked out furiously.

'See?' she yelled, not discouraged by being caged in the pot man's embrace. 'The young gent wants to go with me!'

The young gent in question looked familiar to me. Tompkins had him in his grip and was forcibly walking him back towards the tavern door. His prisoner, like a recalcitrant toddler, was responding by dragging his feet and sagging, forcing Tompkins to haul him up straight again.

Transferring her attention to the lost customer, just before he disappeared, the prostitute urged, 'Don't you take no notice of that sour old misery, lovey! Nor of that bit of old mutton dressed as lamb! You come with me. We'll have a real good time, you and me! I know a place—'

This disrespectful description of her attire had reached the ears of Louisa within the tavern. She flew out like an avenging fury and managed to box the offender's ears.

At this, the girl, with a screech, broke loose of the pot man. Tompkins was forced to release the young man, and it was all the landlord and the pot man together could do to prevent an all-out battle, for Louisa had joined the fray. The landlord pushed his considerable bulk between the two women as things reached the hair-tugging stage.

'Leave it to me, Lou!' Tompkins gasped to his offended spouse. He turned back to the girl who was again in the pot man's grip and doing her best to break free a second time. Unable to do this again, she kicked out at Tompkins instead, and caught him just below the knee. He let out a roar that made the windowpanes tremble.

'Well, he ain't coming with you! I said you was to clear off. And off you go, my girl! What's more, you don't come back, not today, not never! You go ply your trade elsewhere. You're not giving my establishment a bad name!'

The reply from the woman was couched in such language as I personally had never heard from any female. Louisa Tompkins seized the young man and marched him into the tavern. The red-haired woman retreated backwards down the road, still roaring insults.

Miss Eldon, sipping tea by the fire, was as calm as ever when I rejoined her. 'I apologise, Mrs Ross, for the disturbance, but please pay no attention. Mr and Mrs Tompkins don't allow women of easy virtue to seek out customers in the Queen Catherine. Drunken behaviour is common here, I am afraid to say. But mostly it occurs at night. In the afternoon it is less usual.' She smiled graciously. 'Did you say you would take another dish of tea?'

All was quiet in the street below now and I decided it would be a good time to leave. I declined more tea, thanked Miss Eldon for her hospitality and set off down the creaking old stairs to the ground floor. I walked into the taproom to let Mr Tompkins know I was going home and please would he call Bessie from the kitchen.

But Bessie was already in the taproom, as was Mrs Tompkins, who resembled a large parrot, a macaw perhaps, in a gown of a brightly coloured plaid pattern. I understood it would have attracted comment from the prostitute. The macaw's plumage had been ruffled, and the landlady was still simmering from the insults she'd received, but had managed to pin up her hair more or less tidily. Mr Tompkins was with her, and also of the company was the sweating, dishevelled and red-faced young man I had glimpsed from above. He was well dressed, even though at present his coat was askew and his cravat untied and dangling over his waistcoat. Nevertheless, he was recognisable as the dandy who had been demanding champagne the first time I visited the Queen Catherine. He was now slumped on a chair by the wall. Mr Tompkins, purple with rage, was standing over him like a guard. The prisoner, for so he seemed to be, was scowling up at him and still uttering protests that were much weaker than the lively exchange Miss Eldon and I had overheard.

The two old men I had seen in here before were seated by the fire; and watching with amused interest as they puffed on their clay pipes.

'Dash it all, Tompkins, it is none of your business,' the young man was saying again, but with much less force, more in a sulky way, like a resentful child.

'If it's in my hostelry it is my business!' declared Mr Tompkins majestically. 'As you know very well, Mr Temple! I am responsible for maintaining the peace in my house. I got my licence to consider.'

Mrs Tompkins chimed in. 'You've had a sight too much to drink, Mr Temple! The pot man has gone to fetch Michael to escort you home.'

'Can't!' said the miscreant sullenly. 'Can't let the old girl see me like this.'

'If,' declared Louisa Tompkins, 'by "old girl" you mean

your godmother, you ought to be ashamed to speak of her in such a way!'

'I've had a dreadful day,' muttered Temple. 'I had to go to an inquest. Yesterday I had to look at a dead body! It was horrible.'

'We all ends up as dead bodies,' retorted the landlord with simple logic. 'Most of us probably don't look our best at the time.'

'You don't understand!' the wretched Temple cried out in anguish. 'The girl lived in my godmother's house. The whole business is— is unspeakable!'

At that moment someone came in from the street. A large shadow fell across me and turning, I saw, with shock, a great hulking brute of a fellow with tow-coloured hair. For a moment I feared that the prostitute had sent along her bully boy. But then I saw he was dressed much in the style of a footman, although I never was in any house that employed a footman built like a prizefighter.

'There you are, Michael!' exclaimed Louisa, with evident relief. 'Your young gentleman's had a bit to drink. He's rambling about a dead body and an inquest. You'd best take him home and smuggle him indoors somehow without poor Lady Temple seeing him.'

The giant nodded and moved purposefully towards the slumped form of George Temple.

'Come along, Mr George,' he said in a gruff but surprisingly gentle voice. 'It's for the best.'

He stooped and took hold of George's arm. George stood obediently, swaying on his feet for a moment. He muttered a token objection. 'Dash it, Michael, I am not a child and I am not drunk!' But then he allowed himself to be led out. We saw the pair of them pass the windows, Michael still holding the young gentleman's arm, partly in support and partly to prevent his breaking away and making off.

Mr Tompkins turned to me. 'Sorry about that, Mrs Ross. The young gent had a bit too much brandy. He tucked himself away in the snug and I didn't keep a close enough eye on him. Then that doxy slipped in here and joined him. I heard her laughing and guessed what she was, so I pushed her out. He followed and tried to get her away from me, but the state he was in, he couldn't do much. Anyhow, all sorted out now. My apologies to you for any unseemly language you many have heard.'

'Please don't worry about it, Mr Tompkins,' I told him. Secretly I was delighted to have an item of news that would interest Ben. 'Bessie and I will be off now.'

'That was a real dust-up, that was!' Bessie told me happily as we walked back towards Piccadilly. 'Before they got out in the street, Mrs Tompkins threw a jug of water over that hussy because she was rude about Mrs T's gown. You never heard such language, not from him nor from her neither!'

'I did hear it,' I said. 'So did Miss Eldon.'

Bessie frowned. 'Not nice for the poor old lady.'

'Well, I confess I expected her to be shocked. But Miss Eldon didn't turn a hair,' I told her.

'That young dandy,' said Bessie after a moment. 'He's from the house where that poor dead girl lived?'

'Yes, yes, indeed.'

Bessie opened her mouth to give her opinion on that, but I cut her short.

'Oh, Bessie, I do believe there is a four-wheeler cab waiting at the rank, there. We shall get home sooner.'

That evening Ben and I exchanged accounts of our days.

'I knew he was in the pub,' said Ben with satisfaction, on hearing of George Temple's adventure. 'Sitting in a darkened room and dwelling on thoughts of mortality? Hardly likely! But then, she knew he wasn't in the house.'

'She?' I asked.

'Lady Temple, his godmother. I have seen that footman you spoke of, Michael.' Ben looked thoughtful.

'He must be a great worry to her, I mean George must be a worry to his godmother,' I said.

'Rather more than that, at the moment,' Ben replied, still gazing into the fire. 'A cause of considerable distress, I should think.'

After a moment I ventured to ask, 'Ben, do you think it is at all likely that George Temple is responsible for Emily's death?'

'He has to be a suspect. What is more to the point, does his godmother think he had something to do with it? That is the question I know she is expecting me to ask. That is why she had summoned Pelham to attend her when a visit from me was expected. It is the question I somehow can't ask. At least, not until I have real evidence. Otherwise, it's all supposition. I should find myself and any other officer banned from the house and our inquiries blocked at every turn. George Temple is a fool, but he is a fool who is heir presumptive to a fortune. Therefore, there are those in whose interest it is to protect him from his folly. Also, I believe that the old lady really cares about her godson. He is her late husband's nephew. For her, that is reason enough to defend him and his reputation to the hilt.'

We sat in silence for some minutes, watching the fire crackle and snap, sending up sudden flares of scarlet and yellow, before falling in upon itself to reveal its fierce red heart.

'I read the Salisbury newspaper you gave me,' I said at last. 'There is mention of the Bastables in it.' I fetched the paper from where I had put it in my little writing desk, and pointed out the paragraph in question.

'So there is!' exclaimed Ben. 'I had missed that.'

'Do you think that is why Emily kept it? Because it mentioned the new owners of the house she must have thought of as her home?'

'It may well be why she kept it,' Ben agreed. 'But I would dearly love to know how this edition came into her hands. It cannot be by chance. Someone in Salisbury sent it – or brought it – to her.'

Chapter Twelve

Inspector Ben Ross

ON MONDAY afternoon of the following week, I received an unexpected but welcome visitor. Dr Mackay appeared in my office, carrying a package wrapped in waxed cloth. He placed it on my desk and unrolled it carefully. It proved to contain the hammer and the trowel taken from the garden shed.

'I hope you didn't mind my troubling you with this,' I told him.

'Not at all, Ross!' he returned cheerfully. 'Now then, I have examined these two items carefully, been all over 'em! I found mud and rust and insect fragments. But nothing that suggests to me that it is blood. Even if I had found traces I believed to be of blood, and my findings were supported by my own tests, I could not have told you whose blood it was, you understand that?'

'I realise that, Doctor. It was only ever an outside chance,' I told him. 'Thank you for giving your time. I'm sorry it's been wasted.'

'No, no!' exclaimed my visitor, his Scottish accent

becoming more evident in his enthusiasm for his chosen interest. 'Let me tell you something about blood. Well, I dare say you know it already. It gets everywhere. Moreover, it is very difficult to remove entirely. There are spots, splashes, trails . . . well, you will know all that. You have viewed murder scenes. Over time it degrades, of course. But I believe it should still be identifiable.'

'My wife is a doctor's daughter,' I told him. 'He did a bit of surgery, too, as family doctors in small towns do. She has informed me that soaking bloodstains in cold water is the best way to remove them from cloth.'

'So it is. But it can be difficult to remove completely from other surfaces. Blood smears or spots can be very small, tiny, in the form of a spray reaching further than might be expected, and be overlooked at the general scene. You wrote that these items were taken from a garden shed?' He indicated the tools on the desk. 'Do you think it is the scene of the crime?'

'I cannot say. Possibly, or perhaps the body was kept there for a short time awaiting disposal elsewhere. We know it was in a seated position for that period and I had been thinking of a cellar.' I considered briefly. 'But a cold garden shed would seem a very likely spot.'

'Then there could be blood elsewhere in that shed. The fact that I couldn't find any on these tools should not make us rule out the possibility of finding it on another surface. Perhaps only the smallest trace! I should very much like to examine the interior. Could it be arranged?' asked Mackay, as eager as a child wanting to go to a party.

I thought quickly. 'If I ask the owner of the house, she will consult her man of law and he will prevent us, I have no doubt of that. But if you were to arrive unannounced with Sergeant Morris, and he requested the butler to let you both take another look in the garden shed, and ask for the keys, well, that might work. But I should have to consult my superintendent,' I added reluctantly. 'The house owner is not without influence.'

'What?' exclaimed the startled Dunn, when, having introduced Dr Mackay, I put the proposed plan to him. His bushy eyebrows shot up to his hairline. 'Are you quite out of your mind, Ross?'

'No, sir. Dr Mackay here is making a study of bloodstains.'

Dunn made a noise with his tongue against the roof of his mouth, sounding like a child's clockwork toy running down. 'Is he, indeed? I understand tests for the presence of blood are unreliable.'

'I am not referring to the tests using guaiacum, sir, but to other methods of my own.'

This statement first caused Dunn to look alarmed, then doubtful and finally, to my relief, to heave a sigh and say, 'Oh, well, I don't know, we should have to tread very carefully, Ross.' *Tock-tock-tock.* 'See here, it would be better to request the lady's permission before we send a medical man to crawl about in her garden shed taking samples. No offence, Dr Mackay!' he added hastily.

'I understand,' Mackay assured him. 'But the head would have bled at first before the blood congealed. If the victim was in that shed when she received the head wound, there will be some trace of blood, and I can find it.' After a moment's pause, he added, 'Or I am pretty sure of it.'

Dunn put his finger on the weak point in my request.

'Even if the doctor here found some bloodstains, say, on the wall, what of it? I do not wish to appear to challenge your expertise, Dr Mackay. But I understand that bloodstains deteriorate quickly. In any case, we could not declare with confidence they came from the victim. We should be in a most difficult situation, should any halfway competent barrister for the defence question our claim.'

I had to convince him quickly. 'A defence barrister would seek to undermine any evidence we brought forward to show the presence of the victim's blood, certainly, but it would help *me*! I believe Emily Devray died in that shed and if Dr Mackay can't find any bloodstains from her head wound, it's important I know it; because it would indicate to *me* that I am on the wrong track. Dr Mackay has returned to me the tools Morris and I took from the shed. We signed a receipt for them, and gave it to the butler. So it would be quite natural for Morris to go back to the house and return the tools to the butler. There would be no need for him to speak to the house owner. Then, if he asked if he could take one more look, the butler should be appeased at having the tools returned, and there is no reason why he should object.'

'How do you explain the presence of this gentleman?' Dunn nodded at Mackay.

'We don't – or rather, Morris doesn't. The butler will assume we detectives go about in pairs.'

'It's all very underhand,' muttered Dunn. 'Even if we try to make bloodstains part of our case, what are the odds that we shall be told the gardener cut his hand the last time he was in there?'

'It would give me a lead,' I said firmly. 'And we are

sorely in need of a lead, sir. I want to trace the body every step of the way from the house to the refuse bin at the rear of the Imperial Dining Rooms.'

'Oh, very well, then!' snapped Dunn. 'But, I beg of you, Dr Mackay, take the greatest care. Don't say anything, *anything at all,* before the butler. Above all, don't suggest to him you are a police officer. You are not – and it is an offence to pass yourself off as one. I repeat, just say nothing at all!'

When we were outside Dunn's office, I urged Mackay, 'Go at once, if you can. I'll call Morris. Don't delay. Mr Dunn may change his mind.'

Morris returned later in the day. 'Well?' I asked of him with some apprehension.

'It went a good deal easier than I was fearing, sir,' Morris admitted with obvious relief. 'I think that butler is getting used to the idea of the police coming and going. He didn't ask who Dr Mackay was. He was just pleased to see the tools returned. He let me have the keys again without a peep! Dr Mackay crawled all over the shed, as happy as a sandboy, and has taken away some scrapings.'

'From the internal walls?' I asked.

'From all over the place, sir.' Morris shook his head in awe. 'Even from that lawnmower. I never saw a man take so much enjoyment in his work!'

On Thursday morning, however, two things happened. First I received a letter from Colby in reply to that which I had written to him the previous week and also to report on the situation in Salisbury.

Second, we were also notified, in a message from Pelham's clerk, that Emily's funeral would take place on the following day, Friday, at noon. After a short service in the Anglican chapel at Brookwood Necropolis cemetery, the interment would follow nearby.

I attended to Colby's letter first.

Report from Inspector John Colby

I had hoped to have some new evidence to present to you. But if I cannot do that, alas, I can add a little to what is already known.

The sad fate of Emily Devray remains the talk of Salisbury. It inspires sermons and feeds the gossip at ladies' tea parties. Of the sermons I have personal knowledge because I sat through one myself this past Sunday at the cathedral. I had anticipated that some members of the congregation would be eager to speak to me afterwards, or so I hoped. I had a helping hand, as it were, from the preacher that day. Seeing me in the audience and recognising me, he told everyone who I was and asked them all to pray for my success, and that of Scotland Yard, in discovering who was responsible for this dreadful crime.

I was surrounded afterwards by worshippers. All were anxious to know more, and to tell me that they had personally known Mrs Waterfield and Emily Devray, as both had attended morning service regularly at the cathedral.

I can now tell you that the suspicions you and I

both have concerning Carroway's role in the decision to send Emily Devray away, and sever the link between her and her benefactor, Mrs Waterfield, are shared by others. It seems that Mr Anderson, the nephew who was Mrs Waterfield's heir, came down from Yorkshire to pay a week's visit to his aunt some four months before the lady died. Thus he had ample time to take stock of the situation and become alarmed at the affection his aunt clearly had for Emily Devray. (Several ladies assured me of that affection.)

Anderson is known to have visited the lawyer, Carroway, during that time. I should add that there is nothing that can be secret for long in a place the size of Salisbury.

All the ladies assured me they had been astonished that Mrs Waterfield had made so little provision for Emily in her will. They strongly disapproved of the plan to send her off to London. All believe this was done at Carroway's instigation to bolster Anderson's prospects. The matter is the cause of much outrage here, because of what subsequently happened to Emily. Carroway is well aware that blame is being placed at his door. No wonder he was so displeased to see us when we called on him.

He is not the only one out of sorts. Dr Bastable was in the congregation accompanied by his sister, who looks exactly like him: tall, thin and eagle-eyed. He was also anxious to corner me after the service, but in his case in order to complain. It seems that since our visit to him, and the news of Miss Devray's murder being generally known, sightseers line up outside his house and eagerly watch anyone going in or coming out. This notoriety is not to his taste, nor to that of Miss Bastable. It seems her friends are now unwilling to call on her or even leave cards because of the public excitement occasioned by their appearance.

Miss Bastable has a habit of repeating a key word in her brother's speech in order to associate herself with the sentiments expressed. For example:

'This is all highly improper!' thunders Dr Bastable.

'Improper!' snaps Miss Bastable.

'If this is how our police force investigates crime, then it is a disgrace!' says Bastable.

'Disgrace!' agrees Miss B with a look that, had it been the blade of a stiletto, would have gone straight through me.

Dr Bastable concluded his tirade by informing me that if this interference in the lives of respectable citizens is the result of the late Sir Robert Peel's setting up of the police force, then it is a pity Peel had not left well alone.

I promised I would ensure that a constable patrolled the area for a few days, paying particular care to move on dawdlers outside his residence. Unfortunately, that has made matters worse. The constable has confirmed the increased interest.

By Tuesday Bastable was back, this time in my office, to complain that, far from being dispersed, the sightseers seem to believe he is now about to be arrested. But he never even met the late owner nor this young woman who has been murdered. If this continues, he informs me, he will have no choice but to consult his lawyer regarding the intrusion and harassment. His lawyer, it turns out, is Mr Carroway. You will perhaps not be surprised to learn that.

Not only does Miss Devray inspire sermons from the cathedral pulpit, she is the subject of some terrific ranting in local chapels, particularly the one favoured by Fitchett's lad, Ezra Jennings. I ran into him in the street that same Sunday afternoon, He was buttoned into a black coat and, with his pale face, looked like an undertaker. He was eager to know what progress had been made in the investigation; and disappointed I had no news for him.

But I did learn that the sort of public curiosity shown towards the Bastables is also shown towards Fitchett's bootmakers. In contrast to the Bastables, however, Mr Fitchett is not at all displeased. The shop is busier than ever with customers. They come in on a variety of excuses, from vague inquiries as to the cost of new boots to bringing in used boots for repair, even if it's not required. Some, however, have actually ordered new boots in order, in Ezra's opinion, to talk to Tobias himself, because he measured the poor girl's foot and the idea of this personal contact with the victim inspires horror and fascination.

Fitchett has shown himself an astute businessman and the wooden lasts made for poor Emily's feet, and which he showed us, are now displayed in the shop window, labelled *Recently made for a young lady*. Nothing so vulgar as to mention her name, but everyone in Salisbury knows that those are the murder victim's feet.

As a result, says Ezra, two ladies have ordered boots to be made to the exact same pattern as those made for the murdered girl. I tell you, Ross, there seems to be a ghoulish streak in the nature of respectable females that can never cease to puzzle and horrify me. It's bad enough in men, but in the gentle sex?

At any rate, Tobias Fitchett is the only person in Salisbury to whom Emily Devray's murder has brought a measure of good fortune, and he is making the most of it.

I went to see Dunn to show him Colby's report and to let him know about the funeral the following day.

'You'll attend, of course,' said Dunn, 'both the funeral service and the burial at Brookwood. Keep your eyes open.'

'Yes, sir,' I said. I did not need him to tell me that. 'I propose to send a telegraph message to Inspector Colby, to let him know, in case he wants to come up for it. He should be able to arrive in time for the interment at Brookwood, at least.'

'Yes, yes, if you think so, Ross.' Dunn was already fidgeting with other papers on his desk. He did not even complain about the cost of a telegram.

Passing by the open door of the superintendent's office some twenty minutes later, I was surprised to see that, despite his ordering me to keep my eyes open, Dunn had apparently dozed off at his desk. This was an unknown occurrence. It wouldn't do if anyone else saw him. I went in, closing the door behind me, and tactfully cleared my throat. When this didn't waken him, I cleared it again more loudly.

Dunn opened his eyes and stared at me blankly for a second or two. Then he rallied and asked testily, 'Yes, what is it, Ross?'

'I wondered, sir, if you would be attending the funeral with me?'

'Oh,' said Dunn. 'Yes, I might do that.'

I had not expected a great gathering at Emily's funeral service. Mr Dunn had taken up my suggestion and come with me. I felt a little guilty, as he was just off his sickbed, and the weather remained very cold and damp; and the fog still lurked, trapped in nooks and alleys. But I guessed he wanted to demonstrate he was quite fit again. John Colby at Salisbury had telegraphed a reply to say he would certainly be there. He'd heard that several people from Salisbury were also planning to make the journey, despite the early start it would require. They had first to travel to London by train to Waterloo Bridge Station; and then transfer themselves to the Necropolis's own private railway station nearby. From there they would travel in one of the Necropolis railway's own trains to the cemetery. The coffin and bearers would travel on the same train but accommodated in a separate carriage.

In the event, Dunn and I had quite a surprise. Gathered at the Necropolis Station was a large mourning party of about twenty people, garbed in the required black weeds. I thought at first it must be for some other funeral that day. However, it struck me that they all looked fairly cheery for a funeral party.

It was explained when John Colby emerged from the throng and made his way towards us. He had exchanged his tweeds and bowler hat for a formal frock coat and a top hat. I wondered whether the hat belonged to him; it seemed a little large. The others trooped at his heels and took up positions where they had a good view of Dunn and myself. Our arrival had livened up things even more. Even those who had been doing their best to look tragic were now not quite managing it. Their eager excitement kept breaking through. They fidgeted, whispered and nudged each other. John Colby's face wore the despairing expression of a harassed schoolmaster as he came forward to greet us and be introduced to Superintendent Dunn.

'It's not my fault, I assure you,' hissed Colby, under cover of taking off his borrowed top hat. I was now sure it was borrowed because the inner rim was packed with tissue paper to make it fit. 'I'm not in charge of them!' He clasped Dunn's hand. 'I must apologise, sir, but it's really not my doing. This whole business has created such a stir in Salisbury and when word got out somehow that the funeral was to be today, well, frankly, anyone who could come along, wanted to be there.'

As he spoke, the crowd watched our every move. We could overhear them whispering to one another that Dunn and I were 'very important people from Scotland Yard'.

'You've noticed him?' Colby whispered to me, with a nod of his head towards the crowd.

There was no mistaking the pale, expressionless face and the tall, spindly figure he indicated: Ezra Jennings, no less, in a long black overcoat and a bowler hat. He made an excellent mourner, quite the professional, standing aloof from the general excitement. However, seeing my eye on him, Fitchett's assistant raised his hat and bowed slightly. I returned him a curt nod of acknowledgement. This caused another ripple of interest in the crowd and for several minutes Ezra was the subject of intense scrutiny. He appeared oblivious of this.

Neither Dr Bastable nor Mr Carroway had come, and that didn't surprise me. I was more surprised to see no one from Lady Temple's household. But I did mark the presence of a fellow in a crumpled tweed suit who appeared to be conducting a head count of mourners and scribbling the result in a notebook. The information would be conveyed to the London public in one or more of the evening papers.

The visitors fell silent in respect when Emily's coffin arrived, borne by sombre bearers under the direction of Mr Protheroe himself. All the bearers and Protheroe wore silk top hats with mourning veils tied around them. I thought unkindly, but probably accurately, that this was all providing an excellent advertisement for his funeral parlour. Emily's coffin was loaded aboard with quick profession-alism. Then there was a scramble to board the train themselves ahead of another funeral party, which would also be travelling with their coffin, on the same train. Dunn and I, together with Colby, managed to secure a first-class compartment with no other occupant but a reverend gentleman of advanced age, with a small valise, nearly as old as he, on the seat beside him. He studied us for two minutes and then addressed us.

'You gentlemen are from Scotland Yard?'

We told him that was indeed the case.

'My name is Spencer,' he told us. 'I am to conduct the funeral service for Miss Devray.'

After that he spent the twenty-five-mile journey reading his prayer book.

'How many of those people from Salisbury actually knew Miss Devray, Inspector Colby?' inquired Dunn, as we rocked out of London. 'It's an – um – impressive turnout.'

'As many can claim a personal acquaintance with her as you could count on the fingers of just one hand, is my guess,' admitted Colby in some embarrassment. 'I truly had no idea they were all coming. I went to the station to catch the London train and there they all were, awaiting me. There was quite a festive atmosphere. I wasn't quite sure if I was setting off for a funeral or for the races.'

The Reverend Spencer glanced reproachfully at Colby over the top of his prayer book, and then returned his gaze to the printed page.

'Extraordinary!' said Dunn.

'The whole business has caused some excitement in our city, sir,' Colby explained to him.

'Evidently! Who is the fellow with the pasty complexion and the bowler hat? He bowed to you, Ross, as if he knew you.'

'That is Ezra Jennings, from the bootmaker's shop. The owner, Fitchett, isn't here, however. I wouldn't have been so surprised to see him. I understand he has been doing a brisk business in making boots similar to those Miss Devray wore. He, if anyone, ought to pay his respects!'

'Extraordinary,' murmured Dunn again. He made a few

of the *tock-tock* sounds with his tongue against the roof of his mouth.

'Jennings came to tell me, before we left Salisbury, that Fitchett has sent him to represent him and the business. Fitchett doesn't like travelling on trains, it seems. The speed of them upsets him,' Colby explained.

Dunn was looking as though he was regretting his decision to accompany me.

The fog thinned as we moved further away from London. I was glad of it. It was not always the case. A London Particular, when it strikes, reaches its clammy fingers out well into the suburbs and beyond. We were at least spared that.

We descended at one of the Necropolis platforms, the one reserved for funeral obsequies of the Church of England. We had lost the newspaper reporter in the tweed suit, who had amassed enough copy back at the station in London.

Shortly before our arrival, the Reverend Spencer rose and walked out of our compartment with his suitcase, so that he was ready to leave the train as soon as it stopped. He now reappeared fully robed and without his valise. I wasn't quite sure where he'd deposited that, unless there was some clerical left-luggage office here. I couldn't see one.

After some milling about we formed up in a respectable procession. The Reverend Spencer led the way, holding his prayer book. The coffin followed. Mr Protheroe paced behind that. We found ourselves next in the procession, Dunn, Colby and myself. Without warning, Pelham the lawyer joined us. To be precise, he materialised from behind a funeral monument. I must have looked startled. If he had

been on the train he'd been hiding away in another compartment. I guessed he must have travelled on an earlier train
and waited for us to arrive.

'I am here to represent the family,' he said blandly.

I gathered my wits and introduced Superintendent Dunn
and Colby. They exchanged handshakes and Pelham moved
away, carefully distancing himself from us.

Colby looked curiously after Pelham, but said nothing.

The Salisbury visitors arranged themselves as best suited
them, and managed to subdue their chatter. We progressed
in orderly fashion to the Anglican chapel. After a short
service, we exited it to form up again, and proceed to the
burial site where the empty grave was waiting. The gravediggers stood a short distance away, resting on their spades.

I was glad of the Salisbury presence now. Otherwise
poor Emily would have been placed in the earth with no
one in attendance other than the funeral parlour crew plus
myself, Dunn, Colby and Pelham. As it was, I found the
ceremony brief, dignified and touching. Even Pelham stepping forward to throw a token handful of soil into the open
grave on behalf of the family did not strike a false note.

It was done. We all turned away. The gravediggers
straightened up from leaning on their implements and made
ready to be about their business as soon as we were out of
sight. The Salisbury mourners were more subdued now,
but this was partly because some of them were taking the
opportunity to examine other burial monuments and head-
stones along the route back. When we reached the platform
again, however, I saw a figure peel away from the small
crowd and approach us. I was not surprised.

'Well, Mr Jennings,' I said. 'You will be able to report to Mr Fitchett that all has gone well.'

Jennings leaned towards me, his bowler in his hand and held at the level of our heads, as though to shield our conversation from others. 'Mr Fitchett would have attended in person, Inspector Ross.' He spoke in a hoarse whisper. 'He asked me most particularly to explain that to you. He was sure you would be here – and Inspector Colby too. But the very thought of travelling by train terrifies him.'

'He has never ventured to travel by rail?' I asked.

Jennings considered this. 'In the past, Inspector Ross, he has done so. But various unfortunate incidents have ruined his confidence. He has heard of people going mad on trains and attacking all the other travellers. And then, the final straw as you might say, came the terrible derailment at Staplehurst five years ago. Mr Dickens, the novelist, was travelling on that very train at the time, as you will recall. "If Mr Dickens can be on a train and it falls off the tracks," said Mr Fitchett, "then it can certainly happen to any train I might be foolish enough to board." And he never has again. Boarded a train, you understand.'

'Please tell Mr Fitchett I quite understand,' I told him.

Ezra bowed again and glided away.

'Dashed odd fellow!' commented Dunn. 'Come along, or we'll miss the return journey. I don't want to hang about here. To be frank, I can't wait to get back into London.'

'Do you know?' observed Colby. His eyes followed Jennings as he walked away from us with measured pace in the wake of the Salisbury contingent. 'I do believe that is the longest speech I have ever heard from Ezra there.'

Dunn said suddenly, 'Ross! I have seen that lawyer fellow, Pelham, somewhere before.'

'Yes, sir, you remember the Putney murder?'

'Yes, yes.' Dunn nodded, satisfied. 'Mixed up in this, then, is he?'

'So it seems, sir.'

Dunn said no more on the subject, but from time to time on our return journey we heard '*tock-tock . . .*' from his direction as he stared through the window at the London suburbs, growing ever thicker like a brick forest as we rocked past.

Back in London, Dunn set out for Scotland Yard. Pelham vanished as easily and quickly as he had appeared at the cemetery. The Salisbury mourners set off chattering in search of tearooms. It was their outing and they meant to make a day of it. Ezra Jennings was not among them as far as I could see. I presumed he was making his way back directly to Salisbury by the first available train to report to Fitchett.

As I did not live very far from the station, I invited Colby to come to my house, and take some refreshment there before setting off home. We could compare notes at the same time.

I had warned Lizzie that we might come and when we arrived, sure enough, a table was ready set. Although it was gone half past three o'clock by now, Bessie carried in a splendid chicken and ham pie with a raised crust, accompanied by vegetables, and followed by a steamed sultana pudding and custard.

Really, it was quite a jolly little party, despite the sad event Colby and I had both attended. I had to describe the funeral to Lizzie, of course.

I later accompanied Colby on a leisurely walk back to Waterloo Bridge Station.

'Well now, Ross,' he said, 'you believe the answer to the mystery lies in the household of Lady Temple? In other words, you think the young gentleman is the culprit.'

'He is certainly a suspect, although I have no direct evidence on which to make a case against him. That house holds a secret, certainly. I do believe Emily died there, but I cannot prove it. My personal dislike of George Temple isn't enough! In fact, it complicates matters because I have to keep telling myself to be objective.'

I hesitated. 'I would like to know more about Emily's life in Salisbury. Clearly, there are enough people willing to make the journey to attend her funeral to show there are memories of her. I recognise that perhaps some of them were just curious, but if any of them knew Mrs Waterfield, they would have known Emily. Did you have a chance to talk to them on the journey earlier, coming up to London?'

'I couldn't avoid talking to them!' returned Colby. 'Or rather, they were determined to talk to me. Several of them knew Mrs Waterfield. And, yes, they knew Emily. Rather, they knew who she was and had seen her with Mrs Waterfield. Or they had visited Mrs Waterfield and seen Emily at the house. But Emily herself seems to have been a lonely and friendless figure.'

'No suitors, then?' I asked.

'None. Even though it was generally believed she had expectations, Mrs Waterfield being wealthy, and Emily being raised by her from infancy as a daughter. As it turned out, though, she received little from Mrs Waterfield's will, as we know. When that became known, there was much surprise. The more you think about that, the odder it seems. All believe Mrs Waterfield was influenced, with the result that Emily, alone and without money to live on, had to go and live among strangers, in London, where she met her death. The blame for that is largely placed at the door of Anderson, the eventual beneficiary. That's the fellow Carroway spoke of, the one who lives in Yorkshire. No sign of Anderson at the funeral! Well, I suppose it's a long way from Harrogate. His property is not far from there, I understand. Perhaps he feared facing criticism. It is felt he ought to have "done something" for Emily, even if his aunt had not. General feeling is that Carroway had a hand in the matter. Carroway is pretty unpopular at the moment and I have to say that gives me a certain satisfaction. I don't like him, either.'

Colby hesitated. 'It was even suggested to me by one or two of the mourners that there may have been an earlier will, treating Emily more favourably, and Mrs Waterfield was persuaded to change it.'

He lowered his voice although there was no one in the crowd hurrying past us to overhear. 'See here, Ross, this pure speculation on my part. I have been in two minds whether to speak out about it. But I wouldn't have done in the presence of Superintendent Dunn. He's the sort of fellow who'd want chapter and verse, I reckon.'

'Well, go on, then,' I urged him. He was right about Dunn.

'We're agreed that Emily being cut out of the will, more or less, *is* a devilish odd business. I have begun to wonder if there was indeed another will, but it was made *later*, not earlier than the will favouring Anderson.'

'And that it was suppressed, destroyed,' I asked, 'because it made more generous provision for Emily? Destroyed by whom? Anderson – or Carroway?'

'Got to be one of them,' said Colby. 'If that was the case, of course. As I say, it is only speculation on my part. There's not a scrap of evidence for it. But if that did happen, and if the person responsible panicked when there was so much gossip, after Emily was so poorly treated, because questions might start to be asked in earnest, then, well . . .' His voice trailed away.

'It could be very convenient for someone,' I finished his sentence, 'if Emily were to die . . .'

Colby spread his hands but said nothing.

'I'd rather like to meet this fellow Anderson, who inherited the lot,' I said.

Colby beamed. 'I thought you might! I took the liberty of making some inquiries and I have his address here.' Colby produced a folded slip of paper. 'He lives in the country. He owns a rather fine estate and a house to go with it, Ridge House it is called.'

'I'm obliged to you,' I said, taking the piece of paper.

'Might be a waste of time, of course,' said Colby, suddenly cautious. 'What would Superintendent Dunn think about you haring off to Yorkshire?'

'He might be difficult.'

'Thought so,' said Colby, nodding.

We had reached the station. There was a train about to depart and so we jog-trotted down the platform and Colby scrambled aboard just before the guard waved his flag. Colby dropped the window sash and stuck out his head as the train began to move off. 'Good luck!' he shouted and brandished his borrowed top hat in farewell.

'Well,' said Dunn, when I called by his office on my return to the Yard, 'do you think Colby is on to something?'

'I don't know,' I confessed. 'Colby does have a vivid imagination. When I first met him in Salisbury, before we had definitely identified the victim, he suggested an elopement and a vengeful family. Now he imagines a dastardly plot involving wills. But perhaps imagination is no bad thing. It enables one to view the problem in different ways. I remain convinced that we must concentrate chiefly on the Temple household, though it would be foolish not to explore other avenues. Everyone who knew of the late Mrs Waterfield seems dismayed by the way Emily Devray was, while not cut out of her will, left very poorly provided for. I think I should follow this up.'

'How?' asked Dunn bluntly.

'I should like to travel up to Yorkshire and pay a call on Mr Frederick Anderson.'

'He is not a suspect, is he?' Dunn asked this in a suspiciously mild way. 'Unless you can place him in London on the date of the murder.' He raised his eyebrows.

'Hearing what he has to say about the will is a point at which I can start,' I argued. 'I am not accusing the man of anything, just trying to find out more about the victim.'

Dunn beat a rapid tattoo on his desk with his fingers and added in some of those '*tock-tock*' sounds he had taken to making of late. I wondered if I might be bold enough to warn him about that. He was in danger of sounding like one of those clockwork toy orchestras in which model animals, wound up, beat drums and clashed cymbals. No, I had better not say anything. If he had started carrying on like this at home, Mrs Dunn would tell him.

Suddenly, Dunn stopping his distracting behaviour and announced grandly, 'I am agreed.'

'Agreed, sir?' I ventured.

'Yes, yes! It is what you want, isn't it? My permission for you to travel up to Yorkshire?'

'Well, yes, I was hoping . . .'

Dunn made an expansive gesture, sweeping his arm across his desk. 'I shall telegraph a message to the constabulary there, so that they will expect you. One doesn't wish to tread on local toes, eh? Especially if this Frederick Anderson is a man of some property and influence. You will have to stay there overnight, I suppose. Be sure to take a room in a modest hostelry. You will not be on holiday. On your return, you may request reimbursement of your travel expenses, within reason.'

I was so taken aback by his lack of opposition, his offer to send a telegraphed message ahead of me, and even more by the offer of reimbursement, (within reason), that I was speechless for a few minutes.

'Go along, then, Ross!' ordered Dunn testily. 'Better get on with it.'

'Yes, sir, at once!'

'Mr Dunn agreed?' Lizzie asked, as amazed as I had been.

'He was positively keen on the idea. To be honest, Lizzie, since Dunn has returned from his sickbed, he has been behaving a little – strangely. I am beginning to wonder with what kind of medicine Mrs Dunn has been dosing him.'

'Goodness,' said Lizzie. 'Well, if you are to be away for two days, I shall take the opportunity to call again on Mr Bernard, hoping to find him at home.'

'Listen, my dear,' I warned her. 'You cannot go asking the man to donate to a charity that doesn't exist. It's breaking the law!'

'Oh, I won't,' my wife assured me. 'As soon as I am inside the house I shall explain the real reason for my visit.'

'And Mr Bernard will be perfectly entitled to have that manservant you described escort you briskly to the door. See here, Lizzie, I know you are trying to do what seems to you and to Miss Eldon a good deed, but you are proposing to gain access to someone's house under false pretences.'

'I can't think of any other way,' she pointed out, 'or I should not have to do it.'

'For pity's sake,' I begged her, 'do not let him know you are married to an officer of the law. Or I may return from Yorkshire to find I am a police officer no longer!'

'Trust me, please, Ben. I would never do anything to embarrass you,' said my wife.

'Just bear in mind, my dear, that I am relying on that.'

Chapter Thirteen

Elizabeth Martin Ross

ONCE BEN had departed for the North in the early morning, Bessie and I discussed our planned assault on the house of Mr Bernard, the banker, that afternoon. Bessie was full of misgivings and I have to admit I had more than a few qualms myself. Ben thought it a reckless idea and doomed to failure. He also feared it would end by involving him. Another husband might have forbidden me to go. But Ben trusted my judgement and that I wouldn't act rashly. I did not want to let him down. But nor did I wish to disappoint Miss Eldon. She, too, counted on me.

'Perhaps Mr Bernard won't be at home,' said Bessie hopefully, as we walked towards the front door.

'It's possible,' I agreed. In my head a little voice was saying the same thing: *perhaps Bernard won't be at home. Perhaps he has left word with his servant that I am not to be admitted. I can go back to Ruby Eldon and tell her I have done my best.*

I turned my head and looked towards the Queen Catherine tavern standing solidly across the street. It had stood there for two hundred years or more and it was no longer quite square at the corners, as Wally Slater had remarked. Its oak timbers had weathered and settled. The roof dipped. Turning my gaze upward, I saw the large dormer window behind which Miss Eldon spent her days. I half expected to see her form behind the glass, watching me. But there was neither shadowy figure nor any movement.

'Come along, Bessie!' I ordered. I walked up the scrubbed front steps of Bernard's house and rang the bell.

It clanged distantly within. The die was cast. I could not now turn and flee, like a naughty urchin amusing himself with disturbing respectable householders. I couldn't hear Bessie breathing at all. I fancied she was holding her breath. For two pins, as the saying goes, she would certainly have fled.

The following couple of minutes seemed endless. I became acutely aware of my surroundings: the black-painted panelled door, the bricks weathered to a dull shade of a tortoiseshell brown from the original red, the white-painted window frames. Someone must daily wipe them clean of the sooty deposit from the air. Probably that was the task of the little skivvy Miss Eldon had seen. Bessie, behind me, had begun to breathe again. I sensed her growing panic.

There was movement behind the door. It opened and the swarthy manservant stood there again. He recognised me; that was certain. He scowled. But he also reached for the silver tray and held it out silently for my card. I placed the little white rectangle on it.

'Mr Bernard is at home?' I asked as I did so.

'He is at home. Wait, please.' This was the stern reply, following which the door was shut in my face.

'What do we do now, missus?' hissed Bessie behind me.

'We wait,' I said simply.

After some minutes the butler, or at any rate he appeared to hold that office, returned and opened the door to us again.

'Mr Bernard will see you. Come, please!' He stood aside for us to enter.

I took a deep breath and stepped over the threshold. Bessie trailed in after me. The door was shut. We were trapped.

'Follow, please!' The butler ordered this gruffly, and set off down the hall at a smart pace, not waiting to see if we did follow as bid.

Behind me, I heard Bessie's whispered, 'Oh, blimey!' I gestured at her to be silent.

The hall through which we passed so hurriedly appeared expensively papered in a maroon shade with an elaborate damask design. The wide staircase to the left had a similar maroon carpet. The paintwork was cream. I had little time to observe much else because of the butler's brisk step. But we had arrived. The man threw open a door which must lead into a back parlour.

'The lady, Mrs Ross,' he announced into the room. Then he stood aside and gestured me to enter.

I walked steadily past him, Bessie scurrying at my heels. The door closed. We were alone with Bluebeard in his castle.

It was a comfortable room. A fire crackled in the hearth.

Above it, a mantelshelf supported a fine porcelain garniture of vases and candlesticks, set on either side of an ormolu clock. A chandelier hung from the ceiling festooned with glittering crystal droplets. It was the room of a wealthy house owner and there was something un-English about it. The clock was French, I was sure of that. The chandelier too, I suspected, was French. The porcelain vases might be from a Dresden factory. They closely resembled a set belonging to my Aunt Parry.

Bernard was on his feet already. He had been standing with his back to the door, looking out into a courtyard at the back of the house. It appeared largely a paved area, with classical urns, and a fountain, now silent. He was a tall, solidly built figure in a frock coat and stood with his hands clasped behind him. He wheeled to face me quite suddenly, still keeping his hands clasped behind his back. I noticed he wore a diamond pin in his silk cravat.

'Well, now, Mrs Ross,' he said. 'You wish to speak to me.' His voice was deep and resonant. He did not challenge me, nor did he pitch his words as a question. I wished to speak to him; I had told the butler so. It was fact. As a banker, he dealt in facts. He received me now as he would a client of his bank.

Somehow I found my voice. 'It is good of you to agree to see me,' I said, hoping my voice had not wavered. I added more firmly, just to make sure, 'Thank you.'

He gestured towards a chair near the fire. 'Please, sit down,' he invited.

He ignored Bessie, rightly assuming her to be a maid. Bessie, for her part, scuttled further away and stood by the wall. I took the chair indicated and Bernard seated himself opposite to me. I could now see that he was a handsome man, with thick dark hair and strongly marked eyebrows. He had large, brown, striking eyes and the expression in them was quizzical. I suddenly had the horrid feeling he could read my mind. He was a man with whom it would pay to be honest. He would know at once if I were anything other than frank. He would also know if I was not genuine, as surely as he would have spotted a faked bank note.

'Tell me what is on your mind, madam,' he invited. He held up one hand briefly. 'Please, do not speak to me of mistreated cab horses. I have no interest in the subject. Nor do I believe it is that which has brought you.'

Honesty is not only the best policy; it is the easiest course of action. 'I have come on behalf of an elderly lady, Miss Eldon,' I said. 'I am sorry if I said anything else, when I first called. But it is a little difficult to explain. I needed a reason to call and, if it seems shabby, it is because I couldn't think of anything else.'

He raised his eyebrows. 'Do I know Miss Eldon?'

'No, not personally. But she is a neighbour of yours. She lives across the road, at the Queen Catherine tavern.'

Now he was clearly surprised. But he was also intrigued. 'She lives in a tavern?'

'She has rooms at the very top of the building. She is a lady, though in reduced circumstances. Living where she does should not be held against her. She is utterly respectable and of good family. One of her brothers died at the Battle of Waterloo. So, you see, she is a person to be treated with respect.'

'I hope,' said Mr Bernard mildly, 'that I would treat any elderly lady with respect.'

'Of course!' I stumbled, 'I didn't mean to suggest . . .'

'She is very small,' said Bernard suddenly. His eyes lit with recognition and he held up a forefinger. 'And she wears very old-fashioned clothing. Am I right?' The forefinger pointed at me. The nail was beautifully manicured.

'Yes, you are right. That is Miss Eldon.' I felt a surge of relief. At least he knew I wasn't making this up, another fantasy on a par with the cab horses. Miss Eldon existed and Bernard had observed her quaint figure for himself. 'Well, I have come at her behest, Mr Bernard.'

Bernard leaned back in his chair and surveyed me steadily for a moment or two. Then he asked, 'And what can I do to oblige Miss Eldon?'

This was going to be the difficult bit. Gaining entry to the house had proved far easier than I'd imagined. But explaining that he and his household had been spied upon for some time, that was exceedingly awkward.

'From her rooms, above the tavern, Miss Eldon has a very good view all around. She— she has taken an interest in a young lady I— I think may be your daughter.' This was an inspired guess and if I were wrong, it would be an embarrassing moment. I saw at once that I was not wrong, but my assumption was a blatant intrusion into his private life. He looked at first surprised and then his features seemed to freeze.

'Ah . . .' said Bernard very quietly and I knew that now he really was not pleased. His earlier tolerant manner had vanished. I sensed he was on the verge of showing anger, and controlling it with difficulty. I heard a movement behind me from Bessie by the far wall. She had read the signs, too. Her instincts were still to run. But I couldn't do that. I had to sit here and face whatever happened.

After what seemed a long silence, Bernard trusted himself to speak. 'You are correct, Mrs Ross. I have a daughter. But my household is no concern of Miss Eldon's. Nor, may I add, is it any concern of yours, *madame.*'

'I do understand that, Mr Bernard.' I hesitated. 'I know I have upset you and I am truly sorry for that. But may I tell you something of myself?' Without waiting for his reply, I hurried on. 'My late father was a medical man. He knew that there are many good reasons why someone may not leave the house in which he or she lives, medical reasons. It has worried Miss Eldon that Miss Bernard does not leave the house. Her concern is kindly meant.'

'Is it?' Bernard said harshly. 'She is not, perhaps, an old woman with nothing to occupy her but to watch others, and make up stories about them?'

'If you met Miss Eldon,' I replied firmly, 'you would not say that. Yes, it is kindly meant. She is not a— a snoop, nor is she a gossip. She is a gentle soul and, though she lacks worldly goods, she is rich in generosity of spirit.'

'You, too, Mrs Ross, have spirit, if I may say so,' Bernard replied. 'And courage. May I inquire as to the occupation of Mr Ross?'

This was what Ben had feared, but there was no avoiding it. That I had not been shown the door already was due to my being completely honest.

I drew a deep breath. 'My husband is an inspector of

police, based at Scotland Yard. However that has nothing to do with my coming here.'

'Somehow, Mrs Ross, that does not surprise me. Does he know you are here?'

I felt myself redden and hoped Bernard would think it was due to heat from the fire. 'Yes, I did tell him I intended to call. He tried to dissuade me. He was against— against it. He felt it was . . . well, wrong of me to pry.'

'Inspector Ross's instinct is sound. Perhaps you should have taken his advice? Yet you *are* here, against his wishes!'

'Yes, and I realise how odd that must seem. I explained to Ben – to Mr Ross – that Miss Eldon depended on me in this. I had given her my word.'

There was a lengthy silence. Then Bernard said drily, 'I imagine, Mrs Ross, that it is difficult to dissuade you from doing anything you have set your mind on.'

I was too embarrassed to say anything. Bernard gave a brief, faint smile. I felt a flicker of hope.

Then he appeared to have made up his mind. 'The young lady observed so intently by your friend, Miss Eldon, is indeed my daughter. She is deaf.'

Ruby Eldon had seen the girl make strange movements with her hands. I ought to have kept quiet, but I burst out impetuously, 'She signs the alphabet! She understands how to spell out words on her fingers and to understand others in that way!'

Bernard was silent for a moment. I think he was taken aback. 'You know about the signed alphabet?'

'Yes, I told you, my father was a doctor. He learned it himself out of interest. He taught me when I was little. We used to play a game in which he asked me questions, using his fingers, and I replied via the same method. I mean, I know it is a serious thing for your daughter, but to me it was a game. Children learn well in that way.'

'My daughter learned it at the celebrated School for the Deaf in Paris. My late wife was French. My daughter was born in France and raised there. She also learned to lip-read at the school. Unfortunately, although she can make a few words herself in reply, the school was less successful in teaching her to speak. Of course, all of this instruction was in French. That is the language my daughter understands, if it is written or signed. But she cannot mix in ordinary company, certainly not here in England, where she can make out nothing of what is going on around her. She faces two barriers: her deafness and her ignorance of the English language. She is afraid of going out into a world of which she can make nothing, cannot communicate with, nor understand, what anyone might say to her. Could not hear the rumble of approaching wheeled traffic, nor a shout of warning. You can understand that?'

'I speak French,' I said.

'How so?' He stared hard at me. I detected suspicion in his voice. For the first time he doubted my truthfulness.

To prove my claim I replied to him in French. *'J'avais une gouvernante française. Elle m'a fait parler français tout le temps.* I had a French governess when I was a child. She made me speak French all the time.'

'Tell me more about your governess,' he invited suddenly, speaking in French.

Clearly, I was meant to reply in the same language, so

I did, hoping my command of a language I had not had cause to speak for quite a while would not let me down.

'Her name was Madame Leblanc. I am not quite sure how she came to be in England. I understood, from my father, that she had told him she had been employed by another English family, but they had left for India. For that reason, she could give no references.'

Bernard raised his eyebrows. 'And your father gave you into her care, nonetheless?'

'He believed himself a good judge of character. Also, she was desperate to find a new situation and my father was a kind man.'

'And was she a good governess? Clearly she taught you French very well.'

'I must confess,' I said, 'that she did not teach me very much else. She knew some French history, but very little English history, or only from the French point of view. She was a Royalist. She particularly detested Bonaparte.' I hesitated. 'She was not perhaps the best educationalist, but she was a kind listener and good friend.'

Bernard's gaze moved to the window and the view of the silent fountain. 'Yes, yes,' he said, more to himself than to me. 'A young girl needs a friend.' He remained silent for some minutes and I realised it would be better not to interrupt his thoughts. Then he asked, 'Would you like to meet my daughter?'

I was astonished, but said at once, 'I should like to meet Miss Bernard very much.'

Bernard reached for the bell and the butler appeared.

'Monsieur?' he asked.

'Tell mademoiselle Rose that I shall be bringing a visitor to meet her,' Bernard ordered in French.

The butler showed his surprise but only fleetingly. Then he bowed and went out.

'We'll give my daughter a few minutes to make ready,' Bernard said to me.

I was beginning to feel embarrassed. It was clear that the servants here had learned how to communicate with Miss Bernard. Far from her being a prisoner, I guessed this was a household that had been completely arranged to take account of her particular needs.

'I don't want to frighten her,' I said. 'Please believe that.'

'She should not be afraid. I shall be with you. She will be nervous, however. You should understand that.'

'Of course, I understand completely,' I assured him. More hesitantly, 'I do understand you are putting your trust in me, Mr Bernard, and I am someone of whom you know nothing, other than what I have told you.'

'Your father trusted a woman of whom he knew nothing and gave you into her care. I am following his example, am I not?' He stood up and added briskly: 'Come, we shall go to my daughter. Your maid,' for the first time he acknowledged Bessie's presence, 'can wait in the hall.'

He led the way up the staircase and along a corridor until he came to a door at which he tapped before opening it and entering.

I found myself in one of a suite of two connected rooms. This was a detail Miss Eldon had not been able to observe. We were now in a pretty sitting room. Through open doors I could see into a bedroom beyond.

A young woman stood with her back to the window and to the light. It meant I could not distinguish her as clearly as I'd have wished. She was of medium height and slightly built. Her dark hair was twisted into a simple knot on top of her head and she wore a blue gown with velvet ribbon trimmings. I guessed her age at about seventeen.

'Mrs Ross,' said Bernard, pointing to me as he spoke, 'May I present to you my daughter, Rose.'

The young woman, who had been watching his face as he spoke, bobbed a curtsy in my direction. I bowed in return.

'Mademoiselle,' I said to her, 'I have come to visit you on behalf of a friend.'

I spoke in French and she watched my face. At the same time, from the corner of my eye, I saw Bernard move his hands rapidly, spelling with his fingers. I continued to speak, but accompanying my words with the signed alphabet as well as I could remember it.

'My friend is Miss Eldon. She is an old lady and she lives over there.' I pointed at the window behind her.

Rose turned and looked out at the tavern across the road. Then she turned back, looking puzzled.

'Yes, yes, over there! On the top floor, where there is a very large window.'

Rose's frown faded and suddenly she smiled. She glanced questioningly at her father, who nodded, and then she went to fetch a book from the table. She brought it over to me and I saw it was a sketchbook. Now, by common consent, we all three sat down and Bernard watched as Rose leafed through the sketchbook until she found the page she wanted.

Then she held it out to me. And there I saw Ruby Eldon in pen and ink, her diminutive figure clad in old-fashioned clothing, leaving the doorway of the Queen Catherine.

'Yes, yes! That is the lady!' I exclaimed in English, forgetting for the moment. I hastened to repeat it in French. 'That is Miss Eldon, the friend who asked me to call on you.'

Rose was looking puzzled again. Her lips parted and I saw she was about to try and speak. Her father had warned me the school had not been so successful in that area. The first sound she made I did not understand. She tried again and I realised she was asking, '*Pourquoi?*' Why?

I did my best to reply to what was a pertinent question but embarrassing, using actions to accompany my words. 'She can see you, from her window, the big window. She sees you sewing and drawing. She remembers when she was young. Now she is old, she has no one.'

Rose had understood but my reply had saddened her. Rose was young, but she had no one.

'You draw very well!' I said hastily. 'I cannot draw nearly so well as this.'

A shy smile touched the girl's face and her pale cheeks flushed. She began to riffle though the pages again and found another image of Ruby Eldon. This one was drawn when it had been raining. My elderly friend scurried along the street on a rainy day, clinging to a large umbrella that seemed about to sweep her off her feet. It was not a mocking sketch; it was a humorous and kindly one.

She was far from being the only subject Rose had taken. She did not go out, so she drew everyone and everything she saw from her window. Thus people of every sort were captured by Rose's pencil. As the pages turned, I recognised both Mr Tompkins and his wife, Louisa. In another scene, the brewer's dray stood outside the tavern and the men rolled the barrels across the cobbles and let them down through the open trapdoor to the cellar. A pie man went by with his tray of pies suspended from his neck, ringing a bell. And then, to my surprise, I saw myself, and Bessie, on our way to visit Ruby. Rose had seen that I recognised myself. There was a sudden gleam of mischief in her smile.

Ruby Eldon had worried that the artist she saw from her window had few subjects for her pen. But Rose observed London life from her eyrie. The sketchbook was her diary. Each illustration was neatly initialled 'RB' with the date it was drawn.

Now she turned another page and rotated it so that it was the right way up for me. This was a very lively scene indeed; and not a usual subject for a young lady's pen, or indeed one a young lady would have occasion to see. It was quickly sketched because the subjects were in motion; a small crowd in altercation. There was a dishevelled young man in the grip of Mr Tompkins. George Temple, surely. There was the young woman who had been ejected forcibly from the tavern, in the grip of the pot man and kicking out furiously. Louisa Tompkins stood nearby, hands on hips. All had been caught with a few strokes of the pen, a moment in time preserved.

I looked up and met Rose's eye. 'Yes.' I nodded and smiled. 'I saw that scene. I was over there,' I pointed towards the tavern and the upper window. 'I was with Miss Eldon. I looked out and saw all that!'

Rose closed the sketchbook, hesitated, and looked across at her father.

He was adept at reading her mind. 'Mrs Ross!' he said to me. 'I think my daughter would like you to bring Miss Eldon to meet her. Would the lady be agreeable, do you think?'

'She would be very pleased and appreciative,' I told him.

'Then we can arrange something. Not tomorrow, but possibly the day after that?'

He was allowing Rose a day to change her mind. I understood that. It also gave him time to verify my claim to be married to a police officer.

'I will go now and tell Miss Eldon,' I told him. To Rose, I said, 'It has been a pleasure to meet you, mademoiselle.'

Rose turned as pink as her name, and nodded furiously.

Bernard conducted me downstairs, where Bessie jumped up from a chair, clearly relieved to see me.

'Thank you, Mr Bernard,' I said to him. 'Thank you for your confidence in me and for forgiving me the impolite way I invaded your house.'

'Yes,' agreed Bernard calmly, 'it was very impolite, Mrs Ross. But I do forgive you. I hope we shall see you and Miss Eldon the day after tomorrow.'

'I can't tell you, missus,' said Bessie when we were again in the street, 'how pleased I was to see you come back down the stairs safe and sound. Mind you, I wouldn't have left that house without you!'

'I was quite safe, Bessie. Mr Bernard took me to meet his daughter, that is all.'

'Just like that!' said Bessie in awestruck tones. 'And she's his daughter? You're a bloomin' marvel, you are, missus.'

'Thank you, Bessie. Now let us go and see Miss Eldon and tell her all about it.'

We made quite a little party in Ruby Eldon's garret room. Louisa Tompkins had taken note of what was going on across the road. She darted out of the taproom, glowing with excitement to receive me when I entered the tavern. She led me up the creaking stairs to the top of the house, addressing me over her shoulder in a seamless stream of words.

'I said to Tompkins, that Mrs Ross, who visits Ruby, has gone over the road to the big house and talked her way inside! Would you credit it? And Tompkins, he said to me, "Go on, Lou! She never has!" So I told him, I'd seen you with my own eyes, and young Bessie there, as well. "Are we going to have to go over there and rescue her?" asked Tompkins. "Form a raiding party?" He was joking, of course. But he would have done it, if it had been necessary, you can believe me!'

I did believe her. Bessie followed us up the stairs, pattering along in the rear. When we all three reached the top, crowding the tiny landing, and Louisa had announced us, it was clear that both she and Bessie meant to stay to hear the whole story. So we sat before the hearth and I related my adventure to my three listeners.

'Well, I never!' said Louisa. 'Deaf? Who'd have thought it? Poor young lady. I suppose her papa means well. She's drawn pictures of all of us? Me and Tompkins, too?'

'Yes, and the pot man, and the pie man, and the brewer's dray with the horses. She has drawn me and Bessie, coming here to visit Miss Eldon.'

'And she's French? Well, there's a thing. I'd never have guessed any of it! I declare, it's like one of those novels.' Louisa rose to her feet in a rustle of bottle-green taffeta, that being the gown of the day. 'I'll go down and tell Tompkins all about it.'

'You go downstairs, too, Bessie,' I told our maid. 'I need to have a word with Miss Eldon.'

When Miss Eldon and I were alone, Ruby, who had sat silent throughout my narrative, stirred and said, 'I am very much obliged to you, Mrs Ross. I also owe you an apology. On my behalf you undertook a task that could have turned out very unpleasantly. Mr Bernard might have received you with hostility and abuse. I had no right to expect any such heroism from you. But I am very, very pleased to know the young lady is in no danger. I am very sad, of course, for her situation. But it is so much better, far, far more, than I had feared.' She looked down at her mittened hands and added in some embarrassment, 'You will say I have been foolish and let my imagination run away with me!'

'No, you saw something that puzzled and worried you. You felt you should do something about it. There is no shame in that.'

Miss Eldon sighed and nodded. Now I sprang my surprise.

'I am invited to call again, the day after tomorrow, and to bring you with me to meet Miss Rose Bernard.'

Miss Eldon looked up, startled, and for a moment unable to reply. Then she gasped, 'I am to meet her, the young girl I've seen so often?'

'Yes, and it will put your mind at rest. Yes, she is lonely

and I believe her father understands that. But he does not know what to do about it. There is the double problem, you see, her deafness and her lack of English. Do you know some French, Miss Eldon?'

I was fairly sure she must have had a young lady's education and been taught at least one language, other than her native English.

'Oh, yes, I had lessons, of course, when I was a child. Oh, dear!' She clasped her mittened hands as if in prayer. 'Shall I remember it all?'

'I am sure you will remember enough and I shall be there to help out.'

'My goodness,' said Miss Eldon, letting her hands fall to her lap. 'I am sure I shall not sleep a wink now until the time of our visit comes!'

Chapter Fourteen

Inspector Ben Ross

SINCE COMING to London from Derbyshire as a young man I had had but one occasion to travel back north. By chance, that had also been to Harrogate to pursue some inquiries there into another case, that of Thomas Tapley. Now I took the train to the spa town once more, this time not to stay, but to make my way onward across the moors to Ridge House. I was looking forward to the possibility of meeting Inspector Barnes, the local man, again. He had been of great help to me on the previous occasion and he and his wife and had made me welcome at their dinner table.

When I arrived in Harrogate, sure enough, there was the considerable bulk of Barnes, waiting to meet me and pump my hand until I felt the fingers would never function properly again.

'Will you need me to come with you this time, Ross?' he asked.

'Thank you,' I said, 'but I want to make my call on Anderson appear as informal as can be. Is there anything you can tell me of him before I go?'

Barnes nodded. 'As informal as possible is probably best. Officialdom wouldn't impress him. He's a respected man, a judge at livestock shows, and at one time a magistrate. He owns a fair amount of land, most of it let out to tenant farmers. There is also a home farm, of course, attached to Ridge House. I believe he takes a great interest in that. Something of a gentleman farmer, as they say. He doesn't do much except ride round his estate but likes to keep everyone there on their toes.'

He steered me outside to a waiting pony and trap. 'Here's your conveyance. This is Herbert, your driver. The roads outside the town are a little rutted with ice at this time of the year, but Herbert will keep you safe. You won't want to be upturned and it's easily done. Oh, when you get back, my wife and I hope we shall see you at our table again? And I've taken a room for you, as before, at the Commercial Hotel. It was all right last time, was it?'

I assured him I had been very comfortable at the Commercial Hotel and looked forward to renewing my acquaintance with Mrs Barnes. I had not forgotten the excellent table she kept. Barnes beamed at this and clapped me on the shoulder, nearly dislocating it.

When I set out in the trap, driven by Herbert, and we had left Harrogate behind, I soon felt I was in another world. The bright clean air was wonderful to breathe after London's stinking fogs. What I had not perhaps considered properly was the legacy of the heavy winter snows, still much in evidence. In London we had suffered fog. In Yorkshire, Herbert confirmed, they had suffered heavy snowfall that winter.

'Out there . . .' He waved his whip at the open moor. 'You'd have thought you were sailing on a white ocean! Trees poking up bare arms like drowning men calling for help. Some buildings half buried. You could see the chimneys sticking up like markers. That's how you knew where houses were.'

Even now, only the top tiers of the stone walls could be seen, and the sheep, poor creatures, they huddled in what poor shelter they could find.

Barnes's warning that the roads were 'a little rutted with ice' had been an understatement. Ruts there were aplenty, but in other places, Herbert's sea of snow had been replaced with a slough of frozen mud. The strips of firm going were so narrow the trap could often only proceed at walking pace. Several times hidden rocks jolted and shook us severely, making the trap bounce up in the air on one side or another. Then I had to grasp anything I could and hang on, for fear of being thrown out. I wondered more than once whether we'd be flipped over. Yet Herbert knew his business, and, though he gave me a sardonic glance or two when he saw how grimly I was clinging on, we made a steady progress.

Herbert himself so closely resembled William, the driver on my previous visit, I wondered if they were brothers. He seemed slightly perplexed at my presence; and even more perplexed by my having come up from London. After our initial brief exchange, he did not speak again for a while, but then his curiosity overcame him.

'You'll have visited Ridge House before, then?' he bawled at me from beneath the brim of his bowler hat. It was tied on his head with a woollen muffler to keep it in place in the sharp wind; and to protect his ears from frostbite.

'No!' I returned, huddled in my greatcoat.

'It's a fine place!'

This was followed by another fifteen minutes of silence. Then Herbert resumed.

'London, eh? That's where you hail from?'

'I live there now, but I'm a Derbyshire man by birth and upbringing.'

'What are you doing in London, then?'

There was an echo here of my conversation with Miss Eldon when I had met her behind Bellini's restaurant.

'I went there, like Dick Whittington, to make my fortune!' I dared to joke.

'And did you make it, then, this fortune?'

'Not exactly. I joined the police force.'

'Oh, aye?' said Herbert. 'You could have joined the police here, you know. We're quite up to date.'

'Well, I was a youngster you know, and I had a fancy to see London.'

'There's no accounting for taste, I suppose,' replied Herbert. After that he did not speak again and I felt I had blotted my copybook, as they say. At last, however, he drew rein, and pointed with his whip across the landscape.

'There you are, that's Ridge House.'

It was only about a quarter of a mile away but I would have missed it if Herbert hadn't drawn my attention to it, even though it topped a rise in the land that had given the house its name. The wind buffeted it on all sides. Smoke spiralling from it chimneys immediately evaporated in the wind. The simple, elegant, but sturdy lines of the house suggested it had been built in the reign of their Majesties William and Mary. The outer walls were plastered and painted white. This did not help in the prevailing conditions. Herbert turned us off the main track on to another one. Ahead of us now, Ridge House formed a more solid bulk, the tall, regularly spaced windows and a pillared portico to the main door being the most noticeable of its features.

Herbert drew up before the door. A boy ran out from somewhere and took the horse's head. The main door opened and a butler appeared.

He descended the portico steps with dignity and approached us. 'Inspector Ross?'

'Yes,' I told him. I clambered down as best I could, since I was stiff and aching from the drive.

'I trust you had a safe journey, sir. Mr Anderson is waiting for you. If you would kindly follow me?'

I set off in the wake of the butler. As I did, from behind us, I heard Herbert call, 'Of course he were safe, Isaac Gregson! He were driven by me!'

The butler ignored this and continued with a stately tread ahead of me. He appeared oblivious of the sharp wind cutting through the air, so I had to appear as indifferent to it as he was. I would have preferred to cover the ground at twice the pace, to get indoors and find sanctuary. At last we passed through the open front door and the wind was left outside. But the temperature did not strike me as perceptibly warmer.

The interior of the house was dark despite the large windows. Otherwise, it seemed as well built as its outer appearance suggested. The wind battered it in vain. Old family houses tend to be a repository of changing fashions and interests. The cavernous and gloomy hall contained a good deal of furniture serving no purpose but to make work for the maid who had to dust it. The walls were hung with what I guessed were family portraits. They bore a strong resemblance to one another, these Andersons. All of them looked as solid and defiant as the house. There was a large glass case containing some stuffed game birds and, on one wall, between the portrait of a red-faced Georgian squire and a very plain woman wearing some very fine jewellery, was another case with a large trout mounted against a painted background showing a riverbank. I suspected it of being a plaster reproduction of the original. It was dusty and flaking within its glass house. The case seals must have perished. But it wouldn't occur to anyone here to take it down and throw it away. It belonged here as much as that long-case clock, ticking away time dolefully, and the table with the barley twist legs on which stood the box for letters to be taken to the Post Office in Harrogate, if there ever were any. To say nothing of assorted chairs that must each once have formed part of a dining set, but now jostled for space in case anyone should care to sit down in this dark museum. It struck me that the place lacked a woman's touch.

Isaac Gregson relieved me of my hat and coat and hung both on a rack. He then threw open a door and showed me into a large, equally cluttered room, inadequately heated by a single fireplace at the far end. A small dog of terrier type ran to meet me with a brief bark. It then sniffed at my boots and appeared satisfied. From its general appearance it was very old.

'You'll not need to worry about Sammy,' said a voice. 'He'll not bite. He's not got many teeth left that are any use.'

The speaker was a burly man of perhaps five and fifty, wearing a thick tweed jacket and seated in a large armchair before the fire. He had bushy hair, worn collar-length, and still Nordic blond in colour, albeit with streaks of grey. Beneath it, his complexion was red. The crimson could not be from the heat in the room. That was minimal. A fondness for the bottle, possibly? Or wind-weathered from riding round his land, as described by Barnes? A man for whom the force of the storm, or the cold wet kiss of the snow, was to be endured and shrugged aside. A descendant of the Vikings! I thought. His left ankle was in a plaster cast, from which his toes protruded in a woollen sock. It was propped on a footstool. He whistled and the dog trotted back to sit beside his chair.

'Mr Anderson?' I bowed politely.

'You'll forgive me not standing to greet you, Inspector Ross,' he replied. 'I have broken my confounded ankle.' There was a stout walking stick propped against his chair. As for his voice, it was deep and in its own way as weathered as his complexion. But he did not speak uncourteously.

'I am sorry to hear it,' I told him, wondering when he had broken it. I also made a quick estimation of how tall he would stand upright. A good six feet, I reckoned.

'Had a good journey across the moor? Who drove you?' he demanded.

'Herbert Wainwright, sir.' The butler, still behind me,

had taken the last question as put to him. His reply came over my shoulder.

'Good man, Wainwright.' Anderson nodded and returned his attention to me. 'You will be chilled to the bone, I dare say?' he demanded of me, rather than inquired solicitously.

'I confess I am,' I told him.

'Bound to be. Mind you, we've known worse winters, although it's been bad enough. A lot of the farms were marooned until a couple of weeks ago, couldn't get to or from them! One of the tenants had a wife in the family way and she decided to go and give birth to twins in that time. No one to help but her own old mother and she nearly eighty. Still, Yorkshire women are hardy stock. Gregson! Bring us a hot toddy apiece!'

The butler withdrew and Anderson waved me to a chair by the fire near to his.

'Does the ankle mend well?' I asked politely.

Anderson regarded the affected limb with resentment. 'Well enough, but too slow. The surgeon told me it could take up to six weeks for it to mend. Dashed inconvenient.'

'An accident on the ice, perhaps?'

'No,' was the growled reply. 'I fell down my own main staircase on a Sunday morning, two weeks ago. No good reason for it. I wasn't suffering a drunken hangover. I just missed the step on a dark landing.'

This meant the accident had occurred on the day of Emily's murder in London. Was Anderson presenting his alibi early?

He stared at me in a way that was direct but not offensive. 'Come to talk to me about Emily, have you?'

'Yes, sir, I have, if I may. I am anxious to establish the background to her murder. The more I know, the better I will be able to make some sense of it.'

Anderson gave a shout of mirthless laughter. The dog looked up at him questioningly. He dropped his hand to touch the terrier's head. Reassured, Sammy settled again. 'Make sense of a murder, eh?' Anderson's look challenged me. 'The murder of a young girl like that? Good luck to you, Ross.'

'I am a police officer,' I told him evenly, 'but I am not insensitive. It is a dreadful business and I shall do everything possible to see Miss Devray has some justice, even in death.'

Perhaps he thought my words carried some criticism hidden in them, some reference to the will, because he stared very hard at me.

'Will you, now?' he said. He studied me for a minute. Then he shifted in the chair and muttered, 'Dashed inconvenient, this ankle!'

The door opened and the butler brought in the hot toddies. Anderson raised his to me in a silent toast. I responded in like manner and we sat in silence, drinking. The fire of the whisky and the sweetness of the honey coursed through my veins and I did feel much more human. I had been even more chilled than I'd thought.

I took the moment to look around the room. It was furnished much in the style of the main hall with assorted furniture, all of it very good, but much of it dating back to the beginning of the century, as was the discoloured wallpaper. There were more paintings hung around at different levels, but time and smoke from the hearth, and generations of candles, meant they were in sore need of cleaning. The nearest picture showed a man standing with proprietorial pride beside an enormous bull. Its huge solid rectangular body put me in mind of a railway engine. It hardly seemed possible that its short legs could hold it up. A farm worker was at its head, holding a stick, which hooked through a ring in the brute's nose. The proud owner wore knee-breeches and a low-crowned hat, and rested an outstretched hand nonchalantly on the beast's rump. Dimly, through the grime, the landscape behind it appeared to contain a house in the distance, resembling the one in which I found myself.

Anderson had marked my interest. 'Achilles, that animal was named,' he said. 'And the man you see there is my grandfather.'

I was a little embarrassed to realise he had been watching me so closely. He now set down his empty tumbler before I could think of a suitable comment, and changed the subject briskly. 'Getting down to business', he would have termed it himself, no doubt.

'See here, Ross, I took the news of Emily's death very much to heart. Who the devil would want to do such a thing to such a harmless little creature?'

'You must have known her all her life,' I suggested.

'Naturally, I did! My Aunt and Uncle Waterfield took her in as an infant. The original intention was that it would be a temporary solution, you understand, until some relative of the Devrays could be found who would take over the responsibility for her. But none was ever found. Whenever I visited, Emily would be there, growing up, in the background. My uncle and aunt brought her with them when they came up here for a visit one summer. She would have been twelve years old then. It was just before my Uncle Waterfield died, lost at sea. He should have stayed on shore. There was no need for him to go sailing around the globe. He wasn't a naval man. He traded in commodities.'

'I would have expected him to live in London.'

'He couldn't stand the place and I don't blame him. With the coming of the railway, there was no need for him to do so. He could travel up and down as needed.'

'The Waterfields had no children of their own, I understand.'

'None. No more have I!' he added suddenly, fixing me with a direct look. 'I am a widower. I have been so these last ten years. My wife and I had only one child and he was carried off by a fever when he was but two years old. Are you a married man, Ross?'

'I am.'

'Family? Children?'

'No, I – we – have no children.'

'Well, for me, being childless means I have no one to leave this to.' He gestured, indicating the house around us and the landscape visible through the windows. 'It is a matter of some concern to me. I am now fifty-seven.'

He stared past me through the windows again, at the snowy landscape. 'There are labourers working on my land out there, who have a dozen children apiece. Not every family is so large but most have two or three, at least. There is irony in it, is there not? Poor families all around us with a brood of thriving youngsters. Yet I, and my late Aunt Maude down there in Salisbury, both remained childless.'

'Your Aunt Maude, Mrs Waterfield, was your father's or your mother's sister?'

'My father's sister. She and I were the last of the Andersons. If I had broken my neck one night tumbling down the stairs, not just an ankle, and had Aunt Maude still been alive at the time, she would have inherited this estate from me. Given she was nearly twenty years older than I am, that would have been less than ideal! Now only I am left, and the matter is serious.' He reached out and tugged at a bell rope hanging by the hearth. 'We shall have another toddy,' he said.

The one I had drunk had already made its way pleasantly to my head, but I dared not risk offending my host. He seemed in a mood to talk. Besides, I was beginning to suspect where this was leading.

Anderson proved he was not a man to beat about the bush. 'There has been much gossip, I dare say, in Salisbury about my aunt's will. I have been informed that you have been down there, poking around and asking questions. It will be that which has brought you running up here from London.'

I guessed it would have been Carroway who had informed him.

'Yes, Mr Anderson, a lot of gossip, or so I understand from my colleague, Inspector Colby, of Salisbury City Police.'

'Hah!' exclaimed Anderson fiercely. 'I can imagine it! All those old biddies with their tea and card parties – ah, Gregson!' The door had opened noiselessly behind me. 'Another couple of toddies!'

I decided to take a hand in the direction of our conversation. 'It has been suggested in some quarters that Mrs Waterfield changed her will not long before she died. Previously, in another will, she had been more generous towards Miss Devray. After the change, much less so.'

'Well, that is correct enough, as far as it goes,' Anderson agreed. 'Mind you, Inspector Ross, I won't ask you who told you that. I will point out that, legally, my aunt was not required to do *anything* for Emily.'

'But she had brought her up from babyhood,' I protested.

'That's as may be. But Emily Devray was a child no longer. My Aunt Maude was not a sentimental woman, Ross, and neither am I a sentimental man. That doesn't make either of us heartless. Let me explain it to you in simple terms. There you are, Gregson! Set them down.'

The hot toddies were arriving at a speed that suggested a generous supply had been brewed up ready and was waiting in Gregson's pantry.

'I'm a practical fellow. My aunt was a Yorkshirewoman by birth and breeding and she was practical, too. Some months before she died, she wrote asking me to pay her a visit in Salisbury, stay with her for a week or two. I have a competent land manager here. I went to Salisbury. When I had been there a week, my aunt explained what was on her mind, why she wanted me there. I suspected it already. She was getting on in years and her heart was weak. She was concerned about Emily's situation, when she, Aunt Maude, should be gone. She wasn't callously indifferent to Emily's future, as you seem to have decided, Ross! As you were rightly informed, by whichever busybody told you, she had made a will some years earlier leaving the bulk of her estate to me. Emily was, however, generously provided for under this will.

'But Emily was a bookish girl, always reading. She was shy in company. Aunt Maude feared that, left without protection, and with a small but respectable fortune, Emily would see a queue of unsuitable hopefuls at the door, proposing marriage. She could not trust Emily to make a good choice. Probably, in the circumstances, she'd make one she would regret.

'Well, as Aunt Maude pointed out, I am without an heir. Surely the simplest solution would be that I should marry Emily?'

He broke off, because I was so startled at hearing this I couldn't disguise it, and sat with my mouth open like a perfect fool.

Anderson bridled. 'I thought it was a very good suggestion!' he said truculently. 'Emily was young. We could have children. She would have a comfortable home. With luck, I would have another son; or even a daughter would do. There are several landed families around here with sons. A daughter could have been married to any one of them, and the pair of them could have stayed here and taken over from me. But a son would have been preferable, of course. A man likes to see the family name continued.'

Anderson waved a hand at the room around us. 'In return, Emily would have as much pin money as she wanted. She could run the household as she liked, changing all the furniture, curtains, all the rest of it. And she would be safe, protected. She had seen the house when she was a little younger and knew it. She would be well aware of what I was offering. So, I told Aunt Maude I was very content with the idea; and asked formal leave to address myself to Emily on the matter. Aunt Maude was delighted. She thought everything would be taken care of in the best way available. Everyone would get what they wanted, eh?'

Anderson ceased speaking and stared into the dancing flames in the hearth.

'And you did so?' I prompted tactfully. 'You asked Miss Devray to marry you.'

'Aye,' returned Anderson, still staring into the flames. 'I did. And she turned me down flat. No other way to describe it. She didn't mince her words or even try to hide her— her horror at the idea. She spouted a lot of nonsense besides, such as she would not be "bought and sold", that sort of rubbish. That's what comes of a girl having her nose in books all the time.'

'You were angry?' I suggested, after a tactful silence. He must have been embarrassed, furious and confused, I thought.

'I was, I admit it, for a while. But not nearly as angry as Aunt Maude. She was bitterly disappointed. It was her idea, you see, and after all she had done for Emily, the girl had not even considered it. Very well, then, so my aunt told her. Emily would have to make her own way. She could start right away by seeking a situation as a governess or companion. My aunt would support her no longer. My aunt underlined this by writing herself to an acquaintance, Lady Temple, seeking a position for Emily as a nurse-companion. She, my aunt, also changed her will and reduced considerably the amount she had originally bequeathed Emily. She would have cut her out altogether, but I persuaded her this would attract far too much comment. Well, it has attracted comment enough, anyway. I understand the lawyer, Carroway, has had to shoulder much of the blame. It won't worry him. He never cared much for Emily. He saw her as a parasite.'

I was right: Carroway had been keeping Anderson abreast of all that went on in Salisbury.

'Is that how you saw Miss Devray?' I ventured. 'As taking advantage of your aunt's kindness?'

Anderson turned his head sharply and snapped, 'Of course not, damn it! I was very taken with Emily, as it happens. And, at my time of life, a wife who wants to sit reading is perhaps preferable to one who wants to go to balls and parties all the time. Nor do I give up easily!

'I was prepared to wait and try again. But then, as if matters couldn't be made worse, they were. Aunt Maude died suddenly. Lady Temple was prepared to hold the position of nurse-companion open for Emily, until the house in Salisbury was sold. I thought I would wait until Emily had been in London a little while, running around looking after an invalid lady. It ought to bring her to her senses, make her see the reality of her situation. I then intended to present my case to her again. I hoped the second time she might be persuaded to marry me. But, as it turned out, some scoundrel stepped in and took Emily from this world. So I had not the opportunity to ask her again.'

Sammy had fallen asleep and twitched in his dreams,

perhaps remembering chasing rats and rabbits in his youth. Anderson leaned back in his chair, moving his leg a little, and winced. 'Dratted ankle!' he muttered. He looked up at me. 'Heard enough? Got some more questions?'

'No, Mr Anderson, I have no more questions.'

'Do you think I acted badly?' he asked suddenly. 'You can speak freely.'

I was startled. I hadn't thought him a man who would ask a stranger to comment on his private affairs.

'That is not for me to say, sir.'

Anderson jabbed a stubby forefinger at me. 'Don't be mealy-mouthed about it!'

'I'm not!' I protested. 'But I am here in an official capacity, investigating the background of a murder victim. I am only interested in such facts as may have a bearing on my work.'

'Come now, you are an intelligent fellow. In your time as a detective, you must have peered behind the parlour curtains of a good many folk, I'll be bound. I am interested to hear your opinion. I won't hold it against you!' he added drily.

I took a deep breath. 'Well, then, urged on by your aunt, and perhaps believing she had already won over Emily to your cause, you were misled into being overconfident. Perhaps if you had wooed the girl a little longer, not just presented her with an ultimatum . . .'

'Humph!' muttered Anderson.

I decided not to say Mrs Waterfield ought to have shown more sense. She certainly seemed to have lacked insight into her young ward's mind. Tactfully, I added, 'Possibly

Mrs Waterfield felt time was not on her side. It was an unfortunate situation.'

Anderson leaned forward in his chair. 'It was an unnecessary one! My aunt trusted the girl to show some common sense.'

'She was very young and— and the offer of marriage very sudden,' I offered feebly, wishing I had not let myself be drawn into making any comment.

'Head in books!' muttered Anderson. 'Well, well, my aunt bore a degree of responsibility, I have to agree with you there.'

Had I said that? I'd meant it, certainly, but tried to avoid stating it baldly.

'She should have made it clear to Emily much earlier than she couldn't depend on Aunt Maude's charity forever. She certainly couldn't expect an independence from any will,' Anderson rumbled.

'You think Emily did expect what you call "an independence" from Mrs Waterfield's will?' I asked quickly.

'Who knows what Emily thought?' was Anderson's moody reply.

No, I said to myself, nobody knew what Emily thought, or wanted or expected, simply because nobody had ever asked her. But I didn't say this aloud.

Anderson had picked up the walking stick by his chair and was prodding gently at the plaster cast. 'Have to get the dashed surgeon to come out again and take a look at that. It itches like the devil!' He looked up and at me. 'Well, if there is nothing more you want to know from me, I'll have Gregson tell Wainwright to bring the trap around.'

I was not to be offered anything to eat. I was meant to sustain myself with hot toddies. It was probably what Anderson himself did until the roast appeared on his dinner table. But he was also sending me an unspoken message. I was not an invited guest. I was an intruder; into the house and into his business. Perhaps it was my meddling in what he considered his private affairs that he resented most, no matter that I had an official interest in Emily's death. He had dealt with me as briskly as he would his estate manager. Business over. Dismissed.

Sammy woke and followed me to the door, seeing me off the premises. On leaving, I found myself pleased to be in the cold crisp air again. It cleared my head.

As he drove me back across the moors, Herbert Wainwright asked me suddenly, 'Get what you wanted, did you?'

'I think so,' I told him. Around us the early winter evening was drawing in. The failing light caused strange shadows to play among the lingering heaps of snow, distorted and alarming. The pony was stepping out smartly. Perhaps it knew it was homeward bound and wanted to be in its warm stable; or perhaps it didn't like the shadows either.

'Wanted the young lass to wed him, didn't he?' asked Herbert suddenly.

'You know about it?' I replied in surprise.

'Couldn't not know. He came back from that place down South . . .'

'Salisbury.'

'Aye, Salisbury. Mr Anderson came home in a rare old state. Everyone was afraid of him. He's got a temper, as all know. Even Isaac Gregson had to mind what he said or did, and Isaac has worked at Ridge House for years. Mr Anderson told Isaac some of what had happened, one evening when he was in his cups. He's not normally a drinking man. But he was embarrassed, you understand? Made to feel a fool, and he's not a fool. Not him, no. To my mind, the lass should have accepted him.'

'Perhaps the young lady didn't want to leave the South and live up here,' I offered, as I peered, a little nervously, into the lengthening shadows. There was a black shape by the side of the road which looked like a huge mythical beast. It was only a bush, of course.

'Don't talk daft,' said Herbert.

I dined with Barnes and his wife, a cheerful evening. Later, in my bed at the Commercial Hotel, my thoughts were more sombre and I lay awake for some time, staring into the darkness. My sleeplessness was not the fault of the Commercial. The bed was comfortable enough. Nor were my thoughts because of the case I was on.

Old memories had been jogged by the dark shape at the side of the road, glimpsed as Herbert Wainwright drove me back to Harrogate from Ridge House. I had felt again that small boy, sent down into the mines at the age of seven to be a 'trapper'. That is, to sit long hours in the darkness by the wooden doors that open and shut as required to control the flow of air drawn in through ventilation shafts to prevent suffocation in the mine's Stygian tunnels. The law had already been brought in that children under the age of ten could no longer work underground. Mostly pit children were small and scrawny and had the faces of old men. But I was a sturdy child; and if a boy looked near enough ten, then he was reckoned to be ten, as far as the mine managers were concerned.

So I crouched there keeping my lonely vigil in the darkness, ears straining for sounds, even the pitter-patter of rats' claws, because the silence was worse. In it I feared I'd been forgotten and no one would come to relieve me, or send me up to the surface. My father had died in an accident underground and never come up to the surface alive.

From time to time lights wavered in the darkness and my ear caught the crunch of heavy boots. Miners appeared, so blackened by the coal that they were mere shapes in the gloom despite the lamps they carried, shapes like the bush on the moor. Mostly they passed me by in silence. Sometimes one of them would speak to me, but usually they were too tired, and just trudged wordlessly by. Sometimes, making my way to or from my station, I would hear the hooves of a pony hauling a wagon of coal and the creak and rattle of the wheels. Then I had to scramble aside, for there was little room to pass. I was small and I could not be sure they'd seen me. The ponies were small, too, shaggy and near-blind. They hardly ever saw light other than by the miners' lamps. Later, when I was a little older, I was given other work in the pit, harder, but not so lonely.

Dr Mackay had remarked to me, before I left for my present visit to Yorkshire, that 'blood gets everywhere'. So does coal dust. When I made my way home at the end of the day, my mother would weep at the sight of me. She worked washing the floors and cleaning the stove at the house of the mine manager, which was reckoned a good job and a clean one, better by far than sorting coal at the pithead, as other women did. My mother could both read and write and she had taught me, and another boy. Lizzie's father, Dr Martin, saved me from that life: when he learned by chance that I was literate. He paid for me to go to school. He brought me up from the darkness into the light; so that my mother no long wept when she saw me. That is the way I remember it.

They are stricter now regarding children working underground. At least, that's the theory of it. When I look into the fire of an evening, sitting by my own hearth, I don't see the dancing flames. I see the tired men, and the blind ponies, and I hear the rats scrabbling out there in the darkness.

Lying there in my bed at the Commercial Hotel, I could see and hear all these then, but only in my head. As a policeman I have seen some dreadful sights, but none that haunt me so much as those childhood images that lurk in my brain.

I took the train back to London the following morning and went straight from the station to Scotland Yard to report to Superintendent Dunn.

'Well?' he asked. 'Did you discover a plot, such as Colby fancied?'

'I did discover a plot,' I told him. 'But it was not quite as Colby imagined.' I related what I had learned from Anderson.

Dunn listened in silence, occasionally punctuated by the '*tock-tock*' noises. I did wish he would stop that.

'Well, well,' he said thoughtfully when I fell silent. 'So

it was all about a marriage, eh? Or a proposal that was turned down.'

'It was. Mrs Waterfield wanted to provide for Emily in a way she thought suitable, without leaving her vulnerable to the wrong sort of man. Anderson wanted a wife. Mrs Waterfield thought that he was the right sort of man. Nobody consulted the girl.'

'And he was angry at being turned down, eh?' Dunn mused, tapping the desk with his stubby fingers. 'Embarrassed, too, I dare say. Insulted, perhaps?'

'All of those things, I would guess. In his part of the world he'd probably be considered a catch, a man of property and so on. I do wonder if he had not had his eye on Emily for some time, watching her grow up and understanding his aunt's concerns for her. He is anxious to have an heir, but he'd done nothing about it until a year or so ago. To my mind, it's because he'd decided on Emily Devray, as soon as she was of an age to marry. He is the fellow accustomed to have his own way; not many would argue with him. I was told he is known to have a temper.'

'And he admits he intended to go to London and ask the girl again?'

'Yes, when she'd had time to reflect on her situation, that was his way of thinking. He was confident, I believe, in her change of heart. After she had spent some time looking after an invalid lady, and a very elderly one, who might die at any time and leave her without a place, well, she'd be very pleased to be Mrs Anderson with her own home. Plus, as Anderson put it, as much pin money as she pleased.'

'So he'd be furious if she had turned him down a second time! Is he our man, Ross?'

'I am sorry to tell you we have to rule him out. He wasn't able to go to London and ask her again because he broke his ankle on a Sunday two weeks ago. That would be the day we believe Emily died. He was most careful to tell me that before I had been five minutes in his presence.'

'So he could not be in London at the time, putting his renewed offer of marriage to Miss Devray!' said Dunn drily. 'Nor could he be there to react violently to a second refusal. How did he manage this convenient accident?'

'He claims he fell down his own staircase, after stumbling on a dark landing. Well, to be sure, it is a gloomy house. My guess is that he was also drink-fuddled; though he declared he wasn't drunk or hungover. It's feasible enough. The house is as gloomy as a mausoleum and stacked to the rafters with a couple of centuries' worth of clutter. He was probably fortunate not to break his neck.'

I realised what I'd said and stopped short in embarrassment.

'Like the girl, eh?' said Dunn.

I hurried on. 'He mentioned the surgeon coming to attend to the injury. The lower leg and ankle are in plaster. So, if asked, I am sure the surgeon will confirm it.'

'Huh!' muttered Dunn. 'I can't say he sounds the sort of fellow I'd like to see any daughter of mine married to.'

'He is Mrs Waterfield's nephew and heir,' I reminded him, 'so I can see how she and Anderson thought it a good idea. But they went about it all the wrong way. Mind you,

I'm inclined to agree with you that he wouldn't be an easy man for a young woman to share her life with.'

Dunn was silent for a while, then remarked, 'It is a pity about that broken ankle. We should not rule him out, Ross, even so. Anderson, as you describe him, is a man of influence in his district, a man with friends. No doubt the surgeon is an old acquaintance. Perhaps, for friendship's sake, he was willing to slap a whole lot of plaster round an ankle, having declared it broken. As a police officer I have learned to be wary of men with influence, especially in rural areas.'

Eventually, after all of this travelling to and fro, I got home to my own fireside that evening. Lizzie listened to all I had to say and agreed that Mrs Waterfield's plan had been poorly executed.

'Just to produce Anderson from out of the blue, and suggest Emily marry him, what could she have expected?'

'I gave some thought to that,' I admitted, 'during my train journey back to London. You've spoken of your late father a couple of times, during this investigation of mine. Tell me, did he ever have occasion to let a patient know he was dying?'

'Not so bluntly, I hope!' Lizzie exclaimed. 'But people do need time to put their affairs in order, so occasionally he had to suggest that it might be a good idea, just a precaution, to give thought to such things.'

'Exactly!' I told her. 'I fancy that Mrs Waterfield's medical man had just such a conversation with her. Her heart was weak; she knew that. Anderson told me so. She'd made a will some time earlier. That's the will Anderson mentioned in which his aunt had left Emily quite well provided for. But now, with perhaps less time that she'd thought she might have, Mrs Waterfield panicked. Possibly her doctor had dropped a hint or two. She began to review the dispositions she'd made and to worry about Emily. The girl was young. She was unworldly. According to Anderson, Emily always had her head in a book.'

Lizzie was looking thoughtful and a little sad. 'I can see how that might happen. But still, to suppose Emily would accept a man of fifty-seven who lived a rural life in the North of England, when Emily had spent her time in Salisbury . . .'

'She had visited Ridge House,' I reminded her.

'Well, yes, when she was twelve years old! From your description of the place, I suppose it was much the same when Emily saw it. It wouldn't have appealed to a twelve-year-old. She must have thought it a fusty old museum of a house, stuck out in the middle of nowhere, where to pay a simple social call on a neighbour would require at least a pony and trap.'

'All right, all right!' I placated her. 'Mrs Waterfield was foolish and Anderson was overoptimistic. It explains how Emily came to be living with Lady Temple and acting as her nurse-companion, but it doesn't help me much in discovering how she died. Anderson broke his ankle that same weekend. Dunn is sceptical, but I feel forced to accept it as true. Anderson isn't a suspect. But, if I rule him out, then I have nowhere else to look, unless it is in Lady Temple's own house.'

'You suspect George Temple?'

'I can suspect him as much as I like!' I muttered. 'It gets me nowhere.' I realised that I had been so wrapped up in my own narration I had forgotten that Lizzie also had had plans. 'Tell me, did you reconsider your idea to visit the banker fellow, Bernard? I hope so . . .'

Even as I spoke I saw that I hoped in vain. Lizzie's cheeks were flushed a little more than could be caused by the fire. Her attitude had gained some defiance. But also, I fancied, there was a spark of triumph in her eyes. 'Go on,' I said, resigned to hearing the worst. 'Tell me what you have done.'

'I don't see why you should think it should all have been such a disaster!' my wife declared robustly. 'As it happened, it all turned out rather well.'

She then embarked on a long explanation of her day and her success. I was forced to agree she had achieved a good deal. But the past couple of days had been strenuous, the fireside was warm, and I have to admit that towards the end of Lizzie's story, I fell asleep.

Chapter Fifteen

WHEN I awoke the following morning it was to a curious silence. Lizzie still slept peacefully alongside me. I slid carefully out of the covers so as not to disturb her and stood in my bare feet listening for sounds from the kitchen, indicating Bessie was down there, clanging pots around ahead of breakfast. Nothing. The room was cold. It would be colder outside. I went to the window and drew back the curtains.

My hearing was as smothered as was my vision. If there was anything outside in the street, I could neither see nor near it; any view cut off by a grey-white blanket, tinged here and there with pale orange patches. The house was no longer part of a material world. We were cocooned in a cotton-wool silence, so eerie and so isolated that I did wonder, for a moment only, if perhaps we'd all died in the night and floated through some celestial ether. It was, of course, the fog. It had been thinner these past few days. Now it had returned with a vengeance, creeping upriver during the night, reaching out its damp, cold arms, and drawing us all into its maw. So might the whale have swallowed the luckless Jonah.

There was a sound at last from below. The back door slammed. Bessie had been out to the privy in the yard. Within a few minutes I heard her clumping her way up the stairs. There was a knock on the door and it opened to admit her small, sturdy form, carrying a jug of hot water.

Unbothered by finding me standing before her barefoot in my nightshirt, she marched across to the washstand, deposited the jug, turned and announced, 'Here, you can shave. And it's something awful out there. You can't see your hand in front of your face. I don't know how you're going to get to work.' With this depressing news, she marched out again. Lizzie stirred and peered over the blankets. 'What is it?'

'Nothing,' I told her. 'Only Bessie. The fog is back.'

Lizzie groaned and flung back the sheets, reaching for her wrap. So another day started in the Ross household.

Getting to work proved as difficult as Bessie had fore-seen. Fires had been kindled in houses all around, the smoke from the chimneys mingling with the river mist and producing an odorous, suffocating soup, through which I felt my way. There could have been no greater contrast between this and the clear, cold air of the Yorkshire moors I had quitted only yesterday. Even my sense of direction was confused. I listened for the traffic ahead, but the sounds I heard I could not place. When I reached the great rail terminus at Waterloo Bridge, the smoke from the locomotives was added to the mix. Even to draw breath was difficult. Unwarily, I opened my mouth to gasp for air, and swallowed a mouthful. The taste was foul. I coughed and spluttered, hearing, though not seeing, other early-morning

Londoners all around me. We cannoned into one another, muttered apologies, and stumbled onward. As I crossed the bridge I heard, but could not see, the river traffic below my feet. Hooters and foghorns played a melancholy symphony. A clip-clop of hooves and the groan of wheels gave warning of an approaching vehicle, proceeding at a walking pace only. I pressed myself against the parapet and a dark shape loomed up. A hansom cab was taking a traveller and his luggage to the station. I smelt the acrid odour of horse, heard the cabbie swear, and glimpsed the pale face of his fare peering out anxiously, wondering if he would catch his train. Silently I wished him luck.

I found Scotland Yard was emptier than it should have been at that hour, other than for a few tired-looking officers who should probably have gone off shift an hour earlier. I asked the officer at the front desk if anyone had been called out to a scene of crime. He replied that most had simply not arrived yet to take up the day shifts.

'But Superintendent Dunn is here, sir,' he informed me. 'Came in twenty minutes ago.'

Just my luck! I thought crossly. Everyone else was held up, myself included, but Dunn, who had come in from St John's Wood, a fair distance, had managed to arrive already.

'Sergeant Morris?' I asked hopefully.

'Not yet, sir.'

A last desperate throw of the dice. 'Constable Biddle?'

'Can't say I've seen him, sir.'

Just myself and Dunn, then, and a couple of constables near asleep on their feet. I climbed the stairs and first went along to the superintendent's office, to let him know I, at least, was on the premises. I entered on a quite comfortable scene. A fire burned in the grate. Dunn sat in his chair at his ease; and was fortifying himself with a tumbler of something poured from a bottle of murky brownish liquid standing on his desk. It was an odd-shaped bottle, flattened not round, of medium height with a narrow neck. I had seen similar in dispensing chemists' shops. Whatever the contents were, they were no kind of ale or any spirits I could identify. The liquid looked sticky in consistency, like something a maid might use to get scratch marks out of polished wood.

'Good morning, sir,' I greeted him. 'You're early.'

'No, I'm not,' returned Dunn. 'I'm on time. You are late, Ross!' He didn't sound too put out about my tardiness. That was odd. Then he spluttered, coughed, and drained the tumbler. 'Ah, that's better! The congestion lingers in my chest, Ross.'

'Such things are often slow to clear,' I sympathised, venturing to add, 'What is that mixture, sir?' I had understood Dunn to be a member of some temperance society. What on earth was in that bottle?

'It is Mrs Dunn's preferred cough mixture,' he told me. 'She has the pharmacist make it up for her.' He gave the bottle an affectionate tap. 'It is excellent stuff. It got me through this last bout of illness, Ross. You should try it.'

'Oh, I see,' I said. A suspicion had entered my head. 'You've been drinking it regularly, then, sir? Since you went down with that bad chest infection?'

'It is the first thing Mrs Dunn reaches for,' he assured me.

Could the mystery of the odd quirks of behaviour exhibited by Dunn of late be explained?

'Just out of curiosity, sir,' I asked, 'it isn't laudanum, is it? Or something like that?'

'No idea,' was the vague reply. 'The pharmacist recommended it. I understand he sells a lot of it at this time of year.'

Probably at any time of year, I thought. I made my excuses and went to my office.

There, another surprise awaited me. As I approached the door I heard voices. One croaked – that meant Morris had arrived – and one had a Scottish burr. Indeed, Dr Mackay rose to his feet to greet me.

'Good day to you, Inspector Ross,' said Mackay apologetically. 'Although it's hardly that, I mean, the fog . . .'

'Quite, Doctor,' I said. To Morris I said, 'Glad to see you, Sergeant!'

'Sorry to be late, sir,' returned Morris. 'I found Dr Mackay here downstairs at the desk and took the liberty of bringing him up to see you.'

'Certainly!' I said heartily. 'Always a pleasure to see you, Dr Mackay. You're out and about early.'

'I haven't been home,' confessed Mackay, 'or not since yesterday. I was at Bart's and, when the fog began to close in, I decided to stay there overnight. I sought out one of the cots used by the duty doctors, and slept on that.'

'Dr Mackay,' croaked Morris, 'has kindly been giving me advice on my cold.'

'Only commonsense, really, and some old traditional remedies,' confessed Mackay. 'Drink plenty of water. Herbal teas are often helpful: ginger tea was one my own granny swore by. Honey and lemon juice in boiling water also makes a helpful brew.'

'A lot of housewives still swear by laudanum mixtures,' I suggested mildly.

'Well, I do not!' was Mackay's stern reply. 'Laudanum can be very addictive.'

'Good for the nerves, perhaps?' I continued to play devil's advocate.

'Makes 'em happy, I suppose,' agreed Mackay. 'In the short term. But still not to be recommended!'

'Thank you, Doctor, I will bear it in mind. Now then, have you had a chance to look at any bloodstains you may have found in the shed?'

'I have and it is that which has brought me.' Mackay cheered up. 'I had to get down on my hands and knees. There is a well-marked trace of blood on the lower inside wall, certainly – well, at least, to my satisfaction. But also on a lawn-mower!'

'The lawn-mower!' I exclaimed.

'Indeed. By my deductions, someone – I cannot, of course, say it was definitely the young woman – fell in the shed. Let us assume it was she. She struck her head on that sturdy metal contraption, bled from the wound to the back of her head, until it clotted; but died very quickly, due to her neck being broken. That happened, I suggest, because of the confined space. It meant the body did not sprawl but collapsed downwards, in a heap. The back of her head collided with the lawn-mower. This collision acted very much like a rabbit punch.'

'And she remained there, in that garden shed, until the body was moved later, after a period of at least six to eight hours?' I put in.

'Resting against the wall, her head touching it at the point I found the bloodstain.' Mackay nodded vigorously.

There was a silence while all three of us considered the situation. Morris cleared his throat. 'Problem is, gentlemen, as I see it – with your permission, Mr Ross . . .'

'Yes, yes, go on, Morris.'

'A good defence barrister will seek to get the evidence of the blood thrown out. No disrespect, Doctor!'

'Yes, he will, certainly if he is briefed by Pelham.' I sighed. 'I am sorry, Dr Mackay.'

'Don't apologise!' Mackay told me. 'I wish I could prove it in a manner that would convince a jury or a judge. Give me another year or two, and I'm confident I shall be able to do it.'

'I am still extraordinarily grateful to you. Well, I had better go and tell all this to Mr Dunn. Will you come with me, Dr Mackay?'

'Well, well, Dr Mackay,' said Dunn when he had listened to us both. 'We thank you, of course. However, Ross, although I dare say you'd like to go back to Lady Temple's house and interrogate them all afresh, we cannot do so. But it seems that we are looking in the right place. Something else, Ross. There must be something else.'

'Oh well,' said Mackay. 'I've done all I can and I'm obliged for the opportunity to add to my researches. I'll take my leave of you and make my way back to the hospital.'

I decided to take my chance. 'Dr Mackay,' I said to

Dunn, 'has been kind enough to advise Sergeant Morris on his cough and sore throat.'

'Really?' asked Dunn, interested.

'More than happy to oblige,' said Mackay, 'Although it is time rather than medication that will cure him. The symptoms can be alleviated. I advised plenty of fluids, and tea made with lemon juice, ginger, or oil of thyme. They are all very effective. I advised him against laudanum mixtures. I can't recommend those, although they are popular. All these opiate-containing potions are so very addictive.'

'Really?' asked Dunn in surprise.

'Oh, yes. An habitual user becomes as dependent on them as a drunkard does upon alcohol.'

Dunn looked first startled and then worried. 'Really, Doctor?'

I showed Mackay out, leaving Dunn staring thoughtfully down at his desk.

I never again saw the bottle of Mrs Dunn's cough mixture in his office. I can also report that following Dr Mackay's visit Mr Dunn's normal brusque manner returned within a few days.

Elizabeth Martin Ross

I looked out at the fog that morning in dismay. Did this mean I must defer my plans to collect Ruby Eldon and take her across the road to meet Rose Bernard?

'It's going to take a long time to get there,' warned Bessie. 'I can go out and find us a cab, but it will still take a good while. It'll be dangerous on foot. You can't see a hand in front of your face and that's to say nothing of the risk of just getting lost. That's what the fog does, isn't it? It's not just that you can't see which way you're going, you can't tell, half the time, if you're even going in the right direction!' She eyed me thoughtfully. 'You're going to try, though, aren't you, missis?'

'I would like to,' I confessed.

'Will you eat some of that soup, then, before we start out?' asked Bessie. 'And there's half the apple pie left.'

So the matter was decided. But a surprise was in store. We were getting ourselves ready to leave the house and brave the weather. The fog had lifted very slightly, but still remained a severe obstacle to both vision and sound. Then, outside in the street, we heard the creak of wheels and the clip-clop of hooves. It was a closed cab, and it drew up before the front door. Shortly afterwards, the brass horseshoe that formed the doorknocker was sharply rapped. Bessie went to answer it and returned with a stunned expression and holding out a white envelope to me, in silence.

It took a lot to silence Bessie. I took the envelope and opened it.

My dear Mrs Ross,

My daughter and I fully understand you may not feel able to pay the arranged visit this afternoon, due to the weather. However, I have taken the liberty of inquiring of Miss Eldon if she has your address. [I had given Ruby my address, in case she needed to send me a note.] *I am sending this letter with José, my butler, who will bring it to you by cab. If you still feel able to come, as*

*arranged, José will bring you back with him in the cab.
A similar arrangement will, of course, take you back home
again.*

The note ended with a formal expression of regard and
was signed *Léon Bernard*

'Are we going, then?' asked Bessie. 'In that cab?'

'Yes, or at least I am,' I told her. 'You can stay here.'

Bessie's plain features set mulishly. 'If I have to follow
that cab on foot, I'm going along with you!'

She was quite capable of doing that. I went out to find
José and tell him we would accompany him.

I did not think José was French; in fact I was sure he
was not. If I had to guess, I would say Spanish or
Portuguese. But the Bernard household was an unusual
one. If Bernard felt he could trust someone, he could make
a decision that might seem capricious or strange to a chance
observer. I knew this because he had decided he could
trust me, and taken me to meet his daughter. Somewhere,
in his no doubt colourful past, Bernard had encountered
José and his wife, decided they were trustworthy and
engaged them as household staff. Where he had found them
was a mystery. They had probably worked for him for years.
I suspected they had followed him from France to England.
Before that? There was a lot about Léon Bernard I didn't
know, and probably never would.

When we reached the street in which both the Queen
Catherine and Bernard's house stood, we all descended from
the cab and José paid off the cabbie. I told José I would go
up and fetch Miss Eldon downstairs. He nodded silently.

'I did not know whether you would come, dear Mrs Ross!' confided Miss Eldon. She had jumped to her feet as soon as I entered the room and had obviously been waiting for me in a fever of uncertainty. 'But I hoped you would. I was sure you would do your utmost to keep to the arrangement. I beg you will forgive me passing your home address to Mr Bernard.' She peered up at me anxiously. 'I thought, as he is a banker, he would be a man of discretion. I did not like to think of you trying to make your way here through such a terrible fog.'

'I certainly appreciate Mr Bernard sending his butler in a cab to bring me. It is very cold and unhealthy out, Miss Eldon, and although it is only a step across the street from here I hope you won't catch a chill.'

'Oh, no, no!' insisted my friend. 'I really am quite warm.'

I could not say the same of the room in which she'd received me. The fire burned as usual in the grate but it couldn't adequately heat the large attic space, with its high steepled ceiling and dark rafters. Ruby Eldon probably counted herself lucky to have a roof over her head, and indeed she was, in her straitened circumstances. But she was like a bird in a treetop, buffeted by the elements and clinging on to its branch.

One could not but think of a bird when looking at her. She had dressed carefully to make this important visit; and was the picture of fashion of thirty years earlier. We made our way to the foot of the winding, creaking staircase to find Bessie waiting there with Louisa Tompkins.

'He's outside,' said Bessie grimly. 'That butler, or whatever he is. He's waiting for us.'

'Tompkins and I want to hear all about it afterwards,' warned Louisa. 'Don't forget! I want a full description of the furniture, the china, everything!'

Bernard had taken time from his banking business to be there to receive us. He was waiting in the parlour in which I'd met him the first time. He was not alone this time. Rose was with him. He received Miss Eldon with a grace approaching gallantry. Ruby Eldon, for her part, fluttered like a young girl, clearly completely bowled over.

Rose had also dressed with care for this occasion. She wore a silk gown with lace trimmings. We all curtsied, bowed and nodded as if at a court reception.

I wondered if the whole visit was to be spent in this room. But Rose led the way upstairs to her private sitting room. There we found a table spread with a lace cloth and the tea things set out upon it. The silver teapot stood on a little samovar. The china was fragile and not English to my eye. There were several pretty dishes set out with little cakes and biscuits.

Bernard himself did not join us at the table, but retired to a chair in the corner, to keep a watchful eye in case Rose needed help. Bessie had taken her previous chair downstairs in the hall and was no doubt bursting with desire to know what was happening.

As it was, after some initial shyness on Rose's part, and some more fluttering on Ruby Eldon's, we all got on famously.

When we'd drunk our tea and partaken of the delicacies provided I saw Bernard, from the corner of my eye, reach out and tug a bell pull. Shortly after that, the door opened and both José and his wife appeared. It was the first time I'd seen the wife. Like José, she was olive-complexioned, sturdily built, and impassive. Between them, the servants removed the tea things. This included taking off the lace tablecloth, folding down the tea table, which was constructed on the gate-leg principle, and then moving the table itself to stand against a far wall.

This was likely to be the most difficult part of the visit because it all turned on communication.

I leaned forward and indicated Miss Eldon to Rose. 'I have been telling this lady about your sketchbooks.' As I spoke, I mimed opening a large book, and then made movements with my hand as though I sketched. Rose nodded. 'Miss Eldon would like very much to see some of them, I think.'

'Oh, yes!' said Ruby Eldon, nodding in her turn, and smiling.

Rose blushed again, but stood up readily enough and brought over two large sketchbooks of her work. She opened the first of them and placed it carefully on an easel. Ruby Eldon and I stood up and went to watch as Rose slowly turned the pages.

'How wonderful!' cried Miss Eldon. 'You really are very talented, my dear Miss Bernard!' She took a deep breath and added in French, 'You have a good eye!' She pointed at her own eye as she did.

Rose drew a deep breath I recognised as preceding an attempt at speech on her part, and managed, '*Mer-ci!*'

This book was the one Rose had shown me on my first visit. Miss Eldon was clearly enchanted at seeing herself depicted, and the one showing her clinging to the umbrella had her clapping her hands in delight and laughing.

At that, Rose laughed too. It was an odd sound, coming from deep within her throat, but it was very affecting. Something made me turn my head, and look across the room towards her father, sitting quietly in his chair and almost forgotten by all of us. He caught my glance and stood up, gave a brief bow, and left the room. I realised he was deeply moved and did not want me to see his emotion.

We had finished looking at the first book. Rose replaced it with the second and we began to look at a new set of drawings. These I had not seen before. Some were more street scenes, but then came a group of strange sketches that seemed to have been made during the night, when the street was lit only by a couple of gas lamps and a swinging lantern over the door of the tavern.

I looked at Rose questioningly. She shook her head slightly, pointing through the open door into the adjoining bedroom. Then she put her hand to her cheek, tilting her head to mime someone sleeping, before taking it away while shaking her head. She spread her hands in a characteristically French manner.

I understood. She did not always sleep well. When that happened, she got up, went to her window and watched the street as she did during the day. These were sombre drawings with none of the humour of the scenes in the first book. The inhabitants of the night were sad, haunting figures. A dishevelled, drunken man stumbled from the door of the tavern. A homeless person, so wrapped in rags and oddments of clothing it was impossible to tell whether male or female, huddled for shelter in a doorway from driving rain. A young woman in tawdry finery wandered along the street, seeking custom. A child, a little girl no more than twelve years of age, followed behind. She wore a hat with a feather in it. It looked incongruous on her. I realised with despair that this child, too, was on offer. The tragic little soul was serving out a sordid apprenticeship in an ancient occupation.

I glanced at Rose, wondering if she understood the scene she had so vividly captured. She looked sad. The scenes she saw from her window had taught her about life and its horrors. She did not need to go out into the world herself to discover them.

Miss Eldon, beside me, said quietly, 'Oh, my dear, oh, no.'

Rose turned the page quickly. This time I gasped and Ruby Eldon exclaimed, 'Why! What is that?'

This was by far the most unexpected and strangest of all the scenes. The other images had been caught with a few quick, strong strokes. The images in this picture had a soft, almost imprecise line to them and seemed to be seen through a window in need of cleaning. Then I realised that this scene was not only at night; but the air outside was thickened with fog. Despite the fuzzy nature of the subjects, I saw a giant of a figure stooped over a wheeled invalid chair, pushing it along the street. The wheelchair contained a shrouded form, completely covered with a blanket of some sort. I had seen this giant before, and Ben had also seen him when he'd called on Lady Temple. I looked at Ruby Eldon whose face was set in serious lines.

'Yes, Mrs Ross,' she said to me. 'That is certainly Michael, Lady Temple's footman.'

I turned to Rose, who was beginning to look anxious. She realised something had happened as a result of showing us this sketch, but she could not know what. She was sensitive to atmosphere and touched my arm hesitantly, raising her eyebrows in question.

With a mix of gestures and pantomime I asked Rose if I might have this sketch, or rather borrow it. 'I will bring it back!' I promised.

Rose understood what I wanted and willingly detached the sketch from the book, rolled it into a tube and handed it to me.

At that moment, two things happened. The closed cab in which Bessie and I had travelled across the city arrived in the street below and drew up before the front of the house. At the same time, there was a sound from the door of the room. I turned to see Bernard re-enter. He had come to indicate our visit was at an end.

'Mr Bernard,' I said. 'I hope you will not be displeased but mademoiselle Rose has kindly allowed me to borrow one of her sketches. I would like to show it to my husband.'

Bernard raised his eyebrows and crossed the room. I handed him the rolled tube of paper. He unrolled it, frowned at the subject and looked at me in question.

'I think,' I said, 'it could be of interest to my husband in a matter he is investigating.'

Bernard was not happy about this. After a moment, during which I really feared he was going to forbid my removing the sketch from the house, he asked, 'This is really important?'

'Yes, Mr Bernard, I believe it is.'

'I do not want my daughter to be involved in a police matter. She could not cope with that.'

'She will not be involved. The sketch would be of great interest to my husband. But it is not something that would be admissible as evidence. I am sure of that. He would like to see it, that is all. Then I will return it.'

Bernard was silent and I waited anxiously. Then he said, 'Very well, but I am placing great confidence in you, Mrs Ross, and relying on what you have said. My daughter cannot be interviewed by any police officer, even your husband.'

It was Ruby Eldon who spoke up. 'If anyone were to be asked anything by Mr Ross, it would be me, Mr Bernard. I am the one who has identified the figure in that drawing. Miss Rose obviously has no idea who he is. But I recognise him and, if necessary, will tell Inspector Ross so.'

Bernard still hesitated.

'I do understand, Mr Bernard,' I said to him. 'This is what you have always feared if you let the outside world into your house, or your daughter into the outside world. That something may occur you cannot control. But the world cannot be kept out completely forever.'

'I see it cannot!' said Bernard sharply. 'I have trusted you enough to let you into my home. I do not think you repay my trust as you ought.'

'Mademoiselle Rose will not be inconvenienced, I assure you.'

There was a movement behind me, and a voice I recognised as that of Rose spoke. 'Papa?' She split the word into halves as she had done with *merci*. *Pa–pa*.

We all turned to look at her. She moved forward, put her hand on her father's sleeve and nodded.

Bernard smiled at her. Then he turned to me, rerolling the sketch into a tube as he did. He handed it to me. 'The sketch belongs to my daughter and she had made the decision. Do not betray my, or her, confidence in you, Mrs Ross.'

'No, sir, I shall not.'

We took our farewells of Rose. Bernard escorted us both downstairs, where Bessie jumped up from her chair. José was waiting.

'José will escort you home, Mrs Ross.' Bernard hesitated. 'My daughter has been happy this afternoon. Perhaps we can arrange for you to call again with Miss Eldon?'

'I should be delighted to come again!' said Ruby Eldon brightly. 'It has been a great pleasure to make the acquaintance of Miss Rose. She is really is extremely talented.'

Bernard smiled at her. 'Yes, she is, is she not? Allow me to escort you across the road to your . . . lodgings, Miss Eldon.'

As José handed me up into the cab, I said to him, 'I would like, please, for the driver to take me to Scotland Yard.'

José looked startled and glanced across to his employer for direction. Bernard nodded.

Bessie scrambled up into the cab with me, José gave the new direction to the cabbie and joined us, and away we rolled. As we left, I turned my head to look back. I was just in time to see Miss Eldon arrive at the door of the Queen Catherine on Bernard's arm; to be welcomed by

Louisa Tompkins making a curtsy deep enough to receive royalty.

Bessie was delighted to be going to the Yard because she hoped to see Constable Biddle whose absence, since I had banned him from our kitchen, had caused her great distress. When we arrived, I told José he and the cab could go. It clattered away with the butler in it.

'Cor, this is a day, this is!' said Bessie happily, as we entered the building.

'Not very interesting for you, Bessie, you had to wait in the hall.'

'Oh, they gave me a cup of tea,' said Bessie. 'The wife of that butler brought it up to me. Her name is Adela. It was a funny old cup of tea, a bit weak for my liking and tasted different. But it was nice of her. There was a bit of chocolate cake, too, so I did all right.'

Ben was surprised to see me and, I fancy, slightly alarmed.

'What have you done?' he asked.

'I have been very helpful, I think,' I told him. I produced the sketch. 'There, now!' I explained how I had come by it. 'Rose Bernard has a keen eye and I am sure this is as accurate as can be.'

I did not know quite I'd expected him to say. In fact, at first he said nothing at all. Then he looked up and said seriously, 'Lizzie, you will never cease to amaze me! I think we must take this sketch along for Mr Dunn's opinion.'

'Mr Dunn doesn't like me interfering in police business,' I warned him.

'No, he doesn't, but he's used to it,' was my husband's reply. 'He won't be surprised.'

So it was that I found myself in the presence of Superintendent Dunn. Bessie had tracked down Constable Biddle and retired with him to some secluded corner to waste police time.

'Mrs Ross!' said Dunn, when he had studied the sketch. 'I can only say this is a remarkable discovery. Thank you for bringing it to us.'

'I thought you'd be interested,' I said meekly.

Dunn gave me a suspicious glance. 'Yes, interested, I am indeed. Whether we can make good use of it is, of course, another matter. I'll have to discuss that with your husband.'

Ben took the hint. 'I'll put you and Bessie in a cab to take you home,' he said.

'And how is Constable Biddle's cold?' I asked Bessie as we made a slow progress homeward by cab.

'Ever so much better,' she assured me. 'It's nearly gone completely, only a sniff or two. Can he call on me again? I really don't think he's catching.'

It was my private opinion that Biddle was indeed not particularly catching; but he was Bessie's choice.

'Well, yes, tell him he may call again.'

Bessie's smile spread from ear to ear.

Chapter Sixteen

Inspector Ben Ross

WHEN I had seen Lizzie into a cab and returned to Dunn, I found him seated at his desk studying the sketch made by Rose Bernard.

'This is a dashed odd business, Ross!'

'Yes, sir. You will see that the artist has initialled and dated her work. That sketch was made the night Emily Devray died.'

'In court, the defence will say anyone may write any date on a sketch. Let us accept, for the sake of argument, that the date is correct. What do you make of the scene it shows? Are we supposed to think this is her dead body, being pushed through the streets at night, by the footman?'

'I believe it is, sir. That is Lady Temple's wheelchair, to be sure. I don't believe for a moment Michael would be pushing her ladyship through the streets in the middle of the night and at this time of year.'

'Can't see who or what it is in that chair,' grumbled Dunn. 'It's covered over completely. Damn funny shape, too.'

'It isn't someone sitting in a normal position,' I agreed. 'But we know that the body had to be wedged in as best Michael could do it, with or without George's help, owning to rigor having frozen her in a huddled state.'

'Yes, yes, it is all very plausible. But this, as evidence,' Dunn tapped the sketch, 'is on a par with your friend, Dr Mackay's, bloodstains. They and this drawing may well chart the progress of a murder. But there is nothing here we can produce in court.' He leaned back. 'What do you propose to do?'

'I would like to talk to George Temple again.'

'On the basis of this?' Dunn tapped the sketch again. 'We cannot bring him on this alone – even with the bloodstains. That lawyer, Pelham, would have him out of here in five minutes. We would have the devil of a job defending ourselves if Lady Temple saw fit to make a complaint, declaring we have been harassing her godson.'

'I don't believe she would do that,' I said. 'Fear of scandal, you see. People would say "no smoke without fire". She and Pelham would seek to hush things up.'

'And she has the influence to do just that! We need more. We cannot arrest George Temple as things are.'

'I would still like to talk to him again. If he knows Michael was seen – there is no need to name the witness, in fact, it's better we don't. But it would rattle Mr Temple. He might— he might be more forthcoming.'

'You cannot go to that house again, Ross, on this basis alone!' Dunn warned.

'I understand that, sir. What I propose to do is write a note to Mr Temple, asking him to meet me in the snug of the Queen Catherine tavern tomorrow afternoon.' Belatedly I asked, 'Would that be in order, sir?'

'Oh, very well! But be careful, Ross. The young man may or may not be a murderer. He may or may not be a fool. It would be unwise to leap to a conclusion on either point.'

Lizzie had described the Queen Catherine tavern to me in some detail. As a result, when I walked into the place the following afternoon I felt I had been here before. There, by the hearth, sat the two old men smoking their pipes. I was sure they must be the same pair Lizzie had seen here.

Business this afternoon was not brisk. A cold rain, mixed with sleet, was falling outside. It had helped to disperse the fog of the previous day, but visibility was still very poor. Pedestrians were wrapped to the eyebrows in coats and mufflers, hats pulled down over their ears, and many sheltered by large umbrellas. They walked as fast as was possible, given the slippery conditions underfoot, and kept their heads down.

I wondered if George Temple would come in answer to my note. In his godmother's house there would be warm fires. Or he might prefer to join his friends at some other, more select, establishment. He would certainly choose almost any other way to spend his afternoon than sitting with me and discussing the murder of Emily Devray. I felt almost sorry for him. He had worked so hard to distance himself from the whole affair. The moment of sympathy for him was quickly over. *Come, Ross!* I told myself. *That young fellow was not Emily's friend.* Was he then her enemy? The word was perhaps too strong. But, I thought, he had feared her and her influence. All the time she was under that roof, he could not relax. Even if he were not guilty of her murder, sooner or later he would have sought some way to get her out of his godmother's house.

The only other customer in the taproom, in addition to the two pipe-smokers, was a poorly dressed woman of indeterminate age with a red face and greying hair pinned up under a small flat hat decorated with squashed artificial flowers. She wore a stained apron over her skirts and was wrapped up well in a knitted shawl. Asked to place a wager on her occupation, I would have guessed immediately she was a charwoman. Her stint scrubbing floors was over, she had been paid, and was stopping on her way home just to 'wet her whistle' with a drop of, probably, gin. She'd already had more than a drop of this restorative. Her gaze was vague, taking me in with a complete lack of any interest. The door to the snug was open and the little room appeared to be empty.

Behind the bar stood a thickset, balding man, his two meaty arms resting on the counter. Mr Tompkins, the host. He watched me approach warily.

'Good day to you, sir,' he said, his small dark eyes assessing me.

'Are you expecting Mr Temple in here this afternoon?' I asked casually. There was no need for Tompkins to know I had asked Temple to come.

'It's quite possible, sir. I couldn't swear to it, mind.'

'Then I'll wait for him in there.' I indicated the snug.

'Right you are, sir,' said Tompkins. 'Will you take a drink while you're waiting?'

'No, thank you.'

'Ah,' said Tompkins wisely. 'You can't, I suppose, not while you're on duty.'

He knew I represented the law, of course he did. 'My name is Ross,' I told him. 'My wife has paid a couple of calls on Miss Eldon, your lodger.'

'Guessed as much,' replied Tompkins. 'I thought you might be him. Ruby told us Mrs Ross was married to an officer of the law.'

'Indeed she is. I hope you won't hold it against her.' I made for the entry to the snug, but paused on the threshold to look back. 'Don't warn Temple off, will you?'

'Wouldn't do no good, if I did, I dare say!' retorted Tompkins. 'You'd catch up with him some other place.'

'I only want a few words with him,' I explained. 'A little informal talk.'

Mr Tompkins made no audible reply to this, but his expression spoke volumes. He knew what little talks with police officers resulted in.

The snug was heated, indeed overheated, by an iron stove with a pipe to channel the smoke outside. Some fumes still found their way into the room and the air was almost unbearably stuffy. The only light came in through one very small window and on a day like today that was very little. Within a couple of minutes, however, Tompkins appeared carrying a pair of lighted candles in pottery holders. He set one on the table and the other on a small shelf. All this was done in silence. But as he left he paused in the doorway and turned to address me briefly.

'If you're going to run him in,' he said, 'I'd be obliged

if you didn't do it on the premises. It gives a place a bad name.' Then he was gone, closing the door behind him.

I had to wait another ten minutes, in this Stygian little cell, before George Temple arrived. It was with relief I heard his voice addressing the landlord. I guessed he was asking if I was already there. 'In the snug!' came Tompkins's muffled reply.

The door opened to admit the new arrival and I rose to my feet.

'Well, I am here,' Temple greeted me in surly fashion. He shrugged off his greatcoat and tossed it towards the nearest free chair. Then he hung his hat on a peg and seated himself, flicking aside his coat-tails.

I retook my seat. 'I am obliged to you, Mr Temple.'

'I don't know why you wanted to talk to me here!' he grumbled. 'There is no need for Tompkins to know all my business.'

'I thought you'd prefer to meet me here,' I replied as civilly as I was able. 'You would not want me at Lady Temple's door again, I dare say – and without Mr Pelham present to protect your interests. Nor would you fancy another visit to the Yard!' I was tempted to add that the Tompkinses already knew quite a lot about young George's business, and did not need me to tell them.

'I need Pelham here, then?' Temple asked, treating me to a shrewd look.

'Do you have any reason to believe you will have need of him?' I retorted.

Briefly Temple gave the impression of a man about to leap up and flee. He leaned back in his chair, causing it to shift backwards, and the legs to scrape on the bare boards of the floor. He rocked it on to the two back legs and shadow covered his face. I had seen suspects do this before and understood the purpose of the manoeuvre was to escape the ring of candlelight. Then panic was replaced by a cool insolence, as he tipped the chair on to its four legs again, and his features back into the yellow glow. He waved away my question as a triviality. But I was not fooled. George was badly rattled.

I put his mind at rest. 'I am not intending to arrest you, Mr Temple. At least, not today.'

'What's that supposed to mean?' he demanded. 'What the deuce do you want me here for, anyway? I have nothing more to add to what I've already told you about the day Devray disappeared. Don't you have anyone else to quiz about this matter?'

I ignored this question to say, 'I thought you might like to hear the latest information to come my way.'

Temple didn't reply at once; but sat studying me thoughtfully. I studied him in return. He was, I supposed, what is generally called handsome. But his looks were spoiled by a pettishness in the set of his mouth and jaw. *A spoiled brat of a child who had grown into a young man who expects the world to tailor its ways to suit him!* I thought. A young man who, if a penniless girl like Emily had rebuffed his advances, wouldn't take it kindly. But had that happened?

Temple, for his part, had reached a conclusion of sorts about me. 'You know, Ross,' he said. 'You don't look much like a police officer, or not my idea of one.'

'They say that if you cannot place a plain-clothes officer at once, you must have led a blameless life. Tompkins knew my occupation straight away,' I replied.

'He sees all sorts in here, I dare say. He tells me you refused a drink. Does that mean I can't take a drop?'

'You may do as you wish, Mr Temple.'

George gave a sudden, loud shout of laughter. It was so lacking in genuine mirth that it was almost like a cry of pain. It was the last reaction I'd expected and I must have shown my surprise. 'If only that were true!' he said.

'Go on,' I invited him.

'If I could truly do as I wished, I would not have to dance attendance on my godmother as I do. Oh, don't misunderstand me. I have the greatest respect for the old lady and am quite fond of her, though she is a bit of a dragon, you know. A very softly spoken, well-bred, sort of dragon; and that, Ross, is the worst kind! The sort that huffs and puffs and breathes flames is much less tricky a foe. It shows its weapons. My godmother's greatest weapon is her ability to cut me out of her will. My uncle left everything to her, you see. I believe he did not trust me with money. Perhaps he was right. So Lady Temple makes me a generous allowance. I will be fair to her on that.'

'You have no money of your own? From your father, perhaps?'

'Spent it,' said George briefly. 'Cards, so on, you know. It didn't seem to matter when I was sure I'd inherit from her. She has assured me that I shall. But it depends on my good behaviour, steering clear of any scandal. It also entails my presence in the house. She likes to have me around, in a word, so that she can watch me. Make sure I don't stray, or not too far.'

'Or Michael, the footman, is sent to bring you home?' I suggested.

'That's right,' agreed George after a moment's pause during which he eyed me keenly. 'You have a way of knowing things, don't you, Ross? Or finding them out.'

'It is my business,' I explained.

'It is Pelham's business, too,' he muttered. 'He has his spies and they report back to him, and he to her. Do you know why I like to come and drink here, in this rickety old place, and meet my friends here? It is because Tompkins doesn't report on me. Or not directly, not to Lady Temple, nor to Pelham. He might send for Michael to take me home if I've had a little too much to drink. But he doesn't report it to anyone else.' He paused. 'I'd like to know how you know about it!'

'This is London, Mr Temple. There is little anyone can do that is not observed by someone.'

It was difficult to be sure in the poor light, but for the second time I fancied George Temple looked uneasy. 'What is it you have called me here this afternoon to tell me?'

'As I say, I thought you might like to know where I am, as you might say, in my investigation into the death of Miss Emily Devray. She also depended on a will, you know, that of the childless lady who had brought her up. She also had some expectations. But the lady changed her will, and Emily received very little. That's how she came to work for Lady Temple.'

'Really? I didn't know that,' Temple said with a frown.

'But I didn't know much about her at all, other than that she came from Salisbury. I wish you success in your investigation, of course. But there is nothing more I can tell you. Clearly, you know more about her than I do – or did.'

'Yet we have good reason to believe she died in Lady Temple's house, sir. Or rather, perhaps, in the little garden.'

Now, for a moment, George looked stunned. Even in the poor light of the flickering candles, I could he had changed colour. 'What makes you say that?' he asked in a strangled voice.

'Oh, we are tenacious fellows at the Yard and we pry, as you would no doubt describe it, into everything. Little odd bits of information add up. I imagine it is rather like making one of those screens artistic young ladies decorate, with odds and ends of découpage, I believe it's called. They cut out colourful subjects from magazines and the like, and paste them on the surface of a screen, or a workbox, to make a whole pattern. When they are satisfied, they varnish the lot. It's much what I or any other detective does.'

'That sergeant of yours, Morris,' George Temple said slowly, 'now I'd recognise *him* as a police officer anywhere. It's the way he looks at you, and the way he walks – and the way he talks, for that matter. But you, Ross, you are a puzzle. You look like a brigand, you speak like an educated man, and you hunt like— well, I don't know. A fox? No, something stealthier. A tiger? Yes, I fancy a tiger, although I was never in India. But I can imagine you watching, sniffing the wind, prowling silently through the undergrowth, creeping up on your prey.' He leaned forward suddenly and said harshly, 'But I am not your prey, Ross. I am no tethered goat!'

'What are you?' I asked him. 'You have described me at length, as you see me. How do you see yourself? Do you consider yourself a gentleman? A man of honour?'

'Yes, dammit, I do! I am! You are dashed impertinent, Ross!' George had become agitated.

'Then, as a decent fellow, would you allow another, less favourably placed in life, to carry the burden of your misdeeds?'

'No,' said George, his voice sounding thick, as though the word stuck in his throat.

'Emily Devray . . .' I prompted gently.

'I didn't kill her!' he burst out. 'Why can't you get that into your head?'

'Did you chance to find her corpse?'

I thought for a moment George might topple sideways off his chair in a faint. I got to my feet, went to the door and called to Tompkins to bring some brandy.

We waited in silence until the landlord appeared with the brandy bottle and a couple of glasses on a tray. He eyed George and then stared hard at me before withdrawing in silence.

'He is wondering whether to send for Michael to rescue you,' I said. 'You spoke of that as the pattern. When you are in a fix, Michael rescues you, takes you home to safety and the protection of Lady Temple's house?'

George had made some recovery. He poured himself a tumbler of brandy, held up the bottle to me with an inquiring look, and then, when I shook my head, set it down again. He tossed back the brandy and sat silent.

'Let me ask another question, more specific,' I said to

him. 'Did you order Michael to move the body, to hide it? By the way, you should have fetched a shawl or something to leave with the body because the absence of outerwear was the first indication that Emily died in the house. Did Michael, following your orders, put the body in Lady Temple's wheelchair, cover it with a blanket, and later that night manoeuvre it through the garden door into the street?'

George opened his mouth and shut it again.

'And did Michael, following your orders, push it through the darkened streets late that night, or in the early hours, leaving it where it was found behind the chophouse?'

'You cannot possibly know this,' George whispered. 'It is a figment of your imagination.'

'No, no. There is a witness, you see. I told you, a London street is always full of eyes, watching. They themselves may not be seen. But they miss nothing. And besides, Michael is an unusual figure, almost a giant. He cannot be ignored and he is remembered. What is his history?'

George said reluctantly, 'He is a former soldier. He was wounded in the head, when only eighteen years old, in the Crimean business. The surgeon removed the ball and, against all the odds, he survived both the injury and the surgery. But his mind was affected. Never the quickest, he became like a young child. He was discharged from the army, of course, and fell on hard times. My godmother heard of his story and offered him a place.'

'Could he have killed Emily? Not intentionally, perhaps. But he must be very strong and, if he is mentally slow, as you say, he might not know his own strength.'

I waited. I had taken a gamble. If George really was the

selfish weakling I had first taken him for, then he might seek now to throw the blame on Michael. It would be an easy way to deflect me from concentrating on him. Maybe he did consider it for a moment. I fancied I saw him hesitate. Then he shook his head.

'I don't believe he killed her, Ross, but neither did I.'

'Who found the body, and where?'

George helped himself to another brandy 'I did. Just as you— guessed. And it must be a guess on your part. You cannot possibly know. I found her in the garden shed.' He stared fiercely at the brandy glass, swirling the tawny liquid around in a miniature maelstrom, and reliving the shock of that moment.

The candle flames flickered and danced in a draught, and threw patterns across the tabletop. I wondered where the draught found its way in. The window was tight shut, and the door. But an old building like this tavern must be full of chinks and crannies. I wondered whether, through such a tiny gap, Tompkins was able to eavesdrop on this conversation.

'What were you doing there?' I asked him. 'On a wintry evening, outside in the cold, in a garden shed?'

Temple looked up. 'Use your head, Ross! I went to smoke a cigarette. I can't smoke in the house, so I go out into the garden. But you're right, it was very cold and damp that evening. I noticed the key was in the lock of the shed, which surprised me a little because the gardener doesn't come at this time of the winter. Anyway, I tried the handle, and opened it up. I stepped inside for what shelter it offered. Since I had done that before I knew there was – is – a little oil lamp hanging on a hook on the wall. I had a box of lucifers with me, to light my cigarettes, and so I lit the lamp. Then I turned round and— and there she was, huddled on the floor, propped against the wall – and yes, dead. I was never so— so horrified, so shaken, in my entire life.' He drew out his handkerchief and mopped his face. 'Her eyes were open. She was staring at me. I thought at first she could see me. I even spoke her name. But as I did, I knew it was useless. I'd get no reply.'

'What time was it?'

'Oh, not late, but it gets dark so early. I suppose it was after eight. I had been out with friends, and only just returned. But I'm sure it was not yet nine.'

'Was the body stiff?'

'No, no, it wasn't. Or not very.' He spoke reluctantly, unwilling to relive that moment of horror. 'Her head, her head was at an odd angle. I thought, I thought I'd get the blame. I panicked. What do you expect? Good grief, Ross, I'd like to know what any other fellow in my place would have done! Walk into the house and calmly inform Wilson that the nurse-companion was outside in the shed, with what looked to me like a broken neck, and would he kindly clear her away?'

'Send someone to fetch the police,' I suggested.

George gave me an exasperated look. 'I don't know if that is your idea of humour, Ross, or whether you are dense. Well, I know you are not dense. Of course I didn't want the house full of policemen! What about my godmother? She was already worried because Emily had not been there when needed to help her to bed. To be told the girl was dead in the garden shed would have frightened her into fits.'

'Oh, I doubt that. My impression of Lady Temple is that she has seen violent death before. She accompanied a soldier husband on his campaigns, did she not? However, I recall at our first meeting that you explained the delay in reporting to the police that Miss Devray missing as being a question of upsetting the sensitivities of your godmother's social circle. Now it appears that, on your part at least, the reluctance to involve the police was due to your panic.'

Temple glowered at me. 'Oh, I dare say you, in my situation, would have kept a perfectly clear head. I did the only thing I could think of, call on Michael's help. He obeys orders, you know. He'd never question it, if I asked him to move the . . . the body.'

'What about the body? Did you lock the shed door after you when you went to find Michael? Someone else might have stumbled on it.'

'I was aware of that! It was the last thing I wanted!' he snapped. 'I needed time to find Michael; or decide what to do if I couldn't find him. Fortunately the shed key was in the lock. The other key was on the floor. I picked that up and put it in my pocket. Then I secured the shed, put the key in my pocket with the other, and went back to the house before anyone came out into the garden. Not that they would do at that time of year, not normally, too damn cold and foggy. But you never know.'

'What was this other key?' I asked sharply. 'The one on the floor.'

George stared at me, surprised. 'The one into the street,

of course, through the door in the wall. They were usually kept together. I thought, and I still do think, she had helped herself to the keys, and let someone in through the wall door.'

His voice grew firmer, more aggressive. 'See here, Ross, everyone is so keen to say what a Miss Prim and Proper she was. But to my mind, Emily Devray was a sneaky little thing. She knew exactly how to butter up my godmother. I believe, and I can only ask you to consider – and to consider it seriously – that she let the murderer into the garden herself! How else could the keys have got out there? She must have taken them.' He drew a deep breath. 'Anyhow, when I saw the garden-door key, I thought it would be a straightforward enough matter to move her, lose the body, leave it somewhere – somewhere no one knew her. I went to find Michael, and we arranged to move her later that night, when my godmother had gone to bed and so had the rest of the household. There was a further difficulty when the time came. She was much stiffer, made it difficult to manoeuvre her, so we used the wheelchair to transport her, as you appear to know – or your "witness" saw. I would like to know who your "witness" is!'

'I dare say you would,' I replied. 'Mr Temple, I would like you to return with me to the Yard, of your own free choice. You are not under arrest. There you can write out the account of the discovery of the body and the removal of it at your orders, and sign it.'

'And then? If I do this?'

'Then you can go home. If I need you again, I will contact you.'

'Do you take me for a fool?' Temple asked seriously. 'If

I provide you with a "signed account", do I not put a rope round my own neck?'

'No, not if you are innocent, and what took place did so exactly as you describe.'

'You are asking me to trust you,' Temple said, after a lengthy pause. 'But you are under pressure to find a killer, are you not? Once you have my account, written out in my own hand and signed, what would be easier for you? To put it away with all the other scraps of découpage, as you described them, and wait for it to form part of a picture? Or produce it to your superiors as the basis for my arrest on a charge of murder?'

'Yes, I am asking you to trust me.'

Temple got to his feet, took his hat from the peg and picked up his greatcoat. 'You will excuse me, but I feel this is a matter on which I do need to consult Mr Pelham. I already think I know what he will say – and so do you, Inspector Ross. Produce your evidence, your witness, and anything else you have to make a case. Until then, I bid you good day.'

'One moment, sir!' I held up my hand. Temple looked at me suspiciously. 'I shall need to speak to Michael. I'd be obliged if you would send him to the Yard. Lady Temple need not know, at least unless it becomes absolutely necessary. But I must have his version of the story. I take it you don't want an officer coming to the house to bring him in.'

'Of course not! I'll send him,' Temple snapped. 'If you think it absolutely necessary, though I can't see myself that it is. And you must make allowance for his . . . his slowness.'

'I shall,' I promised. 'And on your part, I must ask you not to coach him in what to say.'

Temple scowled at me. 'You have my word!' He walked out.

Well, it had been a gamble, and it had not come off. That is to say, I was fairly certain I knew now what had happened that night, from the moment the body had been discovered in that shed, huddled in a seated form, just as Mackay had deduced. But before that? Had it been exactly as Temple described? Had Emily opened the street door to the garden and admitted her killer herself?

I returned to Scotland Yard and reported my meeting with Temple to Dunn. He listened in silence, then stood up and began to walk up and down his office, with his hands clasped behind his back.

'So, what it comes down to, Ross, is – do we believe him? Do *you* believe him? I know he has been your preferred culprit. But did he kill her, eh?'

'His account is plausible,' I admitted reluctantly. 'I don't think I really ever thought him a fool. A wastrel? Yes. A young man who suddenly found himself in very deep water, far over his head? That, certainly. He panicked. He could have put all the blame on Michael, the footman. I gave him the opportunity to do that. He did not. My opinion of him has, well, not changed exactly. But he's gained a point or two in my estimation.'

Dunn uttered a sort of growl. 'What about this footman?'

I recounted Michael's history.

Dunn growled again, like Anderson's elderly terrier

disturbed in his basket. He had continued to turn up and down the room. Now he stopped and wheeled to face me.

'Why leave the body behind Bellini's chophouse, in that waste bin? How do you account for that as a choice of place? Michael has been told to lose the body somewhere. But he leaves it where it is bound to be found in the morning almost as soon as the kitchens began work.'

'I don't really know,' I admitted. 'Perhaps he felt he had pushed the wheelchair far enough away from the house? Perhaps he feared that the longer he pushed the chair and its contents through the streets, the greater the likelihood he'd be seen? We know from this drawing that Michael's progress *had* been seen already, although he didn't know it, and a detail preserved in Rose Bernard's sketchbook. There are always eyes watching in London's streets, even at night. He might have encountered a police officer on his patrol. Such a sight on so bad a night must make any officer curious. Perhaps Bellini's yard just seemed a good spot? Who can understand the thinking of a man who has had an army surgeon digging into his skull?'

'Fair enough,' said Dunn, adding after a pause, 'Poor devil! Let us hope they found some chloroform to put the patient out before they began. It was in short supply, I believe in the Crimea. Not all the doctors believed in it at that time, anyway.'

Everything had been in short supply in the ill-fated Crimean campaign. The organisational muddle had passed into legend.

Dunn had returned to his desk where he sat and shuffled papers for a moment. 'Despite Temple giving you his word, I am sure he will tell Michael exactly what to say. But, yes, of course you must have a statement from him.' Dunn sighed. 'And, like so much else in this case, it will make for very poor evidence if produced in court.'

I had wondered whether Michael could find his way unaided to the Yard or whether he really would understand what making a statement involved. In the event he arrived late in the afternoon when gloom had fallen on the streets around and gas lamps everywhere were lit. The visitor was announced by Biddle, who appeared abruptly in my office in a fever of excitement to exclaim, 'There's a regular giant outside, Mr Ross! I never did see such a big fellow. Ought I to fetch extra help? He could be dangerous!'

'I do not think he is dangerous,' I assured Biddle. 'Just bring him in.'

But Michael had not come alone. The butler, Wilson, accompanied him; and it was Wilson who appeared first, leaving the footman in the outer office under the nervous eye of Biddle. Biddle has a liking for 'penny dreadful' novelettes. Michael must look as if he had escaped from the pages of one of them.

'You will understand, Inspector Ross,' said Wilson, standing before me in a manner that managed to be both respectful and immovable, 'that all the staff of Lady Temple's household are answerable to me. I, on my part, have a responsibility towards them. That is why I have accompanied the footman you asked to see. Young Mr Temple has, I believe, explained to you the nature of Michael's disability.'

'He has. Does Lady Temple know you are here?'

'No, Inspector Ross, Mr Temple and I are agreed that her ladyship should not be troubled by this. Lady Temple is already much distressed by the sad fate of Miss Devray.'

'Very well. Send Michael in.'

Wilson cleared his throat. 'I should very much appreciate it, Inspector, if I could remain in the room. I will not interfere. But Michael will be very frightened if he is left alone with you.'

I agreed, and he went back to the corridor. He re-appeared followed by the hulking form of the footman. In my small office, Michael appeared even larger. I glimpsed Biddle lurking in the background with his mouth agape.

'Don't worry, Michael,' I said to him. 'Just sit down on that chair.'

The idea of sitting down in my presence seemed to alarm Michael, who turned his head to look at Wilson. The butler nodded. Michael sat down, rested his powerful fore-arms on his knees and stared at me. His gaze was neither incurious nor completely blank but somewhere in between. I realised he was waiting to be given an order.

'Now then, Michael,' I began. 'Just tell me about the evening Miss Devray died.'

Michael looked perplexed. 'Nothing to tell you, sir. The young lady was dead.'

'Were you present when she died?'

In the background Wilson looked disapproving but, true to his word, said nothing.

'No, sir,' said Michael.

'Who told you she was dead?'

'Mr Temple told me.'

'What else did he tell you?'

'That he found her in the garden shed.'

We were in danger of going round in circles. 'Did he come and fetch you?'

'Yes, sir.'

'It must have been very dark outside in the garden, and particularly inside the shed.'

'Mr Temple had lit the little oil lamp. It's always out there, in the shed.' Michael raised his hands; they were broad and bony and when he cupped them it reminded me of a miner's shovel. 'It's a little thing, about this size, and it hangs on a hook in the shed.'

'The sight must have been shocking. You must have been startled.'

'No,' said Michael, after an attempt at thought, signified by a knotted brow and laboured breathing. 'Mr Temple told me, on the way, there had been an accident and Miss Devray was dead. So I knew I'd see her when I got there.'

Now he was so close to me, I could see the long, straight white scar across his skull where the surgeon had sliced through the skin with his scalpel; and the slight dent in the skull's surface which marked where he probed for the bullet. Michael's thick fair hair had been grown longer in the area and brushed over to hide the evidence. I shuddered inwardly at the thought of that army surgeon and his instruments. I hoped they had at least plied the patient with brandy before-hand, if supplies of chloroform had been low. Even if it had been available, it was quite possible they would not have wasted the precious anaesthetic on an eighteen-year-old private soldier.

I forced myself back to the matter in hand: the body of Emily Devray slumped in the wooden shed, and Michael's claimed lack of surprise at the sight. He'd been forewarned on the way there, but nevertheless . . . Yet I was inclined to believe him. To lie, to concoct any invented story, was probably beyond his mental powers.

'Did you wonder why Miss Devray, dead or alive, should be in a garden shed? It was a winter evening, cold and dark. Why should the young lady have gone to the garden shed?' I persevered.

'She had her reasons, I dare say,' said Michael simply.

I sat back and thought about my next words carefully. 'Michael,' I began. 'Had you seen Miss Devray in the garden before?'

'Sometimes,' said Michael.

'Doing what?'

'Walking about.'

'Waiting, perhaps, for someone?'

'Don't know, sir,' replied Michael. 'Just walking up and down.'

'Despite being warned beforehand, you must still have been shocked when Mr Temple opened the shed door.'

Michael looked faintly puzzled. 'Seen dead bodies before, sir. They're all much the same.'

'But, surely, Miss Devray was different. She didn't die of disease or old age. She was a young woman and healthy.'

'So is a soldier, sir,' returned Michael with unexpected

acuity. 'He's fit and healthy, but it doesn't stop a bullet nor a musket ball.'

I decided to move on to the matter of disposal of the corpse. 'Who asked you to move the body?'

'The young master did, sir, Mr Temple. That's why he fetched me.' Michael frowned slightly at me. Perhaps he thought I was the one a little slow on the uptake.

'Did he tell you exactly where to take it?'

'No,' said Michael. 'Only take it away and lose it in an alley, far away as possible, without being seen. I took her away in Lady Temple's chair. That was Mr Temple's idea. It was a good idea,' added Michael, his voice gaining a note of approval. 'I could push her along easy in that. Only, mind you, propping her in the chair wasn't easy because she was stiff and folded up, like, with her knees under her chin. But she was a little thing, so we managed it. The fog had come up too, when I set off with her.'

'And what made you decide to leave her in the yard behind the chophouse?'

Michael gazed at me uncomprehendingly. I realised he didn't know the yard was behind a chophouse.

I tried again. 'What made you leave it where you did?'

'Mr Temple said to leave it in an alley, so I went to find an alley. I'd have gone a bit further, but there were people about for all it was late and foggy. When I saw the entrance to that alley I decided it would do. But it was narrow and I was afeared she'd be found, right off. There was a gate and I pushed it. It weren't locked. It opened right up into a little yard. So I took her in there and left her in a big bin where no one could see her unless they looked right in. She fitted in there just right, folded up like she was. Then I pushed the chair back home.'

It had worried Dunn that Michael had left the body where it would be found immediately in the morning. But Michael had worried more that if he left it on the ground in a narrow back alley it would be found almost at once. To his mind he'd hidden it.

'Thank you, Michael. If you go now with Mr Wilson, there is a constable in the further room who will write all of this down. You need only repeat to him what you've just told me. Then you will sign it. Can you write?'

'Not well, sir,' admitted Michael.

'Do your best. If you cannot, then bring the paper back here and make your mark in front of me. I will sign to confirm that I witnessed it.'

This was a subtlety beyond Michael's grasp. He stared at me and remained where he was.

Wilson left his position by the far wall and came to the desk. He tapped Michael on the shoulder, at which the giant rose obediently to his feet and shambled out.

The butler, however, lingered and turned back to face me. 'Sir?' he said.

I thought I detected some embarrassment in his voice, or something very like it. 'Don't concern yourself about Michael,' I reassured him, 'I am taking into account his disability.'

'Yes, sir, it's not quite that.' Wilson paused again. 'I feel there is something else I should tell you.'

I sat back in my chair and indicated the seat opposite me. 'Well, then, Mr Wilson, perhaps you'd like to take a seat and unburden yourself of what is on your mind.'

Wilson, after more hesitation, took the seat indicated. Looking at him, pale-faced, cautious but obstinate, I was put in mind of a country vicar, determined to do his best by his flock, but mindful that his living depended on the squire up at the big house.

Wilson cleared his throat. 'It is like this, Inspector Ross. I have been in Lady Temple's employment for fifteen years.'

'That is a long time,' I replied. 'You were there in the lifetime of her husband?'

'Yes, sir, but only briefly. I joined the household in the capacity of footman in 1855. The general was posted out to India at the time of the Mutiny in 'fifty-seven. Lady Temple did not accompany him because of the uncertainty of the situation there. The general had not been there very long when we received news of his death from a fever. It was a very great shock to us all.' He paused. 'It is necessary that someone in my position is at all times discreet. It would not do for me to gossip about the household, nor to allow the staff to chatter carelessly away from the house. They all understand that.'

'Mr Wilson!' I interrupted. 'Am I to understand that you are about to tell me something you should possibly have told me before now?'

Wilson flushed. 'That is so, Inspector Ross. But I want you to understand my reasoning. I was not being obstructive, but I did not know it would be of any importance.'

'Let me worry about the importance, if any. If it helps, I understand the delicate situation in which you may have found yourself. Please go on and, please, do not leave out anything.'

'Yes, sir. It is an incident that took place some five weeks *before* Miss Devray met her sad end. That is why I have not mentioned it until now. I had been out to hear the preacher at Evensong at St Martin's. It was cold, dark, and the fog gathering, but visibility was not completely obscured. I was returning home and as I began to walk down the street towards Lady Temple's house, I saw a man walking ahead of me. I did not pay particular attention to him at first because there are always people about. He was a fairly tall fellow, narrow in build, and wore a long greatcoat, I fancy it was black, and a bowler hat, if I remember well. Not a top hat, anyway.'

The butler paused again, so I prompted, 'Would you say he was a gentleman, Mr Wilson, or a labouring man in his Sunday best?'

'Well, neither of those, sir.' Wilson shook his head and considered his next words. 'He had not the bearing of a gentleman. But not a labouring man, either. He had a very steady way of walking. I thought he might be a clerk working in some professional capacity, a solicitor's clerk, or a banker's teller.'

Wilson hesitated again and I urged him on once more. 'Do go on, Mr Wilson!'

Wilson leaned slightly forward in his seat. 'If I had known what he would do next, I would have paid more attention. But he took me by surprise. He had been walking beside the wall of our garden. There is a door in it that is normally kept locked, particularly in winter when the gardener does not come. He stopped by the door and he knocked on it. I began to hurry my steps at once, meaning to ask what he was about.' Wilson's remembered shock echoed in his voice. 'But before I could reach him, the door opened, he stepped through it into the garden and the door was shut again.'

'Did you also knock, to see if it opened again?'

'No, Inspector Ross, I ran down the basement steps to the kitchens. You see, I suspected one of the maids might have admitted an admirer. I was very surprised, because they know it would be strictly forbidden. Besides, none of them is young and flighty. Most of them have been employed in the household for some years. But you never know, do you?' Wilson's formal tone and manner briefly lapsed.

'Er, no,' I agreed.

'I went straight to my pantry, where the garden keys are kept on a hook, and sure enough, they'd gone. So then I went up the basement stairs to the ground floor and took a look through the window of the back parlour. It gives a good view of the garden. I did not make a light of any kind. I did not need one. I know the house like the back of my hand! Sure enough there, in the garden, was the man I'd seen and a woman. I could not see her well, but I thought she might be quite young, on account of her slight build. My first thought was one of relief that it could not be a housemaid. They are all somewhat, well, sturdy. My next thought was that it might be Miss Devray. I was very surprised as I had always found her a very proper young person.'

'Did you go out and face them?'

'No!' said Wilson firmly. 'If I'd been sure it was a house-maid, I should have done so at once. But Miss Devray's position in the household was not that of a servant, you understand. She sat at table with the family. She was not answerable to me.'

'What about Mr George Temple? Was he in the house? You could have told him and he could have investigated.'

'Mr George had gone out to meet friends. He would not be back until later. Then, as I watched the pair in the garden, the man took something from an inside pocket of his coat and handed it to the woman. I could not see what it was but it looked like a package of papers. That was another thing that made me think there might be some legal connection. He gave the package to the young woman and she took it; and appeared to be expressing thanks. Then they stood there chatting—'

'In the cold and mist?' I interrupted.

Wilson looked embarrassed. 'After a few minutes they went into the little shed. She unlocked the door. I think they lit the little lamp in there. It was very— a very awkward situation, Inspector Ross. Rather a delicate one, if you follow my meaning.'

'And so what did you do?'

'In the end, I went back down to my pantry. Whoever the female was, she would need to return the keys. I did not sit in the dark. That would be undignified. I lit a small paraffin lamp and turned the flame down very low, and I waited.'

Wilson looked briefly embarrassed. 'I put my prayer book on the table, so that if anyone else looked in, I would be thought to have been reading it.'

'Was it long before the woman came back with the keys?'

'I suppose,' said Wilson carefully, 'it might have been between twenty minutes and half an hour. The pantry door opened and Miss Devray walked in. She was very surprised to see me! But she covered it well. "I have been outside for some fresh air, Wilson," she said. Then she reached up to replace the keys, said "goodnight" as cool as a cucumber, and walked out. One thing I did notice: she no longer had the package of paper, if that is what it was. She had either returned it to the visitor, or she had taken it up to her room before coming to the pantry.'

'And you never asked her about it, at a later time?'

'No, sir,' admitted Wilson. 'She was so . . . so self-possessed! I did not feel it was my place to quiz her and she never offered any explanation. I did not want to trouble Lady Temple. I decided, on reflection, it might be best not to tell Mr George. I fancy he had a few doubts about Miss Devray and I did not want to . . .'

Wilson's voice tailed away.

'To give him any ammunition against her?' I suggested.

'Quite, sir. I would not have wanted to be the cause of her losing her position. Nor did I want to distress Lady Temple unnecessarily. She was very fond of Miss Devray.'

'Thank you for telling me all this, Mr Wilson,' I told him. 'You have acted quite properly.'

Wilson looked relieved.

'Well,' said Dunn when I had told him all this. 'What do you make of that? A solicitor's clerk? Is there one in the case?'

'You might say there are three solicitors involved in the

matter of Emily Devray,' I said, 'although I've only met two of them. One is Pelham. He acts for Lady Temple. George Temple told me that Pelham keeps an eye on him on behalf of Lady Temple. "He has his spies", is what George told me. Pelham may have had his own concerns about a stranger arriving in the household, and acquiring influence over his client. Perhaps he sent a clerk to sound out Emily, to seek to trap her in some indiscretion, that might result in an excuse to send her away?'

Dunn nodded. 'Possible, I suppose.'

'Second,' I continued, 'there is that fellow Carroway down in Salisbury. He's a devious sort. Perhaps the situation was troubling him? He might have sent someone to make sure Emily was safe and well? Not because he cared tuppence about her happiness, you understand! But he does care a lot about his own reputation; and that has suffered following Emily's departure from Salisbury; and the murky business of the old lady changing her will. He might have wanted to be able to rebuff any further criticism.'

'So,' asked Dunn. 'Who is the third?'

'The third legal person, unknown, could be someone acting on behalf of Anderson, the rejected suitor up in Yorkshire. Anderson told me himself he meant to wait until Emily had had time to think about her new situation before making another approach to her about marriage. He could have sent down someone to test out the ground.'

'And which of them would it be in your opinion, Ross?' asked Dunn, squinting at me.

'In my mind, it was someone from Salisbury,' I told him

promptly. 'Because I can guess the nature of the "packet of papers" Wilson fancied he saw in the poor light. Not papers, but a newspaper, folded to fit into a pocket. The Salisbury newspaper, in other words, I found in Emily's room.'

Dunn rubbed his hands over his face; and from behind them uttered a growl. 'For my part I am not so quick to dismiss George Temple as a suspect. He's run through his own money and depends on his godmother. Money makes for a powerful motive for murder, Ross! Setting aside Wilson's story of a tall dark man tapping at the garden door, at least for the moment, and thinking of the footman's story. What Michael had to say confirms Temple's account of the evening the girl died, I suppose.' He took his hands away and stared at me.

'I never thought it would do anything else!' I muttered.

'Dashed nuisance,' said Dunn. 'If, of course, we accept Michael is not being influenced.'

'He struck me as telling the truth, sir. To lie takes a certain agility of mind and he doesn't have that.'

'He could be taught a story and repeat it?'

'He could. But to make it believable would also require a talent of sorts.'

'Someone's clever,' said Dunn after a moment's reflection.

Someone is very clever, I thought, as I walked back to my office.

The fog had evaporated later that evening when I walked home; and London was busy again. All the activity slowed or brought to a halt by the smothering might of a London

Particular was suddenly released and it was as if everything and everyone wanted to make up for lost time. Newspaper-sellers cried out their wares on street corners. Cabs, carts, omnibuses, the occasional gentleman's carriage, all clattered past throwing up thick sprays of mud, water and filth. Housewives, muffled in shawls, scurried about making last-minute purchases. Petty thieves and pickpockets had emerged, too, about their business. When the citizen stays indoors, they have no target. I saw one or two familiar faces in that line of occupation. They saw me and vanished at once into the hurly-burly of the crowd.

I reached the great bridge across the Thames and the steam from the engines in the railway terminus on the other side rose into the air ahead of me, leaving tracks of dirty white clouds against a night sky tinged with mauve.

I stopped halfway across the bridge and leaned my forearms on the parapet, gazing down at the river. That, also, was alive again now the fog had lifted and craft of all kind passed beneath my feet. I took little notice of them. I was thinking about Emily Devray and my quest to know her story. I had learned something of her life in Salisbury and the circumstances of her coming to London. I had learned about her death. Tonight I had listened to Wilson's story. But of Emily herself, I still felt I knew nothing at all. Yet, as I had explained to Lizzie and to Bessie, I needed to know all about her, for her to be a person and not just a corpse.

With the little I had discovered, it would be easy to draw the wrong conclusions. Miss Eldon, knowing only what she'd observed from her window, had drawn some

287

erroneous conclusions about Rose Bernard. Yet, on the other hand, she had not been entirely wrong. What picture of Emily could I put together?

Three voices echoed in my brain. The first was that of Mrs Bates, the cook, who had known Emily so well. 'An angel,' she'd called her. Then I heard George Temple's angry tones. 'Everyone thought she was Miss Prim and Proper!' And also, 'she knew how to butter up my godmother'. Finally, there was the Emily who received a mysterious visitor under cover of night after stealthily purloining the keys to the garden door. She must have been startled to find the butler sitting waiting in the pantry when she returned there with the keys. But she had 'covered it well', said Wilson, and not lost her poise or shown any embarrassment. 'Cool as a cucumber' was his description. Did that mean Emily was no novice when it came to small deceptions? At any rate, I was left with more than one view of the same girl; and I had no way of knowing which was nearer the truth.

Was Emily the innocent that Mrs Waterfield had feared would fall into the hands of an unscrupulous suitor, if she were left with a large sum of money? Had there ever been such a suitor, a flesh-and-blood reason behind Mrs Waterfield's fears?

Was Emily the unrealistic dreamer with 'her head always in a book' that Frederick Anderson remembered with resentment, the girl who had turned down his proposal of marriage?

Or was she the cuckoo in the nest that George had thought her, scheming, worming her way into Lady Temple's affection, causing Wilson concern? I didn't know. Perhaps I would never know because I could never now meet Emily in person.

'Hullo, there, gentleman! Lonely, are you, tonight? Want a bit of nice company to cheer you up?'

A waft of strong, cheap perfume filled my nostrils. I turned and saw a mop of henna-scarlet hair under a ridiculous hat with silk flowers on it, quite unsuitable for the season. It perched atop a familiar face, though one I hadn't seen in a while.

She recognised me, too, at once. 'Blimey,' she said, 'it's Mr Ross!'

'Daisy Smith!' I exclaimed. 'I am glad to see you well. But I am sorry to see you are still plying your old trade.'

'A girl's got to live!' retorted Daisy. 'I know you was always keen for me to go and learn to be a housemaid or some such. But I didn't fancy that then and still don't fancy it now!' She put up a hand to straighten the nonsense of a hat. 'Anyway, I've got a new feller. He looks out for me.'

'Have you, indeed? Well, when he starts knocking you about, let me know and I'll have a word with him.'

Daisy stared at me at first in horror; then burst into laughter. 'What, and everyone thinking I've got a Scotland Yard man looking after me interests? You don't want to make people think that, Mr Ross! It wouldn't do your reputation no good, would it, now?'

She patted my cheek and then, still giggling, marched away across the bridge.

I had first met Daisy on Waterloo Bridge. She had come

running into me as she fled a horror she only knew by reputation and legend. But that experience had not been enough to turn her away from life on the streets. There had been no persuading her. There had been no persuading Emily, either.

I walked on homewards. Emily Devray had refused to accept Anderson because it would have meant selling herself, as she had seen it, for a comfortable home. She might have come one day to rue that decision. As Daisy had said, a girl has to live. A penniless and homeless young woman might well have ended up selling herself for far less than a large house and wealthy husband. Had Anderson attempted to explain that to her? Or had he just been angry that she couldn't see it for herself? Had Mrs Waterfield attempted to warn Emily? Or had Mrs Waterfield, old and ailing, been angered that Emily had refused what her benefactress had considered an excellent and practical solution, marriage to a middle-aged widower, and simply washed her hands of her wilful protégée?

Did the answer to all this lie in Lady Temple's household? Or on the moors outside Harrogate? Or must I retrace my steps to Salisbury and start my inquiries all over again there?

Chapter Seventeen

I LAY awake during the night, turning the problem over and over. By the morning, I was sure I had to return to Salisbury. 'That's where the answer lies!' I told Lizzie over the breakfast table.

Lizzie looked less convinced. 'I'm more inclined to think Anderson might have sent someone to spy on Emily. Perhaps you ought to go up to Yorkshire and speak to him again?'

'If I don't get anywhere in Salisbury, then back to Yorkshire I'll go. But instinct tells me to go to the city where Emily grew up and was known. I might tackle Carroway again. I'll telegraph Colby to let him know I'm coming.'

'What, off again?' growled Superintendent Dunn, when I approached him with my plan. 'You are employed by the Metropolitan Police, you know, and you are supposed to be investigating crime in London and its suburbs! In difficult cases, particularly in that of murder, we do send an experienced man to help out a provincial force. I recall you yourself went down to Hampshire on one occasion. But if this is to do with the murder of Emily Devray, well then, that took place here, under our noses in London. Here is where you are investigating it and not in Wiltshire. You've been to Salisbury once, to check on the girl's history. What else can there possibly be that necessitates you returning?'

'Wilson's evidence, sir. I am sure it was the newspaper that was handed to Emily that evening in the garden. Wilson saw her with the man five weeks before she died. The newspaper I found was five weeks old. It is too much of a coincidence.'

Another growl from Dunn. 'Well, you may go, Ross. But I want an itemised report on every penny spent. You have also been up to Yorkshire and submitted a claim for that. So, keep down any costs for food and drink. Do not imagine you will dine well at public expense. They have food stalls at the station, don't they? Buy yourself a sausage roll and a cup of tea there. That should see you through the day!'

As I hurried out, Dunn called after me, 'By the way, Ross, I see from the expenses claim you lodged after your previous journey to Wiltshire that you purchased a second-class ticket. That is quite unnecessary. Buy a third-class one. Or, if you insist on travelling in style, pay for the ticket yourself!'

Remembering the pungent smell of the meat pasty being eaten by a fellow passenger on my last trip to Salisbury, I decided against buying a sausage roll from a station stall, as recommended by Dunn. This was for the sake of my own digestion and the comfort of my fellow passengers. On my way to Waterloo Bridge Station, however, I chanced to pass by a bakery. A truly tempting aroma suggested something good had just been taken from the ovens. I investigated and emerged with two freshly baked currant buns in a paper bag. These, together with coffee from a stall outside the station, set me up for my journey in a very satisfactory way.

I arrived in Salisbury in the early afternoon. To my surprise Colby had turned out again to meet me, waving his bowler hat to attract my attention. He wore a coat of heavy tweed and his expression radiated urgency. He didn't quite bounce up and down but he stamped his feet like a warhorse.

'Thank goodness you have come!' he cried, grasping my hand. 'If you hadn't come, I'd have sent for you. Come along, no time to waste! I'll explain as we go.' Colby urged me past the ticket collector, who grabbed my ticket as I rushed past him, and then we were out of the station. We found ourselves under a lowering sky and buffeted by a stiff wind. It all promised heavy rain before too long.

'Where are we going?' I asked. We were proceeding at a headlong pace and it was slippery with mud beneath the feet. We were both holding on to our hats.

'To the infirmary!'

'Who is in the infirmary?'

'Poor old Tobias Fitchett, and in a very bad way. He, oh, drat it!' Colby seized my arm and halted me forcibly. 'We would have to run into him!'

I looked ahead and saw, approaching us, the tall, dignified figure of the Reverend Bastable. He was accompanied by a lean female, clad in a voluminous black mantle that made her resemble a large crow. She had a crow's sharp and pitiless gaze and it was fixed on me. She could only be Bastable's sister.

'Dear me!' said Bastable sourly, and reluctantly raised his hat in greeting. 'Inspector Colby! And the emissary from Scotland Yard. Ross, is it not?' He stared at me and then, even more reluctantly, introduced the female. 'My sister.'

'Miss Bastable!' I said politely, with a bow. 'I am indeed Inspector Ross from Scotland Yard.'

The lady, forced to recognise my greeting, inclined her head and said in a clipped tone, 'My brother has spoken of you.'

And not favourably! I thought.

'I suppose,' continued Bastable reluctantly, 'it is the unfortunate business concerning the shoemaker, Fitchett, that has brought you. Though that would appear to be an entirely local matter, an attempted robbery, no doubt. Hardly of any interest to you, Inspector Ross.'

'Hardly so, indeed,' confirmed Miss Bastable. 'A regrettable matter, of course.'

She was still staring at me as though she would like to peck at me viciously.

'I trust,' intoned Bastable, 'that you are not going to return to trouble us at home again?'

'In our home!' snapped Miss Bastable.

'Oh, I don't think that will be necessary,' Colby assured them.

'I should hope not! We shall not delay you further,' Bastable told him.

He and his sister proceeded on their way.

'For goodness' sake, Colby,' I urged him. 'Tell me what has happened to Fitchett! What was Bastable talking about?'

'The shop failed to open for business on Monday morning. There was no notice in the window advising it was closed or giving any reason. It inconvenienced customers; but didn't raise any alarm. But then it didn't open again yesterday morning. That did beg an answer. A customer, who had placed an urgent order, became annoyed, rather than concerned. This morning the police were informed. We broke down the door to find poor old Fitchett lying on the floor of his workroom, with severe head injuries. He was taken to the infirmary at once. I was about to telegraph you with the news when I received your telegram to me, announcing you were on your way.'

'What about that apprentice of his, Ezra Jennings? Did he not try and open the shop?'

'Missing!' returned Colby tersely.

I stopped in my tracks, seizing Colby's arm, so that the poor fellow stumbled. I apologised quickly, adding, 'Is it your opinion that Jennings could be the attacker?'

'He has to be the prime suspect! For a start, he can't be found. No one has seen him since Friday, not even his landlady. He did not attend any chapel services on Sunday. What's on your mind?' Colby stared at me inquiringly.

'I have become more and more certain that the answer to everything lies here,' I told him. 'Emily Devray's story began in Salisbury and, although she was killed in London, the roots of that crime are here, too.'

Either from cold or from impatience, Colby began to stamp his feet again. 'Listen, we must not waste time.

Fitchett has regained consciousness of a sort, slipping in and out of it, you understand. He's been repeating the name "Ezra" and "Ezra has them!" But what "they" are we don't yet know. He could lapse back into unconsciousness.' He tugged at my arm.

'Even so, I'd like to see the scene of the attack before we visit the victim. Will it take long?'

'Not long at all, if that's your wish. But Fitchett's condition is giving cause for concern, so we can't spend long there.'

A stalwart constable guarded the premises. A small crowd loitered outside but, seeing Colby and myself approach, the constable quickly cleared them away. The sightseers withdrew some distance, where they hovered, resentful but excited. News of our presence would soon spread and an even bigger crowd form. I was reminded of the interest shown in Emily's funeral.

The front part of the shop appeared undisturbed. In shocking contrast, Fitchett's workroom was in complete disarray, and gave all the appearance of a struggle having taken place in it. Fitchett's tools lay scattered everywhere and there was an ominous stain on the floorboards.

'Any evidence of a robbery? Forced entry? Money taken from the cash drawer?'

'Fitchett kept the day's takings in a wooden box under the counter in the front area of the shop. The box is there but empty. Either someone, the assailant, made off with the contents, or the attack took place before the shop opened and there was little or no money in the box. It does not appear to have been robbery, which would have made more sense. Of course, if the assault took place the evening before, there might have been more cash in the box and it could be a case of robbery after all. Fitchett hasn't yet managed to make a really coherent statement. I'm hoping he will – if he survives.'

'Why would Jennings rob his employer?' I mused aloud. Then a thought struck me. 'There are other things to be stolen than money!' I exclaimed. 'Colby, have you checked the contents of the shop window?'

'The shop window?' exclaimed Colby. 'The glass wasn't broken. Who would want anything from the small display there? There was nothing of value, only oddments to draw a customer's attention.'

But I was already on my way to investigate. It was as I'd guessed. The shaped wooden lasts for the boots made for Emily Devray, for a while on display as a gruesome exhibit in the shop's window, had vanished.

'Colby! Where is that order ledger?' I was scrabbling under the counter as I spoke and my fingers touched the large solid tome in which Fitchett had shown us the entry relating to the order for Emily's boots. I dragged it out, opened it on the counter and ran my finger down the pages. 'Look, here! Here's the order Mrs Waterfield placed for Emily's boots and this is the order number. Quick! The storeroom!'

I ran through the shop, Colby on my heels, and into the rear storeroom where the racks of paired wooden lasts stood in neat rows.

'Not there!' exclaimed Colby, who had caught on to what I was doing, and had found the empty space where

Emily's lasts had been. 'If this attack is Ezra's doing, it has to do with those wooden lasts of Emily's feet. That is what poor Fitchett meant, when he spoke of Ezra having "them". They must now be with him, wherever he is! Whatever can the wretch want with them?'

'Let's hope poor Fitchett is able to tell us.'

The matron was an imposing figure, as straight and rigid as a guardsman, with a crisp cap and gown and a collar starched so fearsomely I wondered it didn't cut her throat.

'The patient is semi-conscious, gentleman,' she informed us as she led us down the corridor. 'Because, Inspector Colby, you warned us the assailant might return and attempt some mischief here in the hospital itself, we have put Mr Fitchett in a private room. We took this precaution even though, I assure you, it would very difficult for any visitor to behave in a disrespectful or threatening manner in this hospital. It would not be tolerated for one moment and a stop would be put to it straight away!'

I believed her.

Colby said: 'We do understand that, madam. But I trust the constable I sent is still here?'

'Sitting outside the room, in the corridor, as you ordered.' She pointed as we turned a corner and saw the uniformed man in question: a sturdy figure perched on a very small wooden chair.

The constable jumped to his feet and saluted on seeing Colby and me. 'All safe, sir! No one has gone in, 'cepting the doctor and the nurses.'

The matron swept into the room ahead of us and bent

over the patient. 'You have visitors, Mr Fitchett. Do you understand me?'

A voice mumbled faintly from the bed and a hand was raised and dropped back to the coverlet.

'They are police officers and want to talk to you.'

Another mumble from the bed.

The matron turned to us. 'You should not tire him. He is very weak. Whatever you do, don't make him agitated!'

Considering that the patient was in her care as the result of a violent attack, and we were to question him about it, I thought it would be difficult to prevent Fitchett becoming agitated. But we promised solemnly that we would behave with the utmost discretion.

The matron gave us a severe stare and withdrew. We neared the bed.

Poor Fitchett presented a pitiful sight. I remembered him as a small man, but in this bed he resembled a mummified exhibit in a museum, something found in an Egyptian tomb. His head was heavily bandaged and what could be seen of his face was wrinkled like a walnut. One of his hands was also swathed in a bandage. His gaze settled on us hazily at first. This worried me. However, when his sunken old eyes moved to take in my presence there was a flicker of recognition in them. The unwrapped hand was raised in greeting or acknowledgement.

'London man . . .' came in a whisper from the bed.

I bent over him. 'Yes, Mr Fitchett, Inspector Ross from Scotland Yard. I am glad you remember me, and very sorry indeed to find you in such a state. Are you in pain?'

'Headache . . .' muttered Fitchett.

'I realise that. Inspector Colby here suspects you were attacked by your assistant, Ezra Jennings. Is that right?'

The gleam in the eyes brightened with anger. The hand waved to and fro. I feared that he was becoming very agitated and hoped the matron did not return now. Fitchett said something but I couldn't catch it. I bent over him.

'What was that, Mr Fitchett?'

'Lasts . . . he wanted the wooden lasts.'

'He wanted the lasts of the boots made for Emily Devray? We have ascertained they are missing from the shop, both the window and the storeroom,' I told him.

'Wouldn't let him have them. He set about me. Rogue!'

The word was spat out with unexpected vigour. Then the energy faded and Fitchett closed his eyes. Colby and I exchanged concerned looks.

'Should I fetch a nurse?' whispered Colby.

'Hold on a moment . . .' I bent over the old bootmaker. 'Mr Fitchett? Can you hear me?'

To my relief, his eyelids fluttered and opened. His eyes fixed me blearily, as they had done when they first saw us. But then his gaze cleared. He stretched out his hand and seized my sleeve.

'You must find him! He is mad, quite mad . . .' The voice was weak and hoarse, yet the words were spoken quite distinctly. Though he'd been savagely beaten about the head, Fitchett had his wits, thank goodness.

'Can you tell us about it, sir?'

'The lasts were in the window – on display.' Fitchett's hand waved to and fro. 'My mistake. Wrong thing to do.'

'I understand, sir; what happened to them?'

'They came . . . people came and stared at them. Came in the shop. Wanted boots the same . . .'

He broke off and began to cough. Colby seized a glass of water on a nightstand. Between us we managed to raise Fitchett with care and get him to sip a little. The cough subsided and he sank back on to his pillows.

'I decided . . . I should take them out of the window and destroy them. You understand?' Fitchett's gaze was fixed on me imploringly. 'The interest folk showed in them was bad, indecent . . . I decided to burn them was best, right thing. But Ezra, he wanted them. Begged me for them. I asked him why . . . He said, over and over, he said, "Her feet . . . her feet!"'

'Ah . . .' I was beginning to understand. 'Do you think he was obsessed with the young lady?'

Fitchett threw out his hand and gripped my sleeve with unexpected strength. 'He's mad – mad on account of her! You've got to stop him!'

'Stop him from doing what?' urged Colby. The boot-maker, as if exhausted by the moment of energy, had sunk back on his pillows again, and turned his head to stare at the windows and what could be seen of the outside world.

'Mr Fitchett!' I added my entreaty. 'Do you have any idea where Ezra is now?'

The injured man turned his head slowly on the pillow so that he could look up at me again. 'He's taking the boots . . . to the stones . . .'

'To the stones?' I looked at Colby for guidance but he appeared as puzzled as I was. 'What stones are these?' I made a guess. 'Has he gone to the graveyard? Tombstones?

Fitchett, has Ezra gone up to London to take the wooden lasts to place on Emily's grave?'

'No, no!' Fitchett's gnarled old hand, scarred from ancient mishaps in his trade, pointed at Colby. 'Near here! Ask him. He knows them.'

'Think, Colby!' I urged.

Colby scowled. Then his features cleared and he bent over the bed. 'Do you mean the ancient stones? Stonehenge?'

'Yes, yes, that's where he's gone. He's taken them there . . . the lasts . . .'

'It is not quite twenty miles from here,' Colby said to me. 'You've heard of it, Stonehenge, as they call it.'

'Yes, yes, a prehistoric site, is it not?' I bent over Fitchett. 'Is that the place?'

'Yes . . . the old stones, magical place, ancient beliefs, old practices . . . Pagan, not Christian,' croaked the old man.

'But why take the wooden feet there?'

Fitchett's eyes suddenly opened wide. 'Because the Spring Equinox is upon us! Ezra believes that we are halfway between winter and summer, and so, in his poor crazed mind, halfway between death and life.'

Colby was thumbing through a pocket diary. 'Yes, that's right. The weather's been so foul you wouldn't believe it. But according to the calendar, winter is now behind us.'

Fitchett's fingers plucked feebly at my sleeve. 'He believes, Ezra, the silly fellow . . . He believes if he takes the wooden lasts of her feet there, at this special time, he will see her.'

'See Emily?'

'Yes, she will come . . . She, too, is halfway on her

journey between life and death, so he will have it. Thus her path and that of the seasons will cross. At the moment she is going in the direction of death and winter, when the earth is dead. Spring is even now coming towards us in the contrary direction, on its way to awaken the earth. The wooden feet, placed among the ancient stones, will absorb their power. Then they will draw her to them . . . That is what Ezra believes. She will turn back on her journey to the world of the dead; turn back to life. When spring arrives, so will she! Don't ask me from where he has all this. He is mad, as I told you. He believes all manner of nonsense.'

Exhausted by this long explanation, Fitchett closed his eyes. Colby and I gazed down at him in wonder, hardly able to believe our ears.

Colby whispered, 'By Jove, it's like that old Greek tale, you know the one. Orpheus and his wife.'

'Eurydice,' I supplied the name.

'Right, that one. She died and he went looking for her to bring her back from the Underworld. Ezra thinks he can do the same with Emily: bring her back. He's as mad as a hatter.'

'Mad but sharp,' mumbled Fitchett. Though his eyes were closed, he had been listening. 'He found her in London, you know . . .'

My heart leaped into my mouth, as they say. I bent close to the bed again.

'Found her? Found whom?'

'Young Miss Devray. He went to the house where she was living. Saw her there.'

'How did he find her?'

'Clever fellow, Ezra, even if he believes such nonsense,' muttered Fitchett. 'And he is still a rogue. I was teaching him the craft; he was a good apprentice. But still a scoundrel . . .'

His strength was exhausted now and his voice was fading. There was a rapid march of feet behind us and the rustle of starched linen.

'You will have to go now!' said the matron. Her voice did not brook argument. But we were ready to leave.

'We have to get to those stones, that place, Stonehenge,' I said to Colby. 'If Jennings is there, we can take him.'

It was one thing to agree to the plan in principle and quite another to set it up and put it into action. The stones were in the midst of open ground, a flat deserted plain grazed only by sheep, so Colby told me. The land and the monument belonged to the Antrobus family; and he must send word to them that the police were about to invade their estate in some number.

'The stones are of interest to those who like antiquities. They do attract a number of visitors in the better weather, some of them quite distinguished. There have been all manner of discussions about what to do about them over the years. Some people are for setting upright those that have fallen. Some believe they should be left alone. Others fear they will collapse further. There have been numerous committees, I understand, but you know what happens when things go before committees . . . The thing is this. Jennings, if he's there, will be certain to see and hear us coming. We must take enough men with us to make a cordon around the spot, or we won't have a hope of capturing him.'

By the time we had assembled a party of constables, and found transport to take them, the light was fading and a clammy mist was drifting over the open landscape. It contained a drizzling rain within it, and soaked the thick cloth of my greatcoat. I was soon both damp and very cold. Colby and I travelled in a dogcart. Two charabancs had been found and commandeered to carry the party of constables. Were it not for the seriousness of our purpose, we would have resembled a party of day-trippers. Our strength had been increased by reinforcements volunteered by Sir Edmund Antrobus.

The road itself, though muddy and rutted, was passable. We would have made good progress but for the mist. This was not like the London fog, for it carried no odour of sulphur and of workaday life. It was cleaner, but somehow unearthly. It had thickened and spread extensively, played tricks with objects, transforming them into what they were not and making it impossible to judge distance. Natural light had dwindled to a crepuscular gloom before we were halfway into our journey. This meant our conveyances were hung about with lanterns, though they did little to show the track ahead. If Jennings didn't hear us coming, he'd certainly see our lights bouncing in the mist. Perhaps he would think us mythical creatures, will-o'-the-wisps. Around us the landscape was empty, offering no cover. But there were living creatures out there. Sheep would suddenly appear before us, and bound away, terrified. When this happened, my heart would leap into my mouth, for all my attempts to cling to reason. This was an ancient landscape, largely uninhabited apart from the sheep. Yet I felt, from time to time, that unseen beings marked our progress.

We rattled and bounced on for another couple of miles and then, to add to our troubles, there was a distant growl of thunder, followed a few moments later by a flicker of lightning.

'About three miles away,' muttered Colby. As the thunder rolled again he added, 'And getting closer, confound it!' To our driver he shouted, 'How far away are we now?'

'Almost there now, gents!' shouted the man over his shoulder. He raised his whip and pointed at something. 'There is a fire lit ahead, Mr Colby!'

Colby and I hung over the sides of the dogcart and peered through the gloom. Sure enough, flames danced and flickered at ground level.

'Someone is there!' cried Colby excitedly. 'He has lit a bonfire! How has he managed it in these damp conditions?'

At the same moment a great flash of lightning lit up the whole area. I felt the heat of it on my face as we beheld a fantastic scene. The great stones lay higgledy-piggledy before us. I had not realised the enormous size of them or their power, located here in a wilderness. It was as if giants had been playing a monster game of spillikins and many had collapsed in a ragged heap. Others still stood upright amid their fallen fellows. How had they been brought here? Who had brought them? When? Despite myself, I felt a shiver of awe run along my spine. This was indeed a place of ancient mysteries. I began to comprehend why Ezra Jennings had brought the wooden lasts here to carry out the ritual he believed would bring the dead girl back to life.

In a couple of places two of the stone monoliths remained upright, linked by a third across the top, making a stone lintel. The fire had been lit on the ground between the uprights of one such pair. In this rough approximation of a theatre's proscenium arch, we clearly saw the figure of a man outlined against the writhing, orange-red flames. He was gesticulating so wildly he seemed to be a wooden marionette, manipulated into performing an outlandish wild dance by a supernatural puppeteer. Was this part of his ritual? Or had he realised we were near and, if it were Jennings, guessed who we were and our purpose? His arms were making thrusting gestures, as if he would push us back or at least make us stop where we were.

The lightning had gone, and the thunder rumbled more distantly. The threatened storm was moving away. But the fire had also disappeared quite suddenly with only one last feeble flicker. Either the fuel had been too damp, or it had been stamped out by the man we'd glimpsed, to extinguish the beacon leading us to the spot. If so, he was too late as far as that was concerned. We'd found him; we were however still no nearer apprehending him. If he was our man, he was now somewhere out there in the darkness and the swirling clammy clouds of mist.

'Jennings, do you reckon?' shouted Colby in my ear.

'It could well be. Or it might be a tramp. Or a shepherd? We must stop here and deploy our cordon!' I yelled back.

This could not be achieved without some confusion and delay. But eventually our men and the volunteers had formed a circle around the site, their positions marked by the specks of light that indicated the lanterns they held.

It was far from satisfactory. The man we'd seen had also had time to relocate. He could have slipped away between the officers and now be out there somewhere, who knew where?

'No,' said Colby, to whom I communicated my concerns. 'No, he's come here for a purpose and he must carry it out, or everything he's done to make it possible is wasted. What do you suggest we do now?'

'We close in,' I decided. 'We move slowly forward and, if he is indeed still there where we last saw him, he must be trapped.'

I did not feel nearly as optimistic as I sounded. Colby shared my doubts. He mumbled something. I couldn't catch his words, but didn't need to and didn't bother to ask him to repeat it. Colby blew a single blast on a police whistle and we began our move.

I was acutely aware that we were hunters and we hunted in the way primitive man would have done, seeking to trap our quarry. Moisture condensed on my skin and was channelled down the sleeve of the arm I held aloft with my lantern, to trickle down my neck. It also found its way inside my coat at a dozen points. I wondered how wet Jennings was, if indeed it was Jennings out there. He'd been here some while. But the elements would not worry him. They were his friends, inconveniencing us far more than him. He had but to shelter under one of the great stones and watch us blunder about.

At last we were close enough to form a circle through which he could not escape, if he were still here. But was he? There was neither sight nor sound of our quarry.

One of the searchers gave a shout. He was holding up his lantern and pointing downwards. Colby and I hastened forward. The man had stumbled on the spot where the fire had burned. I swung the lantern around in a circle and my eye caught something that seemed out of place. I moved the lantern back slowly until I came to the same spot. There were some objects on the ground. I walked towards them, held the lantern over them and beheld the wooden lasts for the boots made for Emily Devray.

'He is here!' I called to Colby in relief.

Then I stooped and picked up the wooden lasts.

As my fingers touched them, a wild screech sounded above our heads. 'Put them back!' screamed a voice. It seemed to have come from the heavens themselves. The wind caught it and tossed it out into the darkness. 'Put them back! She is coming!' it howled again with even more urgency.

The nearest man to me surreptitiously signed himself with the cross. I looked up for the source of the cry.

Jennings had managed to scale one of the great pillars that had fallen at an angle and balanced there precariously. It was as if some great bird had alighted on it, sent from another world, who could say where or of what kind. All the power of the ancient stone circle seemed to have focused on him, so that it was truly an unearthly figure towering over us, terrifying and grotesque. He began to wail, a primitive keening. His rage, agony and despair all flowed out of him like an electric current. I was aware that, around me, all the officers with the lanterns had instinctively stepped back. The desperate howls echoed off the surrounding stones, as if the ancient monoliths were alive and joined with him in his agony.

'Come down, Ezra!' I shouted. 'You will fall, man! Just slide down the stone!'

He ignored my plea. 'Put them back!' he cried again with such power in his voice I must admit I, too, was taken aback and, for an instant, almost obeyed him. The officers had rallied and moved forward again. Jennings was caught in the orange beams of a dozen or more lanterns held aloft. His unbuttoned coat flapped wildly, indeed like great wings. He waved his arms above his head. The storm that had moved away made its lingering presence known by a distant rumble in the heavens, like a drumroll attending a circus acrobat.

As if on this cue, Ezra launched himself from his perch. He hurtled through the air like some great owl with outspread wings and wickedly sharp talons stretched out to grasp its prey. He crashed into me, knocking me sprawling to the ground. He clawed wildly at me, seeking the wooden blocks, but I was determined to hold on to them whatever the cost. I clasped them to my chest and rolled over to protect them. Jennings began to batter me with his fists, screaming.

Colby came to my aid, and then other officers. They all piled on to Jennings. But he was on top of me, so I found myself at the bottom of a heap of struggling bodies, bearing the full weight of the lot. I blacked out.

When I came to, I fancy it was only minutes later, I was still on the wet ground. Colby was bending over me, shouting in my ear: 'Where are you hurt?'

I moved my arms and legs awkwardly but without pain. 'Not . . . hurt . . .' I gasped. 'Only winded . . . Give me a hand!'

I was hauled to my feet by several pairs of helping hands.

'Where is he?' I managed to ask, swaying on my feet and clinging to Colby's arm like a child to his nursemaid.

'Oh, we've got him safe,' Colby assured me in his sanguine way. 'The fight's gone out of him.'

It was then I became aware of a wild sobbing. I looked in that direction and saw, in the lantern's glow, a huddled figure sitting on the ground with his head on his knees and his arms about his shins, crying his heart out in despair.

'The wooden lasts!' I exclaimed in a panic.

'I have them here,' Colby assured me. 'We can go back now.'

As I stumbled past the crouched figure, he raised his head and I beheld Ezra Jennings's pale face plastered with his long, rain-soaked hair, his eyes burning.

'You have interfered. You have destroyed the link. You have sent her back!' he croaked.

'She was never coming!' Colby told him unkindly.

Chapter Eighteen

'WELL, WHAT'S your opinion, Ross?' asked Colby.

We had made the return to Salisbury in drizzling rain and at a sedate pace. We ought all to be feeling the elation of success; but we did not. The race to reach Stonehenge and the target of taking our man had fired us all. Now that fire had gone out like the one Jennings had lit by the great stones. There was a general feeling of sadness, not helped by our prisoner sobbing quietly most of the way, but occasionally finding his voice to accuse us of robbing him of Emily. I realised how very tired I was and how hungry.

On our arrival Jennings was consigned to a cell and a constable ordered to keep a close eye on him while we decided what to do next. In cases like this, we were well aware, there was always a risk of a suicide attempt.

'Is he as crazy as he makes out?' Colby had produced a pipe and lit it, puffing furiously and creating a pungent smoke. It swirled around his head and gave me the illusion I was back in the London fog. 'For my money, he's not acting. He's a lunatic. They come in all sorts of guises. But you may have a different opinion,' Colby concluded politely.

'I don't know,' I admitted frankly. 'Perhaps we should

call in a doctor to examine him. It would require one who knew something about lunacy.'

'There's one who attends the inmates at a private asylum nearby,' suggested Colby. 'I could send a message to him. His name is Lefebre.'

'Lefebre!' I exclaimed. 'It's possible I've met him before. Is he a well-dressed fellow with moustaches and a small beard, the sort of chap one hears described as "dashing"?'

'Well, yes,' admitted Colby, taken aback. 'That sounds like him. Where did you meet him?'

'Oh, it was a few years back, a case in the New Forest. I was sent down from the Yard to assist. Dr Lefebre was already on the scene as the family of the suspect had called him in. He is considered a distinguished expert. We could not have the opinion of anyone better.'

'I'll send him a note,' said Colby. Then, brightening, 'But he already knows you! Perhaps you could make a personal appeal to him to help us out?'

Everything about this case was odd; so one more odd thing did not seem to me to be a cause for objection. I wrote a letter to Dr Lefebre, reminding him of our previous acquaintance and apologising for troubling him. It was sent off by hand.

'It will be a while before he gets here,' said Colby. 'We could attempt to question Jennings in the meantime. At least we'd have more information for the doctor when he does arrive. I suggest I question him about the attack on Fitchett.'

I considered this. 'This is your manor, as they say in London, and he is your prisoner. If you think that's in order, yes, it might add to our knowledge. Then, if Lefebre thinks he's sane, and if you can get a statement from the prisoner as to what made him batter poor old Fitchett so ferociously, perhaps I might question him about Emily. It is vital, for me, to find out if Fitchett was right in saying Jennings tracked the girl down in London, because it now seems possible we've found her murderer.'

'Stroke of luck, that, for you,' said Colby, perhaps not tactfully, but accurately.

Jennings had been ineffectually dried out and sat sullenly listening as the charge against him was read out.

'Do you deny you attacked your employer, Tobias Fitchett?' asked Colby.

'He was going to burn them,' mumbled Jennings.

'To burn what?'

Jennings shuffled his feet and glowered at us. 'Her feet. You know it. You've got them now. What have you done with them?'

'We have them safe, if it's the wooden lasts you talk of. They are evidence,' Colby told him.

'I want them back.'

'You shall not have them,' said Colby. 'They are the property of Tobias Fitchett.'

'He doesn't want them. I told you. He was going to burn them.'

'You are still not allowed to have them back. They are evidence. I just told you that.'

But Jennings clearly didn't care about evidence or anything else but the wooden lasts.

'When you've finished with them, can I have them then?'

'What's the matter with you?' demanded Colby, irritated.

'Don't you *listen*? They are evidence and if they are to be returned to anyone, it will be Fitchett.'

'But he doesn't want them! He'll destroy them! Can't you understand?' Tears sprang to the prisoner's eyes.

Colby gave me a look and turned back to the prisoner. 'Ezra Jennings, you are charged with an assault on Tobias Fitchett, with intent to cause grievous bodily harm, and the theft of, let us call it property, belonging to said Fitchett. Do you confess to these charges?'

Ezra leaned forward, his pale features suddenly flushed scarlet in passion. 'Of course I assaulted him! He wouldn't give me the lasts of her feet. I told him, I must have them! He said to me, "Over my dead body," so, if that was the only way I could succeed, I had to kill him. It was his suggestion, not mine! Anyway, I didn't kill him, did I? The old misery is still alive and now you say he's going to get the lasts back, eventually. And then he'll burn them!'

Jennings let out a wail like a banshee and fell to sobbing hysterically again.

'I suppose,' said Colby gloomily, when Jennings had been led away, still weeping, 'I suppose he'll end up in an asylum for the insane. I still believe he's mad, as far as I'm any judge, whatever Lefebre says when he gets here.'

Lefebre arrived within the hour and greeted me cordially, his silk hat in his hand. He looked much as I remembered, very much a gentleman and a fashionable one, but with a keen eye. He was, as it happened, exceptionally well turned out in a dark tailcoat and blindingly white linen. He still wore the neatly trimmed dark beard and moustache I remembered. True, there were a few flecks of grey in the beard that I didn't recall from our previous encounter. But I'd found a grey hair or two of late in my own thatch, though Lizzie had been kind enough not to mention them. In addition to his normal fashionable appearance, I saw that he wore diamond studs in his starched shirtfront. I guessed he had some social engagement that evening and thanked him profusely for coming.

'It is a pleasure to see you again, Inspector! If I can be of any service, I am happy to be here. I remember the case at Shore House very well,' he added. 'It concerned a young married lady in the family. I remember also a companion, a Miss Martin.'

'Miss Martin, as she was then, is now Mrs Ross,' I told him.

Lefebre raised his eyebrows. 'Then you are indeed to be congratulated, Inspector Ross! You will, I hope, pass on my regards to her?'

I promised I would do so, while Colby fidgeted beside me.

Lefebre was aware of his impatience. 'Well, now,' he continued. 'Let us take a look at this prisoner you believe to be mad.'

'How long will it take you, Doctor?' asked Colby.

'At least an hour,' Lefebre told him sternly, 'as a first examination. You must understand that, in matters of the mind, one should never jump to facile conclusions.'

Colby flushed and looked discomfited for an instant. He rallied. 'I must insist on an officer sitting in with you. Jennings has already attacked both his employer and Inspector Ross here.'

Lefebre was implacable in tone and manner. 'The officer can sit outside the door,' he said.

Colby clearly wasn't happy with this arrangement; and I can't say I was. If anything were to go wrong, we should be blamed. But Lefebre insisted things must be done his way.

'You called me in,' he reminded us, 'because I am an expert. I do not tell you how to do your job, gentlemen. Please do not tell me how to do mine.'

So we had to agree.

'At the least sound of any disturbance, you go straight into that room!' Colby ordered the officer designated to sit outside the door.

When all this had been set up, Colby turned to me. 'I suggest I send out for coffee and something to eat. Lefebre says he's going to be at least an hour. I haven't eaten since this morning.'

'Nor I,' I said. I thought wistfully of the fruit buns I'd purchased before taking the train in London. They were but a distant memory.

It took a while for the coffee to arrive, together with two mutton pies. I had travelled about the country by train and by dogcart. I'd been soaked to the skin in a rainstorm, attacked by the frantic Jennings and rendered temporarily unconscious. I suspected that in the morning I would ache from top to toe. If anyone needed that mutton pie and hot coffee, I was that man.

We had only just finished our impromptu repast when the constable who had been acting as watchdog outside the door of the interview room came to say Dr Lefebre had finished his examination of the patient.

'Did Jennings give any trouble?' asked Colby.

'No, sir. At least I couldn't hear any disturbance through the door. He and the doctor seemed to be chatting quite friendly, like.'

'Well?' demanded Colby impatiently, when we saw Lefebre again. 'Is he mad?'

'In my professional opinion, he is not insane, if that is what you mean,' returned Lefebre. 'I agree at the moment he's making little sense. But, come to that, a good many people talk a lot of nonsense without being thought insane. People use the term "mad" very loosely, often quite inaccurately. The subject shows symptoms of delusion. He is also extremely distressed and depressed. It is a case with several interesting aspects to it. But, given time and care, I see no reason why he should not regain his full senses.'

Colby was outraged and moved to protest. 'What about this business of bringing the girl back from the dead, by way of a ceremony of some sort, at Stonehenge?'

'Ah, yes, that is particularly interesting,' Lefebre told us. He leaned back and steepled his fingers, as though he sat in his own comfortable consulting rooms, not on a plain wooden chair in Colby's small office. 'He does believe he could have done that. But that is part of his delusion.

'*À propos* of Stonehenge,' Lefebre went on, 'it is a fascinating place and feeds the imagination. As you may be aware, there have been several committees set up over many years to discuss what to do about the stones; whether to restore them upright or not, for example. I understand the hero of the Napoleonic wars, Lord Nelson, was very interested in them. I hope you will not suggest *he* was mad?' Lefebre turned a mildly questioning gaze on Colby.

'Admiral Nelson, as far as I've ever heard it said, never conducted pagan ceremonies at the site, or believed he could conjure up a spirit from the Underworld there!' Colby defended himself. 'I'm not talking about committees of learned scholars and distinguished gentlemen amateurs. I'm talking of a man I have in custody who has exhibited extreme violence on at least two occasions. His former employer lies in the infirmary as a result. And Inspector Ross here . . .' Colby indicated me. 'He was knocked unconscious.'

Lefebre cast me a professional look. 'Got a headache, Ross? Feel queasy, unsteady? Double vision? You appear to have retained a good memory of the event.'

'Excellent, thank you!' I retorted. 'I am not concussed.'

'Well, if you start showing any symptoms, consult your medical man. To return to the ancient stones. We know very little about them, almost nothing. When we, mere mortals, do not know something, we are tempted to invent. It may be because we are genuinely curious. It may be because we have a romantic streak in our natures. It may be because we fear what we don't understand and we are anxious to grasp at any explanation! We wish to be comforted, however outlandish the form of comfort. The thing is, we should be wary of dismissing what others consider to be explanations.'

Lefebre smiled briefly. 'Many people believe those stones to have special significance; and not all of them are by any means mad. I have been told there are some very respectable people, of standing in the community, who go there and conduct ceremonies of their own invention.'

Lefebre made a vague but elegant gesture of one well-manicured hand. 'They dress up in robes of their own design, and progress around the stones, and so on. They often don't like to talk about it to – outsiders. Doubtless they fear mockery. I do not suggest this unfortunate fellow you have in custody is connected with them. But, like them, he is defensive as regards his ritual. He is an Englishman with liberties of which, as a nation, we are justly proud. His beliefs, however eccentric, seem to me to be his own business. They do not make him a madman.'

'Look here, he carried out a murderous assault on his employer and left him for dead,' argued Colby. 'He also attacked Inspector Ross. That makes it police business!'

'Indeed, it does,' agreed the doctor. 'But, if I may remind you, you did not call me here to talk about *criminal* matters. You asked me here to comment on his state of mind; and his attempt to carry out some ritual or other at Stonehenge. I repeat, I do not consider him to be insane, only extremely confused and deluded.'

Colby simmered in silence.

Lefebre withdrew a handsome gold half-hunter from his waistcoat pocket and consulted it. 'I will send my opinion in writing in the morning. Now, I am engaged to dine with friends and have already had to send a note warning I would be delayed. I should not like that delay to be extended any further. A pleasure to meet you again, Inspector Ross, and my most sincere regards to Mrs Ross.'

'All right, then,' said Colby to me when Dr Lefebre had left in a private carriage. 'Jennings is sane. It doesn't mean we can get any sense out of him.'

Nor could we, for Jennings, having explained himself at length to the doctor, had now fallen into a prolonged sulk and refused to speak to anyone.

'Well, Colby, perhaps you can come up with another idea?' I asked the local man.

Colby thought and then snapped his fingers. 'Worth a try!' he said.

'What is?' I asked suspiciously and a little alarmed.

Colby's new idea was to send for the chief elder of the fundamentalist chapel Ezra was known to attend from time to time. I wasn't at all sure about this, as I have encountered a few tub-thumpers in my time, and have found them difficult to stop, once started. But I went along with it.

The elder turned out to be a very small, very energetic man, with a high-pitched but commanding voice. Listening to him address a congregation must be an interesting experience.

His arrival did rouse Ezra from his gloomy silence. He again admitted he'd attacked his employer, Tobias Fitchett. The quarrel had been over the wooden lasts. Yes, he had taken the lasts to Stonehenge in an attempt to lure Emily's spirit back to the land of the living. The elder grew agitated himself at this point, and had to be prevented from roaring condemnation and hellfire on his congregation member for performing pagan ceremonies. Colby thanked him for his help and sent him about his business. Jennings at last put his signature to a confession of attacking Tobias Fitchett.

This was enough for Colby. He had a perpetrator for the attack at Fitchett's shop. The death of Emily in London was my investigation.

'Do you think he did it?' asked Colby. 'I know old Fitchett said Jennings found the girl in London. But how did he get close enough to carry out any attack?'

'Every instinct I have tells me he killed her,' I muttered.

'You will need more than your instinct, Ross!'

'I believe I do have more. You remember Ezra at Emily's funeral, in his black coat and bowler hat?'

'I remember him,' said Colby, scowling. 'I thought he looked like one of the undertaker's men.'

'But in a different situation, not on the way to a funeral?' I demanded. 'If you had seen him walking down a city street in poor light, tall, slender, black-clad? You might suppose him some kind of clerk, mightn't you? A solicitor's clerk, perhaps?'

'I might,' agreed Colby. 'What are you thinking?'

'The butler of the house where Emily was employed observed such a person visiting Emily secretly in the garden. Fitchett told us Jennings went to London and found Emily there. It was Jennings, I feel sure, the butler observed.'

'Well, he's a dangerous fellow, sane or crazy,' replied Colby.

I sent a telegram to Scotland Yard, asking for it to be delivered at once to Superintendent Dunn, who by now would have gone home for the day. Everyone else's supper had been disturbed; there was no reason Dunn's should be the exception. I explained I was staying overnight at a hotel in Salisbury and requested Sergeant Morris to be sent down the next day to assist me in escorting a suspect, possibly violent, back to London.

So that is what happened. Morris arrived at noon the

next day, saying the superintendent was very worried about the costs involved, but cheered to hear we had a suspect in custody. Jennings gave us no trouble at all. He appeared to enjoy the train ride back to London.

Chapter Nineteen

I'VE MET quite a few killers since I joined the force. If they have anything in common, it is that they believe themselves to be very clever fellows. They are also capable of adopting all manner of behaviour: polite, sullen, angry, charming, anything that suits their present situation. No shape-shifting monster of ancient legend can outdo their gift for metamorphosis.

Thus, when I sat down in London to question Ezra Jennings about the death of Emily Devray, I was not surprised to find he no longer appeared the crazed figure that had felled me to the ground at Stonehenge, nor the weeping creature blaming us for the loss of his beloved. He looked almost exactly as he had when I'd first set eyes on him in Fitchett's shop. His pale face was bland, his manner composed, but for a faint, mocking gleam in his eye. He sat on the other side of the table between us, with his hands neatly folded one upon the other; and raised his eyebrows slightly, as if awaiting my order for new boots.

Morris stood over by the wall and Biddle sat with his notebook ready to record any confession.

I began with a question Ezra was not expecting. 'You

brought a local newspaper from Salisbury to London, to give to Emily Devray. Did you think it would interest her?'

'Yes!' said Ezra indignantly, before he could stop to consider the implication of his reply.

'So, then, you tracked her down to her address here in London. You have already admitted as much to Tobias Fitchett, so I know of it. How did you manage that? It must have been difficult.'

'Oh, no,' returned Jennings serenely, 'it was easy.'

'How did you do it?'

Ezra leaned forward confidingly and with a faint glow of triumph in his expression. That is another thing about murderers I'd noted in the past. It is not enough they believe themselves clever; they want the listener to agree. Jennings wanted my admiration.

'I knew she would be leaving the house in Salisbury where she'd lived with Mrs Waterfield. The cook there, Mrs Bates, she's a member of the congregation at our chapel. She would know the date of Emily's departure, so I got in the way of falling into conversation with Bates after the services on Sunday. I'd ask if the future of the house was decided, and whether she'd be able to keep her place. She told me when it had been sold. She said she would be staying on, as the new owners required a cook. She was very pleased about that. But Miss Devray would be leaving on the Tuesday that coming week.

'I made an excuse to Mr Fitchett about going to see the dentist on account of an aching tooth. I loitered about near the house, keeping an eye open for the carrier's cart come to fetch away Emily's boxes. Sure enough, I saw the fellow carry them out and I followed his cart. He took them to the railway station and they were stacked up on the platform, awaiting the London train, to be put in the goods van. They had big labels on them. I just strolled over and read the address. It was all quite straightforward.' Jennings opened his hands and spread them, as if to assure me of the innocence of his actions.

It sounded devious to me, but it was clever. Fitchett had said his apprentice was sharp. Biddle, in the corner with his notebook, was scribbling furiously. Jennings did not appear to notice him, or care if he had.

'You had struck up an acquaintance with Miss Devray in Salisbury?'

Jennings gave me a look of reproof. 'Certainly not! She was a respectable young lady. I had seen her about the town, of course, and noticed her. But she'd been nicely brought up. I couldn't approach her in the street and begin to chat. She had a quiet, decent way about her, and of course, she was pretty. I never thought I'd ever see her closer. Not even in church, you know, because she and Mrs Waterfield attended the cathedral services. I'm a chapel man. I don't hold with processions with crosses and choirboys in lacy shirts.'

He paused in reflection. 'Then she came to the shop with Mrs Waterfield. That changed things.' A faint smile touched his lips at the memory. 'They ordered the boots and Mr Fitchett drew out the pattern on paper, from her stockinged feet.' Jennings's gaze misted. 'They were beautiful. She had perfect feet. You never saw anything so lovely. I helped Mr Fitchett create those boots, you know,' he added proudly. 'I made the heels. Mr Fitchett said I did a very good job.'

Jennings's look of satisfaction faded and was replaced by a more familiar, accusatory expression. 'What have you done with those boots?'

'They are with the rest of her things: evidence, like the wooden lasts.'

'I still want those back, you know.'

I was not going to be drawn into that argument again. 'After that, did you try to strike up acquaintance with Miss Devray? I understand you didn't try before. But now she'd been in the shop.'

Ezra hesitated, fidgeted, and seemed torn between refusing any further information and a desire to impress me. The desire to show off won.

'Well, I wouldn't have spoken to her before she came to the shop, as I said. But that was like an introduction, wasn't it? Now she'd know who I was. So, yes, I did see her one Saturday afternoon on the cathedral green.'

'You had been waiting outside her house and followed her?' I guessed.

Ezra gave me a sour look. 'In a manner of speaking. Well, anyway, she was walking on the green and I went up and spoke to her very civil, took off my hat. I apologised for the intrusion but reminded her I worked for Mr Fitchett and I was wondering if she was satisfied with the boots. She was wearing them!' added Ezra proudly.

'She said yes, thank you, very satisfied. I said I would tell Mr Fitchett.' A dusky pink appeared on his pale cheeks. 'I told her I had made the heels.'

'Was she impressed?' I asked cunningly.

Ezra smiled. 'Yes, I think she was. She ought to have been. I made them very well. Mr Fitchett had said so. Anyway, she asked me how long I had been working for Mr Fitchett. So I told her. She asked me to give him her regards and then, well, she walked on.'

'Did you tell Mr Fitchett about this encounter?'

Jennings gave a testy sigh. 'Of course I didn't. I'd never have heard the last of it!'

'Did you get another chance to speak to her?'

He shook his head. 'Not in Salisbury, no. Well, the old lady died, of course. And the house was all in mourning and Miss Devray didn't go out much.'

'Now, tell me what happened after the house was sold and Miss Devray left Salisbury. Did you just go up to London and seek her out? Knock on Lady Temple's door?'

'Of course not!' Jennings's shocked expression indicated he now thought me totally ignorant of polite behaviour. 'I saw in the local paper that the new owners had moved into Mrs Waterfield's old house. They were a reverend gentleman and his sister, name of Bastable. Mrs Bates, at chapel, was all smiles about it. I thought Emily would like to know all about it, too, so I wrote to her and told her I would be coming to London on a Sunday, and I would call on her, if she permitted.'

'And you would bring her the local newspaper and answer any questions she had about what was happening at home, in Salisbury, that is.'

He scowled at me suspiciously. 'You know all about everything, don't you?'

'Not everything, no. I'm waiting for you to explain to me. Was she not surprised you knew her address in London?'

'I explained I had it from Mrs Bates. In a manner of speaking, I did, so it was not a *complete* untruth,' Jennings added earnestly.

I should have been more professional in my approach, when Colby and I called on Bastable, I thought ruefully. I should have insisted on speaking to Mrs Bates without her employer present, even if Bastable had objected. As a respectable citizen, he could not, in the end, have refused. I might have learned some of this much earlier and been set on Jennings's track. I consoled myself by reflecting that Mrs Bates probably had no idea that she had done anything wrong. She could not have anticipated that her harmless gossip had resulted in sending a deadly visitor to Emily in London. She might not even have remembered Jennings speaking to her at the chapel.

'And what next? Did Emily reply?' I asked the fellow. My voice sounded weary to my ear. I felt I knew the rest, but I had to hear him tell it.

'Yes, she did,' said Jennings proudly. 'She wrote to me asking that I not come to the house because she didn't want gossip among the servants. She said there was a door into the garden, in the street wall. She would open it up on Sunday evening and let me in. I kept her letter.'

'I know,' I said. 'Your lodgings in Salisbury have been searched. Inspector Colby telegraphed me this morning to let me know they'd found her letter to you.'

'*That letter is mine!*' Jennings shouted, his self-control

evaporating. His dark eyes glittered and his pale face turned scarlet. 'You have no right to read it. It is private.'

Biddle rose halfway to his feet. Morris had stepped forward. I signalled him to go back and Biddle to be seated.

'It is evidence, Jennings, like the boots and the wooden lasts. So, from the letter, I know that what you have told me today, so far, is true.'

'Well, then,' snapped Jennings. 'You will know that's what happened. I took the newspaper up to London. I met her in the garden and told her all the news from home, because she looked on Salisbury as her home. She was very happy to hear it all.'

That must be true, I thought. Lady Temple had told me Emily had spoken of Salisbury in a way that suggested she had been homesick.

'You were seen,' I said.

'Who saw me?' snapped Jenkins. 'No one in London knows me.'

'The butler saw you. He was returning from Evensong and saw you walking ahead of him and knocking at the garden door. He did not know your identity, of course, but you wore a long black coat and bowler hat, did you not? As you did at Emily's funeral?'

Jennings had been disconcerted. He began to chew his thumbnail. I didn't want him falling into another sulk.

'You made a regular thing of it, didn't you? Calling on the young lady?' I prompted.

As I watched I could read the struggle in his mind. He wanted to be careful, but he still wanted to boast. As I had hoped it would, the boasting won.

'I went up again each of the following Sundays until – until the last one. Each time I met Emily in the garden. But it was very cold and damp there, so we went into the little garden shed. Emily was afraid we'd be seen from the house, too. She said the butler was always looking to see what everyone was doing. Now you tell me he did see me. Well, he never said anything to her about it!'

There was a silence. Jennings again appeared to be sinking back into that sullen reverie I remembered in Salisbury.

'Tell me about the last Sunday visit you paid her,' I said gently. 'What happened the last time you saw Emily, in that garden shed?'

'We talked about Salisbury. She was pleased to have more news. Then I left and set off back home.' His dark eyes stared into mine. 'She was alive when I left.'

'I know a doctor here in London,' I told him. 'He is by way of being an expert on bloodstains. I intend to have him examine that black coat of yours.'

Jennings was shocked and couldn't hide it. 'Don't believe you!' he said.

'Believe me or not, Jennings, if there is the smallest stain on that coat, the doctor will find it.'

'And what if I say I cut my hand, the last time I was working in the shop?'

'You don't wear your Sunday best on Fitchett's premises, do you? That won't work as an excuse.'

I knew a jury might think differently, but the more confidence I showed, the more confused Jennings became. He was rattled.

'Now then, let's return to that last conversation you had

with Miss Devray. Wasn't she surprised at the regularity of your visits? Every Sunday evening, there you were! Didn't she find that puzzling?' I asked him.

'Why the devil should she?' shouted Jennings. 'Why shouldn't I call on her?'

'She must have begun to ask herself why you did. Did she indicate to you that she wondered what prompted this attention?'

'I was courting her, wasn't I?' he snarled.

'Courting her? Good grief!' I exclaimed. 'Did Emily Devray realise that was what you were doing?'

There was so much emotion, so many conflicting desires, in the man's face, it contorted physically into grotesque grimaces. I thought of those old competitions where a rustic puts his head through a horse collar and makes himself look as fearsome or strange as he can. I waited patiently. At last, Jennings spoke in a stiff, tortured voice that seemed to be squeezed out of his throat. 'I made it perfectly clear. I asked her to marry me.'

'*To marry you?* When?'

'That last time,' Jennings said sullenly.

'I am sure, Ezra, that she was very taken aback at that. You may have decided in your own mind that she realised you were courting her. For my part, I really can't believe she did.'

An ugly dull red slowly suffused his pale face, creeping up from his neck to his hairline. He glowered at me. 'Why not? You shouldn't be so surprised, and neither should she have been! I had been calling on her, after all.'

'So she *was* surprised, then? She hadn't thought you

were courting her! Let's face it, Ezra. You surely don't think meeting a few times in a garden shed is quite the same as calling to— to advance your suit.'

'Well, I could hardly go knocking at the front door. That spying butler you were talking of, he wouldn't have let me in!'

'Yes, yes, I understand that,' I hastened to say. 'You had to meet in secret. But, well, you were hardly like a suitor. Perhaps she thought you were a kind friend. But marriage . . .'

Ezra leaned forward, his eyes now burning with passion in his pale face. 'I told her I had good prospects. Mr Fitchett said I was the best he'd ever had as an apprentice. I meant to set up on my own. She could come home, come back to Salisbury and live there, where she wanted to be.'

I waited until the echo of his shouted words faded. 'And she declined your offer, Ezra?'

'Yes,' he muttered sullenly.

'She rejected it – and you – out of hand?'

'Yes!'

'And you were very angry?'

He looked defiantly at me. 'I had a right to be angry. I had made her a respectful offer. She would not even consider it!'

'When, at Stonehenge, you were angry with me, you attacked me,' I reminded him. 'When you were angry with Mr Fitchett, because he wanted to burn the wooden lasts, you attacked him. Tell me, Ezra, did you attack Emily when you were angry with her?'

'I had a right,' Jennings repeated. 'She insulted me. She

said cruel things. I may be only a bootmaker, but I am an honourable man, and I had made her an honourable offer! She could have said, at the very least . . .' His voice choked and he struggled to control it. 'She could have replied that she would consider it and write to me with her answer. But she . . .' Jennings's features contorted once more, this time into a terrible expression of agony. 'She *laughed* at me. I loved her. But she laughed at me.'

Oh, Emily . . . I thought. *That laugh was your death warrant.* 'Then you were very angry, weren't you? What did you do, Ezra?'

'I took hold of her shoulders, and I shook her, shook her hard, to stop her laughing, and to teach her a lesson. She needed to realise she couldn't treat me like that. Well, she did stop laughing. She was afraid of me then. I was glad of it.'

Jennings gave a cold little smile at the memory. 'She began to struggle, to get free of me. But I had her; I had her in my power. I wanted her to know it!'

'And?' I prompted because he fell silent and sat with that cold smirk on his face. He looked up at me and I saw the calculation in his eyes.

'I let go of her, because suddenly the touch of her was—unpleasant to me. I gave her a good shove to get her away from me . . .'

This time I waited.

'And she fell,' said Jennings. 'She hit her head on that contraption for cutting grass. She didn't get up. I thought she was faking. You know, playing about, pretending. So I stooped over her and pulled her to her feet.' His voice had become very quiet and I had to strain to catch the words. 'She seemed to stare at me for a moment, just a moment. Then the life faded out of her eyes. She was dead.' He frowned and seemed puzzled. 'I don't know why. If she'd behaved herself it wouldn't have happened.'

'It didn't occur to you to go and seek help?'

'What for?' said Jennings. 'She was *dead*. Didn't you hear me?' He leaned forward and I could see he had begun to sweat. The pitch of his voice rose; that glow returned to his eyes. Morris, moving quietly for such a big man, positioned himself behind Jennings and was ready to restrain him. But Jennings was paying no attention to him, and perhaps did not even realise the sergeant was there.

'She ought not to have died!' Jennings screamed, his voice echoing around the small room. 'I only pushed her away. I did that because she laughed. She had no business to laugh, to torment me so! It wasn't my fault she fell. It was her fault. And it was her fault she hit her head and— died like that!' He leaped to his feet.

For a moment only, I saw again that crazed creature, towering over me atop the ancient stone monolith on Salisbury plain, ready to launch himself at me. But whereas then I had seen a soul crazed by grief, now I only saw a piece of theatre.

Morris had him by his shoulders, and thrust him back down into his chair. Jennings squirmed briefly in the sergeant's powerful grip and then relaxed. He began to cry, real tears running down his cheeks. No theatre now, but an agony of self-pity.

'It wasn't my fault: it was hers! She brought it all on herself!' he sobbed.

'You know, Ezra,' I told him, 'you sound just like any outwardly respectable fellow who, in his own home, is a wife-beater. Or any bully boy who routinely assaults his woman and thinks himself entitled to black her eye. They do it either because they enjoy inflicting pain, or because they're drunk, or because they feel the world outside their own house does not appreciate them, as you felt Emily did not appreciate your offer of marriage.

'They have a dozen reasons, none of them excusing what they've done. Then, one day, they strike a blow too hard and the woman is dead. Afterwards they sit there, like you, and weep and tell me it was all the girl's fault.'

'Well, it *was* her fault,' said Jennings sulkily. 'She scorned me!'

'And what did you do next?'

He shrugged. 'First I dropped her, just threw her down. But she looked untidy, so I pulled her up again. Her head was bleeding and if there is blood on my coat, you will say it was from that. But it seems to me you know too many clever doctors! Anyhow, I propped her against the wall of the shed in a more respectable, sitting position. Then I left her there. There was nothing else to be done, was there?'

'How did you leave?'

'The way I'd come, of course. I went out into the garden, through the door into the street, and went home . . . to Salisbury. No one saw me leave the house. Not even that snooping butler. It was very dark, and foggy. Terrible fog you get up here in London. That alone should make anyone want to leave and go back to Salisbury.'

He had been looking down at the tabletop as he spoke

the last words. There was a few minutes' silence, broken only by Biddle's pencil scratching on the paper. Somehow I did not like to interrupt Ezra's thoughts. It was a sad story, but so many tales of crime are sad. That does not make them the less evil.

Then Ezra Jennings looked up and leaned forward as one about to make a confidence. 'I did make one mistake, you know.'

'Really?' I inquired. 'What was that?'

'Obvious! You're supposed to be a detective, aren't you? Can't you work it out for yourself? I should have taken the boots off her feet before I left her there, in that garden shed. I could have taken them with me back to Salisbury. You would not have known where to look for them. You would not have come to Fitchett's shop; and I would have kept the boots safe. I could have held them in my hands.'

He crouched over the table, a terrible look of cunning appearing on his face. 'I could have taken them to the stones. You'd have been none the wiser, neither you nor that fellow in Salisbury, Colby. You would not have chased after me to the stones and interrupted things. She would have come back. I am sure of it. The lure of the boots themselves would have been even stronger than that of the wooden lasts.'

'Do you still really believe that?' I asked incredulously.

I had to admit I was shaken. I was also aware that, in the corner, Biddle had stopped writing and was listening eagerly. When I gave him a severe look he hastily took up his notepad and pencil again. Only Morris had remained impassive.

'Oh, I see *you* do not,' Jennings told me with a touch of scorn. 'No one else believes it. But that does not matter.

I believe it. That's what would have happened. And this time, she would have been in my power. Because I had brought her back, she would be mine completely. She would have had to behave as I wanted.' He gave a little giggle. 'If she didn't, I would have sent her back again! It would all have been all right.'

He fell back in his seat, sullen again. 'But you spoiled everything: the police, old Fitchett, every one of you!'

Then his manner changed once more. His expression of resentment cleared and the look of cold calculation returned. He even gave a superior smile.

'They will not hang me,' he said confidently. 'I am mad, you see.'

I was stunned. I rallied sufficiently to tell him, 'You were examined by a well-known expert in the field of insanity and he declared you not to be mad.'

'Oh, that fancy fellow with the diamond studs in his shirtfront.' Ezra dismissed Dr Lefebre. 'I don't know where you found him. He wasn't like any doctor I've ever seen. Pleasant enough chap, mind, and he didn't scorn what I said, not like you. Well, anyway, they will get another mad doctor to examine me here in London. Any judge is bound to do that. And another doctor will find me mad. You can be sure of it.'

'A very odd business indeed,' said Dunn, when he had read Ezra's confession and listened to what I had to say. 'Tell me, Ross, do you think the fellow a lunatic? Never mind what Lefebre said. What's your opinion?'

'John Colby at Salisbury is certain of it. But I am not,'

I told him. 'I do believe him obsessed and what Lefebre described as deluded, but also what his employer described as "sharp". Jennings is artful, a clever chap in his way, quite an actor. His defence will insist another doctor examines him. Jennings is right in that. Now he has time to plan what to say, he may be able to fool another expert.'

'Hm,' said Dunn. 'That business at Stonehenge . . . It does suggest he's, well, "deluded", did you say was the word Dr Lefebre used? Does he really believe that nonsense about the wooden lasts calling back her spirit?'

I hesitated. 'I don't know, sir. It's possible. But then, as Dr Lefebre said, Jennings is free to believe it if he wishes. People believe all sorts of things. They are not necessarily mad because what they believe is unusual or strange. Perhaps Jennings is not so very different from those who attend spiritualist séances, except that he didn't sit at a table in a respectable parlour, with a medium summoning the departed on behalf of those present. Instead, he went it alone. He took himself off to Stonehenge to carry out a ritual of his own invention.'

When Dunn looked singularly unimpressed by my argument, I added briskly, 'Emily Devray died at his hands. Tobias Fitchett remains very frail following a savage attack. If anyone commits a crime of violence, it is for us, as officers of the law, to track them down and arrest them. It is not a question of what they believe. It is a matter of what they have *done*.'

Dunn sighed. 'The newspapers will love it,' he said.

Chapter Twenty

I WALKED out of Scotland Yard and into the fog. It had returned in all its malign strength, a London Particular. Out there, hidden in its smoky dank folds, who knew what evils were being perpetrated? The police would eventually learn of some of them. Others would never become known. London is full of secrets. So is the human heart. Many of those secrets never come to light, either.

It took me a good while to find my slow way home to my own fireside where Lizzie waited anxiously.

'I am glad this investigation is over,' she said, when I had told her what had happened. 'I haven't liked you being involved in this case from the start. There has always been something unnatural about it. I know you don't think Jennings is insane. But perhaps others will, and he won't hang. They'll lock him away in some asylum. They might even let him practise his trade there.'

'Using all those sharp knives and other potentially lethal tools?' I exclaimed. 'I hope not! No, no, my dear, that would be extremely unlikely. But who knows what judges and juries and all the business of a trial will decide.'

'He didn't mean to kill her, at least, if what he told you

is true.' My wife had apparently decided to play devil's advocate. She likes a good argument. I don't mean a quarrel. We seldom quarrel. But we do have some very lively discussions, let us say.

'*I* don't know that it is true.' I put my side of the debate forward. 'I do know that he flew in a terrible rage when I thwarted him; and before that when poor old Fitchett crossed him. It is more than possible, at the moment when Emily rejected him, he did want to kill the girl. At the very least, he intended to hurt her badly in revenge. Let others decide that, Lizzie. I only collect the evidence and find the perpetrator of the crime, if I'm lucky. If you want to know what happens next, read about it in the newspapers. Dunn remarked how much the press will love the whole rotten business!'

The fire crackled in the hearth. A distant clang of a saucepan falling indicated Bessie was at work in the kitchen. She would have an account of the story from Biddle when next he called. It was too much to hope he would keep that to himself. Bessie would insist on details.

'Have you been able to visit Miss Eldon, or Miss Bernard, today?' I asked my wife.

She sighed. 'Not today. I took Bessie with me shopping at the vegetable market; and the fog made it so difficult, it took us a full two hours to complete our business. But Miss Eldon and I have discussed that we can do for Rose when the weather improves. It must improve eventually!'

'And what have you come up with?' I asked with some misgiving.

'I have suggested to Miss Eldon that we could take Rose out with us in Wally Slater's cab, just to drive through the parks. She would not meet anyone and have any difficulty. But she would escape the four walls of that house for an hour or two.'

'Have you mentioned this to Mr Bernard?'

'Not yet.'

'Then I suggest you wait a while, until the better weather is here.' I hesitated. 'Lizzie, I know you have the best of intentions, as does Ruby Eldon. But have a care. Bernard is devoted to his daughter, maybe obsessively so. The way he has shielded her from all society suggests that. You have achieved a remarkable amount, you and Ruby. But be very careful. Obsessive love, of any kind, is dangerous. To visit Miss Rose at home, well, that's one thing. To take her away from the house, and her father's watchful eye, and drive her around London, well, that is quite another. It may be a step too far. He could easily refuse and put a stop to your visits altogether.'

'But Rose would be so upset!' Lizzie protested. 'And he loves her! He wouldn't wilfully distress her.'

'Just remember that, sometimes, love and logic don't go hand in hand.' I sighed. 'I have encountered terrible things done, not from hatred but from a twisted sort of love. I sometimes think love is one of the most powerful and dangerous of motives.'

The fire crackled again and, with a rustle, the coals fell in upon one another, down into the scarlet and yellow of the flames. In them, it was easy to imagine pictures. One I saw was of Ezra Jennings, standing atop the ancient stone, in the drizzling mist, the wind whipping his hair as he screamed his defiance.